BLOOD RUNNING HOT

BLOOD RUNNING HOT

ROBERT VALLETTA

ROBERT VALLETTA BOOKS

BLOOD RUNNING HOT
A GASLAMP QUARTER THRILLER
BOOK ONE

ISBN: 978-0-578-99787-2 (hardcover)

ISBN: 979-8-483-30981-9 (paperback)

For Lisa, Ed, Ryan & Taylor,
who provided a comforting light
as I wandered away from the shore

One

Oceanside Hotel

Solana Beach, California

Sunday, May 31st

He stepped carefully from the ceramic tile and steamed glass shower stall, naked and dripping wet, to the plush dry carpet in the bathroom. His exposed flesh was immediately draped by an icy blanket of swirling air that surged steadily from an overhead ventilation duct.

J.P. Ballard's eyes glistened with devilish intent. His mind was preoccupied with a mélange of indecent thoughts as he pictured the beautiful, voluptuous woman in silk lingerie who would be sharing his bed during the evening hours ahead.

He reached toward the towel bar on the wall only to find it empty. With his lewd machinations of erotic desires unexpectedly disrupted, he turned and stared curiously toward the adjacent room.

Was he losing his mind?

He suddenly remembered he had left the large bath towel on top of the bed. He had placed it there after he had dried his hands when the food had arrived.

The honeymoon suite at the hotel included a mini-refrigerator, a raised bar, and a sunken hot tub. An opened, chilled bottle of Napa Valley champagne was set on top of the bar. There were separate plates of jumbo shrimp cocktail with zesty horseradish sauce and of fresh strawberries and whipped cream arranged decadently on a silver tray nearby.

A king-size bed with down-filled pillows was centered in the room and placed against the far wall. Small, foil-wrapped squares of Ghirardelli dark chocolate had been meticulously placed on each pillow.

The room had cost more than double the price of a standard room with two full-size beds. But inwardly, J.P. Ballard was satisfied with his decision. He knew it would make her happy.

She hadn't arrived yet for their intimate, clandestine rendezvous. The sun had set nearly an hour before, and his mind was going mad with an impulsive yearning of escalating anticipation.

How long had he secretly plotted to take her in his arms, to devour her sexy curves from parted red lips to the tender nape of her neck to her luscious, firm breasts to the moistened inner sanctum of her quivering thighs?

He glanced outside the room again to the digital alarm clock on the nightstand by the bed.

Plenty of time to prepare before she's due to arrive.

He planned to shave and to trim his fingernails and toenails. He wanted to look and smell his best for their first time together making love.

He had selected a new short-sleeve polo top and a comfortable pair of lightweight dress slacks that were two inches smaller in the waistline than he had been wearing a month ago. He had hung them in the closet so that they would not wrinkle.

He was nervous, excited, and aroused.

At first, he had felt sharp prickles of anxiety to approach her. He was so pleased with himself afterward when he had finally suggested they get together, privately. Then he was over the moon with pride and wanton lust when she had smiled warmly and touched him on the shoulder to whisper the word *yes* softly and seductively in his ear.

"Why hadn't you asked me sooner?" she had inquired.

He had no immediate answer to that, other than his own lack of confidence in himself and the fear a rejection could somehow be used against him. He had a family and too much in the way of material things to lose. There were secrets he couldn't allow to become exposed. He could never let that happen. He had to protect those things he had worked so hard to attain over the years.

There was a sudden knock at the door.

She was early.

J.P. Ballard hadn't even toweled off yet. His skin glimmered with the moisture of the hot shower. His cock had hardened with the expectation of her arrival. He wouldn't allow her to wait a moment longer than necessary.

He strode confidently toward the door. His smile extended broadly from ear to ear. He pumped up his chest and tried to suck in his belly as much as he could.

Oh, what a night it will be!

Ballard didn't bother to check the peephole in the middle of the door. His dreams of libidinous pleasure over the course of the next three nights with this amazing woman were about to be answered. He turned the knob and thrust the door open wide.

Her appearance was not what he had envisioned.

She grinned amusingly from the darkened threshold outside the room.

"Somebody's happy to see me," she blurted shamelessly. She switched off the beam from her flashlight.

"I've been waiting for this chance to be with you ever since I first saw you dance at the club. You remember when that was, don't you?"

"Yes, of course," she replied. "A long time ago, it seems. A different life. May I come in, or are you waiting for our neighbors to get a good look at you?"

"By all means," he offered. "Please come on inside. I didn't realize there was any rain in the forecast this week. You're all decked out in your waterproof rain gear and heavy-duty flashlight. Are we expecting a hurricane?"

"More like a tsunami," she said and laughed softly.

He shrugged indifferently. Sometimes he didn't understand her quirky sense of humor. He couldn't care less about the generation gap that separated their birth dates. She was nearly half his age, incredibly sexy, and had made her motivations of monetary gain perfectly clear. He knew what she wanted, and he was happy to provide that in exchange for the sexual favors she would mischievously submit to him in return.

He turned his back to her and took a few steps toward the bed. He had a perplexed and puzzled expression marked upon his face. He could have sworn the weather forecast called for a lingering heatwave with clear, sunny skies and temperatures in the upper nineties to the low triple digits over the next few days. He had packed a bottle of sunscreen into his suitcase for that very reason.

"Let me grab my towel," he said. "I had just stepped out from the shower."

"Take your time," she suggested. "We've got all night."

He felt empowered and unstoppable at that moment. He heard the abrupt snap as the door closed shut. She slipped the deadbolt firmly into place.

"Make yourself a drink," he called over his bare shoulder. "There's some snacks on the bar and an assortment of beer, wine, and liqueurs. I opened a bottle of champagne, too. I felt like celebrating our first night together."

"That's so sweet of you," she said.

"I don't mind saying," he replied, "I've been thinking about you all day. You're my dream come true."

"I hope to be all that and more."

"Oh, you are, my dear," he replied.

"The shrimp cocktail looks delicious," she said. "And I know what I'd like to do with the whipped cream."

He bent down to pick the folded bath towel off the embroidered comforter atop the bed. He couldn't wait to gaze upon her nude body. To taste her lips and to touch her all over. To feel himself pulsing inside her.

Calm yourself down, man. There'll be plenty of time for that later tonight.

He began to unfold the large Turkish cotton bath towel that had been dropped carelessly on top of the bed.

Suddenly the room went dark.

There was a helpless sense of apprehension as if he were inside a subterranean elevator shaft after the cable had broken. He felt intense pressure weighing down on him.

He had difficulty breathing. Fear swept over him. There was a ringing in his ears.

When his eyes finally fluttered open, he was crawling on his hands and knees. The hotel room was spinning in circles around him, like a gyroscope that wobbled on its axis. Saliva dripped uncontrollably from his open mouth to the carpet below. He felt inebriated and woozy.

A large black metal flashlight lay on the corner at the foot of the bed. It was the one she had brought for the tsunami. There was a red splotch of liquid oozing over the transparent end of the lens cap.

Was that blood?

His vision was fuzzy and out of focus. His head ached with the worst migraine he could ever imagine.

There was an immediate metallic clicking sound as if a tin can lid were being pried open.

He perceived the comforting caress of her fingers against the back of his neck, and he relaxed. He felt safe.

"What the fuck happened?" he mumbled unsteadily.

There was no reply.

It would be the last question he would ever ask.

Two

San Diego, California

Wednesday, June 3rd

O n an extended lunch break from her downtown Gaslamp Quarter office, Micheline Avila drove her shiny new Ford Mustang hardtop on a vital mission of great importance to herself. She headed briskly along Harbor Drive near San Diego Bay toward the Coronado Bridge.

Time was critical. It was a matter of life or death for the passengers she urgently transported to her home near the naval base.

Micheline smiled contentedly as she glanced to her right. Next to her, a white Styrofoam cooler was securely buckled into the front passenger seat. Micheline was coming from the pet store where she had purchased a dozen freshwater cichlids, including some colorful species of peacock, electric blue, and some aptly named black-and-white-striped convict fish. There were also a few black-and-gray-spotted plecos meant to scavenge the algae in her seventy-five-gallon aquarium. The tank was complete with decorative blue pebbles along the bottom and a sunken shipwreck of a three-masted Spanish galleon for the fish to commingle within.

The fish had been placed by the shop owner into a clear plastic tube filled with fresh water and sealed shut on one end. The bags were essentially elongated water balloons stuffed with the fresh catch of the

Micheline reached into her wallet and extracted her business card. She handed the card to the driver of the garbage truck without the benefit of introductions.

"Please take this," she said. "I've got to run, but I'll be in touch."

"But shouldn't we wait? Don't you need my information? This is a company vehicle."

Micheline held up her phone and took a close-up snapshot of the driver's face.

"I've got everything I need. We'll talk soon."

She abruptly turned and left the garbage truck driver on the roadway in stunned silence.

The Mustang roared to life as Micheline depressed the electronic start button on the charcoal gray dashboard. She maneuvered the muscle car deftly through the obstacle course of displaced northbound traffic.

Then she crossed back into the southbound lane beyond the misaligned garbage truck and raced away.

Three

Oceanside Hotel

Solana Beach, California

Wednesday, June 3rd

Detective Micheline Avila of the San Diego County Sheriff's Department courteously lifted the yellow crime scene tape from across the paint-scratched doorway and obligingly allowed her newly assigned senior partner, Detective Guillermo Reyes, enough clearance to pass into the malodorous and dimly lit hotel room.

Outside, the potent coastal air was stiflingly hot and thick with the raw essence of sea salt blown inland by an arid and unremitting Pacific breeze. The sun's rays glared intensely off exposed windowpanes and reflected sharply from the well-worn concrete pavement. Farther away, faint echoes of seagull cries intermingled with rolling ocean waves as the foaming surf crashed and receded in timeless rhythmic cadence upon the rocky shoreline.

Once inside the suffocating enclosure that loudly announced Death's presence without uttering a single word, Guillermo squinted hard. It was a feeble attempt to adjust his aging eyes to the shadowy darkness that seemed to swallow him whole. He accidentally stumbled forward, and abruptly emitted a staccato burst of rapid-fire wheezes and rasps.

"Smells rank in here," Guillermo noted as he regained his balance. Embarrassed by his lack of youthful grace, the elder detective grimaced and rolled his eyes self-consciously from left to right. He exhaled quickly and wheezed again with difficulty.

"The AC had purposefully been switched off," Micheline remarked candidly from behind him, "presumably by our killer upon their exit from the premises."

"Feels like a goddamn sweatbox in here."

"They left a hot shower running with the bathroom door wide open, too. The humidity inside both rooms is overwhelming, to say the least."

"It reminds me of the Yucatán jungles outside of Mérida during the worst of the summer months."

"The body's over by the bed," Micheline said, pointing forward. "Most of it, anyway. It's not a pretty sight. Are you okay?"

"I'll be all right," Guillermo waved her off. "The heat's got to me today, is all."

"Want me to get you some water?"

"No, thanks," Guillermo responded impatiently. "Let's get on with this. I promised my wife I'd be home at a reasonable hour tonight. Foolish of me for making promises I can never keep."

"Wishful thinking."

"Still, I meant it when I said it this morning. So, I guess that counts for something, right?"

"I suppose," Micheline affirmed. She scrunched her nose at the putrid odor of early decomposition and stepped carefully across the perimeter threshold of the doorway into the active crime scene.

"The M.E.'s already inside," Micheline pressed on. "Blood splatter suggests the victim, white male, fifty-eight, stripped naked as the day he was born, was down on his knees and facing toward the far wall when the carotid artery was severed."

"Ouch! Any chance this was a suicide?"

"Nope. There's no weapon present or accounted for. The room had been swept, too. Our victim was attacked from behind and his body was mutilated after the fact. He bled out on the floor by the bed. The flashlight rammed up his ass also appears to have been inserted post-mortem."

"I like your take on things, Michelle," the venerable detective uttered as he wiped a beaded swath of sweat from his brow. He seemed not to notice he addressed her by the wrong name.

"There's no messing around with you young northeastern Latinas with your fancy college degrees. You're all business, giving me the play-by-play with scrupulous detail. It's like you're a sports announcer down on the sidelines during a football game with the latest player injury update."

Guillermo noticed that Micheline carried a wire-bound notebook and a clickable gel pen with her. Old school. He was surprised she wasn't using a tablet. He had forgotten his own notebook in the car.

"Take my advice, though," he suggested.

"I'm focused on the job and the crime scene," she contended sharply. "There's a dead body on the floor."

"You've got to lighten up some. With me, there's no need to be so by-the-book. It's okay from time to time to say something mellifluous or off-the-cuff. Something unexpected but applicable to the situation at hand."

Guillermo motioned toward the back corner of the hotel room with a casual wave of his hand.

"Hey, what's up this guy's ass? Do you know what I mean? It lightens the mood a bit. Puts us both in the right frame of mind to absorb the shock somehow we never see coming when we first arrive to view another dead body on the job."

"I'm not going to make any bad action movie wisecracks, if that's what you're suggesting," Micheline countered.

She frowned somewhat discontentedly. In her mind, this was not a time or place to be joking around. She was sweating bullets and her nerves were on fire. She was busy surveying the murder scene for the second time that afternoon. To make matters worse, her new underwire bra itched uncomfortably in the torrid confines of the sauna-like hotel room.

Had it not been for the thick veil of steam that enshrouded the room like a San Francisco evening fog, it would have been considered a nice hotel room, too. All it was missing was a direct view to the nearby beach and a wide palm tree-lined oceanfront esplanade on the far side of the building.

It was clean, or at least it had been prior to the events leading up to the murder, and it was relatively private. There was direct access from a side street parking lot and the room, although expensive, was not overly priced by southern California standards.

The headboard of a king-size bed was positioned against the far wall. The M.E. stood in the far corner of the room, next to a wooden nightstand with a digital alarm clock. He was dressed from head to toe in white fluid-resistant coveralls with a hood, face mask and safety glasses, gloves, and boots to cover his shoes.

Directly opposite of the bed, a large screen high-definition television was mounted on the wall above a wide wooden clothes dresser. On the other side of the perfectly made and undisturbed bed, face down, drowned in a pool of congealed blood and other dried matter of indescribable nature, lay a chubby naked white male with a long black cylindrical metal flashlight placed appropriately where the sun is not meant to shine.

"Somebody really stuck it to him good, huh?" Guillermo quipped sarcastically as he peered around the corner of the bed to take a closer look at the victim.

Micheline rolled her eyes and caught herself unconsciously smirking.

Damn, that was funny!

"There you go, partner," Guillermo bellowed with a twinkle of surprise in his eyes. "You'll get the hang of this soon enough. I know it's not in your nature, but you've got to keep your sense of humor, otherwise, the horror and the ugliness of it all will start to eat away at your sanity from the inside."

"Got it."

"I've learned over the years it's always best to ease into it at first. Take your time to absorb your surroundings. It's natural to feel pure dread when you first arrive on the scene."

"I've been doing this for a while now."

Guillermo nodded. "Then later, after you've got your bearings, you lean in hard and crack the case wide open with all the facts you've gathered. You want your presentation of evidence and motive to the prosecuting attorney to be beyond reproach."

"I appreciate the suggestions, Guillermo. Really, I get that. But let's cut to the chase, please. Why did you request for me to partner with you on this case?"

Micheline's tone carried more than a hint of a rough edge to it. She tried to stop the anger from coating her words. Her day had already started off badly and she didn't want to unnecessarily offend the much more seasoned Detective Reyes, especially on the first day of a murder investigation. After all, working for the Homicide Squad was her dream. But several things didn't add up in her mind and she wasn't about to be toyed with.

"You're a well-respected veteran on the force," Micheline pressed on, "and we've never partnered before. I'm a woman and my surname would suggest I'm Latina. So, maybe you think your macho male attitude can pass for California cool out here, seeing as I'm not a born-and-bred local like you are."

"That's not it at all."

"Listen," she continued with a razor-sharp edge to her voice. "My intuition's getting the better of me. The top brass assigned me to investigate fraud and money scams in Financial Crimes after a brief stint in the Domestic Violence Unit this past year. So far, I haven't worked with the Homicide Squad out here in San Diego, even though I've worked as the senior investigating officer on active crime scenes successfully throughout my career back in New York."

"I'm aware," he said.

Micheline's blue eyes narrowed and the small muscles in her jaw flexed with tension. She wanted to make her next point crystal clear.

"So, I must respectfully ask, did your regular partner run out on you and leave you hanging, or did you lose a bet? I'm not at all anxious to be made fun of for the sake of some stupid office pool. It's happened before. Men can be such pricks sometimes."

Guillermo shrugged and looked somewhat serious for a moment.

"First of all," he replied, "pretty much everyone out here came from somewhere else at one time or another. Take me as a perfect example. I wasn't born here, as you may have incorrectly assumed. My accent should have given that away. I was born in Reynosa in northern Mexico. It's just across the border from McAllen, Texas."

"I didn't realize," Micheline said. "Sorry."

"When I first arrived here," Guillermo continued, "I immediately felt like an outsider. My parents moved our entire family to Chula Vista when I was a teenager. We all became American citizens, legally. My dad was a director of the supply chain for a maquiladora, a foreign-owned electronics factory with manufacturing sites in northern Mexico, San Diego, and southeast Asia. He placed a great emphasis on family, education, learning to speak English, and hard work. He believed in the American dream."

Guillermo stopped short and paused a moment to slow his breathing. Then he emitted a heavy whistle as he inhaled another sharp breath.

"I graduated from the police academy right after high school," he said, "and I've been a cop ever since. I've got myself a nice house overlooking a park in Bonita. But most people you meet out here will probably tell you they relocated here for work after they graduated from college in the Midwest or Texas or from someplace back east, just like you."

Guillermo paused again for a moment to let his words sink in. "So, you're not alone, Detective. You'll find yourself talking to plenty of people who live here now, but they have family roots in Minneapolis or Pittsburgh. They come from all over, too. Places like Boston or Philadelphia or even Miami, and they know firsthand what tropical storms and winter snow and freezing temperatures feel like. They don't miss it, either. For everyone living out here in the southwest, it's all about sunny blue skies and palm trees and ocean waves from here on in."

"That still doesn't answer my question," Micheline stood firm. She locked her eyes steadfastly on those of her new partner, who exhibited distinct visual signals of being less than forthright.

Guillermo looked upward and to his left when he spoke, and he hesitated before speaking. He appeared to be nervous and chose his words carefully, even though all that came out seemed to be a ramble of insignificant facts.

He was clearly hiding something. Micheline was on to the ruse Guillermo seemed to be playing, and she didn't want to be the punchline for some internal fraternity department prank.

Obviously, I've got trust issues.

Guillermo appeared to falter under the intense visual stare-down from his new partner. His jaw cringed awkwardly. He knew immediately he had made an excellent choice in selecting the tough and serious-minded female detective who had relocated to southern California from the Hudson River community of Edgewater, New Jersey.

The word around the department was Micheline had been an outstanding member of the NYPD's Homicide Division. She was a female sleuth with incredible instinct, a respectable track record for closing what were thought to be unsolvable crimes, and she came with a pedigree. Her father was a retired FBI special agent.

Micheline had degrees in criminal justice and forensic behavioral science, she was divorced, she had no kids they knew of, she had trust issues, and she had a difficult time fitting in at first.

She hadn't yet learned how to dress properly for the Pacific lifestyle. Her Fifth Avenue sense of uptown Manhattan fashion was obvious. She still looked up at the sky and expected rain. Over time, the sunbaked California climate would force her to consider lighter fabrics and more casual attire.

Guillermo could clearly detect an abundance of admirable traits in his new female partner. He was certain he was only seeing what was immediately noticeable from the surface. There were bound to be so many more interesting and diverse qualities hidden beneath those thick-skinned outer layers once the surface ice was effectively melted away.

Detective Micheline Avila was confident, intelligent, and determinedly fierce. She was a fighter. She would never back down on a murder investigation or during an argument when she knew she was right. Ever.

And damn if she wasn't beautiful, too.

Four

Guillermo straightened his shoulders and looked directly into the empyrean depths of Micheline's unblinking sky-blue eyes.

"I asked for you specifically on this case," he began slowly. His voice softened and became a hoarse whisper.

"You know what?" he asked feebly. "Let's start over, please. How do I pronounce your first name? It's not Michelle, is it?"

Micheline knowingly smiled, just like she had done her entire life when that same question inevitably came up in the conversation.

"I'm named after one of my great grandmothers from Italy," she replied automatically. "But it has a French origin."

"That was thoughtful of your parents. They were respectful of the family's history."

"Yes, they were. And you're correct. It's not Michelle, as you called me before. It's not the same as the tire company you're probably familiar with, either. It's pronounced Mish-el-een."

"That's pretty," Guillermo said. "I like the way it sounds. I've never known anyone by that name before."

"It's not too common. There's an easy way to remember it, though."

"How's that?"

"No matter what I do, I *lean* into it." She paused. "Lean. Get it?"

"Yes, Micheline," he replied, placing additional stress on the final syllable of her first name. "That makes sense. But your surname is Avila. That's certainly Spanish. Was I wrong to peg you as Latina?"

Micheline smiled devilishly again with her pouty lips. Most people could never figure out her cultural background or genetic heritage upon first meeting. She was a beautiful woman who stood five feet four inches tall in flat shoes. She was made up of smooth skin, lean muscle, and well-defined curves.

She had silky jet-black hair that was braided in a knot behind her head and draped down below her shoulders. Her skin was a light shade of mocha caramel, and she had exotic Asian features around the eyes, which were strikingly and unexpectedly bright blue.

"I'm a mix of cultures," she offered pleasantly. "I understand the natural inclination for your unconscious bias, but Spanish is only one part of my very complex genealogy."

"How so?" Guillermo asked, suddenly intrigued.

Micheline inhaled a deep breath. "On my father's side, my great-grandparents originally came from Ávila de los Caballeros. It's a beautiful medieval city in the province of Castile-Léon in northwestern Spain."

"It sounds amazing."

"It is. I've been there twice in the past during summer vacations. But my ancestors later moved to Ecuador. So, you're partially correct about my Latina heritage."

"I sense there are more pieces to this puzzle," Guillermo surmised.

Micheline nodded. "Several, in fact. Their son, my grandfather, met my grandmother in Ecuador. But my grandmother was not originally from Ecuador, either. Her family heritage was a mix of Welsh and Italian. She was born in Siena in the Tuscany region of Italy. She's the relative whom I'm named after. She also had bright blue eyes from what I've been told, just like her mother before her."

"So, you're of Spanish, Italian, and Welsh descent, but by way of Ecuador?" Guillermo asked to confirm he got the facts straight. He was playing the part of the good detective.

"Sort of," Micheline gently laughed. "Again, that's only part of the picture. Shortly after my paternal grandparents were married, they moved to North Bergen, New Jersey, right outside of New York City.

That's where my father grew up. He went to college at Rutgers. He's a former Army Ranger who later became an FBI special agent with the Manhattan Bureau."

"I had heard that," Guillermo admitted, impressed. "You grew up in New Jersey?"

"Yes, in Edgewater. Later as an adult, I moved to the waterfront community in Jersey City."

"And what about your mother's side of the family? I imagine something a little more unique or exotic, right?"

Micheline suddenly felt a twinge of sadness as she remembered her sweet mother, who had passed away from cervical cancer the previous year.

"My mother was biracial," she began, fighting back a deluge of tears.

"My maternal grandfather was African American. He grew up near Philadelphia and later became a decorated fighter pilot for the Navy. He was stationed in Tokyo during his deployment, where he met my grandmother. She was a local girl from a traditional Japanese family. Together, they had one daughter. My mother."

"An international romance."

Micheline smiled. "Yes. It seems to run in the family. My mom grew up in Tokyo and attended American schools, so she was fluent in both English and Japanese. She went to college at NYU."

"That's so interesting," Guillermo said.

"She and my dad met during the winter holiday break at Rockefeller Center when she was ice skating, and he offered to buy her a cup of hot chocolate. They were the sweetest, most loving, and affectionate couple you've ever seen. She became a high school English teacher in New Jersey. She died last year after a brief but very painful battle with stage four cervical cancer."

"I'm so sorry to hear that, Micheline. My condolences," Guillermo said.

"Thanks," Micheline replied. "It really broke my father's heart. Mine too if I'm being perfectly honest. That's one of the reasons I packed my bags and headed to the west coast. I had to get away. I didn't want to leave my dad all alone, of course. But I needed to start taking care of myself. There were too many painful memories left behind."

Micheline gave an intensive, furtive look toward her new partner.

"So, Guillermo, I'm not what I may seem on the surface. I'm a one-in-a-million complicated hot mess."

"Oh, of that I have no doubt," Guillermo chuckled softly. "I see you as a firecracker with a short fuse."

"That's one way of putting it," Micheline agreed, nodding confidently. "I can assure you of one thing. You wouldn't like me when I get angry. Now, why am I here to work this case with you, Detective Reyes? And no bullshit this time, okay?"

Guillermo's eyes widened in surprise at Micheline's candid line of questioning and stern confrontational approach. She would make a fine interrogator.

"You're here specifically because you've already paid your dues back east from what I hear," Guillermo said, "and you deserve your shot."

"I appreciate that."

"I realize you're the underdog among a pack of wild hyenas out here. It's tough to fit in anywhere when you're moving from one place to another, especially moving across the country as you did."

"It hasn't been easy. That's true."

Guillermo nodded. "I requested you to help get your foot in the door. I believe you may have a lot to offer on this investigation. The rest is completely up to you. Don't let me down, okay? I'm sticking my neck out for you on this one."

Micheline nodded slightly and smiled warmly, somewhat satisfied with Guillermo's thoughtful response. She almost believed what he had said. She wanted to believe it.

"Thanks," she whispered sincerely. "I've heard good things about you, too, Guillermo."

As a matter of fact, she hadn't. She simply assumed that anyone of Guillermo's age and tenure within the department, the early sixties by the look of him, had to at least be somewhat honorable and worthy of Micheline's respect.

She had heard through some of her acquaintances in the department Guillermo had started as a beat cop right out of the police academy. He had earned a detective's shield nearly three decades before. He was still at it day in and day out after all that time. Whether there were any great stories of accomplishment during that long and extenuated career were yet to be shared.

"Now you've discovered my weakness," Guillermo squirmed uneasily. He felt put on the spot and uncomfortable telling a white lie to such a smart and beautiful woman from the get-go. That wouldn't be fair to Micheline, he silently conceded, and he had come very quickly to like her.

Better to lay it out there and own the truth than to hold back and allow a sense of mistrust to fester.

"Listen, the truth is," Guillermo admitted sheepishly, "you handled a domestic violence dispute in Mission Valley a while back. The husband was snorting coke and banging the under-aged girl across the hall. He was a real badass with a documented history of getting drunk and using his fists to take out his leftover frustrations on his wife whenever he felt like it."

"It sounds all too familiar," she said.

"Life handed him a few too many curveballs and he was always pissed at the world, I guess. His wife was a real sweetheart, too. He never deserved for someone as good as her to be in his life."

"I remember the case," Micheline said. "Vasquez. Shayna Vasquez. She had a shy demeanor, but a strong spirit. Despite her challenging and abusive circumstances on the home front, she was determined to stay positive and to succeed in life, regardless of what anyone told her to the contrary. I saw a lot of myself in her."

"Yes, I believe that."

"She worked full-time at a commercial bakery on the graveyard shift and was going to school to study nursing during the day. She fought hard to get ahead. You could see that resolute and tenacious look in her eyes."

"Her husband was a mess. He kept her from achieving her dreams," Guillermo said.

"But she had a heart of gold," Micheline added, "as I quickly found out, and I think that kept her from leaving him, even with the abuse she suffered. She kept thinking she could change him and make him whole again."

"That's right," Guillermo said, nodding amenably.

Micheline continued. "The husband, Oscar, was a real piece of work. He was a train engineer out on a disability claim. He was an alcoholic who was hooked on prescription painkillers and other recreational drugs. He tried to put his wife's head through the sliding glass door to the balcony one evening because she didn't have dinner cooked on time. I answered the call and I intervened. What about it?"

"According to the reports I reviewed," Guillermo said, "you showed up on the scene and took charge on your own, even before backup arrived. You didn't wait. You just plowed straight into the storm."

"It was a messed-up situation right from the start."

"Now, Oscar's a pretty tough dude," Guillermo acknowledged. "Six-foot-four and two hundred fifty pounds. He ended up on the floor with a dislocated shoulder and a broken nose. After he was deposed, you helped Shayna to find a safe place to move to."

"Uh-huh," Micheline confirmed, nodding.

"I heard from some of her friends you even bought her some text-books out of your own pocket for the following semester at school. Then I heard, somewhat off the record, I might add, you threatened Oscar and said if he didn't start attending his AA meetings regularly, you'd be back to see him again, and his shoulder and nose would be the least of his worries."

Micheline shrugged her shoulders awkwardly. She wanted to know where this discussion was leading.

"That takes fucking balls to call a man out like that," Guillermo declared. "Especially someone as crazy and dangerous as he was at the time."

"That's right," Micheline stated emphatically. "Oscar was a brute. He was a menace to everyone he met. He ruined the lives of the women around him, and he was headed straight down a dark path to hell. I wasn't about to let that go on any further. Now, what's up here, Guillermo? Why the heavy interest in that case? You knew them, didn't you?"

Guillermo looked squeamish. "Fact is, I've known Oscar his entire life. You see, he's my nephew, and you know how I am about taking care of family. Especially when it comes to my sisters and their kids."

"Oh, shit," Micheline winced.

"No, Micheline, look," Guillermo responded defensively with his hands held openly flat and his fingers spread wide.

"If you're going to advocate on his behalf, I don't want to hear it," Micheline contended.

"It's all good. Honestly, you did absolutely the right thing. Oscar is my flesh and blood. He's my sister's oldest son, and you put him down hard, just like I should have done a long time ago."

"I'm glad we're clear on that. He deserved a lot worse. I think he got off easy."

"Listen, I'm proud of you for what you did. This is my way of saying thanks for helping Shayna to escape from that domestic hell. She's a wonderful woman. I'm glad you were there to help her when she needed it most."

"Thank you."

"And for Oscar, too, believe it or not. You put him on the right path toward recovery. Imagine, a macho messed-up guy like that being beaten up by a tiny blue-eyed Latina with a badge. Sorry, I don't consciously mean to keep trying to label you. I'll work on that. But you understand where I'm coming from, right?"

Micheline looked to the floor and shrugged her shoulders.

"I was just doing my job, Guillermo."

Guillermo nodded his head up and down and pointed his index finger directly at Micheline.

"You could have done much less, Micheline. Many others would have looked the other way. But you didn't. You went in and faced that threat."

"I simply stood up for Shayna, that's all," Micheline declared. "It's called being empowered."

"I get it. And for that show of grit and strength, I'm eager to get to know you better."

"I appreciate the gesture, Guillermo."

"This isn't easy for me to confide in anyone. My conscience weighs heavy on me, and I still feel pangs of guilt for not taking charge of the situation the way you did. You're a true inspiration to those of us on the force who want to make a difference."

Micheline shrugged helplessly.

"What can I say?" she offered. "I was confronted on the job with a bad situation, and I reacted according to the severity of that situation. When I got to their apartment, Oscar was high as a kite and wanted to kick my ass with a broken beer bottle in his hand. I don't even think he knew it was broken. He just started swinging at me and charged toward me like a bull after a red cape."

"That had to be a tough scene to arrive to," Guillermo concurred.

Micheline nodded. "You have no idea. There were holes in the walls the size of fists. There were broken dishes and overturned furniture all over the place. He was a monster out of control."

"Where was Shayna?"

"She was curled up on the cold tile floor in the kitchen all bruised and bloody. She had a black eye and a gash on the side of her face. Her clothes were torn."

"Interviews with neighbors established there was a lot of screaming and shouting going on during the disturbance," Guillermo commented. "It wasn't the first time, either."

"Uh-huh. Oscar was a repeat offender."

"Why didn't you wait for backup, then? You had to know what you'd expect to find when you went in."

Micheline shrugged. "When I entered their apartment, I could see a trail of shattered glass spread between the kitchen and across the living room carpet, all the way to the sliding door to the balcony. There was no way was I going to let Oscar get the better of me, regardless of the shit I might have had to deal with from Internal Affairs afterward. My first instinct was to protect Shayna and to mitigate the situation with Oscar."

"You're saying you went easy on him?"

"I wasn't as tough on him as I could have been," Micheline admitted. "I saw Shayna watching all teary-eyed from the floor, and I put her needs before my own."

Guillermo nodded and offered a warm, confident smile. He had made a good choice to partner with Micheline on this case.

Of that, he was now completely certain.

Five

Guillermo glanced vacantly across the hotel room toward the medical examiner, who knelt on one knee near to the victim's corpse. The M.E. was completely absorbed in his own thoughts. He had not been eavesdropping on the detectives' lengthy introductory conversation.

"Hey Andy," he called out, "do we have an ID on the guy with the flashlight yet?"

Andrew Dadouris, San Diego County medical examiner and chief toxicologist, turned his attention from the decedent's body. He faced the detectives squarely.

"Detective Avila has collected all of the facts you'll need in that little black notebook of hers," the M.E. explained. "Give me another minute, please. I'm almost done here."

Micheline took her cue. "According to the driver's license, credit cards and business cards found in his wallet, our victim's name is John Paul Ballard. He went by the initials J.P. like he was some old-world oil industrialist or Wall Street financier. He was fifty-eight years old and a senior vice president at Fidelity National Savings and Loan Bank downtown in the Gaslamp Quarter. So, I guess the name fits the profile."

"A man of means and money," Guillermo noted. "The name sounds familiar, somehow."

"He's married with a wife and three kids. No one's reported him missing yet, but his cell phone has rung several times during the past thirty minutes I've been here. I've seen his picture on the local TV news broadcasts before. He's heavy into fundraising and charities, and he has connections with both the DA and the mayor."

"Had," Guillermo absently corrected.

"Either way," Andy interjected excitedly, "the two of you are going to have a lot of pressure coming down on you during the investigation. What we have here is a high-profile murder case with some outlandish twists. The media's going to go berserk if they catch wind of how this guy died."

"Have you determined a time of death yet?" Micheline asked.

The M.E. looked toward the ceiling with an indifferent expression marked upon his face. "I'd say approximately sixty to sixty-four hours ago. Let's call it sometime late on Sunday evening for now. It's hard to pin it down exactly. The combination of excessive heat and humidity moved the decomposition process along at a much more rapid pace than you'd normally encounter."

Micheline nodded thoughtfully. "According to the clerk at the front desk, the victim checked into the hotel by himself late on Sunday afternoon for three nights, and he never checked out."

"That's consistent with what I'm able to observe here," Andy confirmed.

"Actually, he did," Guillermo commented.

"He did what?" Andy asked, confused.

"Checked out," Guillermo replied, snickering. "For good."

Andy shook his head from side to side. He had worked on multiple cases with the senior detective in the past.

Guillermo could be such a pain in the ass, sometimes.

"Why didn't room service come in to change the bed sheets and bath towels?" Guillermo wondered aloud.

"The *do not disturb* placard had been hooked onto the outside door-knob," Micheline replied. "Check-out wasn't until noon today. The maid found him like this when she came in to clean the room this afternoon. No one disturbed the room until the local patrol cops arrived on the scene."

"Anything unusual from your perspective, Andy?" Guillermo asked. "What's so outlandishly twisted, as you say? I mean, aside from the fact he's fat, naked, balding, and has a one-and-a-half-inch diameter heavy-duty plumbing pipe planted between his ass cheeks?"

The M.E. looked down at the body again. "The victim has a contusion on the back of his head, and there are traces of blood consistent with that blow on the top of the flashlight. The part that's currently visible."

Guillermo chuckled, then emitted a harsh raspy breath.

"Best guess," Andy continued, "he fell to his knees after being struck on the back of the head by the flashlight. The assailant then pulled his head back and slit his throat with a second object. A knife or a surgical scalpel was used to make a deep incision, from right to left, indicating the assailant used their left hand."

"Did we find a knife or a scalpel at the scene?" Guillermo asked.

"No, we didn't," Micheline replied.

"Significant loss of blood from that wound is what probably killed him," the M.E. continued.

"There are no defensive wounds evident. He got taken by surprise. Then, and you're going to love this. After the victim was already dead, his penis and testicles were sliced clean off and placed in the toilet in the bathroom."

"Jesus Christ!" Guillermo expelled loudly. "Who would think to do such a thing? That's what you'd expect from a drug cartel killing, or a Russian mob hit. Except, they'd most likely shove his balls down his throat, right? Why put them in the toilet?"

"My thought," Micheline offered, "is the killer came to the hotel explicitly to murder our victim. There was a passion fueling their pent-up rage. They knew what they were doing. They were careful to contain the mess as much as possible. They subdued and killed the victim by the bed. Then they carved him up like they were performing some type of satanic ritual or voodoo ceremony."

"That's a good point. We should consider whether there are any religious implications evident from the way cuts were inflicted on the body," Guillermo suggested.

The M.E. nodded.

"Afterward," Micheline continued, "they inserted the flashlight into the decedent's rectum. All these activities took place within a relatively small amount of floor space. Notice there's no sign of blood splatter anywhere in the room other than immediately surrounding the body and from what sprayed directly onto the far wall."

"I agree," Guillermo noted.

"When they were done with the body," Micheline added, "they moved immediately into the bathroom, where they deposited the guy's private parts in the toilet and cleaned themselves up. There's no trace of bloody footprints or handprints anywhere I can detect. No droplets of blood anywhere on the carpet from the body to the bathroom."

"That's almost impossible to believe," Guillermo said. "I'll ask the CSI team to do a complete inspection with a UV light to make sure they don't miss anything."

"Uh-huh. Somehow, the killer was exceedingly proficient in the execution of this crime. As if perhaps, they wore coveralls like our M.E. here, and afterward they splashed chlorine bleach around the areas they may have touched."

"Yes, I can smell that," Guillermo said.

"The bleach disinfects environmental surfaces and destroys pathogens," Micheline added.

Andy nodded thoughtfully. "The killer took their good ol' time with this guy, too. The flashlight was inserted after the victim was already dead and missing his reproductive organs. Someone's poetic way of saying *fuck you*, I believe."

"Was the flashlight turned on when you arrived?" Guillermo asked. At this point, he wanted to identify any aberrant or unusual behavior on the killer's part.

"No, it wasn't turned on," Micheline confirmed.

"They shoved it in there nice and deep, too, just to be certain he got the message," Andy said. "Then they turned on the hot shower in the bathroom and switched off the AC before leaving the room as if to inflict further discomfort and humiliation to the decedent."

"You think they wanted to punish him?"

The M.E. shrugged. "Possibly. To me, though, it indicates they wanted to obscure or contaminate any evidence we might discover at the crime scene. Yesterday's high temperature was ninety-seven degrees. It was one hundred and two the day before that. The hot shower steam with the increased room temperature was deliberately planned."

"Something else seems strange," Micheline added. "Assuming the assailant is left-handed, as you say, they would have struck the victim with the flashlight by using their left hand. I sense intense rage, anger, and a personal confrontation here. Wouldn't it have been more reasonable to continue attacking the victim with the flashlight after the victim was already down on the floor?"

"I see where you're going with that," Guillermo said. "Maybe the flashlight wasn't enough to completely subdue the victim. He's a big man, after all. Maybe the flashlight strike was simply hard enough to stun the victim and to knock him to the floor. He probably recovered and was about to get up to retaliate when his guest switched to a more permanent solution, like a knife to the throat."

"So, then what?" Micheline asked, playing the devil's advocate. "The assailant must have acted quickly before our victim recovered from the initial blow to the back of the head. They would have needed to drop the flashlight immediately to the floor, and then pull out a concealed knife or another type of sharp weapon. If this person had planned to kill the victim in a premeditated fashion, you'd think they would have led with the knife in the first place."

"They probably wanted to keep it out of sight until the right moment presented itself," Guillermo offered.

"That's a fair point."

"The killer waited to be invited into the room," Guillermo suggested, "and then struck after the door was closed and the victim had turned his back to them. I agree with your initial observation. The guest must have witnessed the audacity of the victim strutting around the room completely naked, and launched into a violent and emotional frenzy, which ultimately resulted in this man's death."

"There's trace blood evidence on the corner at the foot of the bed," Andy added.

"See? The killer wasn't so perfect after all," Guillermo insinuated.

Andy nodded. "Again, my best guess is the assailant whacked the victim across the back of the head with the flashlight. As the victim dropped to his knees, the assailant tossed the flashlight onto the bed, and then withdrew a knife or sharp object which was used to sever the victim's windpipe."

"Do you have any thoughts as to what type of knife was used in the attack?"

"Early observations indicate a blade of no more than three or four inches in length. That's all I can say for now. I should be able to provide more details following the autopsy."

"What happened after the windpipe was severed?"

"After the victim was down and obviously not getting up again, the killer rolled him onto his back and removed his sex organs."

"Un-fucking-believable!" Guillermo groaned uncomfortably.

"As I mentioned," Andy continued, "the dismembered organs were found in the toilet in the bathroom. The victim's body was then rolled back onto his stomach, and the aforementioned flashlight was inserted deeply into the anal cavity. It's in there a good eight inches or more."

"Thanks, Andy," Guillermo said. "Is there anything else that might be pertinent?"

"I'll know more after the autopsy," the M.E. responded stoically. "I'm heading back to the County Operations Center in Kearny Mesa next. I'll have a full report for you by tomorrow afternoon. Toxicology will take more time, of course."

"Understood," Guillermo replied. "Thanks again."

Micheline cleared her throat. "Check for fingerprints on the flashlight, will you, please?" She paused. "Both ends."

"Yes, of course, Detective."

Micheline took on a more introspective look. She pursed her lips tightly.

"Something else, Detective?" Andy asked.

Micheline nodded. "Although it's a long shot, check for fluids on the, uh, private parts found in the toilet that may not belong to the deceased, please. He may have had sexual activity prior to being killed. You never know."

"All standard procedure, Detective Avila," the M.E. replied. "I'll have a report to you as soon as possible."

"Thank you, Andy," Micheline replied. "We really appreciate your help with this one."

The medical examiner nodded politely and stepped outside of the hotel room. The two detectives were left alone in the room.

"So, tell me," Guillermo queried, "what are your first impressions on this one, Micheline?"

"It was someone he knew, or someone he expected," Micheline surmised.

"An affair?"

"He was waiting for them, and he thought he was going to get laid. A lover? An escort, maybe? I assume a woman, perhaps even his wife. That's not out of the question. This is the honeymoon suite, after all. Maybe an anniversary getaway that went bad. I'm not sure. But again, we can't rule anything out at this early stage of the investigation. Male or female, the killer wanted to punish this man in the most painful way possible."

"I tend to agree with you," Guillermo confirmed. "What a way to go."

Micheline nodded. "He could have been having an affair. Our killer may have been the boyfriend or husband of the alleged lover."

"We need to identify some clues. Text messages or phone records may help with that."

"I spoke to the concierge at the front desk already," Micheline said. "She mentioned our victim had ordered a bottle of champagne on ice, and separate plates of shrimp cocktail with horseradish sauce, and fresh strawberries and whipped cream. Interestingly, all of that is missing from the crime scene. Not just the alcohol and the food, mind you, but the ice bucket and the plates are missing, too."

"It sounds like killing made them hungry," Guillermo quipped. "The dining room was a bloody mess and they had to settle for takeout."

"Your jokes get more off-color by the moment," Micheline advised. "Our killer took nothing to chance. They probably wanted to ensure they didn't leave any fingerprints behind."

"I haven't had shrimp cocktail or a glass of champagne in ages," Reyes commented. "It almost sounds like it was planned to be some sort of special occasion. A birthday or an anniversary like you suggested, maybe?"

Micheline shrugged her shoulders. "It could have been like that. Or perhaps the victim wanted to make a good first impression with his guest. He may have wanted to compensate for his shortcomings by promoting a sense of style and wealth. The honeymoon suite, the fancy food, and wine. Maybe he had a visitor for an hour or two. A new girlfriend or an escort. Possibly a random sexual encounter that ended consensually and without incident."

"That sounds plausible."

"The visitor may have left after their business was concluded, and a second guest may have shown up and caught him with his pants down. After all, infidelity is certainly a strong motive for a spouse or another romantic partner to lash out in a jealous rage."

"Agreed," Reyes said. "Perhaps he had a mistress and he lied about someday leaving his wife. Or maybe he was gay but wasn't going to come out of the closet. Our killer couldn't wait any longer."

"If we could establish the height of the attacker based on body position and entry wounds, that may help. This was a very personal attack. The victim felt comfortable enough to answer the door naked for his guest and then to turn his back on them as they entered and closed the door. I sense arrogance or bullying on the victim's part."

"I'm inclined to agree with you on that point."

"Whoever came to visit him arrived with a premeditated disposition to kill and humiliate him in the most excruciatingly painful way possible. It could turn out Ballard was expecting a lover or an escort for outcall, but someone he wasn't expecting to see showed up instead and surprised him. Nothing's off the table at this point."

Guillermo continued to nod in agreement.

"We should check the victim's recent phone messages," Micheline went on, "inform the family, canvas any hotel residents who may have seen something on Sunday evening, and check-in with his work colleagues, too. I'd like to know when they last saw him. It would be good to know what his family thought he was doing these past few days, and where they were during his absence as well. Remember, our victim hasn't been reported as missing yet by either his family or his employer, as far as we know. Maybe they all think he's away on a business trip, or that's what he's led them to believe. Maybe he called in sick at work."

"Now, see," Guillermo gleamed brightly, "you're already considering some devious subterfuge on the victim's part and a possible jealous wife or lover as the killer. You really think a woman is capable of hunting him down and carving him up like a wild animal?"

"Like I said," Micheline offered, "I sense rage and high emotion with this one. The kind of rage a woman feels when she's been mistreated by a male who had complete power over her. Maybe a battered wife, a jealous ex-wife, or an abused lover."

"But could it have been a male intruder? Could our victim have been queer? Could he have owed money to a drug cartel or to the mob?"

"A woman is a more likely gender to use a knife," Micheline said. "I think if it had been another male, regardless of their sexual orientation, he would have used a gun instead. It would have been a single shot to the back of the head. Simple, get it over with. Blow the guy away, you know?"

"Sure. That's a classic male response to a psychological or emotional problem," Guillermo said and chuckled. "We're just generalizing for now. There's no clear evidence to suggest the gender of our killer one way or the other."

"In this case, however, notice even though there's a lot of blood splatter near to where the body fell, there are no bloody footprints heading into the bathroom or to the door leading outside. Even the bed looks to be untouched except for trace amounts of blood from where the flashlight had been tossed."

"So, the killer was a neat freak."

"What I note," Micheline stated, "is the killer came prepared to clean up after the fact. Something tells me the crime scene investigators won't find any useful fingerprints, either, other than those of the victim, the cleaning crew, or former hotel guests. But let's make sure they do a thorough sweep of both rooms, nonetheless. I like the UV light idea."

Guillermo smiled and nodded in consent. "I knew I was right to ask for you on this case, Micheline. I've been doing this a long time. I've got a good eye for talent when I see it. I'll bet the NYPD misses having you around."

"Thanks, Guillermo," Micheline said. "I won't just see what I want to see. I'll always observe the facts of the case and allow them to lead me to a solid conclusion that can be backed up with firm evidence and witness testimony."

"That's good to know."

"I'm just hypothesizing for now. I'll consider both male and female suspects, and I'll review all of the evidence before making a solid judgment on a final report."

"Agreed," Guillermo said.

"It hasn't been easy for me out here," Micheline added. "I appreciate you asking me to partner with you on this one. I'm looking forward to getting to know you better and to working on this case with you. I can promise you one thing. I'll do my best. Working the Homicide Squad is my calling."

"You damn well better," Guillermo said with a hearty laugh. He wheezed again as he attempted to catch his breath.

"My reputation is at stake here," Guillermo continued, "and it sounds like we should expect the DA and the mayor might stick their noses directly into this inquiry, too."

"It's certainly a possibility."

"What else strikes you as out of the ordinary with this crime scene? It feels staged, doesn't it?"

"The flashlight," Micheline said. "It just seems so out of place. It's a large size, like something you'd keep on the bedside table for when the power goes out. Doubles as a weapon in case of intruders."

"Really?"

"I'm just thinking out loud for now," Micheline offered. "It's not something you'd think to bring to a hotel room with you unless it was already dark outside. That means after nine o'clock on Sunday night. We should check to see if there's any surveillance footage available from around that time."

"There are multiple businesses across the street," Guillermo offered. "There's a good chance we could catch a glimpse of the killer when they arrived on the scene."

"As for the flashlight, it belongs in the garage or a toolbox, maybe the trunk of a car. It could have some significant meaning between the victim and his assailant. A secret between the two of them. Maybe they liked to play sex games and used it under the covers. In that case, it wouldn't have presented a threat to the victim upon initially seeing it when the guest entered the room."

"You mean, maybe he couldn't get his dick to stand at attention, and he used it as a tool to get the job done and light the way?" Guillermo suggested with a mischievous glint in his eye. "Like a glow-in-the-dark dildo?"

"Stranger things," Micheline replied with a discouraging frown. "I was merely thinking they used the light under the covers to see what they were doing. But being a typical male, your mind went straight to the macabre or the gutter. We've both experienced some weird and aberrant behavior during our careers. Am I right?"

"Agreed," Guillermo nodded in affirmation. "I've come across some weird shit in my time."

"Interesting suggestion, though," Micheline commented. "It might explain why the victim had it shoved up his anal cavity after he was already dead. Perhaps it was payback for something he did to our killer, like anal-copulation. Retaliation for a prior sexual act that was not consensual. Maybe he forced himself on the killer during an earlier encounter, and used the wrong hole against their wishes."

Guillermo nodded agreeably. "That would establish a clear motive, too. C'mon, let's allow the CSI team in here to do their jobs, and for the ambulance attendants to transport the body and the, uh, external parts to the morgue. You focus on interviewing the hotel staff and any guests who may have been staying here on Sunday night. Obtain any video surveillance footage from the hotel or from the businesses across the street."

"I'm all over it," Micheline said.

"It's probably too late but ask the patrol officers on scene to check the dumpsters around the side of the building, too. We need to find the murder weapon and the clothing the killer wore during the attack. It's possible evidence may have been tossed somewhere in the vicinity of the hotel property."

Micheline smiled. "Already done."

"Good. I'll check through his recent cell phone messages, his wallet, and his background," Guillermo continued in a rasp as he struggled to get the words out.

"We'll meet up later at headquarters to discuss our findings," he added thoughtfully, "and we'll arrange to meet with the victim's family, too. This is going to be difficult news to break to them."

"But necessary," Micheline concluded. "We'll need to understand who the victim was. What his personality was like. What interests did he have, or what drove him to behave the way he has? Was he close to his family, or detached with outside hobbies or activities known only to himself?"

"I believe you've got this," Guillermo acknowledged.

"This is just the beginning," Micheline said. "The first few hours after a murder are the most critical. This is already day three. We'll have to be all over this."

Guillermo checked his watch. "It's going to be a late-night working this one. I'd better call my wife to forewarn her. We can interview the victim's colleagues at the bank first thing tomorrow morning. We'll plan to meet with the family after that. Does that sound like a plan to you?"

"I'm on board with it," Micheline replied. "I may be a little late tomorrow morning, though, if that's all right. I need to get my car to the dealership first thing in the morning."

"Is it something that can be put off until later?"

"I had a bit of a scrape on Harbor Drive right before I came on the scene today. There's some damage to the front quarter panel. I'd prefer to get it taken care of as soon as possible. But I'll arrange for a rental vehicle, and I'll meet you as soon as I can."

"How about if I pick you up at the dealership after you drop your car off tomorrow morning? It'll save us some valuable investigative time and give us more time to get to know each other."

Micheline nodded agreeably. "That works for me. I'll text you the details with the dealer's address later tonight. For now, let's go catch ourselves a killer."

Six

The Hall of Justice

Superior Courthouse, San Diego County

Thursday, August 6th

Muted light from a late afternoon Pacific sun shone through the dark tinted windows into Detective Micheline Avila's tiny ninth-floor office. What Micheline liked most about her office space, if anything, was that it was quiet. It was a small, out-of-the-way dry-walled and glass enclosure the detective generally referred to as *The Cube*.

On days like today, when the air conditioning was turned up high, she disingenuously renamed her daily workspace *The Ice Cube*. Somehow adding humor made it seem a bit warmer and more comfortable.

Micheline pulled a navy wool cardigan sweater from her desk drawer. She buttoned it and folded her arms across her chest to help fend off the cold air flowing from the overhead ceiling vent.

Staggered atop her desk, the case file documents of the J.P. Ballard murder investigation were strewn and separated into random piles. More than two months had passed since the investigation had begun. Still, Micheline had little more to go on than she did on the day she first stepped into the darkened and foul-smelling crime scene at the Oceanside Hotel.

Alibis were locked down. No weapon was ever discovered. No fingerprints or forensic evidence other than that belonging to the victim came to light. Video surveillance footage from across the street of the hotel revealed nothing. The killer had been evasive, crafty, and cunning.

More damaging to the case than anything, few people had wanted to talk openly or honestly about the victim, even posthumously. It seemed no one really knew him well or liked him well enough to speak on his behalf.

The wife spoke of events during their marriage as if that constituted legitimately knowing the man from the inside. She spoke of material things he had bought her---the vacation home in Colorado, the gift-wrapped Audi SUV she received for Christmas the year before, diamond jewelry, and the gift box hidden under the bed with sexy lingerie for Valentine's Day she had secretly discovered. It was a few sizes too small for her frame, of course, and it was already summertime. But she overlooked those obvious flaws in the details and pretended they didn't matter.

He was so thoughtful, she kept saying repeatedly. He was such a great guy, and he told the best jokes. Then she crooned about how he often left work early to attend one of their children's school or sporting events.

The wife never once identified a particular personality trait attributed to him, or what books he liked to read, what foods he enjoyed, what television shows or movies they watched together.

It was as if they shared the same address but lived separate lives.

She kept lamenting about how he concentrated on his career, how hard he worked, and how tired it always made him feel. She also had no recollection as to what he did while he was away from the home for business trips, which occurred regularly three or four times each year.

But she fondly remembered the cities he was so fortunate to travel to on banking business, including Los Angeles, San Francisco, Las Vegas,

Orlando, and New York. There were even a few international events in London, Paris, and Hong Kong over the years. He was, after all, an important businessman in the greater San Diego region. He attended political dinners with the district attorney and the mayor. He received community awards for his philanthropic and fundraising efforts.

To that point, during a much more interesting and telling interview, Bill Hudgens, the bank president, had confirmed to the detectives J.P. Ballard had no need to travel to conferences or for business purposes. Ever. He must have taken those trips, Hudgens had suggested, during Ballard's scheduled vacation periods and personal days offered through his employee benefits each year.

"His domestic and foreign travel certainly wasn't related to any work assignments or responsibilities in his role at my bank," Hudgens had confirmed resolutely.

One of the bank's administrators had been somewhat forthright and had made a few accusatory suggestions regarding her fellow colleagues. She had been quick to recant her stories, though, when she realized what she was inferring and asked for anonymity.

Micheline had liked her. The woman hadn't backed away when asked some tough questions about her former boss. She provided insight into Ballard's character when none had been obvious before.

What was her name? Something Italian.

Micheline checked the files across the desktop and found the one she was searching for.

Ah, yes. Jenny Casella, senior manager of operations.

Jenny Casella at least had a few nice remarks to say about her former supervisor regarding his wry sense of humor and his mentoring and management coaching style.

"Sure, he was a creep and an obvious voyeur at times," Jenny had said. "He made the women feel uncomfortable. But he had a softer side, too. He was sensitive at times. He offered encouragement. He talked about career advancement and retirement planning. He took time to explain things when no one else would."

It seemed no one else had liked J.P. Ballard as much as Jenny Casella had. That was the consensus Micheline arrived at after having interviewed more than two dozen employees, colleagues, or acquaintances of the former senior vice president at the Fidelity National Savings & Loan Bank.

Ballard was said to have been an arrogant prick, to put it mildly. He was tough on his employees. He offered preferential treatment to those he liked, usually young and attractive women, and he snubbed his nose at men and women alike who showed determination to advance their careers through education, or who lacked the physical appeal of a beach bikini or fashion runway model.

Ballard was said to have often presented others' work as his own. He generally never provided praise or compliments to those he supervised. He doled out assignments to his staff to keep his workload as light as possible, and he only took interest when a wealthy client was involved.

Ballard had also lied to his family about where he would be on the day he was killed. He told them he would be attending an accounting and finance convention in Las Vegas that Sunday through Wednesday, when in fact he was booked into the honeymoon suite at a nearby oceanfront hotel. His wife of thirty-two years and their three children, ages ranging from sixteen to twenty-seven, were left stunned, flabbergasted, and socially embarrassed.

Now, they just wanted to cover it up, to pretend he had been a respectful businessman, a loving husband, a good father, and to be able to move on with their lives.

Over the years, J.P. Ballard had been a man of numbers. He had started his career as an accountant and CPA. He had ascended through the ranks at the bank as each director or vice president above him had moved on to other more promising opportunities across the bank's many branch locations, or at other companies within the financial world.

At age fifty-eight, J.P. Ballard was on the board of directors for several San Diego-based real estate and biotech companies. He had amassed a personal fortune and real estate holdings worth more than twelve million dollars.

Yet, putting aside J.P. Ballard's unfavorable personality traits and characteristics, and his obvious financial holdings, no one had reason enough to want to kill him. His work colleagues and family members all had tight alibis for the date and time of the murder, and there was no way to connect him through electronic or hard copy communications to other suspects.

There was a well-concealed and hidden part of J.P. Ballard's life missing from the picture, and none of the detectives on the case had been able to solve that mystery. He was a ghost, and his private haunts remained an enigma to those who searched for answers.

"Hey, Micheline. Got a minute?" Assistant Prosecuting Attorney Mark Longfellow asked as he entered the chilly glass cube without knocking or announcing himself beforehand.

Micheline looked up from her reading material. Standing immediately behind Mark was Detective Guillermo Reyes. Both men's eyes exhibited somber expressions of crushing defeat.

It was all about to be over. Micheline could tell without having to ask.

Both Mark and Guillermo approached her desk apprehensively.

"I'm so sorry, Micheline," Mark began. "I know you put your heart and soul into the Ballard murder case. It's given me plenty of sleepless nights lately, too."

"It just can't be as simple as a random online escort service and a disagreement over money," Micheline offered defensively. "They didn't take anything other than the room service food. The victim still had his wallet and cell phone in the room. No cash or credit cards appear to have been taken."

Mark shook his head in disagreement. "There was an obvious connection to some form of deviant sexual activity. The removal of his penis is clearly a statement to that effect. The insertion of the flashlight into his rectum adds further speculation he may have forced himself on an unwilling sexual partner in the past."

"That's just hype for the media and an excuse for the DA's office to win some political leverage by taking on the adult websites and their association with the local hotel industry. I'm not in favor of that approach. The way the victim was killed doesn't fit that M.O. He knew his killer and he invited them into that room with him."

"Agreed," Guillermo piped in. "But we've got nothing else to hang our hats on. We've exhausted all potential leads. Every suspect we've considered has an ironclad alibi, and Ballard was so secretive about his extramarital activities that we're running blind."

"I just need more time," Micheline insisted.

"We've run into a brick wall, Micheline," Guillermo said. "For those incidents, we were able to confirm, he paid cash. We know he must have had a second smartphone, a laptop, or another peripheral tablet device through which he planned his secretive activities. But there's no electronic record of ownership or payments for such accounts."

"We can keep digging."

"I'm sorry. We can only deduce the killer knew about these devices and removed them from the scene to cover their own tracks, the same way they absconded with the bottle of champagne, the ice bucket, and the fruit and shrimp cocktail plates."

"I realize that," Micheline concurred.

"And we found nothing from the surveillance footage taken in and around the area at the suspected time of death," Guillermo mentioned.

"The case will remain unresolved officially," Mark interjected. "We'll give it more time, certainly, but we've got to put it aside and move on to other priorities that have a much higher probability of being solved. Our caseload isn't getting any lighter, you know."

Micheline frowned. "I understand," she replied. She had seen this coming, of course, although she had hoped for a little more time and more resources or latitude than she was being dealt.

"At some point, we'll need to hand everything over to the local FBI field office."

Micheline crossed her arms and locked her jaw in a tenacious display of biting her tongue.

"Take one more day," Mark offered, noting her dejected facial expression. "I know that's not enough. But that's all we've got. Explain it to the wife, and maybe swing by the bank or the hotel for a final look around. Talk to the employees again. But come Monday morning, I'll have some new assignments for you. The Financial Crimes Unit has expressed interest in having you back."

Micheline nodded and conceded to the suggestion. "Of course. Please know, though, I'd prefer to stay with the Homicide Squad if possible. I enjoyed working alongside Guillermo."

"I'll provide a hearty recommendation, Mark," Guillermo added. "Micheline is worthy of the effort, despite the outcome of the Ballard investigation."

"That's duly noted," Mark replied. "I'll speak to the DA, but I'm not sure she'll budge from her position on the matter. She's been in quite a mood lately."

"I appreciate it if you would just make one more strong closing argument on my behalf, Counselor," Micheline suggested.

She turned toward her partner.

"Thanks, Guillermo, for believing in me and giving me a chance to work the case with you. It gave me some great experience, and a chance to meet the members of the CSI team. That alone was worth the price of admission."

"It was my pleasure, Micheline," the elder detective remarked solidly.

Micheline turned back toward the assistant prosecuting attorney. She smiled and raised her eyebrows.

"And Mark, whatever you can do to dissuade the DA into changing her mind will not go unnoticed. Think about how wonderful it would be if Boston cream doughnuts or warmed cheese Danishes were on your desk every morning for an entire week."

"I like that idea," he said. "Bribery might be very effective in this instance."

Micheline nodded with a smile. "I have a sneaking suspicion the male barista at the coffee shop I go to every morning has a secret crush on me. I might be able to swing a good deal on some morning pastries for all of us."

"And would that include coffee?" Mark asked jokingly. "Something fancy, too, like an upside-down salted caramel macchiato with whipped cream."

Micheline smiled again. She was happy to play along with Mark's witty banter.

"And some fancy coffee, too," she confirmed. "That is, if you deliver on my request, of course. Otherwise, forget it. The deal's off. I'm not a fool, you know."

Mark smiled optimistically. "I'll see what I can do," he promised. "For now, it might be best to give you some experience across a variety of cases. Let each of the departments get to see what you have to offer. One way or another, you'll find your niche."

Micheline shrugged. "I'll go where I'm needed, Mark. Now, how about letting me get back to this case? I still have tomorrow and the weekend to break it open before you pull me away for good."

"As you wish," Mark said. He turned toward Detective Reyes.

"C'mon, Guillermo. Let's get out of her way before she bulldozes us over on her way out the door."

Micheline was quickly becoming recognized for her tenacity and her concern for the victims and their families whom she represented.

Seven

The Paradise Gentlemen's Club

Gaslamp Quarter, San Diego

Monday, November 9th

The diminutive man with the faded San Diego Padres baseball cap and polarized, blue-lensed Maui Jim sunglasses sat nervously at the corner table by himself. He hunched forward with his hands clasped tightly in a knot in front of him.

To the strip club regular males seated at the nearby bar, he looked uncomfortable and appeared somewhat feminine in a nerdish or book-worm's sort of way. The dark glasses and unruly facial hair only added to the mystery.

Vanessa Nguyen approached the shadowy corner table with a cheerful smile. New business was always more charitable than the dollar tips left by the auto mechanics and construction and factory workers who frequented the downtown Gaslamp Quarter club on most days during the week.

There was something a bit unusual or odd about this man seated at the corner table today, though. The intuitive word was *strange*. Vanessa couldn't put her finger on it immediately.

The man had a pale complexion that contrasted sharply with a wiry dark mustache and goatee. He was dressed in an oversized hooded sweatshirt and baggy blue jeans with a clunky pair of faded leather work boots that were left untied. He appeared to be a member of one of the local construction crews.

He had long black curly hair that was carefully bunched and concealed under the faded and time-worn baseball cap. He was obviously shy and kept to himself, and he had soft hands and neatly trimmed fingernails. At first glance, Vanessa assumed he was likely an LGBTQ paradox without an immediate answer.

"Hi, hon," Vanessa opened flirtatiously, and purposefully bent low in front of him to show off her surgically enhanced cleavage. "I'm Vanessa. I don't believe I've ever seen you in here before. Is this your first time?"

The man glanced upward and offered a slight nod. Vanessa was a petite Vietnamese girl with dark hair and blonde highlights in her early twenties, he assumed. She was dressed in a thin white cotton tank top T-shirt without a bra that showed off her bulging breasts, and tight blue denim cut-off shorts, and black open-toe high heels. Her nails on both her fingers and toes were painted a matching light shade of pink.

"I'm new in town," the man said softly. "I heard this place would be," he paused for a moment to select the appropriate word, "entertaining."

"Oh, it is," Vanessa replied enthusiastically. "You'll enjoy yourself here. All of the girls are very friendly and sexy, too."

"That's good to know."

"Can I bring you a drink?" she asked.

"A local IPA draft, please."

Vanessa smiled again. "That's a good choice, baby."

The man gazed curiously toward the stage beyond the long mahogany bar. A tall, athletic blonde, completely nude with a shaved kitty and several strategically placed tattoos and body piercings was dancing to the rhythm of the music that reverberated loudly from the ceiling-installed sound system.

As one song faded out and another began, the dancer approached closely to the men seated at the bar and began to pose and stretch provocatively in front of them. She smiled and blew kisses until each customer offered a monetary tip to show their appreciation for the visual spectacle, the personal attention, and the entertainment she provided.

"I'll be right back," Vanessa said.

"Before you go," the man interrupted suddenly, "is there a dancer here who goes by the name Clarissa?"

Vanessa looked uncertain. "No, baby, I'm sorry. I don't think any of the dancers or staff here has used that name."

The man looked forlorn and confused. "But I have a business card from this club. The girl wrote a short note, and she signed her name as Clarissa. I took it to mean maybe she still worked here. Damn, I was looking forward to seeing her tonight."

Vanessa could clearly feel the disappointment in the man's body language. She could sense it in his eyes and his facial expression, even from behind the classic frame dark sunglasses and the tangled scruff of beard and mustache that surrounded his lips and lower chin.

"Let me ask the bartender," she suggested. "I only started here a few weeks ago. He may know something."

"Thank you," the man replied. "Please, let me know. I'd really appreciate it."

Vanessa touched the man's arm gently and felt the solid muscle constrict tensely beneath the fabric of his sweatshirt. "Of course, baby. Let me see what I can find out."

"You're an angel," he said with a bright smile.

"Aw, that's sweet," Vanessa replied. "I'll be back soon with both your beer and an answer. But even if I don't get you the answer you were hoping for, I'm sure we can introduce you to someone else who is here tonight, and they'll show you a good time. You'll be incredibly pleased, no matter what."

The man nodded with an understanding smile and watched as Vanessa turned away. He absentmindedly twisted his palms in a tight knot upon the table again.

Minutes passed. A petite Brazilian dancer who was introduced as Melina took the stage and began to remove one article of clothing at a time to the hoots and shouts of the mostly male audience. To the man's surprise, there were a generous number of female viewers present in the club tonight who were just as vocal and excited as their male counterparts.

He tried to wait patiently but failed miserably at the attempt. His knuckles turned white from the pressure of his fingers being squeezed upon the table.

He observed carefully and nervously as several of the dancers strolled topless through the club with crumpled Washingtons and Lincolns stuck beneath the tiny colorful strings of their bikini bottoms and lace panties. The ladies engaged in whispered conversations with the customers seated at the other tables. Every so often, a dancer led a customer by the hand to a hallway located at the rear of the club, presumably for a private dance.

Vanessa returned to the table out of breath and stammered, "Oh shit, baby. I'm so sorry. I forgot your beer. I'm no use to anyone unless I'm focused on one thing at a time."

"That's all right, darling," the man reassured her quietly. "I can't walk and chew gum at the same time, either. Did you find anything out about Clarissa?"

"Yes, I did," Vanessa replied. "I found out she did work here up until about a year or two ago. But she left."

"Is there anything else you can tell me?"

Vanessa nodded enthusiastically.

"The bartender described her as a gorgeous California blonde with a body that would stop traffic. Movie star material, you know. But one day she just decided to give up dancing at the club. It sounds as though she found herself a steady boyfriend or a rich married guy to take care of her. She left without giving any notice, and no one's heard from her since."

"Lucky guy, huh?"

"Joey, the bartender, said she came from a rich family, too. Sounds like she wanted to be very naughty. You know, to get back at her parents for not understanding her when she was younger. Same sob story for most girls who live this type of life, I'm afraid. They come and they go. Sorry, baby. Maybe I could take your mind off her with a private dance later if you'd like?"

"Thanks, but no."

"Aw, c'mon. I know just what you need, baby. I can see you're all tense and bothered tonight. I've got all the right skills and equipment to make you smile. Besides, I like you. There's something sweet and innocent about the way you carry yourself. I'd sure like to get to know you more intimately. What do you say, baby? Can I be your special girl tonight?"

The man shrugged his shoulders confusedly and looked down at the table, apparently considering his options. Slowly, abstractly, he unclenched his fingers and inhaled a deep breath.

"Did Joey know anything else about Clarissa?" he asked. "Like, where she might have gone to work next, or who this new boyfriend could be?"

"No, he didn't, baby," Vanessa replied. "Sorry about that, hon. Everyone likes to be discrete and keep their privacy in this business. Clarissa's not even her real name. You understand that, right?"

"Yes, of course," the man stammered. "Thank you, Vanessa. I really do appreciate your help tonight."

"Of course, baby," Vanessa answered. "Come on. Let me walk you back to the private rooms. I'll take your mind off whatever's troubling you tonight and give you some sweet release."

The man shook his head sadly from side to side and pulled a wad of cash from the pocket of his hooded sweatshirt. He laid a twenty-dollar bill on the table.

"For your trouble," he said apologetically. "Maybe I'll see you some other time, Vanessa. You're a good girl. I'm just not in the right frame of mind tonight. Have a nice evening."

The man stood without saying anything more and began to walk slowly toward the exit of the strip club.

Vanessa watched him leave and rolled her eyes in a combination of absolute frustration and utter amusement. The man's ass shook from side to side like a lady strolling down the sidewalk in high heels.

Fucking men! she thought whimsically. *They never have a clue what they need until it's too late.*

Outside the strip club, the man walked slowly along the cement sidewalk and crossed the street to a vacant bank parking lot. He checked his surroundings carefully. The only available light was emitted from the drive-through ATM on the far side of the Fidelity National Savings & Loan Bank building. The outer perimeter of the parking lot was blanketed in darkness.

When he was certain he was alone, he approached the driver's side door of a sporty convertible that was parked toward the back end of the empty lot.

He sat back and stared at the dim reflection in the rearview mirror. He was hardly recognizable, even to himself.

Then, after checking his surroundings a final time and feeling certain no one would notice him amid the shadows of the back parking lot, he withdrew a folding knife from the front pocket of the oversized hooded sweatshirt. He carefully placed it upon the front passenger seat. Next, the faded ball cap, a black curly-haired wig, and the dark sunglasses were removed and tossed onto the passenger side seat.

Long straight hair fell across the driver's shoulders. Then, the dark mustache and goatee that had been painstakingly glued in place to the soft skin beneath were gently pulled away.

The driver smiled fiendishly at the sudden change of appearance in the reflection of the rear-view mirror.

"Where are you hiding, Clarissa?" the driver mused aloud. "I've missed you, my dear. But I'll be coming to see you soon. You can bet your life on that."

Eight

Marino's Italian Bistro

Mira Mesa Plaza

Thursday, November 12th

C old water surged from the chrome-plated tap of the men's rest-room into Micheline Avila's cupped, outstretched palms. Micheline stood five foot four inches tall and weighed a solid, well-toned one hundred twenty-six pounds. She leaned over the granite-like solid surface vanity as if she were awaiting a withdrawal of cash from an ATM, and abruptly splashed the handful of water against her makeup-free face.

"Aahhh!" she gasped out loud. "I needed that, let me tell you. Better than a cup of coffee. It's been a long day, toward the end of a pretty tough week."

Micheline's exotic-looking azure eyes scrutinized the smudged mirror set above the vanity backsplash. Her reflection stared hard back at herself. Over time, she had noticed slight signs of maturation and experience that had slowly carved finely etched lines into her buttery smooth, naturally tanned complexion.

Even though more than a decade had passed since her graduation with undergraduate degrees in English literature and criminal justice from Penn State University, followed by a master's degree in forensic behavioral science from Boston College, and the sudden and inexplicable move a year earlier from the east coast to the west coast, she still considered herself to be a relatively young and attractive woman. Mind over body, she reasoned.

After an agonizingly painful divorce she never liked to talk about, followed by the heartbreaking loss of her mother, it was time for a fresh start in sunny, warm southern California. It was a place she had always dreamed of living in. She realized, though, it didn't matter where you ran to. Life was all about enjoying the journey, living in the moment, and less about getting to any specific destination.

She had gained a few pounds over the years. Thankfully it was all muscle and was strategically deposited in all the right places. She balanced her life by running a few miles nearly every day and lifted weights, heavy weights, regularly at a local health club.

She maintained a lean, muscular frame that was enhanced by well-defined curves. Her calf muscles, especially when visibly flexed in high heels, were sculpted like an ancient Greek or Roman marble statue. Her heart rate continued to beat slow and steady, even under pressure when her job demanded it.

Her eyes darted quickly to view the reflection of the urinals embedded against the wall behind her.

One urinal was occupied.

"Stand there any longer," she called out, "and there won't be any pizza left for us by the time we make it back to the table."

"Sorry about that, Micheline," Wade Branigan replied over his shoulder. "I didn't mean to interrupt you or to barge in unannounced. But I had to piss like a racehorse. The popcorn at the theater was loaded with butter and salt, and I finished off a large soda and half of Laura's before I could quench my thirst."

"Sure," Micheline said mockingly. "You've been standing there long enough to fill one of the aquariums at Sea World. You know, if you shake it more than twice, you're just playing with it."

Wade grunted morosely in reply. He zipped his faded denim jeans closed and ran a hand through his dark, shoulder-length hair.

After a moment's hesitation, he said, "Well, this is about the only action it gets lately. And what are you doing using the men's room anyway? I saw Greg coming out the door right before me. You two had sex in here, didn't you?"

Micheline dried her hands with two small paper towels from the wall dispenser near the entrance door. "I'll never tell," she giggled, and winked playfully at him.

"By the way," she said, "what's with the comment about you not having any action lately with your lovely wife? The two of you always seem great together."

Wade depressed the chrome-plated lever to flush the urinal he had used. He turned with an indifferent shrug of his shoulders and approached the mirrored vanity to wash his hands.

"Between you and me," he said, "married life isn't the romantic fantasy I thought it would be. You'll understand someday, maybe. As you get older, it's more about responsibility, settling into a regular routine, and working your ass off just to pay the monthly mortgage and utility bills. Not to mention, the property taxes and the earthquake and homeowner's insurance premiums out here are fucking insane."

Micheline took notice for the first time of the red and black tattoo of a wolf's head on Wade's upper right arm. The artwork was partially concealed by the sleeve of his black graphic T-shirt. Micheline knew a thing or two about body art. She recognized the image on Wade's arm immediately as a jailhouse gang tattoo.

"Meaning what?" she asked sincerely.

"Just that, and nothing more," Wade replied. "I've been working a lot of hours at the auto repair shop the past few weeks. When I get home, there's plenty more work to do around the house. All the while that is going on, I still have to keep track of the kids. We've got a teenager who thinks she knows it all, and two toddlers who have more energy than they know what to do with. By the end of the day, I don't know whether to sit back and watch a movie on TV or to just throw myself in bed."

Micheline settled her hip against the edge of the vanity and folded her arms. "You two aren't splitting up or anything, are you?"

"No, no," Wade replied, "nothing like that. Having a family really does complete me, and Laura's great with the kids, too. But I struggle to keep the business afloat, and she works two jobs for us to almost make ends meet. We always seem to come up a bit short at the end of each month lately. It just keeps getting tougher over time, you know. Like a hamster wheel, we just can't get ourselves off."

Micheline nodded. "Yeah, I understand what you're saying. Life can be like that."

Wade averted his gaze from Micheline and stared benignly at the ceramic tiled floor. Then, somewhat unconvincingly he added, "I'm just stressing, is all. It's all good, really. We're having a nice time tonight with you and Greg and Jenny."

"Me, too."

"Laura mentioned Jenny's feeling pretty damn proud of herself for setting you and Greg up together. Somehow she knew you two would hit it off."

"We don't know each other really well yet," Micheline admitted. "Just a few dates so far. But I like him, of course, and we're both having fun tonight, too. I see Jenny and Laura get along like sisters. I hope I can fit in with them without causing any rifts."

"Yeah, they've really gotten close over the past few years. You'll be fine. They both like working out, iced coffees, reading books, movies at the theater, and a night out to enjoy pizza and beer. All things I hear you like, too."

Micheline nodded. "From what you're telling me, it sounds like you and Laura just need to take a vacation together. Maybe shut down the shop for a day and take the kids to the beach. Or maybe take them to the wildlife safari preserve near Escondido. I haven't been there yet, myself. But I hear they have Sumatran tigers, South African white rhinoceroses, and the huge California condors that were extinct in the wild at one point. I heard they're making a comeback in the wild in some of the southwestern states now. I might be able to snag some free vouchers for you from the police holiday fund."

Wade lifted his gaze from the floor but did not let his eyes meet Micheline's. "Not a bad idea, really. Maybe just to take a few days off from work and to spend some time away from the daily grind would be enough. But the kids have school activities, and Thanksgiving and Christmas are coming up soon. I've got a business I'm trying to run, and Laura's got both jobs to think about, even though one is only a part-time, fill-in gig. It's hard to find the time when our family universe is nothing but pure chaos."

"Things will get better, you'll see," Micheline offered sincerely.

Wade nodded. "I'm sure it will. I've been through much worse and survived. Ready for that pizza?" he asked, hoping to change the subject.

"Yes," Micheline agreed. "I've built up quite an appetite tonight."

"You mean before I walked in on you?" Wade snickered.

Micheline giggled softly. "I told you, my lips are sealed on such matters."

Wade hesitated momentarily and averted his eyes toward the floor again. "Hold up, please. I've been meaning to ask, if you don't mind, Micheline. I noticed that bulge at your left ankle. You're carrying a piece, aren't you?"

Micheline nodded perceptively. "It's my backup weapon. It goes with the job, I guess. I carry it with me most of the time, even when I'm off-duty."

Wade appeared to be keenly interested, Micheline noted.

"It looks very compact," Wade observed. "Is it a nine mil? That's what most women cops go for, right?"

Micheline lifted the pants cuff of her dark blue denim jeans to reveal a leather ankle holster. "No," she replied. "It's a .38-caliber Smith and Wesson Bodyguard Airweight."

Wade smiled. "A five-shooter, huh? Nice. Have you ever had to use it in the line of duty?"

Micheline shook her head. "No, thankfully. I've only ever drawn my primary weapon three times in response to a situation on the job. I've never had to pull the trigger in the line of duty. I've only ever fired the gun at the target range. I was fortunate that the intense situations I mentioned got resolved quickly, and I was able to holster my gun before things got too out of hand."

Wade motioned quickly toward the door. "That's so cool, Micheline. A girl who packs a loaded gun on a date to the movies. And Greg still made a move on you when the two of you were alone in the bathroom. That's brave! Okay, let's get going before my wife and our friends realize we've finally found something we have in common we can talk about."

Micheline understood what Wade had meant by his comments and took no personal offense. They had known each other for less than three months. This was due entirely to a friendship that had been formed between Micheline and Jenny, who had gone out for drinks one evening after the J.P. Ballard murder investigation had gone cold. Jenny worked at the bank, and she and Micheline had gotten to talking when Micheline was tying up some loose ends on the unsolved murder investigation.

Other than her work colleagues, Micheline had few close personal friends. She attributed that to having only recently settled in San Diego.

Jenny had persuaded Micheline to go out for drinks that evening after work. During the conversation, Micheline realized they shared a lot of common interests. She had relaxed and let her guard down. She smiled. She laughed. She ordered a second round of drinks and suggested they should do that again sometime. She felt as though she was finally beginning to make contact and to fit in to her new surroundings.

Jenny was best friends with Laura, Wade's wife. The two women had met at the public library a few years before when both ladies had been taking separate certification or college courses and needed a quiet place to study.

Jenny and Laura had continued their friendship by working out at the same gym and enjoyed a coffee from time to time at a local bookstore or doughnut shop. Due to Laura's busy work schedule, though, this occurred typically only on Sunday afternoons.

Like Micheline, Greg was a relative newcomer to the group. He worked at a luxury car dealership near Carlsbad and had sold Jenny her current ride. Greg was a smooth talker, handsome, tall, clean-shaven, and he had a strong, muscular build. He was the perfect distraction for Micheline at this nexus point in her life. It had been Jenny who had made the introductions and brought Greg and Micheline together.

Micheline hadn't even asked what type of expensive car Greg had been able to sweet-talk Jenny into purchasing yet. But it was a topic she looked forward to entertaining soon.

Greg's ride was a sleek black Mercedes S-Class AMG convertible. Micheline loved the feel of the leather seats and how the vehicle handled sharp turns. She was also impressed with Greg's apparent success in his career. She was looking forward to learning more about him.

For Micheline and Wade, it had been an awkward, rocky beginning. Although Wade was a responsible family man who owned and operated an auto repair and body shop, he was also an ex-con. Twice in his earlier life, he had been on the wrong side of the law.

Micheline by comparison was a career law enforcement officer who worked for the San Diego County Sheriff's Department. Before that, she had spent eight years working for the NYPD. For five of those more recent years in New York, she had been a homicide detective.

This night marked the third time the two couples, with Jenny tagging along with solo, had gotten together for a mid-week early evening movie at the cinema, followed by a serving of multi-topping pizza and a pitcher of light beer.

There always seemed to be something interesting to talk about among the group.

Laura chatted about the customers she served at the pharmacy or at the bar. The pharmacy customers always seemed to be irritated with their insurance companies and payment plans. They typically weren't feeling well, to begin with, and this often translated to rude and impatient behavior toward the pharmacy technicians and the pharmacists who fulfilled their prescription orders.

Conversely, the bar patrons were usually a happier, livelier crowd. They were out to socialize and to enjoy themselves. They smiled often and were eager to chat about everyday mundane things.

Wade mentioned the cars he was fixing at the auto shop. Greg talked about the high rollers who came in and paid cash for cars with six-figure price tags. Jenny complained about the paperwork at the bank and the fact her love life was in the toilet. Micheline mentioned old cases she had worked on in New York.

"It's mostly my fault, I suppose," Micheline admitted. "I can run into a burning building on the job without a second thought, but I struggle at making new friends. I'm more of an introvert. I realize that. It's been awkward for me to get to know you up until lately."

"I haven't made it any easier," Wade replied. "I was so grateful to Jenny for helping me to obtain a loan for the business after all of my troubles in the past. I'd be lost without the auto shop. Still, I was embarrassed for the situation I was in, and for the past that had finally caught up with me. The fact you're in law enforcement made me more than a little uncomfortable, too."

Micheline's demeanor lightened. "There's nothing you can do about that now but put it behind you and move on with your life. You've paid your debt to society. You have a family to think about. There are so many possibilities ahead of you now."

"Easy for you to say," Wade quipped. "I rather doubt you had such a sordid past."

"Maybe so," Micheline offered. "Still, I've made my share of mistakes in life. And believe me, I've paid for them. That's one of the reasons I moved out west last year. I needed a fresh start. C'mon, let's go. I've been looking forward to that pepperoni and mushroom pizza ever since the opening credits of the movie."

The two friends walked casually from the back of the nearly filled restaurant to their table by the front window. Along the way, an attractive blonde who wore a tight-fitting sundress with high heels looked up distractedly from her conversation with a male companion seated across from her and smiled in their direction. Further ahead,

Jenny Casella, Laura Quiñónez, and Greg Slater were hunched toward one another as if entertained by some fascinating tidbit of gossip.

As Micheline and Wade approached their table, Jenny looked up from her discussion with Greg and Laura. She eyed her latest girlfriend with amusement. "Did the two of you get lost?" she asked suspiciously.

"You could say I made a wrong turn," Micheline admitted.

Jenny smiled. "I hope you're not making moves on Laura's man. That wouldn't be cool, Micheline. Besides, I've got dibs on you if anyone does."

"I thought I had dibs," Greg said, surprised.

Wade was quick to respond. "We were just checking out the peephole into the ladies' room. It's amazing what you might see the women doing in there."

"Oh, you wish," Laura said with a hearty laugh.

Micheline seated herself promptly.

Micheline quickly recovered from the astonishment of Jenny's comment. She raised her hands in mock defense. "Blame it all on Wade, not me. He drank more soda at the movie theater than he probably does martinis on New Year's Eve. Is anyone thirsty?"

Micheline lifted a full pitcher of light beer and filled frosted glass mugs all around.

Outside, a light rain began to splatter against the front windows of the pizzeria.

"I really liked the movie," Laura said. "The action never stopped."

Laura was petite and curvy, with a rounded nose, dark features, and sultry brown eyes. Her shiny curled hair was the shade of a cloudless nighttime sky and fell well below her shoulders. She carelessly sat back in her chair and pushed the sleeves of her cotton top halfway up her forearms.

"Actually," Wade countered, "I thought it was too predictable. I never missed a thing, even on my second trip to the concession stand. And the main character looked something like Laura's Halloween costume from last year. Do you remember the party we went to? You wore the pirate outfit with the captain's hat, the eye patch, and the hook?"

Laura tossed her head back playfully and laughed at the memory. "That was a fun time. But I hated the beard and mustache with that costume," she said. "It made my face itch."

"We should try the luxury theater over at Mission Bay sometime," Micheline interjected. "They have the call buttons located on the armrests so you never have to leave your seats. The attendant comes right to your seat to deliver your order."

"That would be nice," Greg added. "The seats are like leather recliners in your living room, and you can order dinner or snacks to be delivered right to you without getting up. Micheline and I went to the one in Del Mar not too long ago. That was our second date, I believe. It's a bit pricier, but there's not a bad seat in the house."

The quintet happily lifted their mugs of beer into the air in unison.

"Cheers, Salud!" everyone called out.

The gentle pitter-patter of raindrops against the window glass that had been falling for some time had suddenly transformed into the frenzied downpour of a severe lightning storm. Twisted bolts of lightning illuminated the darkened sky outside.

A moment later, a booming crack of thunder resounded from directly above and shook the walls and floor of the restaurant with vibration. The lights inside the restaurant blinked off and on momentarily but refused to shut off completely.

"I'm glad we're not caught out in that," Micheline remarked. "That's the loudest clap of thunder I've ever heard. It made me shiver. Funny thing, most people at work have told me they don't even own an umbrella out here. Back east, you always have one tucked away somewhere, just in case."

"I'm sure it will stop by the time we're ready to go," Jenny said.

Jenny had a girl-next-door quality about her, with a fair complexion and smooth skin. She stood five feet seven inches tall, and her face was gently framed by a thick mane of chestnut brown hair. It contrasted nicely with her dark brown eyes and red lips that naturally curled into a beautiful smile.

Jenny's outfit was stylish but casual. She wore a paisley-printed blue and white cotton top with dark denim jeans, a pair of sand-colored wedges on her feet, accented by a fashionable white ceramic wristwatch with gold-tone hands and markers on the bezel.

"So, you had the day off yesterday, right?" Laura asked Jenny, her BFF. "You got your nails done, I see, and I like the way you've styled your hair. It's different from the last time we saw each other. The bangs are shorter. The promotion to assistant vice president seems to be going very well for you. Or is it love, and you've met someone you haven't disclosed to me yet?"

Jenny smiled bemusedly. "Yes, the bank was closed yesterday for Veteran's Day, so I had the day off. And no, I haven't met anyone special lately. Other than Micheline, that is. She offered me a spare drawer to keep stuff at her place, like a toothbrush and clean outfits for work. That's for when I happen to stay overnight for a girl's night after we've had too much wine to drink. Come to think of it, we've been doing that a lot in recent weeks. But something tells me Greg may start needling for a drawer of his own if you know what I mean."

"C'mon, Micheline," Laura inquired anxiously. "Are you and Greg starting to get serious about each other?"

"You're putting me on the spot, Laura," Micheline said, suddenly blushing.

"I'm certainly smiling every time I'm with her," Greg politely added.

"Don't pay Laura any attention," Jenny offered. "All she does is read dark romance and fantasy novels in her spare time. She loves to imagine that chivalry, magic, and fairytale castles with handsome princes still exist."

"Well, I like those types of books, too," Micheline admitted. "I'm also a fan of futuristic sci-fi, horror, and thriller novels."

"I'm with you," Laura said. "Throw in some steamy sex scenes and a few good plot twists while you're at it."

"Oh, I know," Micheline said. "I could get lost in a book for hours at a time, especially if I'm sitting poolside with a margarita in one hand."

Laura turned toward Jenny. "You know I hardly have any spare time as so as it is. When I can steal a few moments for myself, I just want to enjoy some honest-to-goodness fiction. I like to be swept away to another imaginary world, just like I felt when I first met Wade. Now, doesn't that make sense?"

"Oh, you know what I mean," Jenny replied with a hearty laugh. "I know you buy an armload of those thick titles with the flowery front covers every time you drag me into the corner bookstore."

"And I have every intention to read them someday," Laura replied. "Life is just a little too busy lately to find that time."

"If I may say," Greg intervened, "I know I'm jealous to hear Micheline and Jenny are drinking all this wine together, and I wasn't invited to the party."

"I just show up on her doorstep every now and then with a bottle or two of our favorite California red," Jenny replied. "Sometimes she's not even home. She works all these odd hours of the night and day. I should text first, of course."

"Well, let me offer a solution to that problem, then," Micheline suggested as she opened her purse. She withdrew a single house key and placed it on the table next to Jenny's ceramic plate.

"What's this?" Jenny asked, surprised.

"The key to my condo," Micheline replied. "That way if I'm ever held up at work, you can just let yourself into my place when you need to. You can drink yourself silly and fall asleep on the couch. I'll be along to join you for a drink, or to cover your unconscious butt with a blanket when I finally make it home in the wee hours of the night."

"Are you asking me to move in with you?" Jenny questioned, obviously surprised by Micheline's actions.

"Yes, what are your intentions here, Micheline?" Laura blurted loudly with an inquisitive grin. "And are they devious and sexually explicit, too? Is there a three-way going on here I wasn't invited to? I want to hear all the juicy details."

"You girls are too much," Micheline exclaimed with a laugh. "Jenny, honestly, let's just say you've become a very good friend to me lately.

There's no pressure here. I like spending time with you, and you're welcome to come over and visit my place any time. Also, I'm not trying to put a wedge in between you and Laura. I truly enjoy hanging out with all of you."

Jenny smiled brightly and picked up the key to the front door of Micheline's condo. "Thank you," she said. "That's so sweet of you. I'll be sure to make good use of this."

Jenny slipped the key into her purse.

"And I'm sorry I've been stressing so much," Jenny added. "The workload at the bank these past few months has been crazy. Maybe that's why I've been drinking so much wine lately. Every day there are hundreds of pages of documents to review for each of the home mort-gages, and we're constantly transferring multi-million-dollar accounts from one bank to another. Some of the down payments are more than a half-million dollars. Honestly, I don't know where people get that kind of money."

"Rich relatives, most likely," Wade commented. "Obviously not mine, that's for sure."

"Nor mine," Greg offered. "Although I've got plans to make it big someday." He let out a hearty laugh.

"And, as it is," Jenny continued, "my parent's fortieth wedding anni-versary is coming up soon. I'll be flying home to Chicago at the end of next week to see them. Thank goodness my brothers and sisters are taking care of the planning for the party. Yesterday, I took my mind completely off it all and had a very relaxing day shopping at the mall. I even fit in time for a hair appointment and a manicure and pedicure at the day spa."

"Oh, I'm so jealous," Laura said. "I color my own hair and do my nails on the weekends, or whenever I have a chance. I wish I could..." her sentence trailed off.

At a table not ten feet away, the pretty blonde in the tight-fitting sundress and her male companion had begun to quarrel, allowing their private conversation to become a loud and unruly public confrontation.

The girl was stunningly attractive. She had mesmerizing green eyes that were surrounded by generous amounts of makeup, and long, curled blonde tresses that spilled halfway down her back. She angrily jabbed a fork into her Stromboli as if the rolled pizza turnover with ham and cheese needed to be killed.

"You're not even listening to me!" the man yelled at her harshly. The expression on his face registered anger and rage. His tone demanded attention.

He was a tall and husky young man, slightly paunchy at the midriff, and he parted his wavy brown hair on the left side of his forehead. He had shaved his thick sideburns so that they were perfectly parallel with the bottoms of his earlobes. Round, wire-rimmed glasses slid precariously down the bridge of his bulbous nose.

"I *was* so!" the girl stammered bitterly in response. "You were talking about your fucking car."

"For your information," he countered, his face turning various shades of purple and red, "I was commenting on my future plans. Our plans, as a couple. My car was only a reference to... Oh, shit! What's gotten into you, anyway? You're certainly not here with me. Your mind is a million miles away somewhere."

"I've got a lot to think about," she fumed agitatedly and thrust her fork into the abdomen of the Stromboli again.

"Some other guy, I'll bet," he hissed. "Some polished European prick you hope to meet over there for this overseas bachelorette party you've been planning. Someone with a British or French accent, and upper-class savoir-faire."

"Hardly," she responded coolly.

"I can see it!" he accused jealously. "You're smiling over there as if you're fantasizing about something really great."

She laughed at him. "Do you really hear yourself, David? You're being an asshole. Maybe I'm just happy with my life right now. Did you ever think of that?"

David abruptly backed out of his chair and stood with his face all blushed and his arms flailing at his sides like a child throwing a temper tantrum.

"No, goddamn it, Samantha! It's like you're having an orgasm across the table from me, and my cock is still zipped up in my pants untouched."

"Shut up, David!" she spat. "I don't like talk like that, especially in public."

"Oh, go to hell!" he shouted.

"No," she retorted angrily. "You go to hell!"

Samantha stood immediately. She picked up a goblet of red wine in front of her and splashed it at him as hard as she could. The Cabernet Sauvignon splattered across his face and white long-sleeve dress shirt and dripped to the floor.

Samantha replaced the empty wine glass carefully to the table without breaking it. She turned abruptly away from David, lifted the strap of her stylish black leather Louis Vuitton Empreinte handbag from the back of her chair, and firmly placed it upon her bare shoulder.

"Don't let the door hit your backside on the way out," David sneered.

Samantha marched determinedly through the crowded restaurant toward the exit without making eye contact with any of the restaurant patrons. She hesitated for a moment at the front entrance door, and then opened it and stepped boldly into the wind-blown tempest outside.

"Don't come back, bitch!" David screamed after her in a child-like tone. "We're through!"

A few moments of absolute silence followed while the patrons of the restaurant sat motionless in stunned disbelief.

David trembled agitatedly for the length of several breaths. His gaze descended to the floor in both shame and humiliation. Slowly, he reached down and half-heartedly began to clear the area around his table.

"He's lucky she didn't hit him with that calzone," Laura snickered in a hushed tone. "Or that rock on her finger. Did you see the size of that engagement diamond?"

"I did!" Jenny said. "I was quite jealous, and it appears she won't need it anymore."

"He needs his prescription for Ativan or Xanax filled," Laura suggested. "He should take something strong to relieve his anxiety and panic disorder. You can see the way his hands are trembling and he's pacing back and forth."

"Do you see that much at the pharmacy?" Jenny asked.

"More than you would realize," Laura confirmed. "Although, the most frequently prescribed drugs at my store are Oxycontin and Adderall. People form an addiction or a dependence on them, and the HCP's keep renewing the scripts for them. They're extremely popular, and we constantly have to re-order supplies for them to keep up with demand."

"What do you mean by HCP's?" Jenny innocently asked.

"Health care professionals," Micheline chimed in. "They're the doctors or nurse practitioners who write the prescriptions for their patients. I hear that acronym a lot when I'm called to testify at jury trials."

"Oh, I see," Jenny said.

"As soon as the rain lets up, I think we should get going," Laura suggested. "We've all got to work tomorrow, and I told Francesca that Wade and I would be home by eleven at the latest."

"Sure thing," Micheline replied. "Francesca's your eldest?"

"Yes," Laura said. "She's fifteen now, going on thirty-five."

Micheline laughed. "And you have two other children?"

"Yes," Laura replied. "Ray just turned five, and Irina will be three in February."

"You've certainly got your hands full."

"Let's just say I'm never bored."

"I'll see what I can do to ask the waiter for the check," Greg announced. "That is if I can get him away from the mess at our neighbor's table."

"Quite an arm she had, too," Wade commented. The argument and soured relationship situation obviously amused him. "That wine splash was like an under-handed fast-pitch softball move. She could pitch for the Padres."

"I pass by the baseball stadium every morning on my way to work," Micheline offered. "Maybe I'll stop in someday and ask them if they need another ninth-inning reliever for their roster."

"You're right on with that, Micheline," Wade confirmed. "I know you've admitted to being a lifelong Yankees fan, but I grew up watching the Padres since I was in Little League. They may never win much, but they're still our hometown team. Just don't get me started talking about the Chargers leaving San Diego for Los Angeles. They're dead to me now. Man, that girl was really fired up!"

"Actually, I've met both of them at the bank before," Jenny confided quietly. "The girl's name is Samantha Miller. Her father owns a biotech company here in Carmel Valley, and she's got a trust fund set up in her name worth millions. She goes to UCSD, too."

"Isn't she the one you mentioned to me before that had a somewhat disreputable past?" Laura asked.

"Yes, that's her," Jenny confirmed. "Those stories may have only been gossip and rumors, though. I don't know what was true or not. She seemed nice when I talked to her, and she mentioned that she's studying both biology and modern dance at UCSD in La Jolla."

"I wish I had the brains for that," Wade said. "I'm just not college material."

"You do have brains, honey," Laura said, patting her husband affectionately on the shoulder. "You just spend too much time sitting on them, is all."

This brought unexpected laughter from all five of the group members at the table.

David, the young man who had bathed in Cabernet Sauvignon, wrongly assumed they were laughing at him. He reached into his wallet and angrily tossed a wad of cash onto the wine-soaked table. Then, without averting his eyes from the floor ahead of him, he tramped outside the restaurant as oblivious to the violent downpour of rain as was his former fiancée.

"Gosh, he looked awfully pissed," Wade noted. "I hope he didn't think we were talking about him."

"You have to admit," Jenny said, "he did look pretty silly, and he deserved what he got for treating her that way."

"I would certainly never speak to a woman that way," Greg said. "Especially if I know she carries a loaded gun."

"It'll make you think twice, won't it?" Micheline boasted. She smiled.

"You're right," Laura agreed. "He had it coming to him. He had no right to treat her like that. He was filled with so much hostility. Somebody should punch his lights out."

Micheline slowly shook her head back and forth in dismay. "In my job," she pointed out, "anger like that can sometimes lead to physical abuse or something even much worse."

"Like rape or murder, you mean?" Wade asked inquisitively.

"Sometimes, unfortunately," Micheline admitted. "I've seen everything you can imagine on the job from long-term verbal abuse to physical confrontations with bruises, broken bones, and bloodshed. Sometimes people react to highly emotional confrontations by going just absolutely bat shit crazy."

"You've witnessed this firsthand?" Laura asked.

Micheline nodded. "One time, a guy made the mistake of trying to attack me with a broken beer bottle. I just hope this David dude goes home, wherever that is and cools his jets down. He wouldn't want to have to deal with law enforcement after creating a scene like we just witnessed in public."

"What happened with this guy with the broken beer bottle?" Greg asked.

"I broke his nose and dislocated his shoulder," Micheline said. "The asshole mistook my tiny size for weakness."

"Goddamn, girl," Jenny said. "Remind me never to wrestle with you."

"He looked like a pussy to me," Laura commented. "I'll bet that girl could kick the shit out of him if he ever tried to lay a finger on her."

"They didn't look like they were meant for each other anyway," Greg said. "He was way out of her league. You could just tell. She could do much better."

"Don't be so sure," Jenny interjected. "I think he's in med school now, or maybe he's already a doctor and doing a fellowship at one of the local hospitals. His name is David Hawthorne. I know he comes from a wealthy family in the movie business, and he graduated from Stanford before going on to med school. Something like that, anyway. I guess having money helps some people to get by despite the other obvious flaws with their looks or their personal character."

"Money's not always the answer to happiness," Greg said. "Trust and compatibility are much more important in the long run, wouldn't you say?"

"But it would be nice to have," Laura said. "If only I could win the lottery. I'd pay off the mortgage on the house, put the kids through college, and take a long vacation to an island paradise."

"You have to play to win, you know," Wade said.

"I know," Laura replied.

"I'd buy a mansion with an ocean view," Greg said.

"I think I'd quit my job for starters and travel around the world," Jenny said. "I've always wanted to see some faraway places like Europe or Australia."

"I wonder if those two will ever make up," Laura said. "I always dream of a happy ending for the princess. You know, like Romeo and Juliette."

"You realize, they were ill-fated lovers?" Micheline asked.

"Oh, that's right," Laura said. "They killed themselves in the end. I forgot. But you know what I mean. Everybody longs for a love story."

"Well, thankfully not our problem," Wade stated as he sat back in his chair and smiled like a Cheshire cat that had just eaten a canary.

"There's something about seeing the hope and possibilities of the future that gives people something to strive for," Laura commented. "It's why I get up every morning and head to work. Wow, I think I've had a little too much excitement for one night. Now I'm impersonating a philosopher."

"Agreed," Micheline offered. "It's been quite an evening. And Laura, you can be anything you want to be."

Laura smiled.

"We should do this more often," Micheline suggested. "Wade and I are starting to get to know each other better, and we haven't even begun to talk about cars yet."

"A chick that's interested in guns, cars, and broken beer bottle fights, huh?" Wade exclaimed. "Now, that's badass, Micheline."

"I agree," Greg stated. "Micheline is that perfect blend between an angel and the daughter of the devil every guy has ever dreamed of. I'm so lucky I found her."

Micheline smiled and reached for Greg's hand.

"Quite the group we've assembled here," Jenny said.

"And to think, it all started in a quiet library," Laura added. "It was just meant to be, I guess."

Everyone around the table nodded and began to look across the crowded restaurant for the waiter.

Outside the restaurant, the deluge of rain subsided, and the overhead clouds began to drift apart in the nighttime sky.

Micheline lifted her free hand and caught the waiter's attention.

Nine

The Bluffs at Del Mar

Monday evening, November 16th

Samantha Miller swung her head of wildly curled blonde tresses from side to side. She clearly enjoyed the freedom she felt as her hair splayed in all directions. She laid her head on the plush, goose-down pillow and instinctively grabbed the hand of her companion. She delicately placed his fingers over the soft mound between her deeply tanned thighs.

"Again?" he asked cautiously.

"Yes. Again, baby," she responded enthusiastically.

Outside the bedroom, a thin sliver of neon moon pierced the wavering curtains of dark, passing clouds, and silhouetted the bony fingers of nearby tree branches as they scraped against the outer window. She abruptly quivered against his sweaty, sweet-smelling torso.

Moments later, he was completely inside of her, throbbing and pulsing in rhythm with her own pelvic movements. He kept his face hidden from her view, first by burying it between her ample breasts, and then by snuggling between her shoulders and the perfume-scented nape of her neck.

He came with a rush of adrenaline, and then withdrew and rolled onto his back. His breaths were heavy with exertion.

Oddly, she felt as though she were being watched from above. She could sense someone's steely eyes upon her, and they were not the tender, playful eyes of her clandestine lover.

Silly, she thought.

I must be mad!

No one knew they were here. She had taken several precautions to ensure their privacy this evening, the least of which was parking her car several blocks away near a corporate office construction site.

It must be guilt, she reasoned. Still, she felt a nagging sensation that would not let go.

She rose abruptly from the queen-size bed of the darkened two-bedroom condo and tentatively approached the window which faced the main street and the shopping plaza beyond that. The mini-blinds had been completely drawn shut. Samantha knew the general location of the window because she had been the one who had closed the blinds earlier that evening.

Her naked body was generously bathed in perspiration, more so from her recent sexual activity than from the warmth that was evenly distributed throughout the condo. When she came close to the window, she placed her hand delicately on one of the blinds and moved it aside. There was a sense of discomfort which burned uneasily within her as if someone who was filled with jealous rage was watching, and silly as it may have seemed, she felt the only way to clear her mind of this ill-begotten burden was to cast aside the protective shield of privacy which the mini blinds had provided.

"What are you looking at?" she asked him, without turning her view from the window.

"I can't help it," he replied. "You have a great ass."

"And so do you," she said. Samantha turned away from the window, satisfied that no strangers or ex-boyfriends or ex-fiancés were lurking among the shadows outside. She bent down and kissed the matted hairs upon his muscular, tattoo-covered chest and ran her fingers through his dark shoulder-length hair.

"I love you," he said helplessly.

She smiled and kissed him on the lips. "I know you do, baby. I love fucking you. It's not the same thing, I know. I'm sorry about that. I always want to be open and honest with what we have between us."

She turned and walked back to the window. Against her better judgment, she reached out her hand and twisted the clear slender rod suspended alongside the blinds.

Outside, a streetlamp had burned itself off, leaving the weather-worn buildings which lined both sides of the street secluded amid deep shadows. There appeared to be no movement of any kind except for the gentle swaying of small, curbside ornamental flowers and palm trees, and a customer pumping gas at the convenience store on the far corner of the block.

"Something got you spooked?" her companion asked from his prone position on the bed.

"Just my nerves," she replied uneasily, continuing to survey the street below. "I even went so far as to park my car a couple of blocks away, just in case."

"You should relax," he stated matter-of-factly. "No one knows we're here. Not my wife, nor that asshole ex-fiancé of yours. Only your girl-friend, Jacqueline, knows we're here using her place for tonight. It was really great of her to lend you the keys to her condo while she's away on a business trip."

"Yes, it was," she replied. "And for the record, technically, David's not my ex. At least, not yet. I'll have to face him at some point and return the engagement ring. But for now, I just want to take some time to myself and let things cool down. The bachelorette party with my girlfriends in Paris next week should really help to take my mind off things and put some space between us."

Her companion propped up his pillow and rested his head against a hardwood maple headboard. "I get it. I wish I could be with you in Paris next week. It sounds so romantic. Now, come back to me, sexy. You're making me horny again, all exposed like that in the moonlight."

"Really?" she asked, turning to face him fully. She playfully reached both hands behind the nape of her neck, thrust her chest forward, and struck a pin-up pose, as if she were the centerfold-of-the-month in a men's entertainment magazine.

"That reminds me of the very first time I saw you dance at the strip club, baby. You looked at me that same way. Come here and find out what I have for you, my sweet Clarissa," he whispered hoarsely.

She smiled seductively toward him and began to approach the bed with her hips swaying wildly to and fro. Her lover raised his arms to guide her to him.

The sudden ring of Samantha's cell phone from the nearby nightstand broke the sexual spell. Samantha froze. An expression of absolute panic crossed over her face.

She glanced toward the illuminated text on the face of the phone. "It says unknown caller."

"Don't answer it," he instructed decisively. "If it's important, they'll leave a voicemail. It's probably just a wrong number."

The phone stopped ringing. After a tense one-minute waiting period, there was no alert of a voicemail, only one missed call from an unknown caller.

Samantha breathed a heavy sigh of relief. "Wow, I'm really on edge lately, aren't I?"

He reached out to touch her arm. "I think I can find a way to help you relax, baby. Come back to bed, please."

She smiled. He was good to her, always.

"I thought my heart was going to stop," she said breathlessly.

"Relax, gorgeous," he said. "We're not going to get caught together."

"I believe you," she said.

"What you need is a gentle massage, all over."

"I like the sound of that," she said.

"Come here," he beckoned.

Suddenly, her companion's cell phone began to ring. He glanced over to check the number.

"Fuck! It says unknown caller."

He took a deep breath to steady himself. "Don't worry, baby. It's just a coincidence that both our phones rang at the same time, and it was a wrong number, nothing more. Probably just a marketing call or something stupid like that."

"I hope you're right," she said. "As much as I can't stand to be apart from you, I think I'd die if anyone ever learned our secret."

The ringing of the phone ceased, and no further alerts appeared on either of their cellular devices.

Samantha turned abruptly and walked back to the window. She gazed out into the night. Nothing had changed in the street below. The wind continued to blow steadily, and everything was bathed in a curtain of ebon with a slight gleam of moonlight that emitted from between broken clouds above. The convenience store parking lot was now empty.

"Are you okay, baby?" he asked. "I'm worried about you."

She shrugged her shoulders to him without turning from the window. "Gas is getting cheaper, you know."

"No, I didn't realize that," he admitted. "I don't pay much attention to..."

"Do you know what else?" she asked, effectively cutting him off in mid-sentence. "All boxed doughnuts and cupcakes are half-priced with the purchase of a half-gallon of milk. How about we fool around one more time and wander down to the mini-mart for some midnight snacks?"

"You're the only thing I'm hungry to snack on tonight," he commented.

"Really?" she asked. "Maybe I'm not enough for you, it seems. I could go for a bite of something."

"Oh, I'm plenty ready to taste something sweet," he said.

"And what might that be?" she asked.

He was about to reply to her with a sexually explicit comment regarding her vagina when Samantha unexpectedly threw herself against the mini blinds and violently slapped her outstretched palms against the windowpanes.

"My God, what's wrong?" he shrieked. "You're beginning to scare me."

Samantha turned from the window and slunk to a sitting position beneath the windowsill. She began to whimper, and large dollops of tears immediately streamed down her cheeks.

Her companion threw back the bedsheets and raced toward the window. "What the hell did you see?" he demanded as his eyes darted wildly up and down the street below. "There's nothing out there."

"Don't you see it?" she lamented.

"No, I don't," he said. "What am I looking for?"

Samantha began to cry even louder. She twisted her hands tightly in her lap.

"Check out the payphone at the corner of the parking lot by the convenience store," she cried. "It's fucking off the hook, and it's swinging like somebody was just there a few seconds ago to use it!"

And then he saw it, too. It was clearly illuminated by the harsh glare of the overhead phosphorescent light from the parking lot. The telephone receiver dangled from its cord like the pendulum of a clock, as if someone had made a call and then dropped it in anger and hurried away.

Ten

Bay View at Coronado

Thursday, November 19th

Micheline climbed two flights of stairs and approached the front door of her third-floor condo. She paused, then inserted the key into the lock.

Nightfall had already descended. Across the bay, the glow from downtown San Diego illuminated a dark cloudless sky above. Fluorescent light escaped from inside the kitchen window and spilled onto the wooden landing. Soft music could be heard from within.

Did someone throw a party at my place and forget to invite me? she wondered.

Micheline eased the door open slowly. Her on-the-job persona was active and expecting trouble to strike. In the living room, the flat-screen TV had been switched on. A subscription music service channel had been selected entitled *Cool Jazz*.

On the granite kitchen countertop, an opened bottle of California Merlo awaited her arrival. There was an empty wine glass and an unopened bottle of chianti next to it.

Micheline looked closer at the bottle of Merlo. It was half-empty.

Or is it half-full? Ha!

For a moment, Micheline imagined that drinking award-winning California wine in San Diego for $6.99 a bottle from the local supermarket must be the same thing as drinking expensive French wine in Lyon or Marseille.

Oh, whom was she kidding? But then, again...

At least, she reflected whimsically to herself, she felt confident her sense of style, natural good looks, and two years of high school French with Mademoiselle Seydoux would get her by if she ever took the time to journey overseas on such a romantic notion. She needed a long vacation. That much was clear. London, Paris, Barcelona, or Tuscany and the Amalfi Coast in Italy were all on her bucket list.

Someday, she promised herself.

"How was your day, Detective?" Jenny's voice carried from behind the sofa in the living room. She stood. Her chestnut brown hair was a tousled mess of wild abandon. She wore only a tight-fitting dark navy and orange Chicago Bears V-neck T-shirt without a bra. Her toned pale white midriff was fully exposed, and beneath that, she wore only a light blue pair of low-rise cotton and lace hipster panties.

"You've certainly made yourself right at home, I see," Micheline mused.

"I have, babe," Jenny replied with a glint in her eye. "I'm stressed to the max, and I needed some soft jazz and a glass of wine to take the edge off. Do you want to join me, please?"

"You mean before you completely empty the first bottle? Believe me, after the day I've had, absolutely," Micheline let out a long breath. "Did you find the visitor parking spaces without any trouble?"

"Yes, no trouble at all. It's just a short walk down the street to my car. I could get there even if I was totally wasted, which isn't too far off at this rate."

"Glad to hear it. Let me get settled first. I need a glass of red as much as you do tonight."

Micheline closed the front door shut and locked it. She bent down and removed her black flat walking shoes and placed them neatly to the side of the door. Then she walked barefoot through the condo and headed straight for the master bedroom. She set her shoulder bag on top of a small corner desk. She withdrew a pair of high heel shoes that she wore at the office and turned toward the walk-in closet.

Jenny had followed her along the hallway and comfortably planted her toned rear end on the edge of the queen-size bed.

"Time to disarm yourself, huh?" Jenny asked.

"It's the first thing I like to do when I'm finally home for the evening," Micheline admitted. "I don't consider my place child-proof by any means, not that any kids come here to visit. But I do like to put everything away and out of sight. I believe in safety first. Plus, it makes it much easier to find things when I need them in a hurry."

"I like the shoes."

"Oh, thanks. These are Jimmy Choo. I remember I bought them at the luxury mall in Short Hills, New Jersey. A little guilty pleasure to make the day go a bit better."

"But you don't wear them all day long?"

"No, only while I'm in the office, usually. It depends. I always keep a second pair of flat walking shoes with me. There's a pair of hiking boots in the trunk of my car, too. I like to look nice on the job, but I have to be prepared for any condition that may come up."

"You don't lock your guns in a safe at home?" Jenny wondered.

"Not all of them. I keep a few of the handguns in separate decorative boxes at the back of the closet. Each one goes in its own box."

"It looks like you've got more than a bunch of boxes in there, too," Jenny noticed. "That's quite a collection."

"Not all of those boxes are for firearms. Just the ones in the middle, here." Micheline waved her hand toward the closet wall.

"Most of the boxes are for storage. Some for shoes, some for purses or bags, and some for bottles of perfume or cosmetics."

"You don't sleep with a gun under your pillow at night, do you?"

"No, of course not. I keep one in the nightstand drawer, though, just in case an intruder awakens me in the middle of the night."

"Can you take me to the gun range someday and teach me to shoot?"

"Now there's an interesting idea!" Micheline laughed. "Sure. We'll have to plan that for an upcoming weekend. Shooting and shopping. How does that sound?"

"Sounds perfect. With dinner and drinks afterward, too. But not this weekend. I'm flying home to Chicago tomorrow to visit the family."

"Oh, that's right. Your parents' fortieth wedding anniversary party. I forgot about that. Are you excited?"

"Yes, of course," Jenny said. "I haven't been home in a while. This will be a good chance for me to catch up with everyone."

Micheline removed both gun holsters and placed each in a decorative storage box printed with pictures of London and Paris scenery. The boxes were lined next to one another on closet organizer shelves.

She folded her blazer and placed it into a dry cleaner duffle bag on the floor in the corner of the closet. She hesitated for a moment, and then unbuttoned her matching slacks and removed them. She folded them neatly and added them to the dry cleaner bag.

It was girls' night. Micheline felt like loosening up. She wanted to let her guard down with her new best friend after a long day on the job.

Micheline unclasped two of the buttons of her light blue blouse and then opened the cuffs at each wrist. She rolled the cuffs up to her forearms and padded barefoot back into the master bedroom.

"Sexy, girl," Jenny said. "I never imagined you'd have tattoos, and so artistically done, too. Like the suicide girls without the body piercings. I'll bet Greg can't keep his hands off you."

Micheline smiled. Her body art was an expression of her mixed heritage, her personality traits, and her life experiences. Some of the tattoos were multi-colored in vibrant yellow, red, green, and blue ink. Others resembled black and gray charcoal sketches. The illustrations covered a full sleeve of her left arm from shoulder to wrist, the back of her right shoulder, and all her right thigh and lower leg to below the calf. Each individual image embodied a piece of herself to honor and armor herself to carry through life.

Sketched upon her left arm were cherry blossoms surrounding Independence Hall in Philadelphia and a Japanese temple in Tokyo, a stack of books with a steaming mug of coffee, and a female sleuth with a magnifying glass and a revolver.

On the underside of her right forearm, the word *possibilities* was written in cursive scroll.

On the upper portion of her right thigh, there was a Tuscan vineyard scene in Italy. Directly below that, long-stemmed red roses surrounded a charging Spanish bull and a dragon from the Welsh flag.

On the back of her right shoulder was a detailed sketch of the lower Manhattan skyline. Beneath the image, a phrase was written in cursive scroll---*Life is a journey, not a destination.*

The images represented mother, father, home, career, and the places her family had come from. One design was a regret that she was slowly having transformed into something else. There were some things from her past that she didn't want to be reminded of.

"Greg's taking me to dinner tomorrow night," she said. "He should be more concerned with what I plan to do with *my* hands."

Jenny laughed. "Oh, fuck! This girl's going to get herself some action tomorrow night. I want you to tell me all the juicy details when I get back."

"All I know is that he made a reservation at a fancy steakhouse in the Gaslamp Quarter to start things off. We'll meet by the bar for drinks, have dinner and possibly head to a club for some dancing. He's already suggested brunch on Saturday. What comes in between is anyone's guess." She giggled like a schoolgirl.

Jenny stood and together they walked back toward the open concept kitchen and living room area. Micheline poured herself a glass of the Merlo.

"I'm glad to hear the two of you are hitting it off so well," Jenny said.

"I'm more interested to hear about who's been keeping you company late at night recently," Micheline inquired. "You are seeing someone, aren't you?"

Jenny raised her eyebrows. "Ah, you'll soon learn I have a specific type of gentleman whom I like to have entertain me. To drive me wild. Older, wiser, experienced. A little silver around the edges. More settled and financially well-off. And married, of course. It stays less complicated that way."

"But it doesn't last forever, then," Micheline said, taking a long sip of her wine.

"Maybe not. But the sparks always burn hot in the beginning. Plus, I'm a bit materialistic, and the benefits serve my purposes well." Jenny turned and picked up her wine glass from the coffee table in the adjoining living room.

"What kind of materials or benefits are we talking about?" Micheline inquired.

"Oh, you know. Diamond earrings, Victoria's Secret lingerie, a Louis Vuitton bag, a Rolex watch, a pair of Christian Louboutin high heels with red soles. All things to help a girl feel sexier and more alive."

"And what's your family like?"

Jenny spread her arms out wide and nearly spilled her glass of wine on the carpet.

"Oops, sorry! A big Italian affair," she proclaimed. "Mafioso style. Without any broken kneecaps or the horse's head at the bottom of the bed, of course. They'll all be at the party, too. La Familia. All six of my brothers and sisters. I'm the youngest and the only one left who's still single."

"Wow."

"They'll be there with their husbands and wives, and countless nieces and nephews. Plus, my aunts and uncles and more cousins than you can shake a stick at."

"Is anyone famous, or maybe notorious?" Micheline asked. "Any gangsters I should be aware of? I have connections with the FBI, you know."

"Let's see," Jenny replied. "Some are professionals like doctors and lawyers. There are a few cops in the mix. Some work in supermarkets or drive taxi cabs. Others work in offices or retail stores. Nothing too spooky to speak of."

"That sounds nice."

"One of my cousins is captain of a freight cargo ship on Lake Michigan. Pretty cool. And my parents, of course, a retired dentist and an elementary school music teacher, standing there proud of the entire family."

"That's so great."

"My Mi-Mi will be there next to them, too. She's my grandmother on my mother's side. She's eighty-nine years old and still shovels snow from the sidewalks by herself. In the summertime, she plays eighteen-hole rounds of golf with her younger girlfriends. She's truly an amazing woman. She still shaves her legs and dies her hair, too. Image to her is everything, even without my Pop-Pop in her life anymore."

"Your family sounds incredible," Micheline said. "For me, it's just my dad and me now. He's retired FBI. I left him back in New Jersey and came out here on my own. I'm still trying to find my way, I guess."

"Have you eaten yet?" Jenny asked. "There's some slices of Margherita pizza in the box on the counter if you'd like. It's still warm and pairs well with the vino."

Micheline raised her wine glass in the universal expression to offer a toast.

"Grazie!" she said.

Jenny giggled and raised her glass in return.

"Prego, saluti!" she called out.

Eleven

Catalina Mission Park

Saturday, November 21st

Brilliant blinding rays of morning sunshine filtered through the uppermost trees of the suburban park and cast faint shadows across the winding dirt path that led to the Harbor Club to the east, and to an upward-sloping canyon ridge to the west.

Although Micheline Avila lived in a two-bedroom condo in Coronado, a resort city established on a peninsula adjacent to San Diego Bay, and the local landscape offered fabulous and breath-taking views from nearby beaches, the detective liked a change of scenery from time to time. She enjoyed going for long runs in various settings of the greater San Diego area both inland and along the coastline in North County when she had the chance.

She jogged along the tree-lined sidewalk that adjoined the entrance to the community park with the mechanical stride of someone who was troubled and at odds with her thoughts.

She wore a light blue short-sleeve dry-fit top with black runner's shorts, a black New York Yankees baseball cap atop her head, and a comfortable pair of white training shoes. Clamped snuggly around her waist was a thin black canvas belt with a zippered nylon pouch that contained a few personal items. A white cotton hand towel was draped over the belt on her right hip.

Sweat oozed from Micheline's forehead and her taut, muscular frame. Her lungs inhaled deeply at regular intervals and allowed her breaths to escape in short, hard gasps.

She ran hard this morning. Adrenaline rushed through her veins. Greg Slater had called her at the last minute to cancel their Friday evening plans with an overtly weak excuse. Something about a business dinner with his boss he had completely forgotten about and couldn't get out of.

She didn't believe a word of it.

Micheline wanted to smash her fist into something that would break and shatter into a million pieces. Running hard was the next best thing, although she also considered going to the gun range later that afternoon to do some target shooting.

She gathered her thoughts and focused on her recent caseload at work. Investigating fraud, money laundering, auto theft, bank robberies, and kidnappings for a living meant long hours dealing with misdirected truth and less-than-trustworthy felons. Nothing was ever as it seemed. Frustration and doubt were her constant companions.

The key, she had learned over the slow and unremitting passage of time, was motive. Something prompted a person to commit a crime, whether that person's behavior was rational and conscious or not. A reason for wrongdoing was always demanded by the prosecution. Discovering what that something was and establishing it as fact, challenged Micheline's ability to solve any unlawful act that came under her scrutiny. Persuading unwilling witnesses to testify at jury trials was one of Micheline's more notable skills.

Suddenly, a bone-jarring scream intruded upon Micheline's random thoughts and seized her immediate attention. There was no mistaking the sense of horror or panic the sound contained.

A woman's frenzied, protracted cries emanated from the shadowy labyrinth ahead of her. Micheline had no time to think, only to react. She halted in her tracks and reached for the zippered pouch at her waistline. She shifted the belt, so the pouch was settled on her left hip, and then she withdrew her other constant companion: a five-shot Smith & Wesson .38-caliber Chief. Gun in hand, with the raven hairs on the back of her neck bristling with electricity, she charged forward into the unknown.

A lump of fear caught in Micheline's throat. She thrashed through dense foliage and quickened her pace while trying to make sense of the commotion. The woman was either cornered by a wild animal or was fighting off an attempted rape or mugging. Micheline subconsciously wagered her next paycheck on the latter.

The landscape sloped upward into a tiny hillock. Micheline veered off the path into a coppice of trees with a tangle of skeleton-like branches. She urgently fought against the wild-grown thicket of obstacles that impeded her progress.

Her mind was set. The woman's terrified screams beckoned her forward. She struggled up to the top of the nearby slope and sucked in another deep breath. Her legs pounded against the hardened ground and propelled her toward the point of no return.

Micheline ascended the promontory as fast as she could run. What lay beyond scared the hell out of her. The hill dropped thirty feet into the depression of a dried-out pond, and Micheline's foot slipped under a raised tree root. Momentum gripped her body like an invisible hand and cast her down to the bottom of the steep slope. Her body crashed uncontrollably against rocks and broken branches and tumbled, finally, to rest on a bed of dry, rotted leaves and pine needles.

Micheline rose unsteadily to her feet. Her entire body was tensed. Her fists clenched at her sides and her thighs squeezed together tightly. A cold sweat suddenly enveloped her appendages. She shut her eyelids tightly, then inhaled a deep breath and let it out slowly.

Another wailing screech echoed through the woods ahead. This one was higher-pitched and different from the one before. Micheline's confusion was profound. It seemed unlikely that two women would be attacked at the same time. The odds were against it. But there was no debating the hysterical, heart-wrenching cries of a second victim.

Maybe a witness?

Micheline got to her feet and expertly maneuvered between one tree and another as she stormed up to the top of the slope at break-neck speed.

The screams died.

Micheline burst into an open area known locally as Five Points, a clearing in the woods where five separate trails converged. Nearby set an obviously neglected granite sculpture of contemporary art that had been vandalized by a thick covering of bird guano and painted graffiti. A dozen carelessly abandoned empty beer cans and bottles lay scattered at the base of the monument. Five Points was known to be a favorite high school and college party spot.

Micheline leveled her gun steadily with both hands.

One of the women stood off to her right. She wept convulsively with her head bowed and her arms steadfastly encircling her chest. She was slender and athletic, with reddish-brown hair, and she was dressed in a maroon and white North Beach softball team uniform. She was more than likely a college coed on her way to the nearby Carmel Valley Community Park where the tennis and basketball courts and the adjoining softball field were located.

Micheline's eyes scanned the periphery. At first, she detected nothing. Absolutely nothing. She squinted, her aim shifting from side to side. Her nerves were on fire. Her pulse beat like a drum in her ears. She could hear her heart thudding vigorously in her chest.

Then, low to the ground, approximately thirty yards distant, she caught the unmistakable glimpse of a huge man hunched over the motionless body of a woman. She appeared to be naked. Micheline's left index finger rubbed temptingly against the trigger of her gun.

The obese man perceived Micheline's presence, stirred, hastily separated from the victim, and held up a metallic-looking object in the crook of one arm. The object was long and thin. Cylindrical.

A rifle!

Micheline darted immediately to her right and forcefully knocked the female witness off her feet. They slammed to the ground behind the cover of the trunk of a wide magnolia tree with several thick branch extensions.

"Drop the gun!" Micheline demanded in an official tone. "Police!" she shouted. She stretched the truth somewhat with that statement, but she didn't care. She expected to hear shots fired in return any second.

Silence followed.

Nothing happened.

Micheline waited a few moments longer, then thrust herself upon the carpet of dry leaves and rolled five feet from the base of the tree. She sprang to a one-kneed shooting stance.

The suspect was stumbling awkwardly from the scene of the attack in a feeble attempt to escape. Micheline cursed to herself. There were too many trees in the way to get off an accurate shot.

She turned and grabbed the female witness roughly by her trembling shoulders.

"Are you all right?" she asked. She looked directly into the young woman's eyes.

Overcome with trepidation, the girl nodded imperceptibly. No sound other than sobbing escaped from her thin, pale lips. Her face had lost all color. She was in shock.

"Do you have a cell phone with you?" Micheline asked. She pronounced each word separately as if she were speaking to a child.

The girl nodded slightly.

"Call the police and emergency services," Micheline instructed. "Tell them there is an officer on the scene who needs assistance right away. The woman needs an ambulance. She is either unconscious or dead, and the suspect fleeing the scene is considered armed and dangerous. Did you get all that?"

"Yes," the terrified girl replied helplessly. "I think so. There was so much blood."

Micheline helped the young woman to her feet. She made a mental note of the girl's appearance. She was a few inches shorter than Micheline, pretty and athletic, with reddish-brown short-cropped hair. Micheline locked her azure eyes directly onto those of the female witness.

"You'll be all right," she offered. "I've got to check on the victim."

Micheline turned and hustled in the opposite direction. Her palms were sweaty, her heartbeat raced, and her visage became locked in a gritty expression of determination.

Was she crazy?

Maybe, for the confusion within herself was great. At times her philosophy was startling, others she was simply foolish and child-like. She experienced feelings she never understood, emotions she couldn't explain, and underneath her mask of confidence hid scarred memories that only emerged in the darkened depths of sleep. She was a woman faced with a rush of questions, and although she knew the answers to some, her only recourse was to roll the dice and to helplessly watch them tumble.

Fate be damned.

Her senses were at a high state of alert. Adrenaline pumped furiously through her veins. She hurried to the motionless body laid spread eagle on the sunbaked ground.

Micheline gagged when she saw her. She immediately closed her eyes shut and covered her mouth. Vomit clogged agitatedly in her throat. She steadied herself and looked again.

No amount of time on the job could properly prepare someone for the abhorrent display of a bloodied and desecrated body repeatedly stabbed. Fear swept over her.

The victim had been an attractive young woman. A blonde with one green eye open stared blankly toward the sky. She was in her early to mid-twenties and she was completely naked. Long blonde tendrils of hair masked and covered more than half of her blood-soaked face.

Oddly, the remnants of a maroon and white softball uniform, white socks, bra and panties, leather baseball glove, a pair of pink flip flops, and a pair of black and white baseball cleats lay perfectly folded and arranged only a few feet away from the victim's motionless body.

The young woman had been stabbed and slashed dozens of times in several places across her upper torso. Her throat had been slit from ear to ear. The thumb on her right hand had been completely cut off, probably during a defensive struggle. Blood had splattered everywhere and even dripped from the leaves of nearby trees. The murder weapon had been a razor-sharp object, presumably a knife or machete, but neither the weapon nor the missing thumb was within view.

A violent physical assault had taken place. The woman had most likely been raped. She was slender in appearance with large breasts and her vaginal area was completely shaved clean. Her battered, lifeless body lay discarded as if used and then quickly forgotten. She had most likely fought desperately against her attacker and then succumbed to an agonizing and painful death.

Micheline knelt beside the pallid corpse. She gently pressed her index and middle fingers against the victim's throat and waited a few seconds. No pulse. The body was still warm. Micheline carefully stood and backed away from the crime scene.

She noted the visible blood on the victim's body was thin and runny like water, not yet clotted or thick and oily. Micheline felt certain she had heard the young woman's last desperate screams before her death only a few minutes before.

Micheline looked at her own hands. Her fingertips were stained with the blood of the victim. Animosity swelled within her and raged uncontrollably toward the breaking point. There was no time to loiter.

She turned and raced after the girl's killer in a fury of anger and frustration, vowing the fat bastard would pay for his repugnant crime.

Twelve

The willowy branches of trees and bushes whipped relentlessly against Micheline's face and body. She pushed them aside without care and darted along the wooded path in search of her quarry, who was nowhere to be seen. Micheline feared the killer may have escaped.

She kept her revolver drawn, ready to shoot at the first sign of trouble. The Smith & Wesson Bodyguard Airweight featured a light alloy frame and a shrouded hammer to eliminate the possibility of accidental firing due to snags on clothing. Micheline didn't bother to cock the safety switch on her two-inch-barreled backup weapon because there was none. A single pull of the trigger would automatically produce the desired double-action response.

Her fingers curled rigidly around the checkered walnut grips on the rounded butt of her firearm. Perspiration soaked through her palms, loosening her hold on the deadly weapon.

She ran as fast as she could for three-quarters of a mile before finally giving in to exhaustion. The killer had mysteriously vanished. Troubled and out of breath, Micheline leaned forward near the trunk of a tall palm tree and allowed her hands to hang limp against her thighs.

She had not intended for things to work out this way. It was not in her nature to give up a fight so easily or to act dishonorably against her word. She hung her head in despair.

Leaves and gravel rustled nearby.

Micheline reacted immediately. She swung her body in the direction of the noise and brought her gun to bear. There was motion in the shadows ahead.

Something was wrong.

The killer was in a great hurry to escape but seemed disoriented and stumbled and tripped as he fought his way down an embankment toward a divided parkway beyond.

Maybe the victim had wounded him before her death?

Micheline sucked in a deep breath and chased after the man. Two full minutes passed before Micheline approached within spitting distance of her adversary. She had to be cautious. She was not a street cop nor a patrol officer. She was also off-duty, and therefore had no reason to be wearing a bulletproof vest. Her gun and her wits were her only defenses.

Ahead, the suspect scrambled at a quick pace along the sidewalk. He never once looked over his shoulder to see how much distance separated him from his pursuer, and even more strangely, he never turned to open fire with his rifle.

Micheline was puzzled. The suspect was a large man who bullishly fled from any possible confrontation. Instead of carrying his rifle cradled in his arms, he held it out in front of him, like a golf club or a walking stick.

A cane.

Micheline's emotions grew stone cold. She advanced recklessly, eager to apprehend the criminal.

"Stop!" she yelled loudly. "Police!"

The man refused to yield and continued moving forward at a frenetic pace.

Micheline summoned all her strength and leaped forward. She tackled the portly man from behind by wrapping her arms around the man's massive legs. Their intertwined bodies crashed heavily to the concrete pavement of the sidewalk.

Micheline abruptly rolled the man over like a giant tractor tire at the police training obstacle course. She harshly shoved her revolver under the suspect's jaw.

"Police, asshole. Don't move," she growled.

The man's glazed eyes stared back at Micheline, unseeing. His entire body trembled with apprehension, almost identically to the redheaded softball player who had witnessed him attacking the victim.

Micheline instinctively probed for a knife, a sharp object, or any weapon at all. The suspect's shirttails were hanging out, the zipper of his trousers was down all the way, but the experienced criminal investigator's search turned up nothing except for a blind man's carved wooden cane, a wallet, a set of house keys, and a wadded-up cloth handkerchief that was moist and wet. Micheline knew the murder weapon had most likely been left somewhere near to the attack. Crime scene investigators would locate it. With luck, there would be time to search for it before dark.

Micheline rose to her feet.

"You're blind?" she asked hesitantly.

"I didn't do it!" the man pleaded. "Yes, I'm blind. I got scared when I heard you yelling, and I tried to run away. I thought you might be the person who killed that naked girl."

"What the fuck were you doing out there if you can't see? And how do you know she was naked?" Micheline demanded.

"I was walking along the footpath," the man stammered. "I live in the neighborhood, and I come here regularly. I heard a commotion, and I moved closer to observe what was happening. I heard the woman scream, and then someone ran past me. When I found the woman on the ground, oh, I could just tell she was already dead. I felt the blood. I realized she was naked as I was touching her."

Micheline surveyed the situation. A few things didn't add up.

"The zipper of your pants is down, and I notice you had a wet handkerchief in your pocket. Would you mind explaining that?"

"Oh, shit," the man sighed. "All right. I was out for a walk today. I had to take a piss, okay? So, I found a tree when I thought no one was around. I was taking a leak and I heard the woman and her friend. They were fucking somewhere nearby, and she cried like she was really getting it good. Having an orgasm, hot and heavy, you know?"

"You've got to be kidding me, sir? You think she was enjoying it?" Micheline's initial reaction would have been to smack the man upside the head with the handgrip of her firearm, but she held her emotions in check.

"Yes, she was. Honest to Moses. They were fucking like two horny lovers who hadn't seen each other in a long while. I got aroused and one thing led to another."

"What do you mean, sir?" Micheline asked. "One thing led to another?"

"I got a woody and I masturbated in my hands. I used the handkerchief to clean myself up."

"Oh, shit! So gross," Micheline remarked as she realized she had touched the fluid-drenched handkerchief and was still holding it firmly in her hand.

"What about the woman's friend?" Micheline inquired. "You're sure they weren't fighting?"

"Yes, I'm sure," he said. "Can I get up, please?"

The man was built like an elephant, easily exceeding four hundred pounds. He looked to be in his early sixties but was probably somewhat younger. Micheline would check his driver's license in a minute. The man had wan, fleshy cheeks engraved with pockmarks, which were in sharp contrast to the thinning, silvery locks of hair atop his head.

"What's your name?" Micheline demanded.

The man was frantic.

"Please," he begged. "Don't get me involved in this! I'm just an innocent bystander. I was at the wrong place at the wrong time. My wife would kill me if she heard about all this."

"Your name, sir," Micheline growled unapologetically.

"Dominic," the man stuttered. "Dominic Sadoski. I'm telling you the truth, miss. The lady was fucking her boyfriend with wild abandon. When they finished, the guy left. It was all kissy-kissy, and I love meeting you secretly like this, see you soon. Then it wasn't long after, I heard footsteps approaching from the opposite direction than the guy had come from, and the girl let out a blood-curdling scream to wake the dead. There was a lot of commotion. After that, someone ran past me and I went to check on the woman, but she was already dead on the ground."

"I heard those final screams, too," Micheline commented. "You're sure it wasn't the boyfriend she was having sex with? You don't think he doubled back and attacked her?"

"Yes, I'm sure," Sadoski said. "It was someone else. Someone quick and light on their feet."

Police sirens wailed in the distance, coming closer, converging on them with every second that passed.

"She was stabbed multiple times," Micheline said. "Did you hear anything else, or find a knife near the body?"

"No, I didn't," Sadoski said. "I can only tell you I didn't do it. I'm not capable of such a horrible crime."

In her five years working homicide back east, and in all the nine years of her career in criminal justice, Micheline had uncovered some hideous truths about people and murder. Capability had nothing to do with it. Motive, the reason behind the crime, was all she needed to know. If the right buttons were pushed, even the most docile of individuals could be provoked to commit gruesome acts of savagery. No case was ever beyond exception to the rule.

"Why's your fly open?" Micheline asked again. "You expect me to believe you just jerked yourself off in the woods while you eavesdropped on another couple making love in a public park? Get real, man. You had sex with that girl, didn't you? She's a prostitute, isn't she?"

"No way!" Sadoski pleaded. "I'm a married man. I wouldn't do that." He choked and coughed loudly.

"Did you know her?" Micheline pressed on. "Did you follow her here into the woods?"

Sadoski shook his head furiously back and forth. "No!" he cried. "I wouldn't do that."

The worried shouts of patrolmen echoed through the trees.

"Over here!" Micheline yelled loudly. "Situation under control."

"Please, miss," Sadoski cried.

"Just wait here," Micheline commanded. "There's nothing to be worried about. We'll both talk to the police when they get here and sort this out."

Two faces broke through the shadows. Two faces clad in blue with silver shields pinned to their chests. Firearms pointed forward as if they were extensions of each of the officers' arms.

Micheline withdrew her wallet from a zippered pocket in the small pack around her waist and flashed her picture ID card. "Hi, officers. I'm Detective Micheline Avila with the San Diego County Sheriff's Department."

Sounded pretty convincing.

She was mistaken.

"Drop your weapon," the first officer, who brandished a Beretta semi-automatic nine-millimeter pistol with an earth-tone finish, ordered harshly.

Micheline looked confused, with her eyebrows upraised.

"Drop your fucking gun or I'll blow your head off!" the second officer demanded. This cop stood firmly entrenched behind his partner. He obviously had watched too many Clint Eastwood movies as a kid. The only personal features evident were his milky white complexion, a set of bloodshot light gray eyes, and a wispy red mustache which curled slightly around the perimeter of his mouth.

Micheline gently tossed her gun to the ground and held her hands in the air. She knew the drill.

The first officer was a tall man, clean-shaven, with dark, Sicilian features, and brooding eyes. A lieutenant. He snatched the wallet from Micheline's outstretched hand and retrieved the gun while the second officer, a sergeant, pushed her roughly forward, face down on the ground.

"Take it easy, Kev," the lieutenant cautioned. "This lady works for the DA's office. I've heard of her."

Micheline remained silent. The situation would defuse itself soon enough. The city of Del Mar had contracted for law enforcement services from the San Diego County Sheriff's Department. Their patrol division, the North Coastal Sheriff's Station, of whom these officers were a part, was responsible for covering the municipalities of Del Mar, Encinitas, Solana Beach, Rancho Santa Fe, Del Dios, Camp Pendleton, and San Onofre.

"You can get up, Detective," the lieutenant said. "Slowly."

Micheline rose to her feet and followed the lieutenant's directions to the letter.

"I'm Lieutenant Frank Salvatore. My partner's Sergeant Kevin Mc-Caffrey. Do you mind telling us what's going on? We had an anonymous phone call about a girl getting killed near the park."

"There was another witness," Micheline responded. "A young female with short reddish-brown hair. I had instructed her to call it in while I chased after this man here, also apparently a witness to the crime, although he's blind. He was in the vicinity and overheard some of what happened. The victim is a blonde woman in her early twenties. She's naked, and she was stabbed multiple times. There's blood splatter all around the body."

"I was just at the wrong place at the wrong time," Sadoski lamented. "Please, I had nothing to do with this."

"Now hold on there, sir," Salvatore said. "Kevin, check this man's identification, please."

The lieutenant turned back toward Micheline. "Where's the body?"

"Less than a ten-minute walk from here," Micheline responded. She took a deep breath and exhaled slowly. She needed to pace herself and to speak in a calculated tone. She didn't want to leave any detail, however small or seemingly inconsequential, out of the conversation.

"At the Five Points intersection of the park. As I said, it's an ugly scene. The victim is on her back and completely naked. Her throat has been slit from ear to ear. She suffered multiple stabs and slash wounds visible across her face, torso, arms, and even her legs. It certainly appears to have been a very personal and aggressive attack against her."

Lieutenant Salvatore held up his hand to silence Micheline. He turned toward his partner and eyed him curiously.

"This gentleman's name is Dominic Sadoski," the sergeant confirmed. "He's got a handicapped ID and he's legally blind. There are blood stains evident on both of his hands."

Lieutenant Salvatore eyed his partner warily and then turned back to face Micheline. "You caught the suspect in the act?"

Micheline shook her head. "No, sir. Mr. Sadoski was bent over the body when I got there. I believe I heard the victim's final screams a few moments earlier while I was on a run near the park. I heard a second scream from another woman who was present at the scene when I arrived there. That's when I saw this man hunched over the body. I was still some distance away. I yelled police, stop, and that's when he got up and ran away."

"Was there any evidence of a weapon of any kind at the scene?" Salvatore asked.

"No, sir," Micheline replied. "At least, not that I was able to see immediately. I told the redhead to call it into nine-one-one, and then I went to check on the victim. I felt for a pulse, but there was none. She was clearly dead. Then I got up and I ran after Mr. Sadoski, here. I had just caught up with him and was questioning him when the two of you arrived."

"I see," said the lieutenant. He rubbed his jaw thoughtfully and addressed McCaffrey in a decisive tone.

"Let's not take any chances here," he said determinedly. "Cuff the perp. He tried to run from the scene. Escort him back to the squad car until we can take his statement and sort this mess out."

"No!" Sadoski cried. "I didn't do anything wrong."

McCaffrey holstered his weapon and then bent over and wrestled Sadoski to a standing position. Micheline detected a faint odor of whiskey on the sergeant's breath.

That explains the bloodshot eyes. It must have been one hell of a Friday night.

"The man is blind," Micheline offered, hoping to diffuse the situation. She recognized McCaffrey for what he really was, a macho asshole with a gun and a badge. A deadly combination.

The North Coastal Sheriff's Station had given their officers carte blanche in choice of sidearms. McCaffrey carried a Remington .44 Magnum, a weapon with high recoil and muzzle flash. It was categorically prohibited by most law enforcement agencies. Not only was it heavier and bulkier than regulation firearms, but the weapon was meant to destroy, not wound, its potential target. In confrontations of thirty feet or less, where most one-on-one situations were dealt, a hand grenade would have been more practical.

"I've already searched for a weapon," Micheline continued. "I couldn't find anything. Please take the cane with you."

Sergeant McCaffrey handcuffed Sadoski with his hands in front. The standard rule of thumb was to handcuff suspects with hands behind their back. McCaffrey went against the standard protocol because he did not foresee Sadoski to be a threat to retaliate. He also recognized that if Sadoski tripped and fell on the uneven terrain of the park, which was highly probable, there was no way the sergeant was going to be able to prevent the man's fall.

It was safer for everyone present to have Sadoski handcuffed this way. It allowed Sadoski the opportunity to block his fall in the event he accidentally tripped while they walked along the dirt pathway.

As McCaffrey snapped the stainless-steel shackles in place, he read the Miranda word-for-word from a card he had withdrawn from his breast pocket.

Sadoski upheld his right to remain silent until he could meet with an attorney. The only words spoken between officer and suspect thereafter were verbal instructions by McCaffrey to aid Sadoski as they walked through the woods toward Catalina Mission Park.

Lieutenant Salvatore returned Micheline's ID and .38-caliber backup weapon to her.

"Thanks, Lieutenant," Micheline said. She slipped the ID back into her wallet and placed both the wallet and her revolver into the zippered compartment of her cloth waist pack.

"You want to come with us," Salvatore remarked icily, sounding more like an order than a polite request.

Micheline submitted willingly and followed closely in step behind McCaffrey and Sadoski.

Thirteen

"Let's start again from the beginning," Lieutenant Salvatore suggested. "Tell me again, and don't leave anything out, no matter how small a detail may seem to be."

Micheline rubbed her jaw thoughtfully as she and the three men trudged along the walking path toward the entrance to Catalina Mission Park. She thought back to the reason she had come here in the first place.

"I had the day off," she began. "I like to shake up my routine by running in different parts of the city."

"Do you come here often?" the lieutenant asked inquisitively.

Micheline liked the lieutenant. Salvatore had a fatherly, rough-hewn edge to his manner. He was someone you could trust and respect. He got right to the point and listened carefully. He took his responsibility to serve and protect the public seriously. He reminded her somewhat of a cross between Guillermo Reyes and her father.

Sergeant McCaffrey, on the other hand, seemed to like roughness for roughness' sake. He was a loose cannon with a nasty temper and an on-duty drinking problem. He was certainly not a candidate for the officer of the month.

"Once in a while," Micheline responded. "I live in Coronado, and I usually run along the beaches and the perimeter of the Navy base out there. Occasionally I like a change of scenery. So, I parked my car at Pacific West Plaza and went for a run through the outlying neighborhood. I like it here. The sidewalks are extra-wide, and the rolling hills make for a great workout. Today's the first time back since sometime in September, I'd say."

"Go on," the lieutenant prodded.

"I heard a woman scream."

Salvatore listened intently while he kept a watchful eye on his partner, who was nudging Sadoski forward with an occasional elbow to the ribs. He disapprovingly shook his head but said nothing in protest.

"I rushed to the scene," Micheline continued. "I heard a second scream which I believe came from a different woman. The murder scene is at a clearing in the woods just off the walking path to Five Points. I turned to see what the woman had screamed about, and I saw Mr. Sadoski straddled over top of the body of the victim."

The lieutenant nodded thoughtfully. "And you say the body's located at the Five Points intersection of the park?"

"That's correct," Micheline affirmed. "About forty yards away from the granite modern art statue."

"And what happened to this other woman who was screaming her head off?" Sergeant McCaffrey asked over his shoulder.

"I'm not sure," Micheline replied. "I asked her to call for police and an ambulance. She confirmed she had a cell phone with her. I left her there at the scene. My next thought was to check the victim for any sign of life. She was clearly already gone. The stab wounds were extensive. I checked for a pulse, and after I determined I couldn't do anything to help her, I took off after Mr. Sadoski, who had left the scene in a hurry."

"It doesn't look good for you, man," McCaffrey insinuated to Sadoski.

"I didn't do anything wrong," Sadoski said. "I was just fucking scared, and at the wrong place at the wrong time. It will all come out when we talk this through. And stop jabbing me with your elbow, you son of a bitch! My attorney is going to get a full report on how you've been mistreating me. I'll tell you that!"

"One other thing," Micheline said upon reflection. "The redhead who called it in was wearing a North Beach softball uniform. She must have known the victim because there was another uniform just like hers near the body of the victim. Folded neatly, like she was at a picnic and planned to put it on when she was done."

"A naked picnic, huh?" McCaffrey scoffed. "Why don't I ever get invited to one of those?"

"I'll let Mr. Sadoski tell his side of the story," Micheline said. "But from what he described to me, it appears there may have been at least one or two other individuals present at the scene before the murder took place."

"Oh, now it might have been a sexual orgy in a public park during the middle of a gorgeous sunny day," McCaffrey rattled on.

"More likely a romantic rendezvous between two lovers who are married to other people, and a jealous third party who showed up angry and unannounced," Micheline suggested. "I've seen that more than once on the job. But again, let's document all of the statements and call in the crime scene unit to begin their investigation."

"Good point," Salvatore interjected. "The female witness. Did you happen to notice if she had any of the victim's blood on her?"

"No," Micheline responded. "No, she didn't. There were dirt and grass stains, but nothing unusual. When you see how much blood splattered at the scene, you'll understand the killer must have gotten themselves sprayed pretty good, too."

"Do you have any idea as to the identity of either of the women?" Salvatore asked.

"No, sir," Micheline replied. "The players for the North Beach softball team are typically locals from Del Mar or Solana Beach, though. The team likely had a game scheduled today. They're probably at the Carmel Valley Community ballpark right now."

"We'll check into that," Sergeant McCaffrey said.

"You better rouse up the homicide team and the coroner first," Micheline suggested.

McCaffrey turned completely around and leered at Micheline with angry, alcohol-induced vehemence. "Listen here, lady detective. I know what the fuck to do! So, why don't you just put a lid on it and let us professionals handle this from here on in, okay? It's our jurisdiction."

Lieutenant Salvatore looked as if he were about to interject and then thought better of it.

Leave it alone.

Utter silence befell the four individuals as if the first to speak would suffer cruel and inhuman torture at the hands of leftist guerillas during a military coup d'état. From that moment on, what thoughts either of them entertained, they adamantly refused to reveal to one another.

They approached the squad car, its cherry top flickering like a red and blue candle flame. McCaffrey locked Sadoski in the backseat of the cruiser and made the initial report via police band radio. He called in a 10-54, code two. A possible dead body. Respond urgently without red lights and sirens.

Micheline leaned against the front quarter panel of the shiny white all-wheel-drive SUV. Her weekend had started off badly.

A young woman was dead. She had possibly been raped. She had been brutally attacked, murdered, and her identity remained a mystery.

The suspected killer currently in police custody resolutely denied his guilt. Or the murder may have been committed by someone else who had disappeared from the park entirely, and the only other female witness had yet to be found and identified.

But if Sadoski's account were accurate, the killer would have left a trail of blood along their escape path. Forensic investigators would be able to follow that out of the park. Perhaps it would lead them to a nearby house or to a parking space along the road. Someone walking their dog or out for a run may have noticed something unusual. A traffic camera may have caught an incriminating image along with a time stamp.

At this point, there were too many holes in the story. Micheline leaned back and remained quiet while she mulled things over in her mind. Answers were certainly few and far between. She also knew she would not be responsible for delving into this matter further.

Best to let curiosity kill a different cat this time.

Unfortunately for Micheline, her inner alarm was ringing louder than a locomotive's whistle at a busy intersection. She not only *wanted* to know, but she also *needed* to know who the victim and the female witness were.

She wanted to know who the murderer was and why they acted so aggressively in a public park. If answers were not found at the local softball field, a gnawing feeling in Micheline's gut suggested another local establishment where she might find some additional answers on her own.

"Fuck the cat!" she mumbled quietly under her breath.

"Do you think he did it?" the lieutenant asked as he turned his attention back toward Micheline.

"Honestly, sir," Micheline responded. "I doubt it. He had some trace blood on him, sure. He did lean over the body, and I saw him on top of her. But his clothing would have been much messier if he had been attacking her and stabbing her with a knife."

"But he ran from the scene."

"I know," Micheline said. "But that's not an admission of guilt. The victim would have fought back. She may have trace amounts of skin under her nails. The killer would have sustained at least some telltale mark, or a bruise or a wound. Let the crime scene investigators have a go at it. They'll be able to come up with something much more conclusive than my conjecture at this point."

Micheline was a woman of patient resolve. She would hear all the testimony relevant to the case and review the findings from the crime lab before making her own final judgment.

Sergeant McCaffrey came around the side of the police cruiser and brazenly slapped Micheline on the back of the shoulder.

"Relax, Detective," he uttered confidently. "We got the bastard. He's guilty as sin."

Fourteen

Micheline sat quietly by herself at a wooden table in the Hops & Malt Brewing Company tasting room. It was a beverage and grill establishment located in the premier retail development site known as Pacific West Plaza in Carmel Valley. At the intersection of Del Mar Heights Road and El Camino Real, the brewery was a hub for a variety of North County coastal types, including beer nerds, business professionals, affluent suburbanites, college students, and factory workers.

It was also a known hangout and social meeting place for members of the North Beach adult women's softball team. Micheline glanced casually around the large dining room and polished off the last vestiges of her dinner, a grilled double-patty cheeseburger loaded with lettuce, tomatoes, dill pickle, onion, and encased within a toasted sourdough bun. On the side had been an order of crispy onion rings and a creamy mound of freshly diced coleslaw. Her right hand gripped a tall pilsner glass filled with a craft-brewed blonde ale.

She was alone. The Saturday night crowd had just started to trickle in. Several of the tables were occupied by couples, mostly dressed in cargo shorts and flip-flops with hooded pullover sweatshirts. At the bar, a few older gentlemen sat discussing the ingredients and taste of their IPA beers, while at the far end of the bar a mixed group of millennials and zoomers, those of the Gen Z demographic who were of legal age, were drinking a combination of beer and tequila shots.

Micheline looked up to watch the high-definition television screen suspended above the bar. The UCLA Bruins football team was trailing the USC Trojans by seventeen points late in the third quarter. Micheline smiled as the Bruins' defense intercepted an errant pass and returned it forty-seven yards for a pick-six touchdown. She loved to watch an underdog make a comeback against a much stronger and nationally-ranked opponent.

A waitress entered the tasting room from the kitchen at the back of the restaurant and eagerly approached Micheline's table.

"Why is such a sexy young woman looking so sad and serious tonight?" she inquired.

Micheline turned to see a familiar face. Laura Quiñónez was clad in a tight-fitting heather gray Hops & Malt Brewing Company T-shirt, a black skirt, and black canvas sneakers with white rubber soles. She had a nasty purplish bruise on her left eye she had attempted to cover with makeup, and there were bruise marks on her right arm.

"I'm doing okay, Laura," Micheline said. "But what about you? Did you get the license plate of the Mack truck that hit you?"

Laura laughed it off and attempted a weak smile. "I did," she responded. "And it's not what you might think."

Micheline looked concerned. "Did Wade do this?"

"He did," Laura confirmed. "But as I said, it wasn't a fight. We were," she hesitated, "getting intimate, wrestling around the bedroom and such. I got behind him, and he accidentally swung around and hit me with an elbow to the eye. It hurts like hell, but I'll be all right."

"I'm sorry," Micheline said. "It does look painful."

"Not to worry," Laura said. "Can I take your plate and get you another beer? Maybe some dessert? The bakery across the plaza brought some fresh cannolis and tiramisu over tonight."

Micheline nodded. "You can take my plate. I'm finished with my dinner. That was a really juicy burger, too. No dessert tonight, thanks. Although they both sound delicious."

"Sure thing. Another beer?"

"No, thanks. I'm not ready for another round yet. I'm just taking my time tonight."

"Have you spoken to Jenny or Greg at all?"

"No, I haven't," Micheline admitted. "I assume Jenny's got enough going on with her family in Chicago this weekend." She hesitated.

"What's wrong?"

"Greg called late yesterday afternoon to break off our date planned for last night. He gave me a lame excuse about a business dinner he had forgotten about. On a Friday night? I think he's just playing the field, and he's already met somebody else he's more interested in."

"I sure hope you're wrong," Laura said. "The two of you look really cute together."

"Thanks," Micheline said. "I could be wrong, of course. But my intuition tells me he's not sending the right signals. And I'm sorry, it must be so tough for you to be raising a family and working two jobs like this."

"It's a living," she said. "The pharmacy is my full-time career. I just work here three nights a week for a few hours to make some extra income. It comes in handy when the kids need things, and the tips are good."

"I guess," Micheline remarked.

"If you don't mind my saying, you look like you just lost your best friend," Laura said sympathetically. "Tough day, huh? Your girlfriend is out of town, and your boyfriend isn't calling? If that were me, I'd be home alone curled up with a good dark romance novel and a glass of red wine tonight."

Micheline locked eyes with her for a moment to consider what Laura had just said. She had seen similar bruises on women's faces before. It was never as simple as it was played out to be.

"I started with the Domestic Violence Unit when I first came out here to San Diego," she said softly. "I have friends there, people I can reach out to if you feel you need help, Laura. All you have to do is ask."

"Thanks for being concerned, Micheline," she said, turning to see if anyone at the nearby tables was listening to their conversation.

"But as I said, this was an accident, and Wade was as sorry as can be. No harm, no foul, right? Besides, you know he has a record. A charge like wife battery would be the third strike and could land him ten to fifteen years in prison."

"Ah, yes. There's that."

"He'd lose the business. The kids would lose their father. We'd lose the house, and I'd never get laid again, except for conjugal visits at the prison. Not such a rosy picture, is that?"

"I guess," Micheline said. "I just want to be a good friend. I care what happens to you. Jenny really likes you, and I do, too." She was disappointed with Laura's response, but she had expected as much.

Maybe someday she will change her mind. Someday before it is too late.

"I heard you had an exciting morning," Laura said, effectively changing the subject. "A couple of the Del Mar officers came in after their shift ended. They mentioned you by name."

"They were talking about me?" Micheline asked, surprised. "What were they saying?"

"The one was blabbering about how he'd like to see the rest of your tattoos. He's obviously not getting any pussy. The other cop was nice. He mentioned you caught a woman's killer today. You were on the scene before anyone else, and if it hadn't been for you, the suspect would have gotten away."

"Do you know who these cops were, or what they looked like?"

Laura nodded toward the bar. "One had red hair. He was the blabbering fool. The other cop looked like the man coming over here to your table right now."

Laura proceeded to clear the empty plate and utensils from the table. She quickly returned to the kitchen.

Micheline looked up to see Lieutenant Salvatore obviously out of uniform. He was wearing a short sleeve Hawaiian shirt, blue jeans, and blue canvas shoes with white soles as he approached the table. The lieutenant was accompanied by a female detective, also in plain clothes, whom Micheline knew personally from within her own department.

"Lieutenant Salvatore, nice to see you," Micheline opened, and offered her hand. "Detective Van Horn, this is a pleasant surprise."

"Please, call me Frank," Salvatore offered. They shook hands firmly. "Mind if we join you?"

"Yes, of course," Micheline replied. "What are you both drinking?"

"Nothing for me, thanks," the lieutenant said. "I had a few earlier. I'll have a soda if the waitress comes by again."

Micheline turned toward the female detective. "Kelly, anything to drink?"

The female detective shook her head. "No thanks, Micheline. I need to keep my head clear."

Micheline's nerves were lit up like a Christmas tree at Rockefeller Center in Manhattan. She could feel the electricity running through her veins. Salvatore was a lieutenant for the local North Coastal Sherrif's Station, but Kelly Van Horn was a junior detective at the downtown office for the San Diego County Sheriff's Department.

Salvatore was easily a quarter-century, if not more, older than Van Horn. Micheline doubted the dignified Italian gentleman was here with her on a romantic date. They were at the bar and grill for a specific work-related purpose, even if they both were officially off-duty.

Micheline felt certain she was their intended target. She nodded slowly. There was no sense beating around the bush.

"It's no coincidence you're here twice in one day, is it?" she asked.

"Same reason you are, I'm sure," the lieutenant replied with a proud grin. "I thought you might get it in your head to poke around the case, even though I know you're not assigned to it. I'm a local, Micheline. I grew up nearby in Scripps Ranch. So, you're not the only one who knows the North Beach women's softball team members frequent this particular bar on weekends."

Micheline nodded again. "That's very presumptive of you, Frank. But right on the mark. I'll admit, the redheaded witness leaving the scene of the crime today and not reporting back in has me bothered."

"And for good reason," Salvatore said. "The fact is, I've heard some great comments about you since I started asking around. You're quite an investigator from all accounts."

"Sometimes people lie. Sometimes they're just mistaken," Micheline said and raised her bottle of blonde ale to take a long swig.

"Sometimes," the lieutenant agreed. "My gut tells me to believe them, though. You've got that east coast New York minute attitude about you. You push hard. And besides, it came directly from both Kelly and the lead detective on this case."

"From Guillermo Reyes, huh?" Micheline concluded. "I let him down the last time we worked together. I'm surprised he would still go to bat for me."

"Not the way I hear it," Kelly Van Horn said. "You were handed a case with few clues, and it went cold real fast. Everyone knows you pulled more than your own weight on that one. Sometimes you just need to step back and reevaluate. Sometimes you clear the case and others you don't. That doesn't stop the next case from coming in and you need to sort your priorities."

"Thanks, Kelly," Micheline said. "I know what you mean."

Laura returned from the kitchen to the tasting room and began to take an order from a table near the entrance. Salvatore rolled his eyes and his jaw dropped.

"My, she's put together!" Salvatore drooled.

"You're such a cliché, Frank!" Van Horn said and tapped his shoulder lightly in a friendly manner.

Salvatore's stare lasted a few seconds longer before he turned his attention back to his current tablemates.

"I was going to give you points for being a dignified gentleman, Frank," Micheline proclaimed. "But apparently you're just as much a hound dog as your whiskey-smelling partner."

"I'll have you know," he stated, "I'm a happily married man of thirty-five years. I just get distracted from time to time. California babes have that effect on me, the present company certainly included."

Kelly and Micheline both smiled pleasantly and let the remark go.

"She's friends with another woman I met recently," Micheline said. "They work out at the same gym sometimes. I don't know how she finds time, though. She's a full-time pharmacy technician and she waitresses here on the side. Plus, she's married and has a couple of kids, too."

"What's with the eye?" Salvatore inquired.

"I don't know for sure," Micheline admitted. "I asked her about it. She said it was an accident. I told her I used to work in the Domestic Violence Unit, and I could offer to help, but she insisted it was nothing."

"She looks like she can take care of herself," the lieutenant remarked.

"Doesn't make it right," Micheline grumbled agitatedly.

"You're a little on edge tonight, Micheline," Salvatore responded. "What's eating you?"

"Your partner has got a real problem," Micheline said in a steady, accusatory, hard-boiled tone. "That bothered me today, the way he treated the suspect without any provocation. Yanking him around, jabbing him in the ribs. Snide remarks about the guy's weight and his guilt. He clearly had alcohol on his breath. Doesn't that bother you to be partnered with someone who might not be able to give their best performance on the job when it really matters?"

Salvatore drew in a long slow breath and straightened his shoulders. "McCaffrey's all right on most days. He was a little off this morning. I'll give you that. A buddy of his had a bachelor party last night at one of the strip clubs down in the Gaslamp Quarter. No harm done. They had a good time. A cop needs to release stress from the job, or he can end up either in a psych ward or with a loaded gun at his temple. I shouldn't have to explain that to you."

Micheline nodded without saying anything more. She could be wrong, and she would admit it if it came to that. But instinct and years of experience immediately called McCaffrey's ability, as well as his judgment, into question. Micheline felt dead certain that McCaffrey had been drinking that morning, and not just late into the evening beforehand.

"They identified the girl," Kelly said. "Do you want to hear any of the particulars?"

"No need to," Micheline answered. "Detective Reyes caught me up to speed. I don't usually handle homicide cases, but I assist when needed, like the one Guillermo and I worked together before. I gave him a complete statement. Everything from a description of the female witness, whom I was informed had failed to remain at the scene, to my chase through the woods of Sadoski, what personal effects I found on him, and the North Coastal Sherrif's Station patrol officer's prompt arrival to the scene. He filled me in on the rest after the coroner called. Besides, it's not my case, remember?"

"Sure," Salvatore said. He looked uncomfortable. "So, how come you're not out with friends or on a date tonight? Are you really here hoping to spot our mystery female witness?"

"I had been dating this guy named Greg," Micheline replied evenly. "He canceled our date at the last minute for last night, so I'm a bit miffed about that. He's hasn't even called me today to apologize. And one of my girlfriends is away this weekend for her parent's fortieth wedding anniversary, so she flew home to Chicago for a family gathering."

"And you didn't want to join her?" Salvatore asked.

Micheline was beginning to wonder which of them was the detective. She shifted uneasily in her chair.

"She took a couple of days off from work. I'm sure we'll get together for a drink and talk about the trip when she gets back."

Micheline took another swig of her beer. "Anyway, Detective Reyes and his team, which includes Kelly, I assume now, are going to question team members until they locate the girl. She shouldn't be too hard to find. If I see her here tonight, I'll call Guillermo directly to report it. Otherwise, I'm just a single lady out for dinner and a beer tonight. It's mostly couples here tonight, anyway."

"Sounds like trouble in paradise," Kelly stated. "You should call your guy to let him know you're thinking of him. I'm sure he'd like that. I know the guy I'm seeing wishes I was more aggressive that way."

"I'm not so sure if I should," Micheline remarked. "It sends the wrong signal. I come off sounding too clingy or needy. We were getting along fine, but things have been kind of tense lately. My work's been getting in the way, I guess. Too many dinner plans changed at the last minute. Or he's talking to me about sports or car sales stuff and I'm trying hard to listen, but in the back of my mind, I'm trying to piece together clues to a case I'm working on. He sees right through me. I'm not hanging intently onto his every word like other women might."

"That's too bad," Salvatore said. "Your girlfriend, the one who's in Chicago for the weekend. Her name is Jenny Casella, right?"

"Yeah, that's right," Micheline replied, surprised. "How did you know?"

"Guillermo Reyes mentioned it to me," Salvatore said. "He and I go way back. We graduated from the police academy together."

"Really?"

"Yes, it's true. And I've met Jenny, actually. My wife and I re-mortgaged the loan on our house last year when interest rates dropped. Jenny handled the paperwork at the bank. Nice girl, and pretty, too."

Micheline nodded. "Yes, she is. We met on an earlier case, the one that Detective Reyes and I worked on together. Her former boss was murdered last summer. Later, sometime after the investigation had stalled and gone cold, I swung by the bank for a final look around. We chatted and then went out for a couple of drinks. It turned out we had some things in common. Now we're friends, socially."

The lieutenant nodded. "That's interesting. And if all the good-looking single guys don't hound you for your phone number tonight, you could always introduce yourself to the pretty brunette to your left who's been staring at you ever since we sat down at your table."

"I hadn't noticed," Micheline said. She carefully glanced around the room. Too many thoughts were swirling through her head. Too many unanswered questions held her at bay. Again, her mind was focused solely on detective work.

The only thing investigators were certain of now was the identity of the victim. Her name was Samantha Miller, twenty-four years old, a biology major and modern dance student at UCSD in La Jolla. Her family lived in an estate overlooking the beach near Encinitas. She was the same young woman whom Micheline had witnessed angrily douse her fiancé with a goblet of red wine only a little over a week earlier at the pizzeria in Mira Mesa.

After a replay of the nine-one-one tape, a female voice was heard requesting police assistance and an ambulance for a woman who was attacked in the park. The message was brief and to the point.

"She's not moving and there's blood everywhere. Please hurry." And then the line clicked dead.

Micheline turned in her chair and made direct eye contact with the brunette whom Salvatore had referred to. The trained investigator was immediately surprised she had not noticed the woman sitting there before. Her stare lingered for a few seconds to ensure her mind was not playing tricks on her.

She knew that face.

The woman sat at a table with three of her female friends. She wore a pair of diamond stud earrings and a thin gold chain-link necklace, a white blouse, and a navy-blue skirt with matching navy-blue high heels. Classy. Something about her brown eyes gave her away.

"Not bad," Micheline remarked. "Are we betting on whether she'll talk to me?"

Salvatore shook his head. "I'm not a betting man, and I know a losing proposition when I see one." He pushed his chair back and stood.

"I'll see you around, Micheline. Have a good weekend. Kelly, are you coming?"

Kelly Van Horn slid from out of her chair. "Enjoy the rest of your night, Micheline," she said.

"Thanks, Frank," Micheline said. "It was good to meet you today, considering the circumstances. Kelly, I hope you have a nice weekend, and I'll see you around the office sometime."

"Yeah," Salvatore replied. The lieutenant turned and took one last glance at the brunette who had been keeping an eye on Micheline. She was an attractive woman, no doubt about it. But her hair was as black as midnight, and the lieutenant knew Micheline was only chasing redheads tonight. He continued his turn and casually accompanied Detective Van Horn straight out to the front entrance of the restaurant.

Micheline sat back and took a final sip of her pale ale. She preferred the Belgian ales to the taste of most other brands of beer. Leffe Blonde was her favorite, a brand she had discovered a few years earlier while visiting Amsterdam.

Normally she preferred a glass of Cabernet Sauvignon with dinner. Not that she drank alcohol too frequently. A mocha latte with hazelnut creamer in the morning and ice water throughout the day were her usual drinks of choice.

The classy brunette wasted no time once Micheline was alone. She excused herself from the group of girlfriends she had been chatting with and approached Micheline's table directly. Micheline maintained constant eye contact with her during the entire stroll to her table.

Micheline smiled warmly toward her. She appeared slightly older than she first had thought, but not by much. Mature and professional were the adjectives that came to mind. Late twenties, maybe early thirties. Maybe it was the makeup or the stylish outfit that accentuated the curves of her body in just the right way. Or maybe it was the dark color of her hair or the fact that this time she was not wearing a softball cap and uniform.

"Hi," she opened. "My name's Micheline Avila. Detective Micheline Avila of the San Diego County Sheriff's Department. Would you like to join me?"

The brunette smiled in return and said, "I can hardly refuse. You may have saved my life today."

Micheline looked directly into her dark brown eyes. "You changed your hair color. It's a good look on you."

The crime scene witness remained standing near the edge of the table.

Micheline could smell the sweet fragrance of the woman's perfume. The detective was still trying to decide whether she liked the woman's appearance better as a redhead or a brunette.

"I thought I was going out of my mind this afternoon," the woman replied. "I wanted something different, an escape. So, I dyed my hair something closer to my natural color, took a hot shower, got myself all dolled up, and came out tonight for drinks with my friends."

"Please, have a seat," Micheline offered.

The woman bent down low and whispered into Micheline's ear. "Let's get out of here, please, so we can speak more privately. I don't feel comfortable talking to you in such a public place. My friends will be too inquisitive. I haven't spoken to them of the events at the park from earlier today. I still don't know if I feel up to talking about it."

"But I don't even know your name yet," Micheline said.

"It's Jacqueline," she said. "But please, call me Jackie." She took hold of Micheline's hand and squeezed slightly, not letting go immediately. "Outside, Micheline. Please."

"All right," Micheline agreed. She withdrew her wallet from her purse and laid a twenty-dollar bill on the table. She added another five-dollar bill on top of the crumpled twenty and set the empty bottle of pale ale on top of both bills.

As she stood, she smiled and made eye contact with Laura, who was standing idly behind the bar. Micheline waved goodbye, and Laura returned the gesture with a wave of her hand and a questioning glance of her own.

Fifteen

Even though the sun had set several hours beforehand, the outside temperature remained a comfortable seventy degrees. A gentle coastal breeze wafted through the open-air retail plaza. Above, the faint light of stars flickered across a clear dark nighttime sky.

Micheline guided Jackie to a nearby bench along the promenade. "You have an accent," she noted. "British?"

"I was born in east London," Jackie confirmed. "The financial district near Bank Station. But my parents and I emigrated to the U.S. while I was in junior high school. We lived in Boston for a few years, and then later when it was time for me to attend university, we moved to San Diego. My father is an analytical chemist for a pharmaceutical company. Each move to a new city was a career opportunity for him, and my mum and I dutifully followed along wherever that took us. My parents settled into a new home in La Jolla while I attended the University of California at Santa Barbara."

"I'm sorry, Jackie. Could you please tell me your last name?"

"Oh, yes," she laughed. "It's Henshilwood. I'm sorry if I've appeared evasive. I haven't meant to be."

"Ah, I understand. It's perfectly normal. And what do you do for a living, Ms. Henshilwood?" Micheline clearly felt comfortable interviewing the witness with the cool British accent.

"I'm a pharmaceutical sales representative for Systole Biosciences."

Micheline nodded. "And why were you at the park today?"

"You know why," she answered flatly. "I was on my way to the softball field. We had a game today. I heard Samantha scream, but I was still too far away. When I got there, I saw the same thing you did. She was naked and laid out on her back with blood splattered everywhere around. The large man was kneeling next to her and touching her all over from head to toe. At first, I had thought he was raping her. I called the police just like you asked, and then I immediately returned home. I was too shaken up to do anything else."

"Did you know her well?"

"Yes," Jackie said. "Both from the softball team and from work. She had interned at our main office in Carmel Valley for two summers in a row while she was in school. Her father owns the company."

"I see," Micheline said. Missing pieces of the grand puzzle appeared to be coming together.

"Do you know anyone who would want to hurt her?"

Jackie shook her head. "No, I don't. At least, not like that. Not rape or murder. She's had a rough life. I was like an older sister to her. She used to tell me things. She suffered sexual abuse from a neighbor when she was younger, in her pre-teen years, and her parents refused to accept her accusations. She got caught up in drugs and petty theft as she grew older, too. She left home for a few years after high school and worked as an escort and a stripper. There was a huge rift between her and her family."

"I had heard she had her life together now."

"Yes. Somehow, her parents made the effort to reconnect with her and to get her away from that downtrodden life. It wasn't easy at first, either for her or for her parents. But then she started going to school. She took an interest in biology and dancing, tango being her favorite, and sporting activities like surfing and softball."

"Did you meet her at school?"

"No, I met her at work. She was sweet and innocent when we first met. She was somewhat vulnerable, and I joined the softball team because of her, too. We became remarkably close after that, like sisters."

"I'd like for you to speak to the lead detective on the case," Micheline said.

"Can't I just talk to you?" Jackie asked.

"I'm sorry, but no," Micheline replied resolutely. "It's not my case. But I know the detective who is leading the investigation, and he's a good man. We worked on a case together before. He will take your statement. He will ask you questions about the people in Samantha's life. Her relationships. Her family. Her fiancé. Any background you can provide might lead to a clue. You might remember something that didn't seem significant before, but in hindsight could turn out to be important."

"Will you come with me?" she asked.

"I could do that," Micheline answered. "Let me call him, and we'll see how he would like to proceed."

"Thank you," she said. "I can't believe she's gone. And for her to die like that. It's so horrible."

"Had you spoken to her recently?"

"The other day. She was thinking to break off her engagement to David. That's her fiancé. Dr. David Hawthorne. He's a surgeon at Scripps Memorial Hospital in La Jolla. He's also a fucking asshole to everyone who knows him. He and Samantha had a huge blowup about a week ago, and she said she was done with him. Besides, I know she was secretly seeing somebody else, too. Somebody, I think she really liked but could never have. I suspect he was already married."

"Another man in her life?"

"Yes."

"Do you know his name?"

"No, I don't. She never told me. I let her use my condo while I was out of town on a business trip to Arizona and New Mexico recently. I had asked her to water the plants on my balcony. When I got back, I found an empty box of condoms left on the sink counter in the bathroom. There were torn wrappers and used rubbers in the wastebasket, too. Lots of them."

"And you don't think she would have used them with David?"

"No, I don't."

"You seem firm on that. Why?"

"Because she and David had decided they'd wait until the honeymoon to have sexual intercourse. She told me David had admitted to being a virgin when they first met. She didn't know how to respond to that, so she lied to make him feel comfortable. She told him she was one, too. What a fucking prevarication that was!"

"I had seen them together in public once," Micheline said. "I didn't see much chemistry between them."

"She told me their lack of intimacy was one of the reasons she knew she would never be happy with him. But mostly it was because of his temper tantrums. He always had to have things his way. He was a big bully. I recall she once told me she always seemed to be attracted to the bad boys, and then later regretted it."

"I see," Micheline said.

"I'm still shaking," Jackie said. "I miss her so much. I'm worried the killer might be coming after her friends, too. Maybe it's some weirdo who's been stalking women who pass by the park."

"There's no need to be scared," Micheline assured her. "I caught up with the guy you saw on top of Samantha. The police have him locked up. It's possible he knew her and killed her. But I have my doubts about that. I think it's more likely he happened to be close by when things began to unfold, and he stumbled upon the scene just like you and I did."

Jackie remained silent and nervously twisted her hands in her lap. She looked up at the sky.

"So, her killer may still be on the loose?"

Micheline had no firm answers or assurances she could realistically provide to her.

"It's possible, yes. But I'll do everything in my power to keep you safe."

A helicopter with a searchlight droned overhead. They both looked up simultaneously at the distraction.

"I need your help with this, Jackie," she said. "I realize this is an unfortunate tragedy. Your close friend was killed in a very brutal way. That usually suggests a pre-existing personal relationship between the victim and the murderer. Any information you can provide in a witness statement may go a long way toward catching the person responsible for Samantha's death."

Jackie nodded her head. "Can I ask you something?"

"Sure," Micheline replied.

"Why were *you* at the park today?"

"I was out for a run."

"You're not married? I ask because I don't see a ring."

"No, I'm not married," Micheline answered. "I've been divorced for a few years now. I've lived in New Jersey most of my life and only moved out here to California about a year ago. I'm still getting myself settled both at work and in my personal life. I've been dating someone for the past few months. But even that relationship feels like it's on the rocks lately."

"Oh, sorry," she said.

"How about you?" Micheline asked.

"I'm recently divorced," Jackie replied. "I lost the house in the divorce, but at least I got a comfortable financial settlement. It's a good arrangement without any of the drama you might normally associate with a break-up."

Micheline inwardly winced. Her own divorce had been more emotionally dramatic than even she could have ever imagined. She still had fingernail scratch scars on her one hand from when her ex-husband refused to believe her announcement of a loveless marriage and clawed at her to keep her from leaving him. She wanted to move on with her life. Her husband had never shown he loved her. He was more worried and ashamed people would look upon him as a failure.

Micheline had been determined not to be controlled or manipulated by people in her life any longer. She wanted to matter to those she also cared about. She went through with the divorce proceedings. As painful and difficult as it was, she knew in her heart it was the right decision. She would never look back with regret again.

"I'm glad I was able to see you tonight," Micheline said. "I had an inkling this might be a place you'd come to."

"I'm glad you found me," she said. "You're obviously a very good detective. You have a kind soul, too. I can tell that right away about you."

"May I have your contact information, please?" Micheline asked. She withdrew her cell phone from her purse and tapped the notes app on the main menu screen.

Jackie took the phone from Micheline's hands and began to type in her name, address, and phone number. She added a brief note at the bottom, clicked done, and handed the phone back to the detective.

"Thanks," she said. "I'll text you as soon as I hear back from Detective Reyes. He's taken the lead on the investigation."

"I'll look forward to hearing from you again," she said and smiled warmly.

"We'll do our best to keep anything you tell us confidential," Micheline said. "But as you realize, this is a murder investigation. Solving the crime and ensuring we have enough evidence to convict the person responsible for Samantha's death is our primary objective."

"I understand completely," Jackie said. "If it's okay with you, I should be getting home. I just wanted to get out of the house tonight to see my friends for a drink. I'll look forward to talking to you again soon. Have a good evening, Micheline."

"You, too, Jackie," Micheline replied. "I'm glad we had this chance to talk. I'll follow up with you as quickly as I'm able to."

Jackie stood and walked toward the retail parking garage further along the paved concourse. Micheline stayed seated on the promenade bench for several minutes and mulled over what she might do next.

She would call Guillermo Reyes for starters, she decided. She scrolled through the contacts list on her phone and pressed the mobile listing for her good friend and colleague.

Sixteen

M onday morning came all too quickly. Micheline awoke alone in her two-bedroom Coronado condo on the peninsula in San Diego Bay. She inwardly frowned at the prospect of rising to get ready for another tough day on the job. This workday would prove especially difficult, following the dreadful events of the past weekend.

She managed to sit upright on the queen-size bed, then planted her bare feet firmly on the carpeted floor. She showered and washed her hair quickly while the hot spray awakened her from a dream-like state of mind.

She dressed in the bedroom by the light of a small bedside lamp. She chose a light blue long-sleeved blouse with navy slacks and a matching jacket, and a black pair of high heel shoes.

Micheline proceeded to the master bedroom walk-in closet, where she selected two handguns and holsters from separate decorative storage boxes located at the back of the closet. The organized horizontal shelf included five separate boxes with an individual firearm stored in each.

All were handguns of various calibers. Micheline carefully strapped the .38-caliber Chief to the outside of her left ankle and slid a Smith & Wesson .38-caliber Combat Masterpiece with a four-inch barrel and quick draw front sight into a shoulder harness on her right flank. Her preference for carrying dual .38-caliber weapons on the job was due to simplicity. Both guns chambered the .38 Special cartridge, therefore no other type of ammunition was needed.

A southpaw, Micheline kept her guns positioned thus, in order that she could easily draw them in an efficient and rapid movement with her left hand when needed.

For more firepower, Micheline kept a diverse collection of handguns and rifles locked in a steel-encased cabinet that had been fitted to the inner dimensions of a cherry wood hope chest. The decorative wooden furniture with the padded top was placed purposefully and inconspicuously at the foot of the bed. The chest included a fake wooden top shelf with a half dozen cotton and wool sweaters that concealed the locked steel gun cabinet beneath.

Micheline grabbed her car keys and her shoulder bag and headed down two flights of stairs to her separate garage across the cobblestone street from her condo building. She pressed the six-digit garage door code, her mother's birthdate, into a keypad and waited for the heavy wooden door to fully open. The beast inside, recently restored to its original showroom beauty, gleamed brightly even amid the dreary shadows of the narrow and windowless one-car garage.

Micheline approached the late model Ford Mustang EcoBoost® Premium Fastback in Kona blue with white racing stripes and settled comfortably into the charcoal gray leather interior. The car featured a 310-horsepower engine, a 6-speed manual transmission, and 19-inch x 9-inch low-gloss ebony, black-painted aluminum wheels. The muscle car looked like it was going eighty miles an hour even when it was parked and idling at the curb.

Micheline backed the car out of the garage and closed the garage door behind her. She drove to work in silence across the concrete and steel girder San Diego-Coronado Bridge to Harbor Drive.

She swept quickly past Petco Park and turned north into the Gaslamp Quarter district. Her mood was serene. Customarily, she listened to the intermittent buzz of law enforcement lingo on the police band radio while in the car. It was usually a twenty-minute drive to work, and she liked to be in on the action whenever she could.

Not today.

She kept the satellite radio turned off as well. With so much on her mind, she felt she could think more clearly without having to listen to the disturbances of pop music or the tasteless jokes of morning talk show hosts in the background.

As she entered the heart of San Diego's historic Gaslamp Quarter at the intersection of Fifth Avenue and Island Avenue, she came to a stop at a red light. She waited patiently for the red traffic light to change to green.

The Gaslamp Quarter was a lively downtown neighborhood south of Balboa Park with late Victorian and art deco architectural styles. It was known for its nightlife, bars, independent restaurants with global options, and cocktail lounges. It was everything San Diego was known for in *italics*.

For the first time that morning, Micheline stole some moments to notice her immediate surroundings. Off to her right stood the old Imperial Theater. The ancient playhouse was a palatial seven-story structure of solid granite that had been erected during the late nineteen twenties. Its regal interior had once contained only the finest materials imported from all over the world, including Italian marble tiles, Oriental silken tapestries, Austrian crystal chandeliers, and original French Impressionist oil paintings. Even the restroom fixtures had been plated with Tuolumne County gold mined in California.

Architecturally speaking, the theater's magnificent design was one-of-a-kind, constructed to last forever, and had proved to be a profitable gamble for its original owners.

Now it was vacant, stripped of its fine adornments, and boarded over with sheets of thick plywood. It had initially been scheduled for demolition, with plans for modern retail spaces and luxury condominiums. But there was a grassroots effort to fund a reconstruction project to restore the theater to its earlier grace.

The demise of the aging playhouse had come as a slow but certain death. Regular maintenance had been suspended altogether years before. The once-elegant theater began to die from within. Presently, it appeared dilapidated and run-down, with its fancy stained-glass windows smashed and boarded over with a thick plywood façade. The majestic castle that once proudly stood as a monument to the arts now resembled a gothic mausoleum in decay.

The literal nails to the theater's funeral bier had all but to be hammered into the coffin lid. Official notifications of condemnation by the city of San Diego had been posted to the wide front entrance doorways, which remained locked to prevent the homeless from seeking shelter there.

Catty-corner to where her Mustang was parked and idling powerfully, Micheline noted as she turned her head to the left, stood a row of strip clubs, massage parlors, restaurants, and convenience stores. Across the street from those establishments stood an expansive, ultramodern brick-faced structure lined with dark tinted glass windows and a large parking lot to the side and rear of the building. It was the Fidelity National Savings & Loan Bank. This location was their downtown corporate headquarters building and it was the office from which Jenny worked. Her latest promotion, her second in the past five months, had ascended her to the lofty position of assistant vice president of credit administration.

Just as Micheline and Jenny had met, Jenny's career immediately began to take off. Two years prior, she had explained to Micheline during the early days of a bank employee murder investigation, she had been a mere teller working her way through night school for her MBA. She worked hard and spent much of an average hectic day seated in front of a desktop computer while simultaneously fielding telephone calls and personal customer visits concerning corporate financial transactions involving millions of dollars.

The traffic light turned green. Micheline accelerated slowly. The Mustang's engine revved as Micheline shifted from second gear into third. Traffic was already congested at this early time in the morning.

Micheline downshifted back into second gear as she edged closer to the rear exit door of a yellow school bus. She drummed her fingers animatedly on the gray leather steering wheel.

She made a right-hand turn at the next intersection and pulled into the parking lot of the independently owned Coffee & Books Café. She killed the ignition to the Mustang and took a deep breath.

Outside, Jackie Henshilwood approached from across the parking lot. She was dressed in a well-tailored matching fuchsia blazer and skirt, with a white blouse. The jacket had an asymmetric close with gold-tone buttons along one side of the notched lapel. The hemline of the skirt was set several inches above her knees and featured a long back slit, all of which showed off her legs and rose-colored leather high heel shoes.

"Nice ride!" she called out as Micheline exited her vehicle and depressed the button on her keychain to lock the doors behind her.

"Thanks," she said. "I've always wanted a Mustang. After I moved to California, it just seemed like the right time."

"I love that dark navy shade of blue with the white stripes. It's not just a sportscar. It's classy, too."

Micheline nodded. She was accustomed to receiving compliments for her sleek and shiny ride.

"But I'm more impressed with its driver," Jackie added.

This took Micheline by surprise. She nodded and smiled politely.

"I can't thank you enough for meeting me this morning," Jackie continued. "I'm so nervous to give my statement to the detective working Samantha's murder case."

"It will go just fine," Micheline assured her. "I'll be there for support. But I need for you to just relax and say everything that you remember. Take your time. There is no need to rush. Recalling the details is what's most important right now."

"I understand," she said.

Micheline checked her watch. "We have time to grab a cup of coffee and something to eat for breakfast if you'd like."

"That sounds fine," she said.

They entered the coffee establishment through double glass swingout doors. Inside, the café was reminiscent of a library with tall wooden bookshelves along the outer walls and wooden tables and chairs placed intermittently throughout the central floor space. A sign posted near the counter stated *Book exchange, bring one in, take another one out.*

"This place has such nice character," Jackie said.

"It does," Micheline agreed. "I come here most mornings before work. Not only does it have the ambiance, but they make a mean cup of coffee, too."

A stout young man with dark green baseball cap and apron, tortoiseshell-framed glasses, a tiny diamond stud nose piercing, several days' worth of facial hair along his jawline, and a wavy mop of dark blond hair atop his head moved athletically behind the service counter to greet them.

"Good morning, Detective Avila," he opened amiably. "The usual today, Micheline? A large hot mocha latte and an oven-warmed cheese Danish to take with you?"

"Yes, please, Harrison," Micheline replied. "How are you doing today?"

"No complaints," Harrison Murray, the male barista replied. "It's been a brisk morning so far. Everyone seems to need an extra jolt with a shot of espresso today. May I get something for your lovely friend as well?"

Jackie smiled at the barista and studied the menu board posted along the top of the back wall. There were so many beverage options to select from, and she became a bit flustered upon noticing the barista's well-defined chest and arm muscles.

"Perhaps an iced coffee, or a mango smoothie, miss?" Harrison suggested. "And by the way, that color looks great on you."

"Thank you," Jackie replied. She blushed.

"Something to drink?"

"They all look so good," Jackie muttered. "What would you recommend?"

"My preference would be a high-protein blueberry kale smoothie. It's made with almond milk, banana, and honey."

"Don't be daft!" Jackie laughed. "Let me have a medium size tea, please. Earl Grey."

"Hot or iced, miss?" Harrison asked.

"Hot, please," Jackie replied.

Harrison plugged the requests into the digital order system on top of the counter. "That'll be fourteen ninety-two, please," he said to Micheline.

"Oh," Micheline smiled. "A good year for Christopher Columbus, right?"

"I'm sorry, Detective?" Harrison asked quizzically. "I don't follow."

Micheline shook her head. "Fourteen ninety-two, the year Columbus discovered America."

"Oh, yeah, I get it," Harrison replied awkwardly. "Sorry. History was never my thing. I'm more of a science nerd. Maybe I need a few extra shots of espresso this morning, too. I'm a bit distracted lately." He smiled toward Jackie again.

Jackie smiled back at him.

Micheline nodded politely and handed a debit card from her wallet to the male barista across the counter.

"I'll bring everything over to the end of the counter when it's ready," he informed them and handed Micheline's card back to her after it had been tapped to the card reader.

A moment later, Harrison handed Micheline a paper sales receipt.

Micheline accepted the paper receipt and stashed it in her wallet.

"Have a good day, Detective," the barista said.

"Thank you, Harrison. You, too."

He nodded politely and smiled toward Jackie again.

Jackie turned and walked across the floor to purview the selection of hardcover and paperback books displayed on one of the bookshelves. There were separate sections organized by category, including horror, fantasy, science fiction, mystery, thriller, and romance. There appeared to be multiple titles by authors Stephen King, Lisa Gardner, and Sarah J. Maas in their respective genre sections.

Micheline ambled over to the dispensary counter and collected cardboard cup sleeves, hazelnut creamer cups, napkins, raw sugar packets, and wooden stir sticks.

Jackie wandered back to the main counter and said a few words to the barista. There appeared to be a brief conversation between the two.

A few minutes later, the barista brought their beverages and a paper bag with the cheese Danish to the end of the main counter. Micheline and Jackie reached for their items and fixed their coffee and tea to their individual tastes.

Jackie looked up and smiled at Micheline.

"Thank you for the tea, Micheline," she said and winked at the detective.

"I like it hot."

Seventeen

W hite stone pillars stood like lone sentries guarding the entrance to the immense, contemporary-style San Diego County Courthouse. Micheline escorted Jackie Henshilwood briskly along a clean concrete path lined with palm trees, rose bushes, and various types of round and elongated cactus plants. They penetrated the edifice's outer defenses as if they were entering a shopping mall.

Inside the main foyer, however, they approached a security checkpoint with two armed guards. Micheline flashed her badge, which was clipped to a thin belt around her waist, and walked through while the guards checked her shoulder bag. The detective was recognized as an on-duty law enforcement officer and therefore was permitted to carry her firearms within the building. However, she was still required to check in with perimeter security upon her entering and leaving the premises.

Jackie placed her purse in a plastic bin and walked through behind the detective. No alarm sounded. The guard handed Jackie her purse.

"Have a nice day, miss," he said.

"Thank you. You, too," she replied.

Micheline escorted Jackie over to the elevators, and they rode in silence to the ninth-floor offices of the county prosecuting attorney. Jackie appeared concerned, hesitant, and nervous.

Micheline occupied her own office, a small drywalled and glass-windowed cube of a room which included a battered wooden double pedestal desk, a brass banker's lamp, and a black canvas office chair on casters. There were two padded wooden chairs for visitors. A locked steel three-drawer filing cabinet was set along the wall. The desktop included dual large-screen monitors, a wireless keyboard and mouse combination, and a phone.

Micheline set her coffee cup and bag with the cheese Danish on the left side of the desktop, then placed her shoulder bag on the black canvas office chair and hung her jacket on a wall hook. She opened her shoulder bag and connected her laptop computer to its docking cable. Then she withdrew a handful of case files from her shoulder bag and placed them on the far-right edge of the desktop.

She placed the leather shoulder bag neatly in an empty lower desk drawer. Then she sat down in her chair momentarily and began to consider each of the currently active cases in the files atop her desk.

She absentmindedly took a sip of her coffee.

One of the files was regarding a seventeen-year-old missing person case of a girl who had recently argued with her mother. The mother was divorced and blamed her ex-husband, who inconveniently had relocated to Arizona. Micheline had called the estranged father for his viewpoint on the situation and had left several voice messages. The father had not yet returned Micheline's calls.

The detective had reached out to local authorities in Arizona for their assistance to locate the missing teen and the father. She also planned to meet again with the mother, neighbors, and the girl's teachers and friends to determine if they could provide any useful information regarding the girl's sudden disappearance.

All indications were the girl had left home of her own volition following a vocal confrontation with the mother. But Micheline had a duty to investigate all possible scenarios.

Another case that had consumed a large chunk of Micheline's time over the past few weeks was for real estate cyber fraud and money laundering charges against a real estate agent and the owner of a mortgage escrow company. There was a father and son relationship as well as a prostitution or drug tie-in to the case. But not all the clues lined up.

Properties were being sold below market value with suspiciously high closing cost transactions. General contracting estimates for fraudulent property upgrades were included, and loans were being de-faulted. Re-finance documents were then filed with alternative banking institutions. An interesting factor in the case was the realization that every buyer and seller listed in the transactions had a criminal record for prostitution or illegal drug distribution. Digging into the numbers was an absolute nightmare.

A third file was regarding a recent credit union robbery in which three armed assailants dressed in full military tactical gear and face-masks had overpowered an armored delivery van guard on foot outside the bank building. Local surveillance cameras around the credit union building had been temporarily disabled during the heist. The driver of the van had been knocked out by tear gas and the armored van's tires had been slashed.

The robbery occurred on a public street in broad daylight. Two empty money sacks along with radio-controlled dye pack incendiary devices and separate GPS locators were left strewn on the nearby sidewalk. This robbery crew was technically advanced and trained. A quarter of a million dollars had been stolen.

The fourth and final file on the desk was a cold case. Although less than six months old, its probative investigative leads had been exhausted. It was the murder investigation of J.P. Ballard, the bank vice president who was maliciously killed in his Solana Beach hotel room, with his throat slit wide open, his reproductive organs sliced away from his body, and a large metal flashlight shoved up his rectum.

The investigation had turned up several male colleagues who, although more highly educated and experienced than their female competition, were passed over for promotion and recommended for transfers to other locations further away. All the men in question described their boss as a mean-spirited bully but had turned out to have solid alibis on the afternoon of the murder.

It became clear Ballard had a sweet tooth for younger women who were pretty and ambitious, and who wore tight-fitting blouses, short skirts, and high heels. Of those ladies questioned, none seemed to hold a grudge against their former boss, although he was not as well-liked as he may have thought while he had been alive. Jenny Casella had been one of those young women interviewed.

Cell phone and credit card records also did not explain why the bank vice president with a lavish home located only twenty minutes away would have checked into the hotel on the day he was apparently killed. Further interviews with family members and even video surveillance from businesses located across the street from the hotel failed to offer any helpful clues toward the investigation.

His family thought he was away for a few days to attend a banking conference in Las Vegas. Investigators had assumed Ballard was expecting to meet someone at the hotel for an extramarital affair. But no link as to whom that person could have been and how they communicated with each other could be established. Ballard had been crafty. He apparently didn't use his personal phone or email for such lewd behavior.

"Have a seat, Jackie," Micheline offered. "It's not much, but this is where I spend most of my time every day. I just need a few minutes to review some of my case files, and then I'll walk you over to Detective Reyes and make the introductions. How does that sound?"

"Perfect," she said. "I really appreciate you taking the time to help me through this. I'm so nervous, I'm trembling."

"Of course," Micheline said. "That's a perfectly natural reaction to this type of situation. Just remember you're here to help."

Micheline took a long sip of her coffee and pulled the cheese Danish out from the paper bag. She spread a napkin down near the coffee cup, took a bite from the Danish, and set it down on the napkin.

Jackie settled into one of the wooden chairs across from Micheline's desk and took in her surroundings.

"You and Harrison seemed kind of cozy at the coffee shop," Micheline said.

"Well, he may have asked for my phone number," Jackie replied.

"And what did you say?"

"I gave it to him. He's really cute."

"So, it had nothing to do with you staring at his chest and the bulging biceps?"

"Oh, it had *everything* to do with me wondering what he looks like when he takes his shirt off."

Both women laughed.

Micheline began to peruse the top file. Outside the glass walls, the office was coming to life. Incoming telephone calls buzzed in various tones. Office employees scurried between one cubicle and another, poured themselves steaming mugs of coffee or tea, and helped themselves to the contents of doughnut and pastry boxes which sat open atop several desks.

Frosted plexiglass shields surrounded each cubicle wall and reached a height of six feet above the floor surface. This allowed natural light into the office while dampening noise levels. It also prevented airflow horizontally across the department, recognized as a common cause for the spread of viral contaminations.

As Micheline read through an updated bank statement and credit card report from one of the small businesses linked to the fraud case, a shadow fell over the printed page. She had not heard anyone enter her office, so she instinctively assumed Jackie was taking a closer look.

A single sheaf of glossy white paper was dropped to the desktop. Micheline glanced at the colorful document without looking up. Only Assistant Prosecuting Attorney Mark Longfellow entered her office unannounced.

Micheline was familiar with the text and photos printed on the document. The bold headline read:

Courage. Conviction. Commitment to Community and Social Justice. Aren't these the characteristics you want to be maintained by the District Attorney in San Diego County?

"Who wrote this bullshit?" Micheline joked without bothering to look up.

"You did," a gravelly voice with a slight Texas drawl responded without humor.

Micheline's eyes lifted apprehensively. She swiveled in her chair. As she did so, she accidentally knocked her coffee cup over on its side. The cup rolled over the edge of the desk. The top lid popped off as the cup hit the carpeted floor and began to spill its contents.

"Oh, Christ!" Micheline blurted. She reached down and picked the cup off the floor. Less than a quarter of the hot mocha-flavored java remained.

District Attorney Rosalyn Whittaker stood before her with a stern look of impatience etched upon her face. She didn't give a damn about spilled coffee.

"I'm sorry, Rosa," Micheline said, sitting upright in her chair. "I didn't realize it was you. Good morning."

"Good morning, Detective. My weekend turned to complete shit. You realize that, right?"

"I beg your pardon?"

"I'm sorry," she said, suddenly turning sideways toward Jackie Henshilwood.

"Who's this?"

Micheline nodded. "Jacqueline Henshilwood, please meet District Attorney Rosalyn Whittaker. Rosa, Jackie is the female witness I encountered near the murder scene at Catalina Mission Park on Saturday. I'll be taking her over to meet with Detective Reyes in a few minutes to record an official statement."

"I want you to handle that," the district attorney remarked.

"But it's not my case," Micheline countered.

"It is now, Detective."

"But I'm not Homicide, and Guillermo has already taken the lead over the weekend."

"Again, you are now the lead detective on this case, and I have the authority to make that call. You are an experienced homicide detective from your years on the job with the NYPD. You have earned respect from everyone in this department these past several months, the Ballard cold case notwithstanding, and now it's time again to put you to good use. I need you to run point on this investigation."

Micheline sat back in her chair and stared at her boss without saying anything. She was stunned.

The DA turned toward Jackie. "Would you mind, miss, and please step out into the corridor for a few minutes? I need to speak privately to Detective Avila. It won't take long. By the way, I love the suit you're wearing."

"Thank you," Jackie replied. "Yes, of course. I'll leave the two of you to have some privacy."

Jackie dutifully stood and left the office, closing the glass door behind her. She found a chair along a nearby wall in the hallway and settled in with her steaming cup of Earl Grey tea.

"The filing deadline for the next election is December sixth," Whittaker fumed. "The primary is scheduled for early March, and the general election will be next November. This morning's headlines are already calling this the ex-stripper, daughter of biotech CEO high profile murder case, and it is, without doubt, going to put my administration under a very dark cloud. To make matters worse, Thomas Gilford, the former DA, and my rival in the upcoming primary election has stepped in to defend Dominic Sadoski. The media are going to have a field day with this case. It'll be more about two district attorneys fighting to win the popular vote than about the sanctity of the case or justice for a young woman's brutal and untimely demise."

Micheline closed the file in her hands.

The DA looked narrowly at Micheline. "A little history lesson for you, Detective. Gilford held my post over the course of four consecutive terms before I ousted him from office nearly three years ago. He's a lifelong politician who yearns for nothing more than to be back on top again. He has the money, the experience, and a Rolodex full of influential friends to call upon when needed. One of those friends just happens to be Stephen Miller, Ph.D., the CEO of Systole Biosciences, and the father of the victim. Gilford is a serious threat toward my bid for reelection next year."

"If he's a friend of the victim's father, why would he defend the man accused of the crime?"

"Tom Gilford is no fool. He never picks a client he knows can't win. He has a political agenda plain and simple."

"Guillermo Reyes is already neck-deep into this one," Micheline challenged. "I talked to him late Saturday night. He and his team were all over it. What's changed?"

The DA shook her head back and forth slowly and dejectedly. "Detective Reyes suffered a severe myocardial infarction yesterday afternoon while hiking the trails at Torrey Pines State Reserve. He's presently in the ICU at Scripps Memorial Hospital in La Jolla. He's scheduled for triple bypass surgery later this week. Unfortunately, he will not be back to work anytime soon. I need you to step in and take over the investigation. I need results, Detective, and I need them fast."

Micheline observed the district attorney's facial expression closely. Whittaker was an African American woman with Texas roots. She was in her late forties, fit and attractive with smooth skin, and wore her thick dark hair relatively short and straight. She exhibited circumspect behavior within the walls of the courthouse. Outside, however, she reveled in public media attention and was often viewed as overly aggressive and ambitious.

"Very well," Micheline nodded affirmatively. "I'd like to begin by diffusing the political minefield you've stepped into. First order of business, I will take official statements from both Jackie Henshilwood and from Dominic Sadoski later today. Then, unless I receive toxicology reports that link him to the victim, or if I hear anything today that is contrary to what Sadoski has already confided to me off the record, I want him released from custody. He is to be considered a witness to a vicious crime and no longer a suspect in the murder of the young woman. I will offer apologies to Mr. Sadoski and his attorney. I will steadfastly reconfirm the department's stance on justice for the family of Samantha Miller, and safety for the community at large. Are we in agreement on that strategy?"

The DA nodded thoughtfully. "I concur. Mark Longfellow will be prosecuting the case, when and if you identify a suspect and can prove beyond a reasonable doubt they are guilty of the crime. Sadoski's lawyer will be at the jail for a two o'clock interview this afternoon. Meet with him. I want your full attention on this, Detective."

"I'll follow this through," Micheline confirmed, "and I'll ensure the prosecution has enough hard evidence to secure a conviction."

Micheline made direct eye contact with Whittaker. "What about my other active cases?" she asked.

"I've already considered how best to reassign your active case-load," the DA proclaimed. "Hand the missing person case to Caroline Atwood. She's still green but fully capable. It will give her some good experience. For the cyber fraud and money laundering scheme, hand that over to Alejandro Ibarra in Financial Crimes. He's a seasoned veteran with sharp instinct and incredible analytical and data mining skills. I've already spoken to his captain."

"Noted," Micheline confirmed.

"The credit union heist goes to Phillip Kovacs and his team over in Robbery. They'd prefer to have you continue the case, but your talents are needed elsewhere. All three are aware of the cases you will be handing over to them today. I want this all taken care of as quickly as possible so that you can focus your full attention on the Samantha Miller homicide investigation. Are we clear on that?"

"Got it," Micheline responded confidently. She glanced at the files on her desk.

"Ah," the DA continued, "keep the cold case. You may have reached an impasse on the Ballard murder investigation for now, but let it simmer for a while. Return to it when you have a fresh perspective. The killer was smart and cunning, no doubt. They left no discernible or telltale clues. But there was clearly some personal rage and motivation involved. Uncovering that personal connection is the key to solving the case, I believe."

Micheline nodded. She respected the district attorney's authority and intuition. From a human resource personality test perspective, though, Micheline knew DA Whittaker had scored in the dark red zone with the strength deployment inventory (SDI) personality test, whereas Micheline had scored in the light blue-green zone. The blue-green result suggested Micheline was more prone to focus on people and process (she showed compassion for victims and worked in a practical step-by-step manner), whereas the DA showed little emotion toward anyone and strove for results and performance.

In other words, she was a hard-ass bitch with non-stop militaristic tendencies.

Rosa didn't know when to quit or to let things go. When it came to minor details, the DA didn't just dive into the weeds looking for answers. She dove into the dirt and bedrock beneath the roots when a fifty-thousand-foot view was all that was required of her. She continuously kept everyone close to her under the view of a microscope. It was an ingrained personality trait that irritated her direct reports daily to no end.

Micheline did admire the fact the DA was a Navy veteran. Earlier in her career, she had served as a commissioned officer in the Judge Advocate Generals Corp, more generally known as the JAG Corps. She also championed a committee to raise funds to renovate the Imperial Theater downtown. Whether that was a strategically fraudulent attempt to gain votes from the more prestigious sector of society, or if the DA's heart was really in it for the love of the arts, Micheline was not certain.

A year earlier, DA Whittaker had suddenly and unexpectedly divorced her husband of twelve years. She had given up custody of their two children. The news had shocked everyone who worked at the courthouse. Since then, her attitude had changed dramatically. She was exceedingly tough in her command and was known to be in the office or communicating to her direct reports via text or email as early as 5:30 a.m. and as late as midnight, seven days a week, including holidays. She was relentless in her approach to drill down into even the tiniest details of a case.

"I'll be watching you closely on this one, Micheline," the DA affirmed. She turned and exited the detective's office with the door left open behind her. She nodded perfunctorily toward Jackie in the hallway as she treaded purposefully toward her next appointment.

Micheline crumpled the political advertisement flyer in her hands and tossed it with her left hand across the room to the corner wastebasket. It hit the rim of the black wire basket and fell limply to the floor in front of the empty receptacle.

Micheline sighed dejectedly as though she had just missed the final second shot that would have propelled her team to the March Madness tournament championship game. She quickly gathered the various files that lay before her on her battered wooden desk.

She looked down toward the floor.

Cleaning the coffee stain on the carpet is just going to have to wait.

She had a ton of work to do ahead of her and little time with which to accomplish it.

Eighteen

The preliminary autopsy report on Samantha Miller read like the screenplay to a low-budget slasher flick. Micheline scanned the typed pages of the corpus delicti, the body of evidence, carefully. She frowned discontentedly due to the severity of the crime and the lack of the killer's DNA, fingerprints, or a murder weapon to substantiate a link to who might be responsible for Samantha's death. She noted the signatures at the bottom of the final page.

Andrew Dadouris was the medical examiner and chief toxicologist for San Diego County. He was an elected official whose duty was to oversee the mechanics of obtaining a medical-legal investigation of death. He initiated a report based on his findings at the crime scene and what was discovered during the autopsy. A final report would include toxicology results. This information would also be reviewed by a forensic pathologist, Anyssa Ortega, whose duty was to determine the official time and cause of death.

Micheline arched back in her chair and sifted through the medical terminology of the report. She was searching for clues that might tie Dominic Sadoski to the crime. She knew all too well, though, nailing a conviction would be difficult, if not impossible, without a murder weapon or a motive to link the suspect to the victim.

Jackie Henshilwood's testimony, as well as Micheline's own sworn statement, were limited to merely seeing Sadoski astride the victim's body postmortem. Jackie claimed not to have seen anyone else present at the scene until Micheline arrived, and Sadoski could do little more than to describe what he thought he had heard.

Hearsay evidence was generally considered inadmissible in court because it was potentially unreliable and could not be tested or refuted by cross-examination. However, in limited circumstances, it could be accepted if it were determined to be credible and relevant.

Micheline had hoped there might be a break regarding the moistened handkerchief found in Sadoski's pocket and a comparison to cervical-vaginal fluid obtained from the victim's body during the autopsy. Laboratory test results for semen analysis of the fluid ejaculated on the cloth handkerchief found in Sadoski's pocket were still pending. Micheline felt confident a clear determination of Sadoski's innocence or guilt would be made upon the outcome of these specific tests.

But what could the motive for killing Samantha be?

Micheline was perplexed. The victim had been young, beautiful, intelligent, rebellious, and exceedingly wealthy. She was purportedly engaged to be married to the physician whom Micheline had seen her arguing with at Marino's Italian Bistro in Mira Mesa the week beforehand.

Samantha's nude body was found at the scene with her throat slit and her right thumb removed and not recovered at the scene. Examination of the extensive puncture and stab wounds indicated a single-edge serrated knife had been used. It had caused massive hemorrhaging. But a determination of the dimensions of the weapon or the depth of penetration was inconclusive due to the elasticity of skin shrinking slightly on withdrawal of the assault weapon from the body.

The results of the autopsy concluded Samantha had sexual intercourse prior to her death. There were no vaginal tears or defensive wounds that would suggest she was raped.

Could Sadoski's story about a clandestine sexual encounter with a lover, and a separate and unrelated attack from someone else immediately thereafter have been accurate? And if so, why? Was it a rape attempt that had gone wrong? A jealous spouse? A vengeful fiancé? A publicly humiliated CEO, whose personal fortune rose and fell with the confidence of the stock market in his ability to lead the company through periods of crisis?

At this point, Micheline was grasping at straws. Still, she had to consider all viable possibilities.

Follow the evidence.

The telephone on Micheline's desk clanged loudly, awakening her from her mental contemplation. She picked up the receiver following the second ring.

"Detective Avila, Homicide."

The voice on the other end of the line was raw, familiar, and paternal.

"What's up, Dad?"

"I miss you, darling."

Micheline's jaw dropped in honest surprise and her muscles immediately melted like ice cream in the hot summer sun. "I miss you, too, Dad."

"Listen…"

"I don't mean to cut you off, Dad," Micheline spoke softly. "I've got a lot of work to do. I'm running point on a murder investigation. It's a big case, too. Can I call you some other time, please?"

"Sure, baby. I just wanted to say I love you."

"I love you, too, Dad. You'll be proud of me on this new case. I can't say much about it for now, but we can talk after I find some time to catch my breath. I promise."

"I understand," he replied. "I've been in that situation many a time, myself."

"I know, Dad. Where do you think I get my tenacity and perseverance from?"

Her father chuckled lightly on the other end of the phone line. He was thinking how much Micheline reminded him of his late wife.

"Love you, baby. Go get 'em!"

"I'll talk to you soon, Dad. Bye."

Micheline gently placed the phone receiver down onto its cradle and frowned sadly. A single tear welled up in the corner of her right eye.

Did I make the right decision to come out here?

"Having a bad day, Detective?"

Micheline looked up haphazardly and tossed the Miller murder file onto her desktop. She quickly wiped the corner of her right eye with the back of her left hand.

"Don't you ever knock, Counselor?" she asked agitatedly to the unannounced intruder. "Am I ever allowed to have a private moment to myself?"

Assistant Prosecuting Attorney Mark Longfellow walked directly into the office and approached Micheline's desk with a confident smile etched on his face.

"Only when I have to," he admitted unabashedly. "Besides, Micheline, invasion of privacy is my specialty. And I know for a fact you like to be surprised. It's what keeps you sharp and on edge all the time."

"Only when I'm working a case and things are going my way," Micheline conceded.

"You're working one now," Mark said. "And it's a big one, too. A lot of eyes are going to be over your shoulders on this one, Micheline. Media exposure and political pressure. The DA, herself. Law enforcement brass and corporate tie-ins. Lions, tigers, and bears. Oh, my!"

"Yeah, I guess so. What's up?"

"Just wanted to check-in. You're going to meet with Sadoski and his lawyer later today?"

"Yes," Micheline confirmed. "It's all set for two o'clock. I'm meeting Richard Tuller and Kelly Van Horn over at the jail. Together, we'll make for a good investigative team. I know them both. They work hard."

"Good. I've got to be back in court this afternoon. I'll look forward to catching up with you sometime after that, okay?"

"I'll find you, don't worry. If not today, then definitely sometime tomorrow. I'll keep you in the loop."

Mark pointed toward the desktop telephone. "What's with the phone call before I came in? Trouble on the home front?"

Micheline squirmed uncomfortably in her chair. "It was my father. He's a former Army Ranger who became an FBI special agent later in his career."

"Quite a tough act to follow, huh?" Mark surmised.

"Yeah, no kidding. Within the span of three years, I got divorced and then my mother died of cancer. I caved, emotionally. I quit my job and left everything behind in New York to come to live out here. Sometimes I feel like a lost child."

"I didn't mean to pry," Mark said. "Let's stick to the business at hand, shall we?"

"It's all right," Micheline said. "I didn't know if you had talked to Rosa yet or not."

"I did."

"Good. Then you know I intend to release Sadoski this afternoon if I don't come up with anything substantially different than I currently have?"

"Yes, I'm aware. I don't need to tell you, Micheline, establishing a clear motive and locating a murder weapon are necessary for a conviction. It needs to be iron-clad, otherwise, politics will come into play, and neither of us wants that."

"I agree," Micheline said. "I'll follow the evidence. I'll also ensure to check and re-check the alibis of everyone connected to the victim. This case has some unique similarities to the unsolved Ballard murder I worked on with Guillermo a few months ago. I need to consider they might somehow be related."

Mark's eyebrows raised considerably with this improbable but imaginative comment.

"How so?"

"Both victims had their throats slit from right to left, indicating a left-handed killer. Both victims were also found naked at the scene of the crime and had suffered multiple punctures and stab wounds across their bodies."

"True," Mark chimed in. "But that could just be a coincidence. Right now, you have one older male and one much younger female victim, with nothing in common between them."

Micheline was unperturbed. "In neither case was a murder weapon discovered at the scene. Although in both cases it was confirmed during the autopsies to have been a single-edge serrated knife."

"Again, coincidence."

"Both killings were intensely personal. I plan to ask the coroner to compare the angle of the wounds, the approximate dimensions of the weapon, and the depth of penetration for any similarities between the two cases. For now, those results are ruled inconclusive."

Mark nodded as he considered the path Micheline was suggesting to him.

"And although it's a long-shot," Micheline continued, "I believe the victims may have known each other or crossed paths at some point in time through the main bank branch Ballard worked at, and to which I believe Samantha Miller, or her father, invested their considerable wealth in."

"Interesting theory," Mark said, nodding appreciably. "Keep on it. Beware, though. Unless you can prove beyond a reasonable doubt the same weapon was used in both killings, you're just handing the defense evidence that is potentially exculpatory or circumstantial at best."

Micheline raised her eyebrows and nodded in confirmation.

"I like the financial tie-in, though," Mark confirmed. "But it still doesn't give us a suspect to hang our hats on. I must run to court now, but I'll look forward to regular updates on this. Keep at it."

Micheline picked up the Miller case file again and opened it on top of her desk. "You've got it, Mark. I'll be in touch soon. I still have a lot of preliminary work to do. I'll meet with my investigative team. We'll put together a strategy on how to proceed."

"I trust you to make us all look good on this one, Micheline," he said.

"I'll do my best," she replied.

Mark turned and strode from Micheline's office with newfound energy and purpose.

Damn! Micheline just might be onto something here.

Passersby along the hallway noted the urgency with which Mark was walking and incorrectly assumed he was late for a scheduled court appointment. He appeared lost in thought.

In fact, he was subconsciously preparing his opening statement and strategy to present to the future jury.

The case now involved a double homicide enacted months apart that followed a characteristic, predictable behavior pattern. There was a probable match to the murder weapon used in both attacks by a left-handed killer. Perhaps a personal relationship between the killer and the victims could also be established.

Mark took a deep breath as he considered his postulations further.

Possibly even more damaging to the defense's case, a trained and well-respected physician with a specialty in neurology would be called to take the stand. Perhaps the doctor's testimony would provide an undisputable clinical diagnosis of the defendant with a tendency to act in service of abnormal psychological gratification.

Mark stopped mid-stride along the hallway to consider what his imagination had eloquently illustrated.

The details of the case now met the legal definition of a serial killer.

Nineteen

etectives Richard Tuller and Kelly Van Horn were standing outside Micheline's office at 1:50 p.m. Van Horn rapped lightly with her knuckles on the glass door. Micheline looked up from the forensic pathology report she was deciphering word-for-word and casually waved for them to come in and join her.

"Good afternoon, team," she opened expectantly.

"Hey, Micheline," Tuller responded. "It's been a while." Richard Tuller stood six foot one inch tall and was a brawny Black man with a short-cropped military hairstyle, a well-trimmed mustache and goatee, and a small scar above his left eye. He was a former U.S. Marine Corps veteran from Richmond, Virginia who had been stationed nearby at Camp Pendleton. Upon his honorable discharge from active military duty, Richard transitioned to civilian life by joining the San Diego County Sheriff's Department and enlisted in the Army National Guard.

"Yes, it has," Micheline said. "How are you, Richard?"

"I'm well, thanks," he replied.

"Kelly, how are you doing?"

"Doing great," Van Horn replied. "I'm looking forward to working this case with you. As I said on Saturday night, I believe in you. This one's turned out to be a high-profile case, huh?"

Van Horn was a natural California blonde who stood five foot ten inches tall in flat shoes. Her hair was secured in a ponytail by an elastic band. Micheline knew her to be athletic and an avid outdoor enthusiast. She could drop and do twenty-five push-ups or run five miles without getting tired. On her days off, she partook in every imaginable activity, from kayaking to hiking, and from surfing to skydiving.

Micheline closed the file in front of her and leaned back in her chair. "Let's just say, the DA came in here this morning and personally told me to light a fire on this one. She asked me to pass all my active cases over to other departments. It doesn't get any hotter than that."

Micheline took a moment to survey her new investigative team. Inwardly, she was pleased with the selection. The DA meant business on this one. Nominating Micheline to head the investigation was proof that her hard work and effort were beginning to pay off.

Between both Tuller and Van Horn, they were experienced, intelligent, and highly motivated. This case would garner a lot of attention both inside and outside the department for everyone involved.

"Any update on Guillermo's condition?" Micheline asked.

"I spoke to his wife about an hour ago," Richard replied. "He's in surgery now. They weren't going to wait. His cardiologist seemed optimistic."

"That still doesn't fill me with great confidence," Micheline said.

"Triple bypass surgery is serious business," Kelly offered. "My grandfather went through that a few years ago. He'll need his friends and colleagues to rally around him when he gets released from the hospital. He'll need to change his diet and start an exercise routine. We need to show him that he's got good reason to be healthy again."

"Agreed," Micheline responded. "He's a stubborn old guy, though. He's likely to resist."

"His wife told me she knows what she's in for," Richard said. "It won't be easy, but she'll get the message across to him somehow."

"Let's hope so," Kelly said.

Micheline let out a slow breath. "Okay, let's focus now. Are both of you up to speed on the particulars of this case?"

Richard nodded. Kelly looked less certain.

"You have a question, Kelly?"

Kelly Van Horn shook her head. "It's the victim being found naked in the park with her softball uniform folded neatly nearby. Who does that, in the middle of the day, no less? And her thumb was missing. What the hell is that all about?"

"It's got me scratching my head for answers, too," Micheline said. "I also know she was engaged to a doctor. I'd be curious to know if a large diamond ring was recovered at the scene."

"No, it wasn't," Van Horn added.

"You're certain?"

"Yes. There was no bling to speak of. No necklace, bracelet, or rings. No cell phone, either."

"Okay, then," Micheline said. "Robbery is a possible motive. Although the manner of her death would indicate something more personal. Kelly, make a note to track the GPS coordinates from Samantha's phone, if possible. For now, let's assume she had it with her at the time of the attack, and our killer may have taken it with them."

Kelly nodded.

"I want to share a theory I have," Micheline said. "There are similarities between the J.P. Ballard murder case I worked with Guillermo last summer and this one."

"Oh, really?" Richard asked.

"At this point, it may just be a coincidence. The key will be to ask the coroner to compare the knife wounds between each of the victims in those two cases."

"I'm on it," Kelly confirmed.

"Thanks, Kelly. Let's hear what Sadoski has to say today and take it from there. From all accounts, he was closest to understanding what may have really happened at the scene. I need to shake his tree to let the truth out. He seems to have a lot to hide. Involving his wife may become necessary to jog his memory and loosen his tongue."

Micheline stood and picked up the Miller murder file. The three detectives left the office together and rode the elevator to the main lobby.

The courthouse held several courtrooms and numerous administrative offices. The county jail was in an imposing fortified concrete structure across the wide landscaped rock garden between the two buildings. They proceeded along a paved macadam footpath to the entrance of the jail.

"Does Sadoski have any priors?" Richard asked.

"Clean as a whistle," Kelly replied. "I checked. Not even a parking violation. Apparently, he wasn't always blind. He did have a valid driver's license on file with the DMV at one point. He volunteers some evenings and weekends at the Carmel Valley Community Library. He teaches other blind students how to read brail."

Micheline held a solid steel fire door open for Kelly and Richard to enter Central Booking. They each displayed their badges and official police photo ID cards to a desk sergeant. The sergeant then called a security guard to escort the detectives to an interrogation room safely nestled behind three sets of locked iron grates within the prison. Sadoski and his lawyer were already present and seated when the detectives entered the room.

Thomas Gilford stood and eyed all three detectives carefully. Gilford was exceedingly tall at 6' 8" and wore a well-tailored charcoal gray pinstriped suit with a burgundy tie and matching gold tie bar and cufflinks. He wore designer prescription eyeglasses that were handmade in Japan. Micheline recognized the eyewear design as that of a local celebrity who resided in Solana Beach. She assumed Gilford was likely to be either the designer's legal representative or a friend, if not both.

"Counselor," Micheline opened. "I'm Detective Micheline Avila. I'm leading the investigation into the Samantha Miller murder. Along with me are Detectives Richard Tuller and Kelly Van Horn."

"Yes, yes, Detective Avila," Gilford replied impatiently. "Former NYPD, yes. I was advised you would be taking over the case for the prosecution. Is my client being charged at this time? You have nothing on him."

"Right to the punch, I see," Micheline said. "Let me frame my answer this way. Not yet. However, due to the severity of the crime, and the fact your client was observed in direct contact with the victim, and was apprehended by officers at the scene, formal charges may be filed upon completion of our investigation. Does your client wish to make a statement or a confession at this time?"

Sadoski looked tired and scared. His hair was mussed, his skin was wan and pale, and his hands shook nervously at his sides. He feebly sank lower into his chair.

"No, he does not," Gilford responded firmly.

Micheline pulled a chair back from the table and sat down. She laid the file folder on the table in front of her.

"Mind if I ask your client a few follow-up questions?"

Gilford looked as if he were about to vehemently deny any opportunity for his client to even so much as open his mouth. He placed a hand firmly on Sadoski's left shoulder to physically quell the man's response.

Micheline noticed the nonverbal cue from the defense attorney. She needed to establish trust with his client.

"I was there that day," Micheline interjected briskly. "I've had time to consider what I observed at the scene. I recall what Mr. Sadoski said to me directly. Let's remember, a young woman from a prominent family was killed on a beautiful day in a public park in a most brutal way. I believe your client overhead the events of that day, and some of the things he unknowingly observed may unlock clues we don't yet know to look for."

Gilford looked again as though he were about to protest.

"I'll speak to her," Sadoski offered. "She's tough but respectful. I appreciate that."

"No," Gilford responded quickly. "I'm sorry, Dom. For your own good, I advise you to say as little as possible."

"It's all right," Sadoski said. "Please."

Detective Van Horn pulled out a chair and sat down next to Micheline. Detective Tuller took his cue and followed suit. Gilford remained standing for a moment longer. He hesitated, then nodded compliantly and settled himself into a chair next to his client.

"It's okay, Dominic," the lawyer affirmed. "Say as little as possible. Answer the detective's questions directly, and don't provide any more detail than what she asks."

"I understand," Sadoski replied.

Micheline nodded and cleared her throat decisively. "Mr. Sadoski, are they treating you fairly in here?"

"Yes," he said. "It's not a day at Disneyland, of course. I have a cell to myself. The food has been bearable. The guards are strict but still courteous. They've respected the fact I'm blind."

"Did you know Samantha Miller?"

"No."

"Never had contact with her prior to that day in the park?"

"No, never."

"When did you lose your eyesight, Mr. Sadoski?"

"Almost thirty years ago. I was in my mid-twenties. It was due to a congenital disease."

"You mentioned to me you walked that path regularly as part of a daily exercise routine. Is that correct?"

"Yes, Detective. That's right."

"What was different that day? What made you stop?"

"I had to go to the bathroom, and I wasn't going to be able to make it all the way home. I found a nearby tree surrounded by thick shrubbery. I stopped for a few moments to listen for anyone nearby. At first, I didn't hear anyone, and I thought it would be okay. I got up close to the tree and the shrubs and began to relieve my bladder."

"But something happened. You heard a sound, maybe?"

"I was still peeing when I heard the two of them whispering nearby. They were perhaps twenty yards away on the other side of the shrubbery. A man and a woman."

"Did they hear you or notice that you were close by?"

"Not that I'm aware of. I bent low to make sure my head was below the top of the hedge I stood behind. I heard the guy suggest he wanted to pull down her pants and slide into second base for the steal. Then she said something about wanting to keep her uniform clean and she would rather take everything off. I must tell you, I got excited by what I heard in their conversation. It was full of sexual innuendo. He mentioned hitting a home run. I didn't understand why there were so many baseball expressions."

"What happened next?"

"They rolled around a little. I heard grunting noises and heavy breathing. Every now and then she'd say *yes, that's the spot. Right there.* A couple of times she said *oh, fuck!*"

"What were you doing? Just listening?"

"No. I got a woody on. Excuse me, there are women present. I can smell the scent of the shampoos you both use. I got an erection. I started stroking myself. It was like listening to a sex tape or the audio from a porn movie. It got very intense. I came pretty quick, too."

"Then what happened?"

"I reached into my back pocket and pulled out a cloth handkerchief. I wiped myself clean and put the used handkerchief back in the rear pocket. They were done soon after that, talking softly to each other. I couldn't make out everything they said."

"But you remained by the tree and continued to listen to their conversation with interest. Is that correct?"

"Yes, that's correct."

"Did they use each other's names or call each other by a nickname?"

"No, I don't think so. There was something about they could no longer meet at the condo anymore. It wasn't safe. Someone was on to them, and it was probably her fiancé or his wife."

"At that point, did they talk about anything else, or say good-bye to one another before they parted?"

"She said she'd swing by the shop to see him again. Then she must have checked her watch because she said she was late and had to go. The guy left first, though, and I think she stayed sitting there for a minute or two longer. I didn't hear any movement. She wasn't getting dressed right away. I remember thinking maybe she was enjoying the sunshine to get a tan, or maybe she could see me and wondered if I liked the show she had just put on."

"Did you?"

"Did I what?"

"Did you like the show? Was it everything you imagined it might be?"

"It was thrilling, yes. Entertaining, like a live stage play, maybe. I got off on it, literally."

Detective Van Horn touched Micheline's forearm. Micheline nodded her consent for Kelly to proceed with further questioning.

"Mr. Sadoski," Kelly said, "at what point did you hear another person enter the scene?"

"It was right then while she was taking in the moment, I guess. I heard quick footsteps and then something like plastic being crumpled. I don't know how to describe the sound. It reminded me of the sound a kitchen garbage bag makes when you pull it off a spool and you try to open it up to fit over the outer edge of the wastebasket."

"Were there voices?" Detective Tuller asked.

"Not at first," Sadoski said. "It was as if she got taken by surprise, maybe from behind. There was a moment or two of silence. Then the woman announced herself. She said something like *hey, Clarissa, you've kept all your curves in damn fine shape.*"

"I'm confused," Van Horn said. "You mean, Samantha Miller spoke to the other woman first and called her Clarissa?"

Sadoski shook his head. "No, the second woman to arrive called the one who just had sex by the name Clarissa. They knew each other. Then Clarissa said *holy fuck, Hillary! You scared the shit out of me. Why are you dressed like that?* Something happened then because they began to struggle, and then Clarissa screamed to wake the dead. It sounded like they were punching each other. Their breaths were hard and heavy like they were running uphill or rolling around on the ground. There were loud gasping noises, and then a few seconds of complete silence after that. Then I heard the crumpled plastic sound again and only one set of footsteps hurried away quickly."

Detective Tuller looked thoughtful. "Did they exchange any more words? Call each other by name again?"

"No, sorry. Nothing at all."

"What did you do next?" Detective Van Horn asked.

Sadoski looked visibly shaken. "I waited for another minute or two. I thought I heard the girl moan or choke softly. I called out to her. I said hello and asked if she was okay. I got no response, so I walked closer to where I thought she had been. I was so absorbed in all the action I completely forgot to zip up my fly."

Micheline rubbed her jaw thoughtfully. "Was there anyone else present at the scene at that particular time?"

"No," Sadoski offered. "Again, not that I was aware of. I assumed we were alone. Eventually, I found her. I called out to her again, and when she didn't reply I bent down lower. I touched her legs first, then her breasts, her arm and then felt for her face. She was completely naked, and she wasn't moving. I could feel the warm blood on my fingertips."

"Did you do anything else?" Micheline asked. "Did you perform CPR? Did you attempt to revive her in any way?"

"There was no time," Sadoski said, his voice quivering. "Another woman from further off screamed, and the next thing I heard was a woman shouting *police, stop*. That was you, Detective. I recognize your voice."

"Yes, it was," Micheline confirmed. "And we know what happened from that point forward. You're certain that the female attacker referred to the victim as Clarissa, and that the victim referred to her attacker as Hillary?"

"Yes, I'm certain," Sadoski said. "That's what I heard."

Gilford patted Sadoski's forearm gently. "Are you satisfied with my client's innocence now, Detective Avila? Might we conclude this matter officially?"

Micheline faced the defense attorney directly. "Chemical analysis of the residue from the handkerchief found in Mr. Sadoski's pocket, and a comparison of foreign material or fibers from underneath the victim's fingernails, as well as seminal fluid from vaginal swabs, is currently pending review. The M.E. and his staff have been working overtime on this one to provide an update by later today."

"Do we have a firm time when that will be?" Gilford asked.

Micheline did not waver from her position on the matter. "If the results are conclusive and support your client's statement today, I will immediately offer my apologies to Mr. Sadoski and to you, Mr. Gilford, and seek his release without delay. If, however, any inconsistencies come to light, we'll be meeting again under much different circumstances."

"Very well, Detective," Gilford said. He turned toward his client. "Don't worry, Dominic. We'll have you released from custody soon."

Micheline looked again at Sadoski. "Just a few more questions, please."

"Detective!" Gilford stammered.

"Are you right-handed, or left-handed?"

"I'm left-handed, Detective," Sadoski admitted calmly.

"We did not recover a murder weapon at the scene, nor was one found in your possession when you were arrested. For the record, do you confirm you did not find a knife, a razor, or another sharp object on or near the victim's body that day, and you did not transport it from the murder scene and dispose of it along the route prior to your apprehension?"

Detective Tuller looked at Detective Van Horn and smiled confidently. Kelly nodded back toward him in understanding. Micheline was checking all the boxes.

"That's correct, Detective," Sadoski said, his facial expression blank. "I did not have any idea how the woman was attacked, nor did I find any type of weapon when I went to check on her."

"And you didn't find a missing thumb?"

"No, Detective. I did not."

Micheline nodded amicably toward Gilford and placed both of her palms comfortably upon the table in front of her.

"One final question to put this matter to rest," she said.

"The M.E. has established the murder weapon was a single-edge serrated knife."

"Detective!" Gilford objected angrily. "My client has already con-firmed he didn't find any type of weapon at the scene, much less a single-edge serrated knife."

Again, Micheline pressed on without delay.

"So, Mr. Sadoski, as you may not be aware, earlier this morning officers questioned your wife and executed a search warrant of your home. Your wife invited them into the kitchen and offered them coffee or tea. I'm told it's a lovely home you have."

"Yes, it is," Sadoski replied.

"Granite countertops and stainless-steel appliances in the kitchen. You and your wife have very good taste."

"Thank you."

"During their discussion," Micheline continued, "your wife let it slip that a rather expensive style of a steak knife with serrated edges was clearly missing from a wooden block on the granite countertop in your kitchen. Would you care to explain that?"

Both attorney and client gasped alarmingly in unison.

Micheline had struck a raw nerve. The undeniable expression of fear and guilt that spread across Dominic Sadoski's face confirmed it.

Twenty

"**H**oly shit, Micheline!" Richard Tuller shook his head wildly in abject disbelief. "The look on their faces was priceless."

"I agree," Kelly Van Horn laughed. "You pulled that zinger from out of nowhere. I thought Sadoski was going to have a heart attack. No offense toward Guillermo, of course."

"I almost fell off my chair," Richard continued. "Gilford's face turned all shades of purple and looked like he was about to have a stroke. How did you know to inquire about a missing steak knife from Sadoski's own kitchen? There was no mention of it in the file."

The three detectives sat comfortably in the air-conditioned black and white police cruiser along the cobblestone and Belgian brick curb of a private driveway in Encinitas. The cruiser was parked in the shade near a clustered row of tall Italian cypress trees that lined the driveway perimeter for three-quarters of a mile to the main coastal road.

"With a little bit of luck," Micheline admitted reluctantly. "I called Lieutenant Frank Salvatore of the North Coastal Sherrif's Station earlier today. He and I had met at the murder scene, and I wanted to let him know the DA had assigned the case to me. When I mentioned we still had Sadoski in custody, he told me another officer in his department had informed him the officer had gone to the Sadoski residence once before. But no official report had ever been filed. The officer recounted how Sadoski and his wife had a dispute with their next-door neighbor in Sadoski's kitchen. Apparently, Mr. Sadoski loved to walk barefoot in his backyard, and the neighbor had three large German Shepherds that liked to do their business in the tall grass."

"No shit!" Richard exclaimed.

"Yes, that's exactly what they did," Micheline confirmed with a sly grin. "Lots of it, too. Sadoski stepped right into a fresh pile and flattened it like paper mâché. Then he proceeded to track it back into their kitchen, which fueled his temper even hotter."

Kelly and Richard grimaced at the thought.

"When the neighbor came over to see what Sadoski was yelling about through the open windows, Sadoski pulled the knife out of the wooden block on the countertop and chased the neighbor out into the backyard. Sadoski slipped again on another doodle pile and threw the knife over the neighbor's wooden fence. Of course, he was angry as hell, and he didn't know exactly where the knife would land. He's lucky no one was hurt. Not surprisingly, the weapon, if you want to call it that, was never recovered. I would imagine the neighbor retrieved it from his own backyard later and tossed it in the garbage."

"The neighbor didn't file assault charges afterward, did he?" Kelly asked skeptically. "That would have created a complaint file."

"No," Micheline replied. "The neighbor felt bad about the whole episode. They talked it over later while the officer was present and when everyone was calmed down. The neighbor found the hole beneath the wooden fence the dogs were using to gain access to Sadoski's backyard. He offered to secure it with steel rebar stakes and chicken wire, and to place large ceramic pots with cactus and rose bushes in front of it on both sides of the fence. He also offered to remove the doggie piles from Sadoski's backyard himself and to pay for a professional cleaning service to disinfect the entire Sadoski house from top to bottom. It all ended well and was forgotten until I reminded Sadoski of that bitter incident in the prison interrogation room."

Micheline sucked in a deep breath and let it out slowly. "The lawyer sure did look like he was about to shit red bricks, didn't he?"

"Absolutely," Kelly agreed.

"Good," Micheline said. "I want him to take us seriously. I want him to know we're all over this."

"Well, if he didn't know it before, he sure does know it now," Kelly suggested.

Richard looked sideways to the immense double wooden and stained-glass front entrance doors to the Miller estate. "So boss, what's our next move here?"

Micheline nodded solemnly.

"We express our condolences to the Miller family, and we attempt to find out any information we can relate to Samantha's personal life that may be relevant to the case."

The detectives exited the police cruiser and immediately felt the warm breath of a Pacific breeze envelope them. They were greeted by a uniformed Filipina maid in her mid-to-late fifties at the front entrance. The maid escorted the group to a room off to the left of the wide marble floor foyer. Before them, an elaborately designed wrought iron staircase with matching marble tiles placed across the front face of each step rose to the second-floor landing. An expansive crystal chandelier hung from the cathedral ceiling above. Large glass windows allowed abundant sunlight to illuminate the extravagant home interior.

To the side of the main doorway, a red Pullman suitcase with a black extended handle stood sentinel over the room.

As they entered Stephen Miller's home office, Micheline noted the rich dark tones of the wooden bookshelves that lined the inner sanctum's walls and the colorful silken tapestries that were resplendent with sunshine streaming through stained-glass windows. To the back of the room, an intricately carved cherry wood double pedestal desk with an old-world globe and laptop computer faced the entrance.

On the left, a green marble fireplace and mantle displayed family photographs in silver frames, and to the right, a matching set of hunter green leather couch, loveseat, and a reclining chair was positioned to surround a silver and glass coffee table set upon a thick burgundy Persian rug. Behind the couch, a floor-to-ceiling window allowed a spectacular view from atop the bluff to the ocean and the wide sandy stretch of beach below.

A large-screen television on the far wall was set to a local news channel. The story of a severe Pacific storm coming across the Bering Sea and down from Alaska along the northwest coastline, disrupting airline flights and commercial shipping routes, was being reported from the port in Seattle.

Most striking of all within the room, though, was the beautiful woman with long curled brown hair cascading over her shoulders. She sat casually and comfortably upon the leather loveseat with her short skirt showing off muscularly defined tanned legs and black high-heeled shoes. With only the hint of an obligatory smile, her mouth was outlined by dark red lipstick, her hazel eyes highlighted by pale blue eye shadow, and a white cotton sundress clung tightly against her lithe body. The dress was unbuttoned from collar to sternum, allowing an oblique view of the full contour of both rounded and unfettered breasts. Her soft skin was void of any tan lines.

Micheline looked curiously at the woman.

"May I introduce Miss Elena Dobrovic," the maid said flatly. "Miss Dobrovic is a professional writer who specializes in obituaries. Professor Miller had her flown in from Detroit to write a feature and memoir for his daughter, Samantha."

"How do you do?" Micheline began. "I'm Detective Micheline Avila of the San Diego County Sheriff's Department. With me are Detectives Kelly Van Horn and Richard Tuller."

"Hello," she said calmly.

"A writer who specializes in obituaries," Micheline said. "That's fascinating. How did you ever decide on such a career?"

"It truly is a unique career choice," Elena replied confidently. "It's a position with an unlimited market that is never impacted by economic or social distress. I also take great pride in my work. I provide comfort and sympathy to those in need."

"I see," Micheline said. "I'd love to hear more."

Elena's dry expression melted into a warm smile. "My work puts me in the throes of my clients' grief," she offered. "As painful as that may sound, it allows me to hear the re-telling of interesting tales, to listen to the anecdotes, and to patiently wait out the awkward silences. In the end, I attempt to give them back a story that is resplendent and as alive as their memory can conceive."

Micheline nodded thoughtfully. "Have you met with Dr. Miller yet or anyone else from the family?"

"No, not yet," she replied. "I just arrived a few moments ago by Uber. We've scheduled interviews with various family members over the next two days in order that I may have a presentation available for the newspapers and the funeral service. They don't know when that will be just yet, I believe."

"That's correct," Micheline confirmed. "Due to the unfortunate nature of their daughter's death, the medical examiner's office is still continuing its investigation. They'll release the body to the funeral home as soon as their work is completed."

Elena nodded. "I'm familiar with the formality and procedure, Detective. It's not my first rodeo."

"May I suggest," Micheline said, "we meet again after your interviews with the family and your presentation have been completed? You may uncover information we otherwise may not have been privy to. I would very much appreciate your insight on the victim and her relationship with family members."

Elena smiled warmly again. She had already inwardly decided she would welcome an opportunity to speak directly to the female detective in charge of this murder investigation. She reached into her leather purse and withdrew a white printed business card.

"I would be delighted, Detective. Please, take my card. I'll be in town over the Thanksgiving Day holiday. Perhaps we could meet over dinner or drinks one evening to discuss my revelations or conclusions."

"That would be splendid," Micheline replied. "I'll look forward to catching up with you and to compare notes. Are you staying here in Encinitas?"

"No," she replied. "I'll be at a hotel near the airport in San Diego."

"Very good," Micheline said. "I'll plan to give you a call the day after tomorrow if that works."

"Yes," she said and smiled again.

Micheline withdrew a blue and white printed business card with the San Diego County Sheriff's Department seal from her pocket and handed it to Elena.

"Here's my card," she offered, "in case you feel the need to speak to me sooner, or if we get our schedules mixed up. I will value your contribution relative to this case."

"Very well, Detective. I look forward to our conversation."

"I see you've all become acquainted," Dr. Stephen Miller announced as he, his wife, and another man who looked vaguely familiar to Micheline entered the study.

"Yes, sir," Micheline replied evenly. "Dr. and Mrs. Miller, please accept my condolences on the loss of your daughter. My name is Detective Micheline Avila of the San Diego County Sheriff's Department. Along with me are Detectives Kelly Van Horn and Richard Tuller, and we've just been introduced to Elena Dobrovic."

"Thank you, Detective," Miller replied. The benevolent and widely respected CEO was tall and lanky, with a deep tan and long reddish-brown hair. He wore a brightly colored Hawaiian print shirt, beige cargo shorts, and flip-flops. He clearly exemplified the typical California surfer, cyclist, and ocean swimming enthusiast.

Micheline had reviewed Dr. Miller's biography on his company's corporate website. Early in his career, he was solely responsible for the creation of two FDA-approved drug treatments for orphan diseases, rare neurological conditions, or degenerative brain disorders that require long-term use of expensive medications to control clinical symptoms.

He later provided laboratory data to identify proteins for promising drug targets and established an experienced core team of medical experts and business professionals to attract and manage investor spending appropriately. This later led to his becoming CEO and major shareholder of a biotech start-up company with laboratories and offices located in San Diego.

"May I present my wife, Beverly."

Mrs. Miller was of medium build. She had curly brown hair and was dressed in a USC Trojan cardinal red and gold hooded sweatshirt and matching baseball cap, a pair of black yoga pants, and white Nike running shoes.

"And this is Dr. David Hawthorne, a close friend of the family." Dr. Miller appeared tight-lipped beyond that statement and made no mention of Hawthorne's engagement status to his deceased daughter.

Miller stepped forward to the hunter-green loveseat. "Elena, it's so nice to meet you. Thank you again for agreeing to come all the way out here on such short notice. I can be quite pushy when I'm agitated. Or in this case, stricken with grief. Many say I have no filter and I just say whatever's on my mind at the time. I hope you won't judge me too harshly."

Elena nodded politely. "I'm here to listen and to help you through this difficult time, Dr. Miller. Whatever you need."

"Thank you, my dear," he replied. He turned toward the doorway, where the maid stood at dutiful attention. "Esmerelda, would you please escort Ms. Dobrovic to the family room?"

"Yes, of course, Professor," Esmerelda replied.

Miller turned back toward Elena. "My brother-in-law and his wife, and their two daughters, Samantha's cousins, are waiting for you in the family room. The girls are both nearly the same age as Samantha, within a year or two. I thought it best you speak with them first. Beverly, David, and I will join you after the detectives have gone."

"Yes, Dr. Miller. That would be fine."

Elena stood carefully and picked up a shoulder bag that had been set on the floor. She looked straight ahead and began to walk toward the doorway as Micheline and Dr. Miller stepped back to allow her passage across the room.

"Detectives, please take a seat on the loveseat and the recliner, and make yourselves comfortable," Miller offered. "The three of us will take the couch if that's all right."

Micheline sensed immediately Dr. Miller was very methodical and overly conscious about order and alignment. He had Ph.D.'s in neurology and psychology, but he would likely notice immediately and become somewhat irritated if an object or a piece of furniture were ever moved from its designated place.

Everyone seated themselves appropriately to Dr. Miller's initial suggestion. Mrs. Miller sat to the right of her husband, and Dr. Hawthorne sat to the left of the man who may have become his father-in-law had fate not intervened.

"How can we help you, detectives?" Dr. Miller asked politely.

Micheline surveyed the expressions of those individuals seated across from her. There was a subdued manner, but also stability and strength to their demeanor. Grief and sorrow were not necessarily evident.

"Frankly, sir," Micheline began, "we're perplexed and challenged by the manner of your daughter's death. It was clearly a very personal attack, most likely by someone known to her. We've come to ask for your help to better understand who your daughter was, why she was at the park that day, whom she might have been meeting, and who might have reason to want to murder her."

Beverly Miller was the first to speak. "Samantha was a lovely young woman with an incredibly bright future ahead of her. She was an avid softball player, and her team had a game scheduled that afternoon. She had many friends and no enemies. She was simply at the wrong place at the wrong time."

"Had you seen your daughter earlier that day?" Detective Tuller asked. "Did you note any difference in her mood or a change in her appearance?"

"No, Detective," Dr. Miller said. "There was no change. Nothing out of the ordinary. It was Samantha's turn in the rotation to pitch that afternoon. She was looking forward to the game. We had an early breakfast together and then she left the house."

"Was she wearing her uniform when she left the house?" Detective Van Horn asked.

"Yes, she was," Beverly Miller responded.

"What time did she leave?" Detective Tuller asked.

"I'd say about nine-thirty that morning," Dr. Miller replied.

"And I understand your daughter was engaged to be married," Van Horn continued. "Was she wearing an engagement ring that morning?"

"No," Beverly Miller replied. "She wasn't wearing it that morning. It is rather large and exquisite. David had exceptionally good taste in selecting it from a jeweler on Rodeo Drive in Los Angeles. That's how much Samantha meant to him. Besides, Samantha didn't wear jewelry during sporting activities. The ring is upstairs in the jewelry box in her bedroom."

"You've seen it?"

"Yes, I have. I spent several hours in her bedroom yesterday while selecting an appropriate dress for her funeral. The ring is still there in the jewelry box on top of the dresser."

"Did Samantha keep a journal or a diary, or perhaps an online blog post?" Micheline asked.

"No, Detective," Mrs. Miller said. "She loved to read romantic comedies and fantasy novels in her free moments. But she preferred to keep her private thoughts to herself. She did, however, post photos of herself and her friends across many different social media sites. She was exceedingly popular in that respect. She had followers in the tens of thousands. Quite remarkable, really."

"Did you happen to notice her cell phone in her bedroom?"

"No, I didn't," Mrs. Miller replied. "Samantha would have taken that with her to the softball field. She always posted photos of her teammates on social media sites both during and after her games."

"I see," Micheline said. "Her phone was not found at the crime scene. You're certain she had it with her when she left?"

"I can't imagine her not taking it with her," Mrs. Miller confirmed. "It's not here. I'm sure of that. Perhaps she left it in her car."

Micheline jotted another notation in her notebook relating to the missing cell phone. Kelly was following up on that lead. Micheline didn't want to tip the family off they were investigating GPS coordinates linked to the phone.

"Samantha's car," she continued, "was found in the Harbor Club parking lot near the entrance to Catalina Mission Park. That's quite a distance from the softball fields. It's a mile and a half away, to be precise. Can you think of any reason why she may have chosen to park her car in that location rather than somewhere closer to the ballfield? There's a community parking lot down the hill on the far side of the playing fields, for instance."

"I can only assume she preferred the security the Harbor Club parking lot offers, Detective," Dr. Miller replied. "We have a family membership to the club, and Samantha played tennis or went swimming there often. She met her friends there as well. She drove an expensive Astin Martin Vantage convertible, you see. So, I'm certain she preferred to park the car in a less public setting that offered better security and protection for the vehicle."

Micheline nodded politely and turned her attention to Dr. David Hawthorne who, to this point in time, had continued to sit comfortably and quietly. He remained aloof and stared straight down at the coffee table during the entire conversation. He made no mention of the engagement ring.

"Dr. Hawthorne," Micheline opened. "You were engaged to Samantha?"

"Uh, yes," Hawthorne replied unevenly.

"There's a noticeable age difference between the two of you."

"I'm thirty-three," he offered. "So, yes. There's a nine-year gap between us."

"How did the two of you meet?"

"At a Christmas party last year. We were introduced by mutual friends."

"Less than a year ago," Micheline stated the obvious. "The relationship must have been very strong."

"Yes, it was," Hawthorne replied.

"No problems between the two of you recently?" Micheline asked pointedly.

"We had our differences from time to time," Hawthorne admitted, "but we were very much in love and looking forward to the wedding next June."

Micheline took a deep breath and locked eyes with Hawthorne. "You may not remember me, Dr. Hawthorne. Do I look familiar to you?"

Hawthorne fidgeted uncomfortably.

"I don't recall seeing you before, Detective. No. I have not had any run-ins with the law, nor have I seen you before at the hospital. You're very attractive, too. I think I'd remember seeing you before if we had met."

Micheline straightened her shoulders. "I was having a late dinner with some friends at Marino's Italian Bistro in Mira Mesa last week during the thunderstorm. You may remember the events of that evening."

Hawthorne's body immediately stiffened. The color drained from his face.

"I witnessed you and Samantha publicly having a difference of opinion, as you say. You both appeared," Micheline paused, "agitated. Samantha splashed a glass of wine at you. She walked away in an emotional state and left the restaurant by herself. She was obviously more than a little upset."

"It was simply a misunderstanding between us," Dr. Hawthorne stated.

"Really?" Micheline said. "I got the impression the engagement was called off. The expletives you used were quite colorful and were not of an affectionate nature. Are you now saying you spoke to her afterward and patched things up between the two of you?"

"Not exactly," Hawthorne mumbled weakly.

"How exactly would you describe it, then?" Micheline asked, maintaining a level professional tone.

"I texted several times," Hawthorne replied. "But she wouldn't respond. I worked long shifts at the hospital. It was difficult for us to make a connection."

"So, you hadn't actually spoken to her since the night of the incident in the restaurant. Is that correct?"

"Yes, Detective. That's right."

"Had you gone to see her at any time, even though the two of you hadn't actually spoken?"

"No, nothing. It's been the darkest of days this entire past week or so. I've been depressed and beside myself."

The expressions on Dr. and Mrs. Miller's faces showed concern, shock, and empathy.

Poor David!

"David," Mrs. Miller began, "we had no idea the two of you had a quarrel. Why didn't you come to us?"

"I thought we could work it out amongst ourselves," he replied. "She was terribly angry with me. I said some things I wish I could take back. She stormed out of the restaurant before I could offer an apology, and we had not spoken since. I was certain we'd be able to straighten things out in time."

"Oh, poor dear," Mrs. Miller said.

"Forgive me, please," Micheline said. "But I have to ask. First, Dr. Hawthorne, where were you on Saturday morning?"

"I worked a twenty-four-hour shift at the hospital until seven that morning. I went through the drive-thru for a breakfast sandwich and then went straight home."

"Where is home, Dr. Hawthorne?"

"In Carlsbad. I have a townhome located close to the premium outlets."

"Was anyone home with you that day?"

"No, Detective. I was alone."

"You didn't go out for any reason, or drive down to the Del Mar and Carmel Valley area that day?"

"No, I didn't."

"Which hospital were you at that day?"

"Scripps Memorial Hospital in La Jolla."

"I'm familiar," Micheline confirmed. "We have a colleague there for a coronary artery bypass operation."

"Yes, that's a good choice. The hospital is ranked among the nation's best for cardiology and heart surgery."

"What is your medical specialty, Dr. Hawthorne? Is it cardiology?"

"No, it's not. I'm an obstetrics and gynecological surgeon. My focus is on minimally invasive robot-assisted surgery, including hysterectomy and myomectomy."

"I see. But you did drive through the Carmel Valley area on your way home from the hospital then, correct?"

"Yes, that's correct."

"And you didn't stop along the way?"

"No, I didn't. I only stopped at the fast-food restaurant near the hospital for coffee and a breakfast sandwich. Then I drove directly home."

"Did anyone see you when you left the hospital that morning? Other doctors or nurses, patients or their families?"

"I spoke to several patients that morning, and then two or three other staff members on my way out the door," Dr. Hawthorne replied. "I can provide you with their names if you'd like."

"Yes, of course," Micheline said.

Micheline made some notations in her notebook relative to photo surveillance of automobiles located within a wide perimeter of the crime scene. Then she looked up to face the Millers.

"Did Samantha have a laptop computer?"

"Yes," Mrs. Miller replied. "It's in her bedroom upstairs on her corner desk."

"We'll need to take that with us, with your permission, of course," Micheline said. "It may help greatly with our investigation."

"Yes, of course, Detective," Dr. Miller replied. "We will help you in any way possible."

Micheline nodded. "Dr. Miller, were you and your wife home all morning on Saturday?"

"After breakfast, I left for a golf outing with some of my colleagues. I was away most of the day."

"And your colleagues can confirm this?"

"Yes, of course."

"What time did you leave your home, sir?"

"I'd say it was sometime after ten that morning," Dr. Miller said.

"Mrs. Miller, were you home then by yourself on Saturday morning?"

"No," she replied. "I had left for a salon appointment around ten-thirty. I had my hair styled, did some shopping after lunch, and returned home later that afternoon."

"Were you with anyone during that time?"

"I met one of my girlfriends at the salon, and then we met two other friends for lunch."

"Thank you," Micheline offered. "We'll need names and contact information for each of the individuals you've mentioned having spent time with on Saturday. That should include a list of all the places you visited, such as the hospital and fast-food restaurant for Dr. Hawthorne, the name of the golf course Dr. Miller played at, and the name of the salon, restaurant, and shopping plaza that Mrs. Miller went to. It's all standard procedure to provide a timeline of events and to rule each of you out as suspects."

"We understand, Detective Avila," Dr. Miller said. "We're grieving the loss of our daughter. Anything we can do to help you catch her killer would bring us at least some semblance of peace in this matter."

"Thank you, Dr. Miller," Micheline said. "We were greeted at the door by Esmerelda, your housekeeper. Was she here at the house for breakfast on Saturday morning?"

"Yes, she was," Mrs. Miller confirmed. "Esmerelda is our full-time housemaid. She lives in the guest house on the other side of our property. She's been with us since Samantha was a toddler."

"We'd like to speak to her before we leave, then," Micheline suggested.

"Yes, of course, Detective," Mrs. Miller replied. "I'll ask Esmerelda to show you to Samantha's bedroom next. You'll be able to see some of Samantha's personality from how she has decorated her place of comfort. You'll be able to see the types of books she's read, the music she listened to, photos of friends, and places she's visited."

"Thank you, Mrs. Miller," Micheline said. "If you don't mind, I'd like for Detectives Van Horn and Tuller to meet with Esmerelda upstairs. They will let you know before we leave today of any articles, such as

Samantha's laptop computer, they will be taking with them as evidence today. All items will be returned to you in due time, I assure you."

"And you, Detective?" Dr. Miller asked. "Do you have other plans?"

"Yes," Micheline replied. "With your permission, I would prefer to walk the grounds outside your home by myself. I would like to gather my thoughts and view the surroundings that Samantha was so familiar with her entire life. It may allow me to put everything we've learned so far into better perspective."

"Ah, I see," Dr. Miller said. "Very well, Detective. Please allow me to see you to the sliding doors that lead out to our backyard patio."

Micheline stood and made eye contact with both Detectives Van Horn and Tuller.

"We've got this, Micheline," Detective Van Horn said.

Micheline nodded. "I'll meet you both out front in about thirty minutes. If you come across something of interest and you need more time, don't hurry on my account. Let's be thorough, please."

"Yes, we'll see you then," Detective Tuller replied.

Dr. Miller stood from the couch and looked toward Micheline. "Detective, if you'll please follow me."

"Thank you, sir," Micheline said as she stood. "I'm curious. During our investigation, the names Clarissa and Hillary were mentioned. Do either of those names sound familiar to you? Perhaps they could be girlfriends of Samantha?"

Dr. Miller shook his head. "No, I don't believe so."

"Oh, Clarissa," Mrs. Miller spoke up. "That was the name of Samantha's favorite childhood doll. She was an American Girl doll, a collector's item now."

"I see," Micheline remarked. "But to your knowledge, Samantha did not go by another nickname at any time, such as Clarissa or Hillary?"

"Oh, no," Mrs. Miller stated matter-of-factly. "Just Sam or Sammy to some of her friends, but mostly by Samantha."

"Did she have any friends who were known by those names? Clarissa or Hillary?" Micheline asked.

"Not that I'm aware of," Mrs. Miller confirmed.

"Thank you for your time today," Micheline said. "Again, I'm sorry for both of you on your loss."

Micheline paused. "Dr. Miller, if you'd be so kind as to show me to the backyard, please?"

Dr. Miller extended his hand toward the exit and offered to show Micheline through the house. Micheline was busy absorbing all the details she could, including not just what was said, but the body language and facial expressions of those she questioned as well.

The words spoken by loved ones expressed grief and loss. The body language exhibited during the interview told another story entirely.

Twenty-One

Daylight faded swiftly into dusk as the sun crested beneath the calm Pacific expanse to the western horizon. Across the bay to the east, the San Diego city skyline was illuminated brightly.

Micheline fumbled with her keys as she climbed the steps to her third-floor condo. Matching solar-powered lanterns on either side of the entranceway provided enough light to allow her to see clearly. Oddly out of place, she noticed a silver two-door BMW with a black convertible top parked further down the street along the curb in a no parking fire zone.

The entrance door to the condo was slightly ajar. There was no light or sound coming from within.

Something was wrong.

Micheline immediately dropped her keys into her pants pocket and withdrew her primary weapon from its shoulder holster. She let herself into her quiet retreat and switched on the interior light. She detected movement in the bedroom and heard drawers being opened and closed.

"Police!" she announced loudly. "I have a gun. Come out slowly with your hands held above your head."

The stirring in the bedroom suddenly ceased.

"Fuck you, Micheline!" Jenny's voice called back harshly.

Micheline slipped the gun back into its holster and snapped the leather restraint button in place.

What the hell's going on?

"Jenny, I'm sorry," Micheline called out in a concerned voice. "I wasn't expecting to see you tonight."

"Other plans, huh?" Jenny remarked callously. "Another brunette, maybe? Or is it blondes and redheads only this week? God knows you dropped Greg like a hot potato, and now I hear you're out on the town flirting and picking up other women. I didn't realize you were into that sort of thing."

Micheline peered around the door frame into the bedroom. Jenny had a cardboard banker's storage box under one arm and was pulling lingerie from a dresser drawer.

"What's going on?" Micheline asked. "You seem miffed about something. Greg hasn't called me once all weekend after he canceled our Friday night date at the last minute with a lame excuse."

"You didn't think to call him?"

"I'm not chasing guys. That sends the wrong signal."

"So, you decided to switch things up. You're into ladies now, huh?"

"I don't know where you would've gotten that idea. Really, Jenny. I'm not into women. I've been neck-deep in work all day. I was requested to take the lead on an active, high-profile murder investigation. A woman was killed on Saturday morning. It was the same woman we saw at the pizzeria having a fight with her fiancé."

Micheline was proud of how much she and her team had accomplished toward the investigation in such a short period of time.

Sadly though, once again, neither Jenny nor Greg was a priority among her immediate thoughts. Micheline was at a loss as to how to answer her friend's agitated and aggressive behavior.

Sometimes I can be a clueless idiot. I mean well, but that is obviously not good enough.

"I'm not back from Chicago for one day," Jenny stammered, "and I hear you left the Hops & Malt Brewery the other night with another woman who was dressed to kill. She must have thought you were something special, all alone and available. You go to a place where you know my best friend works, and then you leave in the company of a sexy brunette. I heard you were holding hands and you had this dreamy smile on your face as you made your way out the door together. I mean, what the fuck, Micheline! Doesn't our friendship mean anything to you?"

"Of course, it does," Micheline replied calmly and evenly. "I was interviewing a witness to the murder that had occurred that same morning. She had left the scene of the crime earlier, and I was lucky to have found her again. There was no funny business going on, Jenny. Honest. It was all work-related. I really missed you this weekend. I've been looking forward to hearing how things went with your family."

"Oh, I'll bet," Jenny spat. "I heard the two of you looked pretty cozy and that she was a real hottie. You got laid, didn't you? Did you bring her back here and fuck her on this very bed, or did the two of you go back to her place?"

"Can we just calm down, please?" Micheline asked. "I'll open a bottle of wine. We'll talk."

Jenny shook her head adamantly. "Let's just take a break for now. Okay, Micheline? I've had feelings for you. Maybe you didn't see it. But I thought we had an emotional connection. I thought we had trust."

"We do have trust between us," Micheline contended. "Nothing's changed."

Jenny shook her head in dismay. "A BFF is supposed to make me feel safe and secure. We're supposed to be a comfort to each other. We should be able to tell each other anything. Instead, you make me feel like last week's microwave leftovers."

Micheline hung her head in response. "I don't know how to respond to that, Jenny. Really, I'm sorry you feel this way. I never intended for you to feel left out. When you were in Chicago for your family's events this past weekend, I figured you were busy with that. I didn't think you had time for me."

"Oh, now it's my fault?" Jenny reflected irately. "It doesn't matter, Micheline. It's over between us. I'm just getting some of the clothing and stuff I left here. Don't bother calling me again. Let's end it here peacefully and remember we did have a few good times together. I shared my heart and soul to you over so many glasses of wine. It just wasn't meant to be, that's all."

"I really wish you'd let me explain," Micheline offered.

"Look, Micheline," Jenny began. "You're a nice person, good-looking, successful in your career, and mature. But you're responsible for yourself only. You're emotionally unavailable and you're definitely not a friend or relationship material in my eyes. You've never even talked about your past. You're all closed inside. You're just someone to have fun with for now, and that's no longer enough for me."

"But..." Micheline had no rebuttal. Jenny was right. Micheline hadn't made Jenny a priority in her life, and she kept her past life securely locked away from everyone she knew.

Jenny stared back at her without comment. She shook her head dejectedly back and forth and proceeded to stomp toward the doorway.

Micheline stood aside and watched as Jenny left. She followed behind her friend slowly while Jenny marched along the hallway and crossed into the kitchen and living room areas.

As Jenny passed by the couch in the living room, she dropped the house key next to a lamp on top of an end table. Then she was quickly outside the front entrance door and clambered angrily down the staircase.

Jenny walked along the street down below and placed her box of silky lingerie and an assortment of hair products into the trunk of the silver BMW that was parked along the curb.

Micheline watched quietly from the top of the staircase.

Alone again. Damn it! You would think after a painful divorce and a few years of being single that dating and relationships with friends would start to get somewhat easier.

Micheline leaned against the doorframe and crossed her arms. She was still waiting for her lifelong dream to come true. If only she knew what that was.

For now, her work was all she had left to put her mind to.

Twenty-Two

Early morning fog swirled threateningly across the San Diego-Coronado Bridge. Micheline traversed the bridge daily on her way toward Harbor Drive. She continued her drive north through the sophisticated, cosmopolitan backdrop of the Gaslamp Quarter in downtown San Diego.

In the early morning hours, thick condensation formed naturally from the ground upward. The fog typically burned off well before noontime to reveal a cloudless sky above. As Micheline drove to work, visibility was less than thirty feet. A rising sun failed to penetrate the gray shroud so much as a glimmer of first light.

The detective's frustration needed to be bled like excess steam from an industrial boiler. Jenny's unexpected departure from her life the evening before left her with mixed feelings, both good and bad. She felt sorrow, guilt, and surprisingly, a bit of relief. Keeping close friends and staying in touch across long distances had always been a challenge for Micheline throughout her life. This time appeared to be no different than before.

"You'll make new friends," her mother used to tell her whenever she changed schools or was transferred to a new department within the NYPD.

The narrow blacktop lane became a racecar driver's final lap to the checkered flag. Surface conditions changed along with the weather. Micheline dared to live life on the edge.

She downshifted into third gear and mentally urged the 310-horsepowered stallion toward the approach of a sharp curve. Her right foot pressed the accelerator to the floor. The white tachometer needle raced into the danger zone.

Micheline's expression grew taut. Her fingers gripped the leather steering wheel inexorably tight. Her breaths became shallow.

The sharp curve came and went. A cloud of dust exploded in the car's wake as the tires hugged the outer edge of the road surface at high speed.

Micheline shifted into overdrive and felt the tension of the car's engine settle into a perfectly tuned rhythm. She allowed herself to relax momentarily. She was in total control.

With her thoughts more than somewhat distracted, Micheline switched on the police band radio. The lingo spoken was something that had taken her weeks and months to get used to when she first began training in the field of criminal justice. Messages were short, cryptic, and garbled by static.

A female dispatcher named Anastasia Kapileo, who liked to be called Ana, was confirming updates with various squads on patrol. Micheline had met her once at an office party. She was an attractive young woman from the Northern Mariana Islands. She had long dark hair below her waistline, a friendly disposition, and she was a single mother. Micheline had liked her.

Anastasia had this recurring trait whereby she would constantly cup her hand, palm out, and smile flirtatiously at the men at the party as she tucked her long silky hair back over one ear. Micheline had once attempted to replicate the gesture in the bathroom mirror before a night out but had failed miserably in her attempt.

Micheline decelerated as the city traffic became more congested. The city was beginning to awaken from its slumber. Here and there, pedestrians strolled along the sidewalks.

Micheline stopped at the intersection of Fifth Avenue and Island Avenue in the heart of the Gaslamp Quarter. She glanced at the dashboard clock for the time. Seven twenty-eight. She waited patiently for the red light to change to green.

Her eyes darted to the Fidelity National Savings and Loan Bank parking lot on the left. Jenny's silver BMW convertible was parked there along with a half dozen other vehicles. This was unusually early for Jenny to be at work as far as Micheline knew. The bank would not be open for another ninety minutes, or so she assumed.

Micheline did all her banking online or with the banking app on her smartphone. She seldom used an ATM for cash withdrawals or felt the need to stop by a branch location to deposit checks or cash in person. Even the documentation and paperwork for the mortgage on her condo had been handled electronically through email and verified signature processes. Such was modern technology.

A white unmarked van was parked directly in front of the bank's main entrance doors. This was also unusual for the early time of morning, although the strip clubs and a grocery store across the street were all open.

Strange, although the driver was probably getting some one-dollar bills at the ATM to tip the exotic dancers at one of the clubs across the street. Why not use the drive-thru ATM, though?

Micheline's thoughts returned to the evening before. She assumed the breakup with Jenny was all her fault. She had never been one to fall into a jealous rage or to care how many friends her other female acquaintances had. Maybe it was because she never got too close before. She turned her head and looked away toward the abandoned Imperial Theater across the street.

The traffic light changed to green. Micheline shifted from first into second gear and merged with the traffic ahead of her. Part of her wanted to stop in at the bank to talk to Jenny. Another part of her said to leave it alone and move on without any further uncomfortable and awkward conversation.

Several cars lined up on Micheline's rear bumper. She was driving too slowly, allowing her mind to wander. She kept thinking about how things with Jenny all had come undone.

Was it really her fault alone?

She didn't want to believe that.

Still, Jenny was the one who left town for the long weekend. Neither Jenny nor Greg had bothered to call Micheline during that time. It was not as though Micheline had simply forgotten about Jenny, either. Micheline was at first out for a run, and then later working a murder investigation. The two women drifted apart in what seemed less than a microsecond.

C'est la vie!

An image of her eighth-grade French class with Mademoiselle Seydoux snapping her fingers excitedly to extract verb conjugations from her students suddenly came to mind.

Vite! Vite!

Quickly! Quickly!

The car directly behind Micheline began to honk its horn. The guy behind the wheel was in an obvious hurry. Micheline was royally agitating him by driving slower than the posted speed limit. Micheline gestured with a slight wave of her right hand to kindly acknowledge the asshole behind her and grudgingly gave the car's accelerator a little more gas.

Clearly upset, Micheline abruptly pulled up on the emergency brake. She slammed on the brakes with her right foot and spun the steering wheel counterclockwise. This propelled the car in a wild U-turn into the opposing traffic lane.

Her tires squealed and smoked. Oncoming traffic swerved to the side of the road. The driver immediately behind her gave Micheline the middle finger salute as he drove on past. He scowled angrily at the seasoned detective who now faced in the opposite direction in her shiny muscle car.

Micheline immediately lowered the emergency brake and slammed the stick shifter into first gear. She backed off the clutch and pumped the accelerator to the floor. She kept it there.

When the tachometer hit the red zone less than a second later, Micheline shifted into second gear and made a sharp right turn and then an immediate left into the bank parking lot. She narrowly missed hitting a white Volvo XC-90 SUV and a red four-door Jeep Wrangler Rubicon with a black hardtop roof. Both vehicles were parked a few spaces from each other in the center of the near-empty lot.

Micheline noticed exhaust plumes emitting from the tailpipes of both vehicles. But she could not see either of the drivers through dark tinted windows.

Probably going to use the drive-thru ATM first thing in the morning. Getting their deposits in order before they head to work.

Micheline circled around the outer circumference of the macadam lot and parked her Mustang sideways with the front wheels turned at a sharp angle. The shiny muscle car took up four open parking spaces. Micheline killed the ignition.

Parking outside the lines won't bother anyone this early in the morning.

She hopped out of the car and began to walk around the building toward the front entrance. Her watch read seven thirty-five. The front entrance doors would be locked, but some employees were likely already inside the building with Jenny. Micheline planned to knock and to wait for someone to let her in.

Although her badge and her primary weapon were outwardly concealed by the folds of her cotton blazer, Micheline knew having a detective's metal shield stamped with her badge number and clipped to her belt, as well as an official law enforcement photo ID card in her wallet, could come in handy on occasions such as this. But Micheline only intended to flash those credentials if she needed to. She would attempt diplomacy first.

And if that doesn't work, I could always pull my Combat Masterpiece out of its holster for a little extra persuasive consideration.

Micheline smiled wickedly at the thought. She noticed immediately the white van was parked by the curb with its engine running. Exhaust fumes seeped from the rear tailpipe.

That's odd.

Micheline turned to see if anyone was seated inside the van. Almost as if on cue, the double glass entrance doors to the bank swung open.

A tall, Black, barrel-chested uniformed security guard stood in the half-opened doorway. His eyes questioned Micheline's presence in front of the bank at such an early hour of the morning with silent reservation.

The top of the guard's head was completely shaved bald. His mustache and beard were well-trimmed and short-cropped. Micheline could smell the sweet essence of lavender moisturizer on his face. He reminded her somewhat of Richard Tuller.

"Can I help you, miss?" he asked politely. He flashed a perfect grin of straight white teeth to greet her.

Micheline faced the guard squarely and read the name tag clipped to the man's left breast pocket.

Marcell Landry.

"Yes, Mr. Landry," she opened in a friendly manner. "Good morning. I have an appointment to meet with Jenny Casella today. This is the only time she could fit me into her schedule."

The guard's facial expression remained stoic. "I'm sorry but Miss Casella has not arrived for work yet. She's due in at nine o'clock. Perhaps you could call back then."

Micheline stepped closer to the guard. She detected the smell of coffee on the guard's breath.

"I see her car is in the parking lot. Are you sure she's not already inside the building?"

The guard didn't blink. "I'm positive, miss. Perhaps she went for a cup of coffee or breakfast before work. There's a café just down the street. There's a Mexican restaurant, too. I seem to remember her mentioning she likes the burritos and fish tacos there."

"Very well," Micheline said. "Do you mind if I wait inside the lobby until she arrives?"

"Uh," the guard hesitated. "No, miss. I'm sorry. The bank is closed. You'll have to call back later, please."

Micheline took an aggressive step forward. She realized suddenly Jenny had likely warned the guard to expect an uninvited female visitor. A woman who might show up at the bank that morning to ask for her. A woman who would never accept the word *no* for an answer.

Micheline was not about to be deterred by a mere security guard. She knew Marcell Landry was lying to her. She was not going to be put off any longer. As she looked closer, she also took note of a small tattoo on the side of the security guard's neck. It was hidden just beneath the top edge of his shirt collar. The image was oddly out of place for someone in this man's line of work.

Micheline reached toward the bottom hem of her well-fitted blazer. Maybe her detective's credentials and shield would provide the appropriate leverage she needed to gain entry to the bank right now.

From behind her, the cold hardened steel of a handgun muzzle was pressed tightly to the side of Micheline's neck, just under the right earlobe. Her body immediately tensed and froze.

"Easy now, lady," beckoned the gritty male voice from behind her. "Take slow steps forward into the bank."

Micheline stood still and refused to step forward.

"Now, goddammit! I've got a loaded nine-millimeter Walther pistol at the back of your neck. Move inside, or I'll clip your ass right here on the sidewalk. Your family can mourn your loss for an act of sheer stupidity. What do you say?"

Micheline complied and edged her feet forward slowly. She knew all too well what type of damage the discharge from a Walther nine-millimeter bullet could do. She kept a similar model of her own back at the condo.

"All right," she replied. "Take it easy. I hear you loud and clear. I'm moving forward."

The security guard immediately backed away from the front entrance doors and allowed his accomplice to direct Micheline into the bank. After they were completely inside the building's entranceway, the guard securely locked the front entrance doors.

"Eyes straight ahead," commanded the unseen gunman from behind her.

Micheline was escorted up a dozen stairs and came to the open foyer at the top. Her eyes scanned the marble lobby for any sign of Jenny. Further ahead, on the far side of the central wooden check-writing stand, three bodies were spread face-down on the cold tile floor. There was no movement from either of the victims. Blood pooled near gaping head wounds. Two females, one male. Neither of the women was Jenny.

Micheline froze in her tracks. She had inadvertently stumbled upon a bank robbery in progress. The white van was obviously the get-away vehicle. Still, there was no sign of Jenny. Micheline scanned the periphery. Jenny's office was located on the second floor, accessible from an open-air staircase toward the back of the building.

"Move forward toward the roped-off teller line and get down on your knees," demanded the gravelly voice from behind her. Micheline glanced down at the marble tile floor and observed a pair of heavy black boots and matching black pants.

"What should I do now?" Marcell Landry, the security guard, asked.

"Change into your tactical gear," the gravelly-voiced gunman instructed. "It's time to take this party to the next level. Be quick about it, too. There's no telling if this lady's just an unlucky bank customer or not. There might be someone waiting for her on the outside. Better safe than sorry, I always say."

Micheline moved slowly and predictably. She had gotten a good look at Marcell Landry, who appeared to be the inside man and noticed a small tattoo on the side of the man's neck. A red and black wolf's head. It was the same design Wade Branigan had tattooed on his left upper arm. Micheline recognized it from mug shots as a prison gang tattoo associated with inmates who had served time at the Lompoc Federal Correctional Institution. It was a medium-security penitentiary with an adjacent minimum-security satellite camp located just north of Santa Barbara.

"There's no one waiting outside for me," Micheline said. She attempted to open a line of communication with the gunman.

"Please don't hurt me. I'm here by myself. I just stopped by to pick up my new checkbooks. Honest. I'm no threat to you."

"Down on the floor, lady," the whiskey-laced voice commanded angrily from behind her. "I won't ask again. Do it now."

Micheline complied obediently and got down on her knees. She turned her head around as she did so to get a good glimpse of the man holding a gun on her. What she saw scared the hell out of her.

The gunman was dressed in black from head to toe, including a steel facemask, like a hockey goalie, body armor, and gloves. True to his word, he gripped a nine-millimeter Walther pistol in his gloved right hand.

To be staring down the barrel of a loaded weapon at close range was not what Micheline had envisioned when she rose from the bed that morning.

Somehow, I've got to turn this situation upside down.

Carefully and unseen by the perpetrators, Micheline gently maneuvered her left hand inside the fold of her cotton blazer. She reached toward the grip of her six-shot primary weapon.

"Turn and face the other way," the gunman shouted.

Micheline mentally prepared herself to withdraw her weapon and fire it at a moment's notice.

Damn it! I haven't even had my morning cup of coffee yet.

Twenty-Three

The Paradise Gentlemen's Club

Gaslamp Quarter, San Diego

Tuesday, November 24th

It was barely seven o'clock in the morning after a tedious double holiday week shift, and Lieutenant Frank Salvatore felt an immediate sense of satisfaction as he abruptly downed a tequila shot and gripped an ice-cold bottle chaser of Bud Light beer in his hand.

Sergeant Kevin McCaffrey had already downed six fingers' worth of single malt whiskey and was cradling a bottle of Modelo Especial lager beer as if it were a long-lost friend.

Surrounding the officers at two separate round tables that had been pushed together, still in their navy-blue uniforms and radio and weapons heavy, sat four of their friends and associates from two other San Diego area patrol departments.

Representing the Clairemont district were Ezekiel Zorzetto and Hayley Rawlins. Sitting opposite them from National City, a southern district adjacent to Chula Vista, were Stanley Holloway and Vickie Diamantes. Each of the officers was wearing their patrol uniforms, were officially off-duty, smelled like the inside of a gym locker room, and were tired and thirsty as hell.

Vanessa Nguyen, wearing only a black slinky string bikini with a thin gold necklace and black leather high heel shoes, approached the police brigade and offered a perfunctory smile. She reached toward the back of McCaffrey's head and tugged intimately at the red strands of hair, effectively pulling his face into her abundant cleavage.

"Tough night?" she asked the group while Kevin inhaled deeply and enjoyed the foreplay of Vanessa's seductive advances. She was expecting a big tip from the foul-mouthed and drunken police officer who frequented the club on his off-duty hours.

"It was a long one, that's for sure," Frank admitted. "We all pulled double shifts last night. That's what happens when you get to a holiday week toward the end of the year. Everyone in the department starts taking whatever leftover vacation time they had accumulated throughout the year. Sorry saps like us have to make up for the open shifts. The overtime pay is about the only benefit, I guess."

The young Vietnamese beauty let go of Kevin's hair and eyed his companions. She especially liked the shoulder patches displayed on the uniforms of the National City patrol officers. The embroidered design included a small colorful circle with a picture of Minerva, the Roman goddess of wisdom, gazing over a miner who works near the Sacrament River. A grizzly bear rests at Minerva's feet and ships ply the river. The Sierra Nevada Mountains rise in the background, and the state motto, Eureka, sits over the top of the mountain range, which refers to the discovery of gold in California in the 1840s.

"What would you all like to drink?" she asked. "Ladies first. Hayley?"

Hayley Rawlins looked thoughtful. She pulled an elastic band from her dark brown ponytail and allowed her hair to cascade across her shoulders. "A bottle of Blue Moon White Belgian, please."

"Okay. Vickie, what about you? Some of that black licorice liqueur you like so much?"

"Coffee, black," the pretty female patrol officer replied immediately. "No ouzo today. Let me have two breakfast burritos with hot sauce on the side, and some slices of buttered toast and strawberry jam. A couple of aspirin, too, if you have any."

"Got it," Vanessa confirmed. "You've got a headache from spending too much time with these wise guys, and you've worked up an incredible appetite."

"Oh, she's got such a wicked sense of humor," Kevin commented. "I'd like to start some funny business of my own with her if you know what I mean."

"Gentlemen, what will it be today?"

"Coors Light," Zeke Zorzetto replied.

"Same for me," Stan Holloway added.

"Very good," Vanessa said. "Any other food while I put your orders in at the bar? Benito grills up a mean batch of chorizo and tomato scrambled eggs. They come with a stack of hot freshly made tortillas and mild salsa."

"Sure thing, doll," Kevin said. "Bring some for everybody. Make sure the salsa is extra spicy. I'm feeling good about today."

"Load some feta cheese on top of mine, will you please, Van?" Vickie Diamantes requested.

Vanessa smiled and winked toward Kevin as she turned and swung her hips on her way toward the bar.

"Are you getting a little action on the side that I don't know about?" Frank asked his partner warily.

Kevin smiled slyly. "I'm working on it. I think she likes me."

"I think she just likes the fat wad of cash from your back pocket," Zeke called out. "And now she knows you're picking up some extra overtime pay this week. Christmas is coming early for her."

"You know, guys," Hayley said, "as much as I like your company, a strip joint isn't exactly the sophisticated hangout spot I like to spend my off-hours time in."

"We get it," Zeke replied amicably. "This place isn't a chic bistro or a five-star restaurant. But it's not just a male macho thing that brings us here. By coming here regularly on our time off, we stay connected with the more shady and felonious elements of our society. It keeps everything, including the rules of justice, in perfect balance."

"Oh, bullshit!" Vickie spouted with a laugh. "You just like the free ass and titty show. Admit it."

Zeke threw his hands up in mock defense and smiled. "Guilty as charged, okay? They have some of the best-looking women in San Diego working here, the present company already included and accounted for. If I were a movie talent scout, this is the place I'd come to check resumes and phone numbers for my next R-rated action flick."

Stan laughed. "That's certainly why I love coming here with all of you. I mean, you guys are great and all, but check out Melina up there on the stage. That woman has some fine curves. I'd love to take her home with me and never let her go."

"I just want her high heels," Hayley remarked.

"And I might consider a tattoo like the butterfly she has painted on her ass," Vickie offered.

Frank looked concerned. "Hey Vickie, how come you're not having any alcohol this morning? Are you feeling all right? You normally have a couple of shots of ouzo or that tree resin wine you like so much."

"Yeah, well," the female officer blushed and shrugged her shoulders. "Turns out, I'm going to have a little Athena to take care of by next summer."

"Oh, fuck! You're pregnant!" Kevin exclaimed. "That's incredible. The baby's not Zeke's, is it? She'd be ugly in all sorts of ways if that's the case."

"Ha Ha!" Zeke laughed appreciatively at his friend's banter. "I'm not that fortunate, of course. Vickie's been dating a corporate attorney for the past few months. He's a real cool guy, too. He got drafted by the Raiders as a running back right out of college, then tore up his knee in a motorcycle accident. He went back to school to get his law degree. He's got a condo overlooking the ocean near La Jolla Cove. This young lady's going to be living in style someday soon."

"Well, congratulations, my dear," Frank said and raised his beer. "I'm very happy for you."

"We all are," Stan said.

"Thank you," Vickie replied.

"I take it this attorney does know about the baby, right?" Hayley inquired.

Vickie smiled cheerfully. "Yes, he does," she said. "He's incredibly happy about this unexpected blessing. He asked me to take a trip with him to Catalina Island next weekend. I'm hopeful that he's going to propose."

"He'd be a fool not to," Stan said. "We'll keep our fingers crossed for you."

Vickie was about to say something else when suddenly the officers' radios squawked with the voice of the female dispatcher on call.

"All units, we have a 211 at Fidelity National Savings and Loan, Gaslamp Quarter, at the intersection of Fifth Avenue and Island Avenue. Be advised, we have received reports of shots fired. There may be hostages inside."

"Jesus, that's right across the fucking street!" Kevin stammered alarmingly.

Frank locked eyes with his companions and then steadied his gaze on Zeke. "We've got this, right?" he asked.

"Damn straight, we do," Zeke responded without hesitation.

"All right," Frank said. "Kevin and I will go around to the back parking lot and surveille the situation from there. The rest of you, position yourselves across from the front entrance on either side of the building. We'll effectively form a triangle perimeter to prevent them from getting away, and to prevent any innocent bystanders from accidentally wandering onto the scene."

"Got it," Zeke confirmed.

"I'll call it in," Stan announced.

Vanessa approached the tables with the officers' drinks.

"Sorry, doll," Kevin called out. "We just got an emergency call from the bank across the street. A robbery is going down and the bandits have real guns. Do us all a favor and keep everyone inside the club until the commotion is over. I'll be back later to get a drink and your phone number. You and I are going to have some fun later on."

"Oh, my!" Vanessa cried. "Please, be careful!"

The patrol officers rose from their seats. Adrenaline was already rushing through their veins like steam from a hot tea kettle. They headed as a single unit immediately toward the front entrance of the club with their eyes alert and their guns drawn.

Twenty-Four

Inside the bank, Micheline made a mental note as a third gunman dressed in full black military tactical gear, including black steel face-mask and body armor, emerged from the open bank vault with two large Pullman suitcases. He struggled to maneuver the gray metallic suitcases with silver handles across the bank foyer floor.

One or the other of the cases kept turning sideways awkwardly as the robber attempted to make his way to the rear entrance of the bank. The luggage cases were obviously heavy and loaded with cash or the contents of safety deposit boxes from inside the vault.

But wasn't the white van parked out front meant to be their getaway vehicle? This made no sense.

"Let's go, guys!" the criminal clad in black shouted with his voice garbled almost unintelligibly by the protective steel facemask.

Oh wait, don't forget about the two SUVs in the back parking lot.

"The missing bitch was hiding in the back office. She tripped the silent alarm before I could stop her. We need to move up our time-table. We have less than two minutes. Set everything in motion as we planned."

Micheline assumed that Jenny may have been the unfortunate victim in the back office who had set off the silent alarm.

Had they hurt her? Had she met the same fate as her former colleagues? Was her motionless body spread on the cold tile floor in a crimson pool of her own blood?

206

Micheline was not about to let these men get the drop on her completely. She needed a plan, and quickly, as the fingers of her left hand burrowed deeper into the recesses of her jacket.

Almost there.

Micheline noted the Sig Sauer nine-millimeter pistol holstered at the waistline of the man who was busy rolling the suitcases across the bank foyer.

She wanted to act immediately. The bandit was preoccupied with the heavy and unruly suitcases. But instinct told her to hold back and to be patient. She was still uncertain how many intruders had entered the bank, or where they were located. She also needed to know if there were any more employees in imminent danger inside the bank whose lives could yet be saved.

Micheline looked upstairs to the rear of the bank.

Thank God, she's alive!

Jenny was being escorted by two robbers clad in full black tactical gear from a second-floor office. These thieves matched the description of the gang who had robbed the credit union armored car a few weeks before. They were proficient, methodical, well-armed, and appeared to have skillsets that came from military training.

Each of the two assailants on either side of Jenny cradled an M4 carbine military assault rifle in their hands. Micheline recognized the model as one she had previously test-fired at the gun range. The standard M4 carbine rifle had a selector switch for semi-automatic and three-round-burst firing modes. Micheline knew that a variant of the M4 designated the A1 model included a fully automatic firing mode and that both models could be accessorized by mounting a grenade launcher to the lower handguard.

This bank robbery crew had come prepared for close-quarter engagement with law enforcement. Each member of this unit wore a full bulletproof tactical body armor protective suit, including steel facemasks and ceramic level III ballistic plates to cover all vital and sensitive body parts from head to toe. The bulletproof plates could stop a round fired from an AR-15 or AK-47 rifle burst. The suits were sleek and ergonomic, designed for comfort and agility. Wide panels on both their belts and thigh modules were packed with extra ammo cartridges.

They were fully prepared to battle it out with SWAT units or police patrol forces if it came to that.

Micheline focused her attention on Jenny. From the distance, Jenny's facial expression was void of emotion. Her movements were rigid and stiff. Her complexion was pale. A trickle of blood ran from a gash on her forehead down upon her cheekbones. Droplets of blood had noticeably splattered across her white silk blouse, too. She appeared to offer no resistance to the heavily armed criminals and was obviously obeying their commands by marching in step with them under duress.

The robber who had been manhandling the two suitcases across the marble foyer suddenly stopped and stared at Micheline on her knees on the floor.

"Hey, how the fuck did she get in here?"

"She's an uninvited guest," the gunman behind Micheline barked back. "She's just a customer who wanted to pick up her new checkbooks. She showed up at the front door out of nowhere. Don't worry, I've got her covered."

"Did you disarm her?"

"What do you mean?"

The shrill sound of police sirens wailed from the street outside the front of the bank. Officers had arrived on the scene and were beginning to create a protective perimeter around the bank building by blockading the nearby cross streets.

Marcell Landry, who was now dressed in full-body combat gear, brandished an Uzi Pro submachine gun. He moved briskly around the corner from the front entranceway and crouched low to the marble floor.

"Everybody out the back, now!" he commanded loudly. "The police are already taking up flanking positions out front, and they'll be moving in around back soon. The package is now armed. Let's go!"

The armed assailants who escorted Jenny down the stairs simultaneously grabbed her by the arms and propelled her toward the back entrance of the bank. Jenny turned her head and caught momentary sight of Micheline on her knees and held at gunpoint. Her eyes widened in sheer terror and surprise.

They were taking her as a hostage!

"What about this one?" the gunman behind Micheline asked. "Should we bring her along for extra insurance?"

"She's a cop!" the robber with the suitcases yelled. He tugged on the suitcases and accelerated his stride toward the back entrance of the bank.

"Shoot her now and let's get out of here!"

Micheline gritted her teeth and squeezed her left hand around the contoured butt of her six-shot double-action .38-caliber revolver. It was now or never.

"Oh, shit!" the gunman lamented loudly. He turned his body to face squarely toward Micheline.

Suddenly, multiple three-shot-bursts of gunfire could be heard in quick succession from outside the back of the bank building. A shoot-out with police on the scene was already taking place.

Micheline pivoted and withdrew her primary weapon in a single motion. She recognized that her assailants wore bulletproof tactical gear. Any shot to the face, the upper body, or legs would be useless. It had to be a clear shot to an exposed body part or appendage to wound them or to put them down for good.

Micheline tumbled onto her side and placed the muzzle of her Combat Masterpiece directly to the back of the kneecap of the man standing over her. She pulled the trigger and fired a single round.

The gunman immediately screamed in agony. Blood, bone, fabric, and cartilage exploded across the floor tiles. The gunman collapsed backward heavily and writhed in extreme pain.

Micheline wasted no time. She immediately got back on her feet and steadied her aim toward the front entranceway of the bank.

Marcell Landry knelt against the far wall around the corner from the front entrance stairway. He was nervously checking his watch and counting down in one-second intervals with his fingers.

A loud explosion detonated from outside the front exterior of the bank. Moments later, a concussive shock wave penetrated the interior foyer of the bank along with a hail of shattered glass, broken wood and bricks, and a thick darkened cloud of concrete dust.

The white van. It must have been packed with explosives to create a defensive diversion.

Micheline quickly regained her balance and aligned her aim toward the front entranceway. She pulled the trigger and watched as the back of Marcell Landry's head burst violently into a viscid red cloud of blood and brain matter. His lifeless body fell limply forward onto the top steps in the debris-laden marble foyer.

The assailant with the bloodied missing kneecap grabbed Micheline by the ankle with his gloved left hand. He was still lucid and had regained a firm grip with his right hand of the Walther pistol that he had trained on Micheline.

Micheline blinked momentarily as the thought occurred to her that two of the robbers carried similar firearm models to those she had in her own collection at home. They were popular models for self-defense, but the coincidence was unnerving, nonetheless.

The seasoned detective quickly swiveled on her right foot and kicked the nine-millimeter pistol out of the gunman's hand with her left foot. The double-action German-made handgun released from the bank robber's grasp and clattered harmlessly across the tile floor.

Micheline realized that shooting the man cloaked in full body armor from this angle and close distance would be futile. She reached down with her right hand and, using her legs to squat as if from a power lift position, she heaved the man up and over onto his side. She grabbed the man's facemask harshly, ripped it away from his face, and flung it like a frisbee toward the open bank vault.

"You're an ugly motherfucker, aren't you?" Micheline sneered bitterly. She gave her assailant a steady hard glare.

"Don't worry," she said. "I'll get you something for the headache later."

The gunman attempted to thrash wildly on the floor. Micheline carefully adjusted her left-handed grip on the barrel of her Combat Masterpiece. She raised her clenched fist up above her head and then slammed the butt end of her firearm across the back of the criminal's exposed skull. The man's face slammed against the marble tile floor and the bank robber's body went limp into unconsciousness.

Micheline turned without hesitation and rushed toward the rear exit of the bank. She had to reach the three bank robbers who had exited into the parking lot before they were able to force Jenny into their getaway vehicle to drive away.

That was their plan, right? To escape in the two SUVs that were parked in the back lot. But what if they had a helicopter waiting or some other imaginative scheme planned for their escape?

Micheline had no time to consider the myriad of alternative getaway options the robbers may have devised. She burst through the rear exit door and felt her own adrenaline kick in. Her heartbeat was throbbing fast, and her breaths were steady and strong. She was right behind them and gaining ground with each second that passed.

Bright sunshine was the first thing Micheline noticed as she stepped openly into the unprotected zone of the macadam parking lot. She was momentarily disoriented as her eyes adjusted to the streaming sunlight.

Next, as she looked down to the pavement, she saw a pool of blood and a patrol officer's body laid prone on the ground. There were multiple gaping gunshot wounds to the victim's chest and abdomen. An earth-toned nine-millimeter Beretta handgun lay on the ground near to the body.

Micheline gazed more closely. She recognized the victim. It was Lieutenant Frank Salvatore.

"Oh, no! What was the lieutenant doing in this part of the city this early in the morning? Fuck!"

Three police cruisers had parked sideways to form a blockade near the street entrance to the parking lot. Officers had exited their vehicles and crouched defensively on the far side facing inward toward the bank. Some held assault rifles, others their service handguns.

Two of the bank robbers with M4 carbine assault rifles took cover behind the white Volvo SUV, and a third gunman stood behind the red four-door Jeep.

The two assailants who had taken Jenny hostage had already ushered her into the backseat of the white Volvo XC-90 SUV with dark tinted windows. One of the robbers had climbed into the backseat to guard their hostage, while the other slid into the front passenger's seat and slammed the door shut. The engine was running.

But where could they go? The police barricade had them securely hemmed in.

The rear passenger window of the white SUV was lowered several inches to expose a view of a bloodied hostage with the muzzle of a rifle pointed at Jenny's head.

One of the robbers who had exited the bank, and who had called Micheline out as a cop, had loaded the suitcases into the rear of the white SUV. Micheline noted at least six suitcases piled into the back of the Volvo cargo area before the rear tailgate was slammed shut. She briefly wondered if there were more suitcases piled into the back of the red four-door Jeep Rubicon.

Micheline stopped short and aimed at the back of the man's legs. She pulled the trigger. The bullet screamed closely past the intended target and ricocheted off the rear bumper of the SUV.

The bank robber turned quickly with an M4 carbine assault rifle in his grasp. Micheline's eyes widened in shock and terror. An M320 grenade launcher had been mounted to the lower handguard of the weapon.

Micheline instinctively pulled the trigger of her K-38 Combat Masterpiece one more time and swiftly dove to the ground as a grenade shot past her toward the rear of the bank building.

There was an incredible incendiary explosion, a burst of white light, a concussive blast, and a thunderous avalanche as bricks and concrete blocks from the building's outer wall cascaded down to the ground below.

The air was immediately sucked from Micheline's lungs. She rolled across the macadam lot for several seconds, stunned, with her ears ringing and her head aching intensely.

Micheline heard muffled shouts and more gunfire exchanged ahead of her. She positioned herself onto her side. She picked up her primary weapon and agilely raised herself up on one knee.

She recognized Sergeant Kevin McCaffrey in his patrol uniform. The Del Mar patrol cop was attempting to surprise the gunman taking cover behind the red four-door Jeep. Combined, all three of the bank heist gunmen were facing toward the street and were engaged in heavy fully automatic gunfire at the three police cruisers near the parking lot entrance.

"Stop firing, or we'll execute the hostage!" the gunman behind the red Jeep called out.

"We're leaving now, or she's dead. Do you hear me? Clear a path to the street."

There was a momentary lull in the gunfire exchange. One by one, the police officers behind their patrol vehicles lowered their weapons. A tense silence ensued. No one was about to expose themselves by getting into the driver's seats of the parked patrol cars.

The gunman with the grenade launcher was crouched low behind the white SUV. He reloaded another grenade into its chamber, then popped up unexpectedly and turned toward the three police cruisers.

He immediately discharged his weapon. The officers who had used the patrol cars as a protective shield were now directly in the line of fire. They spread away from their vehicles in a panic as all three squad cars exploded in a blaze of fire and were lifted several feet into the air. The skeleton frames of the demolished patrol vehicles tumbled and crashed back down to the ground with a deafening series of overlapping auditory quakes.

McCaffrey fired a shot at the gunman taking a stance by the red four-door Jeep Rubicon. The bullet struck him solidly in the middle of the back. There was an intense muzzle flash. McCaffrey's hands were noticeably pushed upward and back from the resulting concussion of the revolver being fired.

The impact of the .44 Magnum bullet to the ceramic shielded vest forcefully thrust the robber awkwardly against the rear door of the Jeep but did not draw blood. McCaffrey adjusted his position accordingly and aimed slightly higher. He pulled the trigger a second time. He watched intently as the back of the gunman's head exploded like a ripened tomato. The steel facemask crashed against the top of the red Jeep and clattered to the pavement along with the twitching corpse of the dead gunman.

Micheline immediately took aim and fired two shots in rapid succession at the gunman with the grenade launcher. He stood to the right side of the white Volvo. The bullets hit their intended target in the upper body, but the protective armor worn by the gunman effectively repelled both rounds.

With six shots fired, Micheline's Combat Masterpiece was depleted of ammunition. There was no place to hide, and Micheline had no time to reload her weapon.

The gunman to the left opened the driver's side door to the White Volvo SUV and climbed in. Seconds later, the sport utility vehicle's engine began revving with more power.

McCaffrey crept closer to the white SUV and focused his aim on the gunman with the grenade launcher, who had dropped his weapon and was reaching for the handle of the rear passenger door.

"No, McCaffrey!" Micheline yelled at the top of her lungs.

"They have a hostage! Don't shoot!"

Micheline instinctively dropped her Combat Masterpiece and reached down to her left ankle. She removed her five-shot backup revolver and immediately turned toward the uniformed Del Mar patrol cop.

"Sergeant!" Micheline barked one final time.

"Don't do it! I'm begging you."

Within seconds, two separate gunshots erupted in quick succession from the bank building behind her. Micheline felt the high velocity of both bullets sail over her left shoulder. The first struck McCaffrey in the side of the neck. As the Del Mar patrolman's body twisted awkwardly around, the second bullet caught the sergeant in the middle of the chest, and McCaffrey collapsed to his knees, then fell face forward to the parking lot pavement.

Micheline whirled around. She was shocked. The gunman with the missing kneecap had survived the grenade blast. Even with the limited use of one leg, he had painstakingly crawled through the chaos and broken rubble to reach the outdoor battleground in the parking lot.

The gunman steadied himself and fired three more shots with his Walther nine-millimeter pistol. There was a momentary pause separating each individual pull of the gunman's trigger.

One Mississippi. Boom!

The first round struck Micheline in the upper chest area on her right side. She was knocked back a few steps, and she breathed in heavily.

Two Mississippi. Boom!

The second bullet struck her in the upper right shoulder. Micheline grimaced in extreme pain. She raised her backup weapon with her left hand and squeezed the trigger.

Three Mississippi. Boom!

The gunman's third shot clipped Micheline in the upper right thigh. She witnessed her own shot strike the perpetrator in the throat, right before the third bullet ripped another hole in her tender flesh. She collapsed to the ground heavily and slammed her head against the hardened macadam surface of the parking lot.

Blood began to course like a slow meandering stream on the pavement around Micheline's crippled body.

The clear blue sky suddenly spun in ever-widening circles. Micheline felt drugged. Her vision clouded. She overheard the strained but professional voice of Ana on dispatch emanating from the police band radio clipped to Sergeant McCaffrey's duty belt.

"All units," she beckoned. "We have a two-eleven in progress, Code nine-nine-nine! Officers down. Multiple gunmen with automatic assault weapons and artillery. SWAT and Bomb Squad are enroute. Fidelity National Savings and Loan Bank in the Gaslamp Quarter at the corner of Fifth Avenue and Island Avenue."

The passenger side windows, front and back, of the white Volvo SUV, began to slide down further. Two M4 fully automatic carbine rifle barrel muzzles protruded from the darkened interior. An abrupt three-round burst of gunfire from each rifle exploded in overlapping sequences. The gunmen appeared to be laying cover fire toward the street entrance to the bank parking lot. Police had repositioned themselves behind vehicles parked on the opposite side of the street.

Micheline heard another body collapse to the pavement nearby but saw nothing. Voices shouted. There was a distinct smell of burnt fuel and smoke. Micheline was in a delirious state of mind. She was drifting into unconsciousness fast.

I can't lose her! Not like this.

The engine of the powerful white Volvo XC-90 SUV roared high. Suddenly the vehicle accelerated toward a chain-link fence at the back of the bank property. It crashed through an eight-foot-wide section as though the perimeter fence had been cut beforehand and sped sharply down a narrow alleyway.

Micheline felt nauseous and weak. For a moment, she thought she observed a heavy crack of thunder and lightning in the sky above. Then her eyes closed tightly, and everything faded to black.

Twenty-Five

Quick flashes of brilliant incandescence surged through Micheline's temples and burned red hot. Beads of perspiration rolled intermittently from her forehead, soaking the heavily starched pillow beneath her head.

She attempted to thrash violently but remained immobile. Her legs and arms appeared to be locked under great pressure she was unable to break free from. Everything moved in slow motion. Blackness faded ploddingly as if it were an endless void in a nebulous cloud from which tiny stars of firelight ignited one by one.

Micheline sucked in a deep lungful of air and forced her to escape from oblivion with all the malevolent rage she could summon. Scratchy cotton sheets twisted in knots, warm and moistened with sweat.

Micheline struggled to open her eyes toward the light. She groaned in agony as the pain of her gunshot wounds returned across her upper right torso and the upper portion of her right leg. Explosions rippled through her mind as she neared consciousness. Her eyelids fluttered open convulsively. Blurred images slowly settled into focus.

She reclined stiffly upon a lumpy mattress. Her surroundings were stark and austere. There was a sterile smell of disinfectant permeating the surrounding air.

She was in a hospital room by herself, she reasoned. An intravenous drip line was attached to her left forearm. Her right arm felt heavy and weighed down as if someone were holding her in place. The sounds of nearby monitors beeped in rhythm with her racing heart. She tried to relax her breathing.

One step at a time.

Sharp pains jabbed various parts of her body, especially her upper chest, her right shoulder, and her upper right thigh. She felt light-headed and weak. The anesthesia was beginning to wear off. The pain from the surgical incisions and the stitching of her wounds was beginning to increase like an electric shock.

A nurse in blue scrubs entered the room. She smiled brightly. Micheline blinked several times to ensure she wasn't dreaming.

"Hello, Micheline," the nurse said warmly. "It's nice to see you finally awake. How are you feeling today?"

Micheline was confused. "Shayna?"

"Yes, it's me," Shayna Vasquez replied. "I'm so glad that you're back with us. I was hoping that you'd wake up on my shift."

Micheline was still heavily sedated. "But you work in a commercial bakery, and I don't see any flour or dough."

Shayna laughed. "That's the meds talking. But you're right. When we first met, I used to work in a bread bakery. It's good to know that your memory is still intact."

"I don't understand," Micheline mumbled incoherently. "Where am I?"

"You're a patient at Scripps Memorial Hospital in La Jolla."

"Okay, but how is it that you're here?"

"Since we last spoke to one another I earned my LPN degree. I'm now a licensed practical nurse, and I'm still working toward my R.N. degree. I left the bakery a few months ago after you helped me to move on with my life."

"It's nice to hear a friendly voice," Micheline said.

Shayna smiled at the injured detective. "The hospital offered me a job. They're even paying for my education now, so it's been a double win for me."

"That's wonderful."

"And I have you to thank for helping me to get started with all of that. If you hadn't come along when you did, I might be dead right now, or still suffering under Oscar's control. I'm happy that I can offer to take care of you while your wounds heal."

"I still don't understand," Micheline said. She felt groggy and off-balance. Her forehead throbbed with a jabbing ache. She attempted to raise her right arm, but it was tethered to the right bedside railing.

"Handcuffs?" she asked alarmingly. "What the hell's going on?"

"Try to stay still," Shayna said soothingly. "You were brought into surgery early on Tuesday morning. That was two days ago, Micheline, after the bank robbery downtown in the Gaslamp Quarter. The story made the national TV news. The police reported that you killed several people at the bank, and they want to question you when you wake up. I'm sure it's only a formality."

"Oh, shit!" Micheline grumbled. "Everything hurts. My head, my chest, my leg. What day is today, Shayna?"

"It's late on Thursday afternoon. Today is Thanksgiving Day. The football games are already over from what I hear. But it's good that you had a chance to rest and that you're coming around now. The surgeon was able to remove two of the bullets that penetrated your chest and leg. The gunshot to your shoulder was a through-and-through. You're all patched up now."

"I ache all over."

"Amazingly, none of the bullets struck any of your tattoos, even the one that passed through the back of your shoulder. You're quite an art exhibit when you're naked if I may say so."

"You now know more about me than I do about you, Shayna," Micheline said with a soft laugh.

Shayna smiled. "The good news is that you're expected to make a full recovery over time. You'll need physical therapy, of course. But thankfully, there was no major tissue damage. Each of the bullets that were removed had struck thick muscle. You can credit your weight-lifting and workout routine for protecting you."

"I'm happy to hear that, of course. But I only took down the men attempting to rob the bank. Why would the police restrain me?"

"I heard them say they have evidence against you. I believe in you, Micheline. Just rest, please. You need to get your strength back. The police will be in to speak to you shortly. I'm sure it's just a misunderstanding that you'll be able to explain when you're feeling back to normal again. Let me record some updates on your chart."

Micheline inhaled another deep breath. She had lost two precious days, and this day had not started out anything like she would have hoped. Shayna smiled at her again while making notations on a clipboard chart attached to the bottom of the bed.

A doctor entered the room abruptly without comment or introduction. He was a dark-skinned Indian with a thick black beard and a white turban wrapped neatly atop his head. His white lab coat was badly wrinkled, as was his pale-yellow dress shirt.

He looks as bad as I feel.

"She's conscious?" the doctor asked LPN Shayna Vasquez.

"Yes, doctor," Shayna replied. "She woke up a few minutes ago. The anesthesia is beginning to wear off, and she's feeling the pain from her surgical incisions."

"Uh-huh," the doctor mumbled acidly.

He must be an intern. His bedside manner is a joke, and he still can't afford to send his laundry out to be pressed.

The doctor checked the heart monitor first, then looked toward the nurse. "She's coherent?" he asked.

"Yes, doctor," Shayna replied. "She's lucid and her memory appears to be fully intact."

The doctor hesitated to get too close to his patient. He kept his distance and looked in both of Micheline's eyes with a penlight that he pulled from the breast pocket of his wrinkled dress shirt.

I don't know what you expect to see from that far away.

The doctor appeared satisfied with the results. He nodded toward Shayna, acknowledging her presence and her bravery for attending to the needs of a criminal, and then turned immediately and left the room.

The hospital room door swung open as the doctor made his hasty exit. A uniformed police officer stood guard outside the doorway. The doctor motioned with his hands to someone waiting in the hallway, just past Micheline's line of sight.

"Not much for bedside manner, is he?" Micheline remarked.

"Sorry about that," Shayna said to her. "He's not usually like that. He's an intern doing his surgical residency here. I think the police presence in the hallway and the handcuffs put him on edge."

"You think?" Micheline replied in a mock tone. "He's not the surgeon who operated on me, is he?"

"Oh, no, Micheline," Shayna replied. "The attending physician performed the operation. Georgie, er, I mean Doctor Sharma-Raval, whom you just met, is on rotation and is only conducting his rounds tonight. Your surgeon was Dr. Mukund Ramesh. He's known to be one of the finest surgeons on the west coast and an avid tennis fan from what I hear."

"I get it," Micheline accepted. "Your buddy Georgie didn't seem to like me too much."

"He'll get over it. Don't worry about that."

"Can you get me something for the pain, please?"

"Yes, of course. I'll see what I can do about that. I'll be back soon to check on you, Micheline. Get your rest for now, please. I'm worried about you."

"Thank you, Shayna. It feels good to have you here, the present circumstances notwithstanding. I'll be okay. Promise."

Shayna smiled warmly at her recovering patient and gently touched Micheline's arm before she left the room. As she turned down the hallway to tend to her other duties, Micheline noted that the uniformed officer outside her room gawked unabashedly at Shayna as she walked away.

Checking out her ass, I'll bet! He'd better be careful. I'll kick him in the balls if he even thinks to look at me that way.

Twenty-Six

The door swung open sharply. Four familiar individuals entered the hospital room, including District Attorney Rosalyn Whittaker, Assistant Prosecuting Attorney Mark Longfellow, Captain Phillip Kovacs, head of the San Diego County Robbery Unit, and Detective Kelly Van Horn.

"What, no flowers?" Micheline asked, attempting to lighten the mood that was clearly communicated by their collective deadpan facial expressions.

"What could possibly be going through your minds right now?"

Micheline's spirits rose in anticipation that she might get a laugh, then faded quickly as the visitors' dispirited countenances left the room more vacant than before. Micheline could smell the trouble and conflict that was brewing in their minds darker than any coffee she had ever tasted.

District Attorney Rosalyn Whittaker glared at Micheline with a venomous stare. "I'm asking myself right now," she opened maliciously, "how it is someone I put so much trust in could have so disastrously failed all expectations? You have single-handedly created a media shitstorm of unprecedented proportions, Detective Avila!"

"I can explain," Micheline attempted to interrupt.

"To make matters worse," the DA pressed on, "I missed the Cowboys' game earlier today. Why? Because I have to be here to question you on Thanksgiving Day instead of being at home enjoying a succulent roast turkey dinner slathered in garlic herb butter and all the fixings."

"I don't understand," Micheline replied evenly. She knew enough to keep her temper in check, even though the emotions were rising inside herself like an erupting volcano. All she wanted to do was to break free and to scream *"What the fuck is wrong with you people? I'm innocent!"* at the top of her lungs.

"Micheline," Assistant Prosecuting Attorney Mark Longfellow interceded. "What were you thinking? We have you on closed-circuit surveillance footage from across the street from the bank parking lot. You were clearly seen exiting the rear of the bank along with your co-conspirators."

"Again, I can explain," Micheline pleaded.

Mark shook his head and index finger at the detective. "The tapes show you discharging your weapon at one of the bank robbers, and then attacking a uniformed off-duty police officer outside in the parking lot. An officer, I may add, that you've encountered previously during the Samantha Miller murder investigation."

"He aimed his gun toward the backseat of the SUV and prepared to fire. He was obviously inebriated and carried a .44 Magnum. He could have killed the hostage."

"I don't want to hear it. Then, after Sergeant McCaffrey went down, you turned around and shot the gunman who killed that brave off-duty officer. Plus, there are more bodies inside the bank. It's just a matter of time before the forensics report comes back and links you to those bodies as well. How the hell did you think you'd get away with this, Detective?"

"You're jumping to conclusions here," Micheline interjected. "Yes, I took down one of the robbers inside the bank and disabled another. Then I followed the others outside as they attempted to flee the scene. I tried to stop them. They were taking Jenny Casella, a bank employee, as a hostage, and they had at least a half dozen suitcases that I assume were full of cash piled in the backs of the two SUVs."

"Your assumptions are wrong," Mark Longfellow said. "The suitcases were filled with, guess what? Fucking clothes, and nothing else."

"And how is it that you came to be inside the bank at least ninety minutes before the bank was due to open?" asked Captain Phillip Kovacs, head of the Robbery Unit for the San Diego County Sheriff's Department.

Micheline considered Kovacs to be both coach and mentor. He was a former Navy Seal and an experienced investigator with more than twenty years of service to the police forces in both Los Angeles and San Diego.

"Phil, it's no secret around the department that Jenny Casella and I are personal friends. We had a fight the other night. When I returned home the evening after the visit to meet with Samantha Miller's parents, Jenny was already inside my condo. She had a box with her, and she was removing her personal items. She was jealous that I was seen out in public with another woman, who happened to be a witness to the Samantha Miller murder. Jenny wanted to put an end to our friendship. That would've been Monday night."

"That still doesn't explain your presence at the bank on Tuesday morning," Kovacs huffed.

Micheline pressed on unperturbed. "I pass the bank every morning on my drive into work. I drive straight through the Gaslamp Quarter. I noticed Jenny's car was in the parking lot that morning, so I made a U-turn and headed back to the bank. I wanted to talk things over with her. She had left my place in quite a mood the evening before, and I wanted to apologize to her."

Micheline noted that Detective Van Horn was taking notes on a tablet.

"And then what?" Kovacs queried.

"Looking back, I saw a couple of things that didn't present themselves as anything unusual at the time. For instance, in the back parking lot, I noticed two SUVs with dark tinted windows, and their engines were running. One was a red four-door Jeep, and the other was a white Volvo. Then in front of the bank, I noticed there was a white Ford cargo van parked, also with its engine running, but with no driver in sight."

"Okay," Mark Longfellow commented. "We have each of those vehicles on video, at least from angles across the street as they approached the bank parking lot. The videos from the bank itself were disabled and destroyed during the heist. We have no camera view of you as you apparently entered the bank from the front entrance."

"I see," Micheline said. "I parked my Mustang in the back lot and walked around to the front of the bank building. I headed straight for the front doors. I was greeted by a uniformed security guard. His name tag said Marcell Landry. He wasn't about to let me in. He was telling me that Jenny hadn't arrived for work yet, and maybe she went somewhere nearby for coffee or breakfast. He tried to get me to go away. I was about to flash my badge when a second gunman came up from behind me and put a nine-millimeter pistol to the back of my head."

"So, your official statement is that you're not part of this?" DA Whittaker asked suspiciously.

"Of course not," Micheline answered flatly. "I was there to see Jenny, and for that reason only. They forced me inside the bank building at gunpoint. When we got to the top of the entryway staircase, I could clearly see three bank employees down on the floor with blood puddled all around them. They had been executed, each with a shot to the head. It was a grisly sight."

"And what happened next?" Kovacs prompted.

"Neither the security guard nor the gunman recognized who I was. They didn't know I was a detective or that I was armed. They must have assumed I was just a businesswoman there to do my banking that morning. They ushered me over to the check-writing table and told me to get down on my knees. I complied with their demands and waited for the right moment to strike."

"How was the security guard dressed?" Detective Van Horn asked.

"Just like a uniformed security guard at first," Micheline recalled. "There was nothing out of the ordinary. His uniform looked authentic. Then the gunman told him to go put his tactical gear on. I turned at one point and noted that the gunman wore bulletproof body armor from head to toe, and he had a nine-millimeter Walther pointed at me."

"You recognized the Walther?" Van Horn asked.

"Yes," Micheline confirmed. "I have a similar model at home."

"I see," the detective replied. "And then what?"

"Things happened very quickly after that. I saw Jenny being escorted down the staircase by another two bank robbers in full tactical gear. They brandished M4 carbine rifles."

"Was she in distress, Detective?" the DA asked. "Was she being dragged kicking and screaming?"

"No, ma'am," Micheline replied. "Jenny had blood on her face and across her blouse. They were taking her as a hostage. She was docile and compliant as far as I could tell. I immediately remembered the description of the gang from the credit union armored car robbery a few weeks ago. This unit had the same physical description and the same M.O."

"Had Jenny been shot?" Kovacs asked.

"I don't believe so," Micheline replied. "It looked as though they may have hit her across the forehead with a rifle butt. Blood had splattered across her face and her blouse. It was a white silk blouse, and all I remember thinking was that she'd be pissed to high heaven because the stains would never come out."

"They headed for the exit door at the rear of the bank, then?" Mark asked.

"They were on their way, yes," Micheline confirmed. "Then another gunman came out from the vault with two Pullman suitcases. He was having a hard time controlling them. They kept twisting as he pulled forward. It appeared they were loaded with something heavy. I assumed it was cash from the vault. As he approached closer to me, he noticed me, and somehow, he knew who I was. He called out that I was a cop and asked if they had disarmed me. That's when things really got interesting."

"How so?" Van Horn asked.

"Two of the assailants had already forced Jenny out the back entrance, and the guy with the suitcases was struggling to catch up with them. While that was going on, Marcell Landry, the security guard, had changed into his body armor. He cradled an Uzi submachine gun, too. He was yelling for everyone to hurry up because a package had been armed."

"Did you know what he had meant by that?" Mark asked.

"No, I didn't. Not at the time, he said it, at least."

"And then what happened?"

"The gunman who stood near me was about to shoot me. I made my move right then. I unholstered my primary weapon and shot the guy in the back of the exposed kneecap. While he went down screaming, there was a huge explosion out front of the bank. The force of the concussion knocked me back a bit. But then I adjusted my balance and shot Marcell Landry to the back of the head."

"You didn't recognize him, did you?"

"No. I had seen his face when I first approached the bank. He didn't look familiar to me."

"So, you shot him."

"Yes. He went down hard, too. Then the gunman with the Walther came at me again. I was able to kick the gun out of his hands, and then I pistol-whipped him across the back of the head after I forcibly removed his metal faceplate. He went out cold."

"And had you ever seen the man you pistol-whipped before?" Kovacs asked.

"No, sir," Micheline replied. "After that, I exited the back entrance of the bank. I wanted to pursue the bank robbers and to stop them. I wanted to save the hostage."

"Your friend?"

"Yes. Jenny Casella is my friend. She was in extreme danger, and I wanted to save her."

Kovacs thoughtfully and deliberately stroked the hairs of his well-groomed beard. "From the video, body language tells me something different than the way you're spinning this tale, Detective Avila."

"I'm telling you the truth, sir."

"Assuming you were in on the robbery, taking out some of your cohorts could be viewed as a means to ensure a higher profit."

"I was not in on this heist, sir."

"At one point, you clearly turn toward a uniformed officer with your weapon extended, thereby thwarting his attempt to stop the white SUV from leaving the scene. You're going to need a skilled defense attorney, Detective. No one here is going to help you."

Micheline laid her head back on the moisture-laden pillow. The shock of what Captain Phillip Kovacs was saying had begun to settle in.

Fuck me!

Assistant Prosecuting Attorney Mark Longfellow leaned in close to her. "I thought I knew you, Micheline. I've always been on your side. But this time, you really let us down."

"I'll figure out a way to make this right," Micheline proposed. "I wasn't part of any bank heist, and the only reason I turned my weapon on Sergeant McCaffrey was that he held a .44 Magnum in his hands. He was going to shoot at the occupants in the backseat of the white Volvo SUV. Jenny Casella was inside the SUV at the time, and I didn't want her to become collateral damage."

"I'm afraid you'll have to consider how to do that from the inside of a cell, Detective Avila," the DA remarked caustically.

"No, please," Micheline cried.

The DA shook her head. "After the medical team at the hospital deems you fit for transport, I'm going to have you remanded to the San Diego Central Jail for the booking process. You'll be officially charged on multiple counts, fingerprinted, and photographed."

"Rosa, c'mon now. I didn't do this."

The DA remained in a stern and furious state. "I'll pull every string I need to with any judge who winds up with your name on their docket. I'll ensure that bail is categorically denied. Then I'm going to have you shipped off to the Vista Detention Facility so that I don't have to see your sorry face until your trial date."

"But..."

"We're done here," the DA announced flatly.

The four representatives of social justice and law enforcement abruptly turned on their heels and abandoned the wounded detective in hushed silence. The door slammed shut behind them.

Micheline looked to the ceiling as if prayer or silent reflection might ease her physical and mental anguish but to no avail.

Twenty-Seven

Micheline twisted uncomfortably in the hospital bed with the lumpy mattress. Her neck was stiff, her body ached all over, and her brain buzzed with insane scenarios as to what might happen next. She took a long, deep breath and slowly began to organize her thoughts as she would for any work-related case she investigated.

First, she would need a defense attorney. A damn good one. She might stand to lose her job and her condo. Her life savings. Her retirement account. Her beloved Mustang. Hell, she might even go to prison.

"Oh, fuck me!" she blurted out loud in the sterile confines of the lonely, darkened hospital room.

A short time later, Micheline became aware of activity in the hallway immediately outside her room. She noticed through the tiny square window as Shayna passed by the doorway and stopped. She was speaking to the uniformed officer on duty. The guard appeared to be incredibly pleased that she had noticed him. Shayna was smiling brightly and laughing like a schoolgirl.

Great! Now she's flirting with the officer who's keeping me prisoner in here. And right in front of my face, too!

The door cracked open a bit, but Shayna remained on the outside of the room in the corridor. Micheline could hear the sexy giggle of Shayna's infectious laugh as she continued to speak flirtatiously to the guard.

The aroma of roasted turkey wafted through the air. Micheline's stomach began to grumble and churn.

"Thank you, Shayna," the officer was saying. "I really appreciate the coffee. The chocolate doughnut was a special touch. That was so thoughtful of you to think of me while you were down at the cafeteria. A guy like me could really get used to such nice treatment. May I ask, is there any chance that you're single?"

The small talk continued for a few moments longer between the nurse and the officer while the hospital room door remained cracked open slightly. Micheline listened intently and wanted to vomit. She had nothing against the guard. Hell, she hadn't even been introduced to or spoken to the man yet.

I'm sure he's a nice guy. It's just the principle of the matter.

Eventually, Shayna respectfully excused herself and entered Micheline's room. She placed a food tray in front of the imprisoned detective and frowned.

"You're in a world of trouble, Micheline," she admonished.

Just rip the bandage right off the wound, why don't you!

"I know," Micheline replied dejectedly. "But I have to keep myself in a positive frame of mind. I'll get a lawyer to defend me. After I give my statement and the forensics come back from the crime scene lab, it should all start to look better for me. Hopefully, they'll release me on house arrest, or they'll clear me altogether. It's just going to take some time to sort it all out. It's embarrassing more than anything else now. But I'll get through it."

"You really think that?" Shayna asked incredulously. "I overhead what those lawyers and detectives were saying after they left your room. They feel confident they've got an open and shut case against you. That's what the older Black woman was saying. Then the other guy with the beard was talking about the bank statements and the guns that are registered to you with your fingerprints on them. It all links back to you somehow. They've even got you on videotape pointing your gun at a uniformed officer at the scene. I saw that part on the TV news the other night. They're never going to let you go, Micheline."

"Bank statements? Guns with fingerprints on them?" Micheline asked dumbfounded. "Because I bought a condo and a new car recently?

I don't even own them. I've got a thirty-year mortgage on the condo and a five-year loan on the car. And the only guns I touched at the crime scene were my own. What's that all about?"

"I'm not sure of the details," Shayna replied. "They've already got the evidence back from the ballistics lab that they need. They said everything is a perfect match, and they mentioned something about a governor's moratorium coming to an end, and that the last execution in the state of California was back in two thousand and six. They were referring to the death penalty, Micheline! I'm so worried for you right now."

Micheline inhaled a deep breath and let it out slowly as she shook her head disdainfully in frustration and apprehension.

"I've come up with a plan," Shayna said. "And you've got to follow my instructions to the letter. Understand? You need to eat now to get your strength back, and then you need to rest. I'm serious now, Micheline. Eat the Thanksgiving dinner that I've brought for you from the cafeteria. There's roast turkey, stuffing and mashed potatoes, and steamed carrots and broccoli. There's even some cranberry sauce in there, and a slice of pumpkin pie, too. Drink plenty of water to wash it all down. After you're done eating and rehydrating, close your eyes and rest for a while. Take a long nap. I'm working a double shift tonight because of the Thanksgiving holiday. It's just a skeleton crew on duty tonight. I'll be back in a few hours to check on you."

"I can't eat, Shayna. I can't even think about resting, either. I did nothing wrong. I was just at the wrong place at the wrong time, and my entire future is about to be stripped away from me because of what happened there. I've got to focus my full attention on planning what comes next. I've got to fight for my life with everything I've got left to defend myself with."

"There will be plenty of time for that later," she said. "For now, follow this nurse's orders and eat something good for you. Do it for me, Micheline. Please. Then make sure you close your eyes afterward and fall asleep for a while. I'll be back for you when the time is right."

Micheline nodded dutifully and appreciatively toward her friend. She trusted in Shayna's intentions. She had no idea what Shayna was talking about, of course, but there was a blend of kindness, strength, and confidence in Shayna's demeanor, and Micheline felt comforted by her mannerisms and instructions.

"Can you check on something for me?" Micheline asked.

"Yes, of course. What would that be?"

"There might be a surgical patient in the ICU here at the hospital. You probably know him. His name is Detective Guillermo Reyes. He suffered a heart attack several days ago. Last I heard, he was scheduled to have triple bypass surgery. Could you check his status, please?"

"Reyes, you say. You mean, Oscar's uncle?"

"Yes. Guillermo Reyes."

"I'll see what I can find out for you, Micheline. I don't mind telling you, I never cared for the man. He protected Oscar through the worst of it."

"Thank you, Shayna. I understand your concerns. But believe me, I've spoken to him about you, and he feels regret for never standing up for you."

"It takes more than words to earn my trust."

Micheline watched sadly as Shayna turned abruptly and left the room.

Presently, Micheline surveyed the food set on a plastic cafeteria tray before her. Her stomach suddenly grumbled again, and the smell of the roast turkey beckoned her to attempt to eat. The first forkful tasted delightful, and Micheline continued chomping on the meal until the contents of the tray were completely devoured and the tall cup of ice water was empty.

Her stomach satisfied, Micheline laid her head back on the stiff pillow, closed her eyes heavily, and allowed the blackness of the swirling void to swallow her up.

Twenty-Eight

Micheline awoke abruptly sometime later. She had no sense of how long she had been asleep or where she was. She felt a gentle pressure against her uninjured left shoulder.

The hospital room had remained quiet and dark with a blurred image of Shayna enshrouded further away by the surrounding cloud of darkness. Shayna gently massaged Micheline's left shoulder to bring her back from unconsciousness.

"Hey Shayna," she mumbled groggily as she returned to reality. "I was just having a nice dream. We were together at Balboa Park enjoying an ice cream. I think you brought along a boyfriend, too. He seemed nice."

"It's time to go," Shayna whispered quietly.

"They're taking me already?" Micheline asked alarmingly as she struggled to force herself awake. "But I need more rest. You said so."

"No, Micheline," she replied calmly. "I'm sorry. Things have heated up since we last spoke. You need to get out of here, and the sooner the better. I'm helping you to escape from police custody. You need to clear your name. You won't be able to do that if they put you behind bars."

"But I haven't even figured out who my lawyer should be yet."

"A lawyer won't be able to change their minds, or even a jury's decision, with the evidence that they've stacked against you. You're all over the TV news. You need to leave the hospital tonight, with my help."

"But how?" Micheline asked, still confused. "I'm handcuffed to the bedside railing and there's an armed guard stationed right outside in the hallway. The one you brought a large steaming cup of coffee and a chocolate doughnut before you came in to see me."

Shayna smiled a mischievous grin. "Jealous, are we?"

"No," Micheline scoffed. "Well, maybe a little."

Shayna reached into the front pocket of her colorful smock. She withdrew a tiny metal handcuff key.

"What the fuck?" Micheline shook her head in disbelief.

"I pretended to flirt with the guard earlier this evening," Shayna admitted unapologetically. "I slipped half a bottle of codeine into his decaf coffee from the cafeteria earlier tonight. He's fast asleep in his chair outside your door right now. He's not likely to wake up anytime soon."

"But what about the other nurses and doctors? Someone will surely see me if I try to leave."

Shayna shook her head. "It's nearly two o'clock in the morning right now. The hallways are deserted. Let's get you dressed and out of here before the codeine wears off and the guard starts to wake up."

"It's too risky, Shayna," Micheline said. "What if he wakes up while I'm trying to tiptoe out of here? I don't want you to get into trouble. You've worked too hard to get where you are now. I couldn't live with myself if that all fell apart because of me."

"Don't worry about me," Shayna replied. "I'll put the key back on the belt loop where I found it, and I'll be the one to wake him up after you're long gone. We'll lock the handcuffs back in place on the bedside railing. They'll think you purposefully dislocated your thumb and slipped your hand through the cuffs."

"That's doubtful," Micheline conceded. "But again, it's a better theory than nothing at all."

Shayna grasped Micheline's hand tightly. "I believe you're innocent, Micheline. I know you're a good woman with a wonderful heart. You've done so much to help me. This is my chance to help you out of this crazy mess you've found yourself caught up in."

Micheline attempted to open her eyes wider. She felt weighed down, even after the handcuffs were unsnapped from her right wrist.

She breathed in deeply. "I may not have said it before, Shayna, but you're an absolute angel. I truly appreciate what you're offering to do for me."

Shayna's expression toughened into a serious and resolute façade. "That's all well and good. Now, listen carefully. They took all your things. I managed to pull the cash and a business card out of your wallet, but that was it. The police bagged all of your clothing, your shoes, your wallet, car keys, and your cell phone, too."

"What am I supposed to do?" Micheline wondered out loud. "Walk out of here barefoot in a hospital gown with my ass hanging in the wind?"

"Not to worry," Shayna said. "I went down to the lady's locker room. One of the female interns left a pair of sneakers, a T-shirt, sweatpants, and a hooded sweatshirt on a bench near her locker. She's off for the long holiday weekend, so no one will notice them missing right away."

"Still," Micheline wondered, "where can I go? Where should I be investigating? And even if I figure that out, how do I get there? I have no means of communication or transportation. And as you've said, my picture has been plastered all over TV and social media. I can't go back to my place, and I can't check into a hotel. I'll be noticed wherever I go. I'm royally screwed!"

Shayna smiled at the detective and turned off the monitors near Micheline's bedside. She carefully removed the monitor leads and placed a bandage over the top of the vein where the IV drip line had been attached to Micheline's forearm.

"Let's start with getting you dressed. Don't be shy. I've seen it all before."

Micheline rose unsteadily from the bed and removed the hospital gown. She tossed the oversized cloth napkin on the bed. She stood naked in front of Shayna and carefully stretched to relieve her tightened muscles.

Shayna noted that Micheline had a series of intermingled color tattoos from shoulder to wrist on her left arm, and wrapped around her right thigh and calf, too. There was a skyline image sketched on the back of her right shoulder, and smaller images on her right side.

Micheline's right chest and shoulder ached the most. Without hesitation, she reached for the sweatpants and pulled them on. She had difficulty lifting her right leg. But she managed. She pulled the T-shirt slowly over her head, and then slipped on the hooded pullover sweatshirt.

"This is exhausting," she said.

"It's good that you're increasing your motion. It will take time, but you'll recover."

Micheline wiggled her feet into the athletic training shoes. They were a size too large.

"Everything's a little bulky. But it'll do for now."

"She's a big girl," Shayna commented. "Sorry, but beggars can't be choosers, right?"

"No doubt."

Shayna turned toward the wide windowsill and picked up a black zippered lunch cooler. She placed it inside a larger backpack and zippered the compartment closed.

"Take this," she said, handing the backpack by its padded nylon strap to Micheline.

"Inside the cooler is another turkey dinner from the cafeteria, plus the cash and business card I had taken from your wallet earlier. The doctor had already prescribed a combination of Toradol and Vicodin for the pain. There's a two-week supply of each in the bottles I've left for you inside the pack."

"I'd better solve this case quickly, then," Micheline said.

"I've also included a bottle of antiseptic, a roll of gauze, and sterile bandages to keep your surgical incisions clean and safe from infection. It's not much, but it will help you to get through the next few days at least."

Shayna reached into her pants pockets and withdrew a set of car keys and her cell phone. She handed them to Micheline.

"Take these, too. The passcode for the phone is 1226. Just remember the day after Christmas. It's my birthday. My car is a gray Honda Accord. It's located on level 3C of the parking garage. Just don't get any traffic tickets, okay? You may not be able to get me out of them this time."

Micheline looked as though she were about to cry.

Shayna touched Micheline's forearm gently and laughed softly. She was trying to lighten the mood. Her genuine concern and sincerity allowed Micheline to relax somewhat. Micheline began to feel more confident about what she was going to do next.

"I don't know what to say, Shayna. Thank you."

"Unfortunately, I can't offer for you to stay at my place," she said.

"That's all right."

"I wish I could. But I have three roommates. Although they're wonderful, strong, and independent women, they've all been through some rough times. I don't think they'd be as supportive or understanding of your situation. They would need to know you better. Harboring criminals from the TV news wouldn't be their thing. Trust me."

"I get it," Micheline replied. "I'm thankful you even considered that for me."

"Of course."

"Anyway, I know what I need to do first. It's best to do it during the nighttime while the coast is still clear."

"Do you know where you're going?"

"Not yet specifically. But I'll figure it out. Everything you've done will help to get me started."

"Okay," she said. "You'd better hurry."

Micheline leaned forward and hugged Shayna tightly. A single tear dropped from the corner of Shayna's eye.

"By the way," Shayna said. "Earlier you asked me to check on Oscar's uncle, Detective Guillermo Reyes."

"Yes?"

"I have some good news. He's out of the ICU. He was placed into a private room down on the third floor, room three eleven. They didn't perform the surgery yet. It's on the schedule for Monday morning."

"That's good to know," Micheline acknowledged.

"Now, let's not waste any more time. You need to leave soon. I'll go out to the nurse's station to make sure everything is clear. Wait two minutes after I leave your room, and then it should be okay for you to step outside into the hallway."

"You'll let me know if you detect anything unusual?"

"Of course. Just act normal. No one will question you at this late hour. Keep your head down and just keep walking straight ahead like you know where you're going. Take the elevator down to the third floor and follow the hallway signs to the parking garage. It's located on the other end of the building."

"Thank you, Shayna. I'll get word to you somehow when this is all over."

"Focus on clearing your name and staying out of sight for now," she beckoned. "I'll put the handcuffs key back on the guard's belt loop after I've left your room, and I'll tend to my other patients. You should have a few hours head start before anyone notices you're gone."

Micheline hugged her friend tightly again. "Gracias, mi amiga."

"De nada querida," Shayna replied. She looked worried.

"Good luck to you, Micheline." Shayna turned then and left the darkened room without saying anything more.

Twenty-Nine

Micheline escaped quietly from the elevator on the third floor and walked at a slow pace along the hallway to her left. She didn't want to attract any more attention than was necessary. She kept her head down and her hands tucked into the front pocket of the hooded sweatshirt.

No attention at all would be even better.

She noted the nurse's station on her right looming ahead and carefully checked the patient room numbers above the open doorways as she walked on by.

Three-oh-five. Three-oh-seven. Three-oh-nine.

A nurse in blue scrubs exited from a room farther down the hall. She paused for a moment to check the time on her wristwatch, then continued to the next room farther away. She immediately disappeared from view.

Micheline peeked through the doorway to room three-eleven. Two beds were occupied. A tablet light illuminated the occupant on the far end of the room by the window. In the first bed, a middle-aged man lay sleeping on his stomach. He faced the hallway and looked to be resting peacefully.

Guillermo Reyes was fully awake and sat upright in bed. He read from a small handheld tablet device. A pair of black plastic reading glasses hung precariously halfway down the wide slope of his nose. Micheline turned the corner and entered the room slowly.

"Hey, Guillermo," she whispered. "Would you mind some company tonight?"

"Micheline, what are you doing up at this late hour?" he asked as though nothing had changed.

"And why aren't you in handcuffs? I don't let just any criminal mastermind come to see me in my pajamas like this," he joked.

Micheline winced, more from the pain of knowing that Guillermo knew about the pending charges against her than from the pain of her gunshot wounds.

"Just had to see my mentor one more time," she said. "How are you feeling?"

"Oh, you know," he offered. "I got my heart broken, and now they're going to have to stitch me back together."

"Always the jokester," Micheline concluded.

"The doctor's telling me I've got to have the surgery on Monday. Then after that, he wants me to go on this low fat, low salt, low fucking taste diet for starters. Then he wants me to start a daily exercise program. Like that's going to happen, right?"

"Give it time," Micheline offered. "You need to take care of your health. Make it a priority, please."

"Are you breaking out tonight?"

"I need to clear my name, Guillermo. Everything they have against me is circumstantial. But there's no way to prove it. No easy way, at least."

"You're not likely to get too far, you know. Even a short-sighted old man like me can see you're limping and favoring your left side. I heard you took three rounds before you went down. That's mighty impressive."

"I'll get by. I've got to do this on my own. No one is going to sacrifice themselves to save me."

"You're fierce as a tiger on the hunt, I'll give you that, Micheline. What can I do for you?"

"Do you have any advice? I have to believe that my being framed at the bank robbery is somehow tied to the Miller murder investigation, which I also believe is somehow linked to the Ballard murder from last summer."

"Oh, really? And how did you put those two murder cases together? One victim's an older white male and the other was a sexy young blonde. Not much in common there, if you ask me. Which you are asking of me, by the way. That's my two cents."

Micheline sat on the edge of Guillermo's bed. Her blue eyes focused on the window overlooking the heart of downtown San Diego.

"Both victims were stabbed repeatedly and found naked at the scene. Both were attacked viciously with a knife by a left-handed assailant, as though the killer knew them and had a personal grievance to settle. Both were wealthy and either worked or did their banking at the same branch bank location in the Gaslamp Quarter."

"You don't say? That's mighty fine detective work, Detective."

"I need your advice, Guillermo. Seriously, I don't have much time. You can leave the sense of humor at the door if you don't mind."

"I can't help you, Micheline. It's not that I don't want to. I would, of course. But I'm laid up here and I'm not going anywhere for a while."

"I just want to know if you were in my shoes, where would you start? I'm kind of short on resources at the moment. It's hard to think straight."

Reyes chuckled softly. "My sense of humor has rubbed off on you, huh?"

"I'm not joking, Guillermo. I'm in the loneliest and most devastating situation of my life right now. Worse than my divorce or when my mother passed away from cancer. Whom can I turn to?"

Guillermo nodded knowingly. "You've got more friends than you realize, girl. Give a call to Kelly Van Horn or Richard Tuller. Tell them what you know and what you believe to be true. They'll rally behind you once they start putting the puzzle pieces together."

"I don't know," Micheline said. "Kelly was here at the hospital with the DA, Mark Longfellow, and Phil Kovacs. She wasn't giving me any nods of approval."

"You didn't expect her to go against her senior commanders, did you?"

"I guess not."

"Give it some time."

"I'm afraid I don't have too much of that to spare."

"Trust your gut on this one," Guillermo suggested. "Kelly and Richard will pull through for you. They're both good kids, like you, and they know you well enough now to stick with you through thick and thin. You've earned their trust. Take the necessary step to put your trust back in them."

"Thanks. I think in the back of my mind, that's exactly why I needed to see you tonight. I needed that extra push to tell me to believe in what I was already planning to do."

"Good girl," Guillermo said. "Now, go on. The cards are stacked against you on this one. You'll have to be smarter and wiser and faster than you've ever been on the job before. And you've got to do it while you're wounded and the whole damn department is chasing after your sexy ass."

"You're a dirty old man, Guillermo. You know that?"

"And proud of it, too. Good luck, chica."

Micheline smiled agreeably. "Thank you, Guillermo. You take care of yourself. I hope the surgery goes well. I'll see you later."

Micheline rose from the bed and turned to leave.

Now, what am I going to do?

Thirty

Except for a thin sliver of a crescent moon that hung high above the Pacific Ocean swells, the night sky was dark and absent of clouds. A mild breeze blew steadily across the walkway outside Micheline's condo building.

To the east across the bay, the illuminated skyline of the Gaslamp Quarter and Waterfront Park in downtown San Diego shone brightly. To the north, an oscillating searchlight scanned the star-laden heavens from atop the control tower at San Diego International Airport.

Micheline parked Shayna's gray Honda Accord outside her garage door and checked the time on the dashboard display. Nearly three o'clock in the morning. She silently wondered how many people were out enjoying their early Black Friday shopping sprees at the premium outlets or the retail chain stores on this first day of the Christmas holiday season.

She left the car's engine running and got out and walked over toward the covered display panel to the left of the garage door. She punched in the six-digit security code, her mother's birthdate, and waited for the door to open. Then she got back in the car and parked it in the garage. She switched off the engine.

She opened a toolbox located on a middle shelf along the side wall of the garage and found what she was looking for. A spare set of house keys to the condo.

She reentered the security code to close the garage door and hoped that none of her neighbors would be awake this early in the morning. She didn't see any signs of light from the windows other than from condos located further down the street. She would try to be as quiet and stealthy as she could be.

Micheline slowly climbed the stairs to her third-floor condo. The entryway door was heavily covered with yellow crime scene tape with black *Crime Scene Do Not Enter* lettering. She peeled away some of the tapes along the outer edges and let herself into her private sanctuary.

Micheline frowned discontentedly as she viewed the interior living room and kitchen areas of the two-bedroom condo. The rooms had been tossed during the execution of the search warrant. Drawers and cabinets had been left open. Pillows and chair cushions were strewn across the floor.

Micheline entered the master bedroom and walked directly to the walk-in closet. Each of the three handguns from the drawers at the back of the closet had been removed. She walked back toward the bed and opened the lid to the hope chest. The folded sweaters had been tousled, but otherwise left undisturbed. The fake shelf beneath the sweaters had not been uncovered.

Micheline wasted no time. She walked back into the walk-in closet and withdrew a Pullman suitcase and a zippered shoulder bag. She laid them on top of the bed, which had the comforter and sheets pulled back, and the mattress and box springs turned sideways.

She stripped out of the oversized clothing she currently wore and folded them neatly on top of the bed. Then she selected clothing from her own drawers and got dressed. She packed the suitcase with extra clothing and toiletries. She included a wide-brimmed sunhat and a pair of Ray-Ban sunglasses to help conceal her identity while she would be out in public.

She walked back into the kitchen. She raided the pantry for some chocolate chip and high-protein granola bars, a box of blueberry pop-tarts, and a half dozen bottles of spring water.

Then she walked back to the master bedroom and removed the sweaters and fake shelf from the hope chest. She unlocked the steel gun cabinet beneath and selected a high-powered semi-automatic rifle and two nine-millimeter pistols with holsters, several magazines and boxes of ammunition, a bulletproof vest, and a black zippered canvas bag to conceal the various equipment. She added a nylon holster belt with Velcro enclosures. The belt held a half dozen tactical two-ounce pepper spray throwing grenades.

She was prepared to fight back with everything she had.

Micheline placed the suitcase and each of the bags on the landing deck outside her condo and locked the door behind her. She took a moment to smooth the crime scene tape around the edges of the door-frame before she left.

Then she made three separate trips up and down the staircase and placed all the bags into the trunk of Shayna's car.

Thirty-One

Micheline's head throbbed with a dull ache. She needed to stop and rest.

But where could she hope to go that she could possibly be safe?

She was a fugitive of the law, and it would be daylight in a few hours' time.

She filled the gas tank at an empty service station and paid cash inside. The attendant had been too absorbed in watching a cartoon on a small countertop TV to take notice of the young woman wearing a hoodie and sunglasses during the overnight hours.

Micheline drove away from the station and parked the gray Accord in a vast parking lot near the San Diego International Airport. She pulled out the cell phone Shayna had given her. She used the password she had been provided and dialed the only number she had with her from the business card in her pocket.

She looked hesitantly at the clock on the dashboard display. It was nearly four-thirty in the morning.

What were the odds the person she was calling would even be awake to answer her call?

The phone rang several times.

"Hello?" asked a distrusting and wavering female voice.

"Hi," Micheline began hesitantly. "I'm so sorry to be calling at such a late hour. Is this Elena?"

"My goodness, Detective Avila," Elena Dobrovic's voice responded immediately and breathlessly.

"I certainly hope you're not thinking to make this a booty call, are you?"

"That was not my intent, no," Micheline replied stiffly.

"And why aren't you calling from the cell number you gave me the other day? You're goddamned lucky I even thought to answer in the first place. I hate answering unknown caller calls, especially when I'm traveling away from home."

Micheline expelled a heavy sigh of relief. "First off, Elena, I apologize from the very bottom of my heart. To be completely honest and upfront with you, I'm in a terrible predicament and I have no one else I can turn to. I realize this is most inconvenient for you. I'll understand if you hang up on me. But right now, I need you."

"You used your one and only phone call to call me?" Elena asked curiously.

"I'm no longer in police custody," Micheline said.

She wasn't exactly lying.

"They released you from custody, then?"

"Not exactly."

"Oh, fuck!" she gasped.

"I'm in a difficult situation, Elena."

"I can only imagine what you're up against, Micheline. I've seen you on the TV news. It's not exactly the best way to make a first impression with me, you know."

Micheline winced inwardly. Everyone she knew had watched her become defamed on national television.

"If I hadn't made a good first impression with you at the Miller estate, we wouldn't be having this conversation right now at four in the morning."

"Touché," Elena replied. "So, you need me, huh?"

"I need a place to stay," she said. "Just…"

Elena abruptly cut her off. "The Harper Hotel," she offered quietly.

"Near the airport. Room four fifteen. I'll be expecting you."

"Are you sure?"

Micheline heard a click on the other end and looked at the phone in her hand. The call had ended.

"I'll take that as a yes," she said to herself, and a slight glimmer of hope sparked like an ember of flame within her.

Thirty-Two

Micheline felt bleary-eyed and physically drained as she knocked softly on the door of room four fifteen at the Harper Hotel. For a moment, her breathing stopped, and she felt as though her heart were stuck in her throat.

The metallic sound of the deadbolt being unjammed and the door handle beginning to turn brought her back to reality. She let out a short breath of relief.

"My, look what the cat's dragged in," Elena said. "Come in, Detective."

Micheline pulled her carry-on luggage behind her and entered Elena's hotel room.

Elena wore an Oriental silk embroidered robe and sheepskin-lined slippers. She stepped tentatively out into the hallway to check for any uninvited nosey bodies.

The coast was clear. The hallway remained quiet and deserted.

Elena quickly stepped back inside her hotel room and placed the *do not disturb* placard on the outside doorknob. She quietly shut the door. Then she set the deadbolt and locked the door. Satisfied they were both safe, Elena turned to examine her early morning guest.

Micheline appeared as though she had caught a winter flu bug. She looked pale, achy, and sweaty. Her eyelids resembled the thin slits of a slightly opened shell of a pistachio nut.

"This is no time for talk, Micheline. You need to get your head on that pillow and rest," Elena commanded as she pointed toward the bed.

"You've been through so much over the past few days. I'm happy to help you. But this is not the way I had planned to spend my Black Friday holiday shopping spree. I'll tell you that."

Micheline nodded and frowned dejectedly. "I need to take my pain medication."

Elena stepped into the bathroom. "I'll get you a glass of water. You take your meds and lay down on the bed and get some sleep. We'll order room service when you're feeling alive and refreshed again."

"If that's even possible."

"After you wake up, you can take a nice hot shower to revive yourself. Then you and I are going to have a serious discussion about who you call when all the odds are against you. Got it?"

Micheline nodded compliantly without uttering another syllable. She accepted a glass of water that Elena offered to her and downed two fifty-milligram capsules each of her prescribed pain medication.

She needed to lie down and rest. Her entire body ached from head to toe.

She looked around the room vacantly, kicked off her shoes by the doorway, and crossed the room to lie down face-first on the bed. She was fast asleep within seconds.

Thirty-Three

Micheline awoke to the sun streaming into the hotel room through the outer window. Heavy dark blue fire-resistant blackout drapes with a white tree branch design and floating golden flower petals had been pulled closed. The curtain panels crimped apart in places and allowed suffused light into the spacious hotel room.

Elena sat comfortably in an easy chair by the other side of the bed. She was reading the hardcover edition of a new bestselling psychological thriller novel she had purchased at the airport newsstand in Detroit. She had removed the dust jacket of the thick tome and had placed it on the nightstand by the bed.

"Is it time for breakfast?" Micheline groaned.

Elena smiled and emitted a soft girlish laugh. "You slept right through lunch, babe. We'll order an early dinner for both of us after you get yourself cleaned up."

Micheline sat upright on the bed. She was still wearing the clothing she had arrived at the hotel in the morning before.

"How long have I been out?"

"Almost twelve hours straight."

"Really? Wow, I was so tired."

"You needed your rest. You've been through so much these past few days. I think my part in this diabolical scheme earns me exclusive rights to your story someday, wouldn't you say?"

Micheline awkwardly brushed a strand of hair away from in front of her face.

"I don't recall if I said this to you. Thank you, Elena. I can't express strongly enough how much it means to me for you to take me in and to offer me protection like this. You're putting yourself at great risk."

"Oh, don't worry. I'm counting on using this as leverage someday to provide me with witness protection, to cancel some overdue parking violations, or to hide a dead body."

Micheline glanced sternly at Elena.

"I'm kidding! Sheesh. You need to take your meds. Then off to a hot shower. That always works for me. You'll start to feel better in no time. I promise."

"First, we need to eat," Micheline suggested. "I'm starved. I have a leftover roast turkey dinner from the hospital cafeteria in the cooler in my bag. Have you got a microwave oven in here somewhere?"

"You're in luck," Elena exclaimed. "This room comes complete with a fridge and a microwave. I'll heat everything up for you. Why don't you get undressed and take a shower? It'll help to wipe the cobwebs away."

Micheline pulled the comforter and sheet back and swung her legs over the side of the bed. She attempted to stretch her muscles.

"Ouch! I literary ache in places I never knew I had," she said.

"I'm certain getting shot several times has something to do with that, huh?"

"I suppose," Micheline agreed. She trudged across the floor toward the bathroom and closed the door behind her.

Thirty-five minutes later, Micheline exited the bathroom with only a large white cotton towel wrapped around her torso. The aroma of hot roast turkey and mashed potatoes filled the hotel room.

The TV was on. A local San Diego weathergirl with Pacific Islander features was confirming sunny skies and temperatures all week long in the low eighties. She looked familiar to Micheline.

"What's the weathergirl's name on the TV?" Micheline asked. "Justice? Something like that. She looks familiar to me."

"It's Freedom," Elena replied. "I've seen her reports every night this week. She's a first-generation Filipina. Her parents must be so proud. You know, the two of you look somewhat alike."

"Ah, that's right," Micheline nodded. "She interviewed me on camera for a story once. I'm not Filipina, though. I have some Japanese in my blood. When my grandparents got together, they tossed everything into a blender. Then my parents added the final ingredients."

"By everything, what do you mean?"

"I have more than just one or two races in my gene pool."

"Such as?"

"A mix of Japanese, African-American, and European."

"It makes you unique. A bit exotic. I can see that reflected in your body art, too.

The view on the television switched to a different weather team reporting from Seattle. A Siberian cold front had collided with warmer temperatures over the Pacific Northwest from Alaska down to Sacramento. This created a devastating monster storm that included high winds, violent ocean swells, torrential rainfall to the west, and significant snow accumulation to the east.

Airline flights were canceled, ocean shipping routes were delayed, and power outages across vast inland regions of western Canada, Washington, Oregon, and Montana were expected to last for several days.

"I may need to extend my trip anyway," Elena said. "I wouldn't want to be flying into that mess of weather. Just wait until it hits the Great Lakes region."

"I do hope you'll stay," Micheline suggested.

"I may have reason to now."

"Yum! That turkey smells just like my mom used to make," Micheline said. She wriggled her nose.

"Except, we had appetizers of steamed dumplings, sushi rolls, and mozzarella cheese wrapped in prosciutto. I grew up in quite an eclectic household."

"It sounds divine," Elena said. "We would watch the Lions' game every year, and my grandmother would cook the entire meal for a dozen relatives. My mother made the best pumpkin pie. My favorite, though, was a chocolate pudding pie with a graham cracker crust and whipped cream on top."

"I miss my mom," Micheline confided. "It's been just over a year now since she passed away."

Elena nodded. "I'm sorry to hear that. I lost both of my parents on the night of a high school dance. They had gone out for dinner and were involved in a multiple-vehicle accident on the highway. It was the same night I had my very first goodnight kiss from a boy."

"I'm sorry," Micheline said. "It must be difficult to put those two images side-by-side. One sweet, the other so unimaginably sad."

"I try to remember all the good times we shared. Family vacations. Hiking in the mountains. Swimming at the lake in the summertime. Times like those that evoke a smile."

Micheline nodded. She picked up her suitcase by the door and placed it on top of the bed. She unzipped the outer cover and searched its contents for a suitable outfit.

"Dinner's ready for you," Elena said. "You can have it all. I'll order room service. They have surf and turf on the menu with a thick filet mignon steak and buttered Maine lobster tail."

"That sounds delightful," Micheline said. "I'll have to try that later this week. If I'm fortunate enough to still be here, that is."

"You will be, you'll see. I could tell the very first time I met you, Micheline. You're intelligent, hardboiled, resilient, and determined. I don't expect an entire statewide law enforcement manhunt would stop you."

Micheline burst out laughing. "Oh, fuck! Now that you put it that way..." her words trailed off.

"One step at a time, Detective. One clue at a time. You've got this."

"I sure hope so," Micheline conceded. "It's only my life on the line, you know. And the life of my friend, Jenny. My God, what if they've hurt her? What must she be going through right now? They whisked her away at gunpoint."

"First things first," Elena suggested. "Eat and get your strength back. I'm here to help you any way I can."

Micheline smiled. She picked an outfit from the suitcase and began to get dressed.

"Tell me about your interviews with the Miller family, would you please?" Micheline asked, quickly rekindling her role as a detective.

"Ah, a quirky bunch," Elena began. "Tightlipped, rich, and mostly concerned about their public image. Dr. Miller is a neurological and chemistry genius, of course. His mind is on running his business. The daughter's passing seemed more of an inconvenience than a horrific event that would scar him for the rest of his life. I got the impression he was concerned about the stock price of his company falling because of the scandal."

"Really?"

"Yes, that was my take on him. The wife was even more locked into her fairytale trophy wife life. She is nothing but a social butterfly who plans her days based on who's paying for her lunch or tennis club outings. I think she's having an affair with her tennis instructor, too. The sister-in-law accidentally let that little morsel of gossip slip out during our heart-to-heart talk."

"What about Samantha's life? Did anything unusual or interesting present itself?"

Elena shrugged. "As I said, they were rather tightlipped. It was hard to get them to spill the beans."

"And yet, they invited you there and paid your expenses to present her story for their memories."

"All a matter of playing a part, if you ask me," Elena replied. "I was there to paint a beautiful portrait over top of the canvas of an agonizing and miserable story. I got the impression Samantha went through some very difficult times in her life. She was only recently on the verge to develop that story in a more positive way when her life was suddenly taken."

"How so?"

"They presented a fiction known as Miss American Pie, all smiles and world travels and cocktail parties. What I perceived hidden under false layers was a tormented young woman who was raped repeatedly by a family friend at an early age. A family who ignored her troubled pleas for help, a daughter who sought confirmation of her existence by stealing expensive handbags in luxury malls. A young woman who later turned to drugs and indiscriminate sex partners to quell her longings and secret desires."

"Yet, she turned her life around. I saw her stand up for herself the week before her death. She was a fighter."

"I believe over time she learned to love herself. She gained confidence. She read books. Big thick technical books, too. And scientific journals. She left fantasy behind and became a realist."

"And someone killed her for it."

"Yes. Or something like that. You must remember, she was an only child of a couple worth over a hundred million dollars. She had what everyone wants, and her killer wanted it all for themselves."

Micheline nodded solemnly. "I believe you're right."

"So, you're working multiple cases right now?"

"There are three separate cases. Two murders and a bank robbery. I may be batshit crazy, but I believe they're somehow all connected to each other."

"No fucking way! How so?"

"The bank is the common denominator," Micheline stated. "Both of the murder victims either worked there or did their financial business there. The way they were killed is another clue. Both crime scenes were filled with blood splatter and a sense of methodical rage. Both crime scenes were ugly and bloody, but at the same time, they were contained and controlled. The killer wanted both victims to be on display when their bodies were discovered."

"That's gruesome."

"No doubt about it. I'm searching for someone who is both highly intelligent and equally mad. They're driven to extremes, and they're not done yet. Not until I catch them in the act and take them down."

"So, where do you plan to begin?"

"I'm searching for a serial killer. But I'll begin with the bank robbery itself."

"I don't understand," Elena said.

Micheline nodded. "Jenny was taken hostage against her will. She was covered in blood and held at gunpoint by masked intruders who carried automatic military-style rifles. Solving that case will solve the murders, or at least get me closer to the truth, I think."

"I'm glad I don't have your job," Elena said.

"I was born into it," Micheline said. "And I wouldn't have it any other way."

Thirty-Four

Balboa Park

Sunday, November 29th

Micheline took a long sip from a large ceramic mug of cappuc-cino. She sat quietly at an outdoor café table. She had pulled her hair forward and wore her wide-brimmed sunhat. Her eyes remained hidden behind a stylish pair of darkly tinted Ray-Ban Wayfarer sunglasses.

She pretended to read a hardcover book Elena had lent her. She savored the flavor of her steamy caffeinated Sunday morning beverage amid the cool morning air.

The overhead sky was clear of any sign of clouds. The temperature was mild, and a soft breeze blew gently across her back. All around her, pedestrians strolled in every direction. Birds chirped from the nearby trees. The hum of automobile traffic blended with a hubbub of voices and a symphony of other urban sounds.

As much as Micheline wanted to solve the case and redeem herself in the eyes of her law enforcement colleagues, and forego spending any time in jail, she admitted stubbornly she couldn't do it all by herself.

She needed outside help. Someone who would be willing to grant her access to police investigative information. Someone she could trust with her life. Someone who wouldn't play both sides of the fence and turn her in to the authorities.

She was on a slippery slope, and she damn well knew it.

She had pondered a long time over the decision to stake out this specific café on a Sunday morning. Everyone she knew from within the department had their favorite morning coffee shop haunt, whether it be located near to their place of residence or closer to the Hall of Justice where their offices were located.

For Richard Tuller, it was a bakery across the street from his fitness gym in Point Loma. Mark Longfellow preferred a Mexican restaurant near Mission Bay. Guillermo Reyes enjoyed the local pancake house in Bonita, and Kelly Van Horn raved about Rashida's Caribbean Coffee-house at Balboa Park near the Gaslamp Quarter. The corner sign outside the family-run café displayed a picture of a tortoise drinking a hot brew. Kelly lived in an apartment building across the street from the café.

As much as Micheline would have preferred to make a phone call from a safe location instead, she realized the only way this would work would be if she met face to face with Kelly. She needed to make a convincing case for her friend and colleague to trust her. They needed to see eye to eye, literally.

Micheline had to put it all on the line. Otherwise, she was just running in circles from her problems.

Be strong and resolute. Believe in the possibilities.

Across the way, the front entrance door to the apartment build-ing swung open. Richard Tuller, in an orange short-sleeve lapel collar shirt, tan shorts, and flat white leather retro sneakers stepped onto the curb. He was followed closely by Kelly in a light blue printed chambray dress and flat sandals. She was smiling. Her right hand was entwined within the crook of Richard's left arm.

No way! They're sleeping together.

Micheline was silently happy to see her colleagues were hooking up romantically during their off-duty hours.

Richard and Kelly made their way across the street and walked inside the busy coffeehouse. Micheline kept her head held low and pretended to be immersed in the novel on the table. Her heart began to beat faster.

Minutes passed. Micheline was perspiring. She didn't know how much longer she could take to wait like this.

Play it cool, right?

Kelly stepped outside onto the sidewalk while she spoke over her bare shoulder to Richard, who was directly behind her. Richard was commenting on the magnificent aroma of the coffee and the warmed blueberry scones they had just purchased.

Micheline suddenly recognized the novel in front of her was upside down. She immediately attempted to flip it around. Her forearm inadvertently brushed against her cappuccino. The ceramic mug tumbled off the tabletop and shattered into several pieces on the sidewalk.

"Goddamn it!"

"Micheline?" Kelly asked in a shocked tone as she approached closer to the table.

Micheline looked up and nonchalantly removed her dark sunglasses.

"Hey, Kelly. How's your Sunday going?"

"Are you crazy, hanging out here in public like this?" Kelly reprimanded her sternly.

"Half the force is looking everywhere for you right now. The other half is just waiting until their next shift starts. They've got officers assigned to watch your condo, and to watch Jenny Cassella's place, too."

"I need your help."

"Micheline," Richard said, "the best thing you can do is to turn yourself in. Quietly and peacefully."

"I'm not looking to make a scene, Richard. I'm innocent of what they're accusing me of. There's no way I'll prove that while I'm locked up in custody and awaiting a trial six months or a year from now. I need to act now while everything is still fresh in my mind."

"This is why we have a justice system," Richard argued.

"Why did you come here, Micheline?" Kelly asked, attempting to diffuse the situation.

"We could call this in and arrest you right now," Richard said. He clearly was attempting to calculate in his mind how he would drop his coffee and scones to subdue his suspect.

"I'm putting my trust in the two of you. I need to identify who the crew members of the bank heist were. I need to save Jenny before they harm her, and I believe both the Ballard and Miller murders are somehow linked to the robbery."

"That's ludicrous!" Richard scoffed.

Micheline shrugged her shoulders. "I'm risking it all by coming here to see you. I'm asking both of you to trust me, and to help me get to the bottom of this."

"You've really gone over the deep end now, Detective," Richard said. "We could lose our jobs over this. Hell, we could be arrested if we're not careful."

"You know in your hearts I didn't do this," Micheline said.

"The evidence is overwhelming," Kelly said. "Your fingerprints are on the guns. The money is verified in your bank account statements. How do you explain that?"

"The fingerprint trail is clear. I fired six shots in all with my primary weapon. I took out the fake security guard to the back of the head and shot the guy from the bank in the back of the kneecap. Once I was outside in the parking lot, the first shot missed and the other three hit the bandit with the grenade launcher before he escaped in the white SUV. His body armor protected him from being injured. I only got off one shot with my backup weapon before I went down. I hit the guy with the missing kneecap in the throat, I think. It's all still a bit of a blur."

Kelly's eyes were wide open, stunned. "Micheline, three bank employees were executed in the main lobby with single headshots and double taps to their chests for good measure. Ballistics confirms the gun used was your nine-millimeter Walther. Your prints are the only ones on the pistol. Another employee was killed in the back room. She was killed the same way."

"I knocked the Walther out of the gunman's hand before I pistol-whipped him to the back of the head. Maybe I touched the gun during the altercation. I don't recall that, though. He was wearing gloves, so of course, his prints wouldn't be on the weapon."

"Micheline," Kelly said, "you're not listening to me. The Walther is *your* gun, registered to *you*. The serial numbers match!"

"What the hell? No way is that even possible!"

"The employee killed in the back of the bank was shot with a Sig Sauer P320 AXG Scorpion nine-millimeter pistol. That same gun is also registered to you. It was discovered in the parking lot outside the bank. Again, your fingerprints are the only prints on the gun."

"That doesn't make any sense."

"There's more," Richard said. "The balance on your mortgage was recently paid off. Four hundred sixty-five thousand dollars. It was paid in a single lump sum wire transaction from Samantha Miller's trust fund account the day before the bank heist. There's another two hundred eighty-five thousand that was deposited into your personal savings account. In total, that's exactly seven hundred fifty thousand dollars. The transactions occurred after Samantha was already deceased, and before the bank heist. Were you planning on early retirement?"

"It's not mine, Richard. Honest. I was going to assume that the bank robbers somehow forced Jenny at gunpoint to initiate the financial transactions from her office at the bank. But the timing doesn't align with that theory now."

Richard looked undeterred. "That's correct. The money transfer requests were made via Samantha Miller's mobile device the day before the bank heist, and not from a computer. In other words, someone either knew Samantha's passwords or used a severed thumbprint to initiate access to her accounts after she was already dead."

"Oh, my. This is beginning to make more sense. But why they chose to frame me, I don't know. I'd need further review of the documentation or the evidence that's been collected so far."

"It gets worse," Richard said. "Kelly tracked the GPS coordinates of Samantha Miller's cell phone. It had been shut off between the time of the murder until the day before the bank heist. It was found, along with Samantha Miller's missing thumb, in a storage box in your master bedroom walk-in closet."

"Again, there's no way that's possible!" Micheline pleaded. "Are my fingerprints on the phone?"

"No," Richard confirmed. "The phone had been wiped clean of any prints."

"Let's focus on what we do know, then," Kelly suggested. "Micheline, do you have any leads the investigative team may not be privy to?"

"Looking back," Micheline said, "there's something I may have missed before. Do you remember the night you and Frank Salvatore found me at the Hops & Malt Brewing Company? I was waiting to see if our mystery redheaded female witness might show up."

"Yes, of course."

"That was the evening of the Samantha Miller murder at the park."

"That's right."

"I remember suggesting that Dominic Sadoski was likely not our killer. But whoever killed Samantha may have sustained physical injuries during their scuffle. Scratches or bruises, perhaps."

"Yes, of course. That's a reasonable expectation. Oh, wait!"

"Right? That same evening, Laura Quiñónez was waitressing. She had a black eye and bruises on her arms. I assumed those injuries were due to domestic spousal abuse. She told me her husband accidentally struck her with an elbow to the face when they were fooling around in the bedroom. Wrestling is what she called it."

"I remember that clearly, too," Kelly replied.

"What if Laura killed Samantha? As a follow-on to that question, what if she and her husband, who's an ex-con, by the way, are also somehow linked to the bank heist?"

"That's a stretch, don't you think?"

"Not really. I happened to notice the fake security guard from the bank heist had a jailhouse gang tattoo on the back of his neck. A black and red wolf's head. Wade Branigan, Laura's husband, has the exact same tattoo on his right shoulder."

"Oh, my!" Kelly replied. "He doesn't own an autobody shop, does he?"

"Yes, that's him," Micheline confirmed.

Kelly's eyes went wide. "The name Wade Branigan came up before during the Miller murder investigation. A review of Samantha's cell phone records indicated she had placed multiple calls to an autobody shop called The Classy Chassis, owned by Wade Branigan. The calls were always under two minutes in duration, so we assumed she was simply scheduling appointments to have her car serviced. We can check deeper into that possible relationship. You say Branigan is an ex-con?"

"Yes, that's right. He served time at Lompoc for drug possession and intent to distribute."

"I'll cross-check his background against the thieves who were killed at the bank. Maybe we'll find a connection."

"Excuse me, miss. Is everything all right?" the café waitress asked as she approached the table Micheline was sitting at.

Micheline quickly slipped her dark sunglasses back onto her face.

"Yes, I'm sorry. I was being clumsy. It was an accident. I'll clean this up."

"Would you like another cappuccino?" the woman asked pleasantly.

Micheline looked at both Kelly's and Richard's faces. She was silently asking them for their trust in this matter, and she worried they would consider turning her in. Under the circumstances, that could lead to commendations and promotions on the job for each of them. They would be considered heroes.

Richard initially looked flabbergasted he had to make such a decision on the spot. He took a long sip of his coffee. He looked over toward Kelly, who eyed him back with a steely glare.

Then Richard caved. He quietly nodded and shrugged his shoulders.

Kelly smiled and immediately winked back at Micheline.

"Yes," Micheline said to the waitress. "Make it an extra-large to go, please."

Thirty-Five

Fidelity National Savings & Loan Bank

Monday, November 30th

The outer façade of the bank entrance had crumbled during the bomb explosion. Temporary scaffolding had been assembled and the sidewalk was blocked to pedestrian traffic.

The branch bank itself was closed indefinitely for customer transactions. But the upstairs offices where the headquarters of the bank were located remained open for administration and staff. Employees entered through the rear entrance at the back of the battered building.

Micheline watched carefully from the smudged display window of the convenience store across the street. She wanted to interview a specific individual who was known to maintain a precise schedule every day. All she had to do was to wait for that person to arrive promptly.

William Hudgens, the bank's president, was seventy-two years old. He had held his present position for more than a quarter of a century. He drove a black Cadillac Escalade and arrived at the bank's back parking lot precisely at ten-thirty in the morning.

Micheline looked carefully both ways across Island Avenue and quickly maneuvered into the blind spot behind Hudgens' passenger side front door. She grasped the door handle firmly and yanked the door open wide.

"What's the meaning of this?" Hudgens snarled.

"Good morning, Mr. Hudgens," Micheline said as she clambered into the front seat. "I'm calling shotgun today if you don't mind. I have a few follow-up questions for you, and I thought it best to keep our conversation private."

"You!" he scowled angrily. "I've had four funerals to attend in this past week. There's one missing employee taken hostage and feared dead, and more than thirty-five million dollars in transferred funds from investors to answer to. You have the nerve to accost me in my car and to make jokes. For shame, Detective Avila."

"I apologize for today's intrusion, sir," Micheline said. "I'm terribly sorry. I'm not responsible for the murders or the bank heist. I've been framed. I don't know how they did it yet, but I'm going to figure that out in due time. For now, I need your help."

"Fuck you!" he snapped angrily. "You're nothing more than a villainous thief hiding behind a badge."

Micheline withdrew a nine-millimeter Glock 19 from her shoulder holster and set the gun comfortably upon her lap. A little friendly persuasion never hurt.

"I'm innocent of all charges, Mr. Hudgens. I wouldn't be here if I had all that money safely stashed away someplace. I need for you to trust me on this."

"And yet, you're pointing a gun at me. Maybe you're just fucking looney-tunes crazy," he suggested.

"Maybe you could just listen to what I have to say."

"Haven't I given enough already?"

"I didn't rob your bank, sir. I didn't kill your employees. Nor did I take your mistress as a hostage against her will."

That statement brought a shocked expression to Hudgens' face.

"How did you know?"

"A lucky guess," Micheline replied. "Jenny confided in me she always chose the bad boys. The older gentlemen who were secure in their financial affairs and who were always interested in screwing a much younger woman. It's no coincidence Jenny received two promotions in the past five months, is it? You were sleeping with her."

"Yes, I was," he confirmed sullenly. "But it was more than what you think, Detective. I loved her."

"I'm happy to hear that. Now, I'm most interested to find her and getting her safely away from her abductors. To do that, I need to identify the robbery crew members who escaped from the bank."

"I can't help you with that. The bank's surveillance system was shut down during the heist. Each of the robbers who managed to escape wore full combat armor to protect them against police gunfire. They were all wearing masks. How can we identify them if we never saw their faces? They left no fingerprints or DNA evidence of any kind. They're ghosts."

"Could they have forced Jenny to use the bank's resources to transfer the funds you mentioned were stolen?"

"Yes, that's the most likely scenario. Jenny had intimate knowledge of who our wealthiest customers are. It appears she initiated electronic transactions that transferred funds to private corporate accounts in the Cayman Islands. Those records are completely untraceable, even to the FBI."

"Whoa! I didn't realize that," Micheline said.

"Three days passed before we even knew the money was illicitly missing. I've spent the past two days going over all our accounts to ensure nothing else was stolen. Somehow, the thieves targeted Jenny for her knowledge in this area. They lured her to the bank earlier than she would normally arrive under the auspices of a loan application."

"Do you have a name associated with that application? Is there an Outlook calendar notation from Jenny's computer terminal, perhaps?"

"Yes, there is," Hudgens replied. "But it's an alias, as fake as the security guard who apparently showed up in an authentic uniform and forced his way inside the building. We even identified an incoming phone call which we believe was used to schedule the early morning appointment. The problem is it came from a public payphone at a location that did not have video surveillance."

"I see," Micheline said. "Thank you for your time, Mr. Hudgens. I'm sorry for everything that's happened. I can't bring those innocent people back, but I'll do my best to resolve this matter, to save Jenny, and to bring the remaining perpetrators to justice."

"You're going to get yourself caught, Detective. There's nowhere for you to run, and there are no clues to shed further light on the thieves' true identities. The forensic accountants and the police investigators all agree they're a gang of extremely dangerous ghosts. They're nowhere to be found."

Micheline slipped the Glock back into her shoulder holster. "I don't intend to get caught, nor to be that careless. As it stands, my only way out of this mess is to crack the case."

"Well, good luck with that. Even the investigative team working the case can't come up with anything definitive."

"I've got to try. Jenny's life may depend on it."

"I appreciate what you say you're going to do, Detective. But it's not enough. We lost some very good people last week."

"I know, sir. You have a good day now. I'll be in touch soon."

Micheline opened the door and jumped down to the macadam lot. She swung the door closed behind her and walked at a fast pace toward the storefronts across the street.

Her stomach grumbled agitatedly. Investigating multiple homicides, a kidnapping, and a bank heist had made her hungry.

Hungry for the truth.

Thirty-Six

Every Monday evening like clockwork, Laura Quiñónez was scheduled to work at the Hops & Malt Brewery Company in Del Mar for her part-time waitressing gig. Her work period ran from five-thirty in the afternoon until closing time at midnight. She did this following an 8:00 a.m. to 4:30 p.m. shift as a licensed pharmacy technician at Hildenbrandt's Pharmacy in Clairemont.

She worked at the pharmacy regularly on weekdays Monday through Friday and filled in for an occasional weekend shift when they needed extra coverage. She worked at Hops & Malt every Monday, Wednesday, and Saturday evening. She had three children. A house to take care of. A husband to clean up after.

Micheline was considering all of this as she sat on a bench along the pathway outside of the Hops & Malt establishment.

When you do the math, it just doesn't add up.

Could Laura have been responsible for Samantha Miller's death? It couldn't be a coincidence that on the same day as the murder, Laura turned up at work with a black eye and bruises on her arm, could it?

Yet, what possible motive would Laura have to kill the beautiful young socialite? Did she see Samantha's death as a financial opportunity to climb out from under a mountain of debt? Had the pressures of modern-day life simply become too much for her, and she finally just snapped?

The more that Micheline mused and pondered the questions, the more uncertain she became. She waited patiently and kept her head tilted down to avoid eye contact with anyone passing by.

At 5:24 p.m. Laura hurried along the paved walking path toward her part-time employer's restaurant. She immediately stopped in her tracks as if she'd seen a ghost. She recognized the familiar face of the woman sitting awkwardly on the wooden and wrought-iron bench. She stepped forward slowly.

"You shouldn't be here," she said. "I've seen you on the television news. The police are looking everywhere for you, Micheline."

"I need to know something, Laura," Micheline stated.

"Anything, Micheline," Laura said. "I've always considered you to be a friend, and I don't believe for a second you've done what they're accusing you of. What do you need?"

"How is it you knew Samantha Miller?"

"I don't understand. Who's that?"

"The young woman whose murder I was investigating. The pretty blonde who was having dinner with her fiancé at the pizzeria when they got into a heated argument, and she splashed her wine at him."

"Oh, *that* bitch! I didn't know her, Micheline. It was more like what I found out about her."

"What does that mean?" Micheline asked.

Laura shrugged helplessly and stared down at her well-worn sneakers.

"I'm not sure what the truth is," Laura responded. "This goes back to more than a year ago. I was doing the laundry on a Tuesday night. I remember that because it was a night off from the bar. I had worked at Hops & Malt the night before, and I recall Wade had gone to a sports bar with some of the mechanics from his auto shop. Just a boy's night out to have a few brews and watch the football game is what he told me."

"What does that have to do with Samantha Miller?" Micheline grilled her.

"I always pull the pants pockets out to make sure they don't have any tissues or papers tucked inside. Makes an awful mess in the washing machine when that happens. Sometimes I find a few dollars in bills or loose change, you know?"

"Yeah, I suppose."

"Well, I found a business card in the pocket of Wade's blue jeans. It was a white card with black print on it. The picture logo was a silhouette of a naked woman with big boobs, and it was from a strip joint down in the Gaslamp Quarter. On the back were a hand-written note and a phone number. It said *call me*, and it was signed *Clarissa*."

Micheline's eyes widened in surprise as she recalled the name from Dominic Sadoski's witness testimony.

"I thought about confronting Wade, and I thought about calling the number to tell her to fucking leave my husband alone."

"That's only natural, Laura," Micheline said. "What did you decide to do?"

"I wrote the name and number down on a scratch piece of paper, and I held onto it. I stuffed the business card back into Wade's pocket after the jeans came out of the dryer. I pretended I had never seen the card. I didn't want to know any more about it, and I never wanted to ask Wade about it, either."

"Then, how did you connect a stripper named Clarissa and her phone number with Samantha Miller?"

"It's not important, Micheline," Laura said. "I didn't want to know what it might mean. I was afraid I might be losing Wade. I thought he was having an affair. I stuffed that piece of paper into a junk drawer and tried to forget about it."

"Bullshit! There's more to this story. What is it?"

Laura shrugged her shoulders and relented to Micheline's interrogation.

"I met Jenny at the gym one Sunday afternoon not too long ago. We went to the coffee shop after our workout for fruit smoothies, and I told her about it."

"Yes. And?" Micheline was quickly becoming impatient.

"Jenny said she'd look into it. She said the strip joint was across the street from the bank where she works. She knew the bouncer. He was a customer at the bank."

"So, she figured it out."

"Jenny made inquiries, yes. She found out the girl's real name was Samantha Miller. She was a rich girl on the wrong side of the tracks. But she had quit dancing at the strip club and was turning her life around. She wouldn't be interested in Wade anymore. That's what Jenny said."

"That's it?"

"Yes, that's it. I didn't give her another thought until that night at the Italian bistro. I could see how humorous Wade found the whole situation. It really pissed me off. I could see there must have been something between them, even if it was only in his wild imagination. It made me sick."

"Did you do anything about it?"

"Do anything? What the fuck do you think I did? I confronted Wade about it. I threatened to leave him. He got physical with me. You saw the black eye and bruises he gave me."

"Why didn't you tell me this before?"

"I thought I had it under control, Micheline. I told Wade I'd leave him, and I made him promise he'd be loyal to me from now on. I told him if he ever lied to me again, I'd go to the police, and he'd go back to prison. He gave me his word and I haven't thought about it since. I've got enough to worry about in my life. Shit! I'm sorry, Micheline, but I'm late for work now."

"I understand, Laura. Thank you for talking with me."

"I don't mind, Micheline. I've always liked you. How about you, though? Are you all right?"

"I will be," Micheline said. "I've got to find a way to prove my innocence."

"Well, I wish you the best. And I hope you find Jenny, too. My two best girls have left me and I'm all alone now."

"I'll find her," Micheline acknowledged. "One way or the other. I will."

Laura hurried along the footpath and went inside the front entrance of the Hops & Malt Brewing Company to start her work shift.

Micheline let out a heavy sigh and began to walk back toward where she had parked the gray Accord.

Thirty-Seven

Micheline walked briskly along the pedestrian pathway. She headed directly toward a divided highway along the outer perimeter of the retail plaza. She moved quickly at a determined pace and kept her eyes cast downward, more to clear her head of a hurricane of wayward thoughts than to escape from being seen in a public space along the busy traffic corridor known as El Camino Real.

She had left the car in a large parking lot near to a hair salon and a dry-cleaning store. Both businesses were closed at this time of the evening. Still, the parking lot remained active due to an open supermarket, several restaurants, and a movie theater.

As her hand reached for the door handle of the car, she suddenly turned and looked around the dimly lit lot. In the far corner, on the opposite side as the supermarket, stood a non-descript, square-shaped building made of glass and cinder block. It was painted white with black trim. There was a yellow illuminated sign with red scripted lettering suspended near the flat roofline.

The Classy Chassis Autobody Shop.

Micheline smiled as the realization came to her. This was Wade Branigan's auto repair shop. She quickly seated herself in the car and drove across the parking lot toward the darkened automotive business. There was an interior light turned on in the front office and waiting area, and there were four closed bay doors of glass and steel supports. Otherwise, the building was left dark and deserted.

Micheline stepped from the car and checked her immediate surroundings. Other than a few patrons coming and going from the supermarket across the parking lot, there was a calm sense of nothingness.

She peered into the front office area and then began to walk along the front edge of the building. She inspected the vehicles parked inside the individual work bays. There was a red BMW three-series sedan with a dented hood and a cracked windshield, a gray Chevrolet pickup truck with a flat tire, and a shiny black Volvo SUV that looked as though it had just been delivered from the dealership showroom floor.

Micheline had considered buying an SUV when she had first arrived in California but had opted for the Mustang instead. She loved its classic styling and brute power.

She looked more closely at each of the vehicles in their work bays. The shop was fully equipped with tooling. Despite that, it was clean and organized.

A little too clean, maybe.

Micheline wandered around the front corner of the building and headed toward the rear lot. There was nothing back there but two large metal trash dumpsters and a debris pile of discarded metal parts. There were a few old tires stacked neatly in a column, a rusted muffler and tailpipe, and various pieces of mangled quarter panels that were peppered with cavities and abrasions.

Cavities?

Or bullet holes?

Micheline pursed her lips tightly. Alarm bells were clanging loudly in her head. She reached into her pocket for the cell phone and made a call.

"No dice, Detective," Kelly Van Horn's voice advised immediately upon answering the call.

"What do you mean?" Micheline asked.

"Your friend Laura has an airtight alibi for the Miller murder. She was clocked in at the pharmacy in Clairemont on that Saturday morning. I have sworn statements from the pharmacist on duty and the store manager. That black eye and the bruises on her arm must have come at the hands of her dirtbag husband if you ask me."

"I found some evidence I think you should check out," Micheline advised.

"Physical evidence?"

"Yes. Laura's husband's name is Wade Branigan. He's the ex-con who owns and operates an autobody shop in the Westwind shopping plaza."

"I'm aware of that," Kelly said flatly. "So?"

"In one of the bays in the shop is a black Volvo SUV, model XC-90. It looks brand new like it just rolled off the dealer's lot."

"Again, so what?"

"Imagine if it were originally white and was recently re-painted a darker color. I found a pile of banged-up white metal body parts behind the building. They're peppered with holes. Now either we have a condor-sized woodpecker on the loose, or those are bullet holes from the bank heist. You should have a crime scene unit get down here to check it out."

"Damn, girl! You may be on to something here."

"Another thing."

"Name it."

"Jenny Casella. You checked into her background, right?"

"Yes, Micheline. She's clean. I checked back five or six years. She's got good credit history. She makes a nice salary at the bank. Always paid her rent on time. Same with her school tuition, auto loan, and utility bills."

"I need you to look back further. Confirm family history. Mother, father, brothers, and sisters. Confirm her recent flight back home to Chicago, dates, and times. Does she have any current debt or upcoming vacation plans booked? When did she earn her degrees? Things like that."

"I can look into that, Micheline. But what angle are you driving toward?"

"Nothing specific yet," Micheline said. "I just have an uneasy feeling in my gut. Something doesn't add up."

"I was never good at math, either."

"Have you gotten any new details from William Hudgens, the bank president? He mentioned that thirty-five million went missing in wire transfers on the day of the heist."

"You spoke to the bank president while you're on the lam from the law?"

Micheline pursed her lips tightly.

"I can't just sit still and hope this case solves itself, Kelly. Imagine yourself in my shoes."

"Got it. Is there anything else I can help you with?"

"While you're doing background checks...,"

"Yes?"

Micheline took a deep breath.

"Do a check on Greg Slater, too. The guy I was dating. Same deep dive as with Jenny Casella. Work history, credit history, school, family, and known associates."

"You really need to get a life, Micheline. Doing a background check on your boyfriend is truly beneath you."

"That may well be," Micheline replied. "But my life has turned upside down lately. Those guns found at the bank came from the walk-in closet in my condo. Only two people I know of could have known they were there. I think it's worth checking into. Hopefully, I'm just being paranoid. But what if I'm not?"

"I'll look into it, Micheline. Anything else?"

"No, that should do it for now. I'm going to continue sniffing around. There's one more lead I want to follow."

"Be safe, Detective. I'll rally to your side, but we've got to uncover some solid evidence to prove your innocence. Otherwise, Richard and I are committing career suicide, and all three of us will get flushed down the toilet together."

"He's on board with this?"

"Yes," she said. "He came around. He's told me so."

"Good. Get the crime scene unit down here to the Classy Chassis Autobody Shop, pronto. If those are indeed bullet holes, then either Wade Branigan or one or more of his employees may have been involved in the bank heist. I'd suggest a more thorough background check on anyone connected to the autobody shop."

"I'm on it, Detective. You stay safe, you hear?"

"Thank you, Kelly. I owe you one, and probably much more."

The phone call disconnected. Micheline turned and headed back through the shadows toward the car. Her stride was full of purpose.

She was on her way to a late-night date with an ex-convict.

Thirty-Eight

Wade Branigan and Laura Quiñónez lived with their three children in a tiny two-story duplex with three bedrooms. There was a master bedroom for Wade and Laura which had its own walk-in closet and private bathroom. The children shared a separate bathroom on the second floor. The girls, who had a twelve-year age gap between them, shared a room with two twin beds. Raymond, who was only five, had a room to himself.

The twenty-four-year-old Spanish-style home had a narrow one-car garage, a kitchen with granite countertop and stainless-steel appliances, and a backyard patio the size of a postage stamp. The next-door neighbor lived on the other side of the adjoining wall which separated the mirror image duplex. The house was positioned near the end of a tree-lined cul-de-sac and offered less than eighteen hundred square feet of living space.

The house had cost slightly over a million dollars. It was more than either of them could afford in two lifetimes. They had barely scraped together the five percent down payment necessary to obtain the thirty-year mortgage in the first place by borrowing money from Laura's parents. But they had selected the cozy home because it offered their children the opportunity to attend one of the best school districts in southern California, it was located relatively close to the beach, and the mild year-round coastal region weather was too delightful to pass upon.

Sometimes they just made bad choices and learned how to live with them. It kept them on a perpetual hamster wheel of continuous debt from which they would likely never get ahead of. In the end, though, they preferred the location and accepted the severe financial consequences that came with the decision.

Micheline stood furtively on the sidewalk across the street. She noted lights coming from rooms on both upper and lower floors. Her wristwatch indicated it was nearly 10:00 p.m. Laura wouldn't be home for another two and half hours when her shift at the Hops & Malt Brewing Company ended. That left Wade to watch the children. Make dinner. Make sure the kids did their homework. Give the little ones their baths. Tuck them in and read them a bedtime story.

Micheline silently doubted Wade did any of that good father stuff like her old man used to do for her. She smiled at the tender remembrance of her loving father but had to stay focused on the here and now. Her life was falling into a bottomless pit from which there might be no return. Somehow it was up to her and her alone to find a way out.

Solve the three separate crimes and how they tie to one another. Earn your freedom.

One by one, the upstairs lights turned off. A short while later, the flicker of a television downstairs also turned off in the living room, leaving only a single lamp illuminated from behind the front bow window.

The front porch lights turned on.

Maybe Wade was leaving a light on for when his hard-working wife returned home later that evening. That's so sweet of him.

Micheline strolled slowly back to the car. She planned to maintain her evening surveillance vigil until Laura returned home. She would head back to Elena's hotel room afterward. She needed to consider one lead at a time, and she wasn't certain what she should do next.

The front door to Wade and Laura's house opened and softly closed shut. From across the street, Micheline crouched low on the other side of the hood of the car. She could hear a set of keys jingling in the latch, securely locking the door closed. Wade was leaving the house unattended with the children asleep upstairs.

Where the fuck does he think he's going at this time of night? Out for a drink while the children are home alone?

Micheline was forced to make a quick decision. She could stay with Wade and pursue on foot from a safe distance away. Or she could take the car and drive around the surrounding blocks in a figure-eight pattern so as not to be detected. She decided to pursue her quarry on foot. Wade didn't drive, after all. The fresh air might help to quell her nerves.

She waited patiently until Wade was well out of view down the street. He moved steadily and with purpose.

Micheline moved cautiously through the neighborhood along the wide sidewalk. No one was outside at this late hour. The street was clear of traffic.

Ahead, she glimpsed Wade turn left down a side street. He continued until he reached the middle of the block. He came to a complete stop suddenly and looked around in all directions. Micheline abruptly ducked low behind a parked car and kept to the shadows so as not to be seen.

Wade crossed into the street and approached the driver's side of a dark Cadillac sedan parked along the curb. Micheline heard the jingle of Wade's house keys again. With the press of a button, the car doors unlocked, the parking lights flashed on and off, and Wade slipped into the driver's seat.

What the hell?

Micheline took several steps closer. She couldn't make out the license number, but she recognized the special interest design of the vanity plate. The image displayed green palm trees, a blue ocean, and an orange sun setting on the horizon. It was a standard-number arts plate, used to support arts education programs across California through grants from the California Arts Council, a state-run government agency. It was the type of license plate the DMV charged an annual fee for.

What's going on?

The engine started.

Micheline turned on her heels immediately and raced back around the block toward the parked gray Honda Accord. She jumped in, started the engine, and pulled ahead toward the intersection. As much of a hurry as she was in, she reminded herself to take it slow and easy.

Don't let anyone take notice of me.

The Cadillac pulled away from the curb and proceeded east on a direct route toward the major freeway interchange. Wade passed immediately ahead of Micheline on the cross street.

Micheline turned right at the stop sign and drove ahead slowly. She held back as far as she could. She didn't want to catch Wade's attention, but at the same time, she didn't want to lose sight of where he might be going.

Wade drove south on the San Diego Freeway and stayed closer to the right lanes on the six-lane highway. He never went above the posted speed limit. He exited at Route 163 and headed south along Tenth Avenue. Then he turned right onto Island Avenue and drove into the Gaslamp Quarter. He crossed the intersection at Fifth Avenue and began to slow down. He used his right turn signal and pulled into a parking space along the curb.

Micheline continued driving past him for another block and then pulled into a parking space along the curb. She quickly killed the ignition and got out of the car. She would have to be fast. From the distance, she saw Wade exit the Cadillac and proceed to walk along the sidewalk down Fifth Avenue.

Further on, he entered a Mexican restaurant.

Is he meeting someone? Is he cheating on Laura?

Micheline pretended to be window shopping and wandered casually along the street. Inside the restaurant, there were a dozen or more patrons seated at square wooden tables with red tablecloths. Wade stood near a takeout counter off to the side of the dining area.

Micheline crossed the street and chose a strategic position from which to watch for Wade's movements. Fifteen minutes later, Wade walked outside onto the sidewalk. He carried a six-pack of beer in his left hand and cradled a large grocery-sized paper bag in the crook of his right arm.

Fish tacos, I'll bet. That's a lot of food for just one guy, though. He looks like he's on his way to a party.

Wade continued to walk further down Fifth Avenue to the corner of Island Avenue. He suddenly veered left into the main entrance of the abandoned Imperial Theater complex.

Micheline quickened her pace and stayed close to the retail storefronts lined along the avenue.

What would he be doing at the theater? It's all boarded over and locked up tight as a drum.

Wade jiggled his keys again. He unlocked the main entrance door to the theater and went inside. The heavy wooden main entrance door closed behind him.

Micheline stood on the sidewalk and considered her next move. There were too few options to think of. If she wanted to find proof of her innocence, she would have to follow the clues wherever they may lead.

Even if it meant breaching the inside of a dark and abandoned fortress in the dead of night.

She turned abruptly and walked back toward the parked Honda Accord. She opened the back hatch and reached for the canvas straps of the large black zippered carry bag. The bag was full and heavy, but it contained everything she might need to protect herself in the upcoming confrontation.

She placed the bag on the sidewalk, gently closed the back hatch to the car, and clicked the button on the key fob to lock the doors.

Am I really doing this?

Micheline looked intently around the street to absorb her surroundings. The muscles of her jaw locked stubbornly with tension. She was certain of what she must do. She was going to spend an evening at the theater.

She may not have had the proper dress or a ticket for admission. But that would never stop her from making an uninvited appearance.

Thirty-Nine

Micheline crouched low in the shadows along the sheer granite blocks that formed the outer walls of the Imperial Theater. From this angle on the ground, the building's structure presented a foreboding and impenetrable fortress.

Yet somehow Wade had the keys to the front door.

Micheline checked and inventoried her gear from within the black zippered carry bag carefully. She slipped on a bulletproof flak jacket and a canvas belt lined with canisters of pepper spray throw grenades.

She carried a nine-millimeter Glock 19 in a waist holster on her left side and tucked a backup handgun into a Velcroed pocket on her lower left pants leg. She clipped a police radio to the canvas belt on her right hip, with the hand mike attached to the top of the right shoulder strap of the flak jacket.

She hesitated.

She had to consider the possibility she might be walking into a deadly trap. She smeared black, military-style camouflage paint onto her face and neck. Then she snapped her detective's shield onto the left front side of the belt around her waistline.

She picked up a black Smith & Wesson M&P 15T semi-automatic rifle. The gun fired 5.56mm shells from thirty-round magazines. She inserted an ammunition clip and added four more magazines to the Velcro pockets in her lower pants legs.

Then she attached a combination rail-mounted LED flashlight and red laser device to the handguard of her rifle. This would allow her to see clearly in darkened spaces in front of her without having to free her hands from the grip of her primary weapon.

Micheline inspected her gear one final time. She was ready to go to war.

But before she would race into harm's way, she steadied herself to calm her nerves and pulled her cell phone from a zippered pocket. She dialed Kelly Van Horn's number. It went straight to voicemail. She tried Richard Tuller's number next.

"Detective Tuller," he answered immediately. "Micheline, is that you?"

"Hi, Richard."

"Jeez, you've set off a wildfire of activity tonight, you know."

"Did I?"

"Kelly's already got a judge's signature on a search warrant in hand. There's a CSI team at the body shop right now. They're going through the metal scraps outside the back of the building. It's all circumstantial, of course. But I'd bet next month's salary you've located the getaway vehicle from the bank heist."

"I'd make that same wager," Micheline admitted. "Richard, I need a little more to go on. Is there anything you can tell me about the heist?"

"Not much, I'm afraid. Phil Kovacs and his team are all over it. I can only give you some scuttlebutt I picked up from Kelly."

"That'll do for now."

"Very well. They identified four of the bodies at the bank. Those wearing military body armor."

"Who were they, and how were they related?"

"First off, they were all military veterans, highly decorated and with some interesting skillsets. They all left military service and got themselves in trouble with the law later on."

"How so?" Micheline asked. "Tell me about them," she demanded.

"Two were Army Rangers. Donny LeGath was the 1st Ranger Battalion stationed at Fort Benning in Georgia. Jeff Breedlove was also a Ranger, but he was 2nd Ranger Battalion stationed at Fort Lewis in

Washington. They both saw action in the Middle East, which is where their paths crossed."

"So, I'm supposed to like them? My father was a Ranger, you know."

"They served their country, Micheline. The same way you and I do every day. They put their lives on the line."

"But they couldn't function outside of the service. Civilian life just wasn't for them. They killed cops and executed innocent bank employees. Is that it?"

"At some point, they went rogue, yes. In the service, they performed covert reconnaissance operations. They were part of an elite airborne light infantry combat formation. They did combat drops and captured enemy airfields, things like that. They knew weapons, tactics, and explosives."

"And the other two?"

"Former Navy, stationed out of Coronado. Similar backgrounds. These were some tough dudes."

"My neighbors. Just my luck."

"Our Army Rangers were part of a bank robbery crew that got busted in Carlsbad a way's back. They served four years in Lompoc."

"That may explain the jailhouse gang tattoos I noticed."

"You're spot-on with that, Micheline."

"Who were the Navy guys?"

"The fake security guard was DeAngelo Johnson. He went by the moniker D.J. His buddy was Albert Glenning. They were SARCs."

"They were what?"

"It's an acronym. It stands for special amphibious reconnaissance corpsman. They did their field medical training together at Camp Pendleton. After they left the service, both men were busted on drug trafficking charges. They served eighteen months at Lompoc, at the same time as our Army crew. And there's more."

"Do tell."

"When the drug bust went down, Wade Branigan was part of their crew. So, he knew DeAngelo Johnson and Al Glenning from the outset. He would've had contact with Donnie LeGath and Jeff Breedlove in prison. They were all part of the same jailhouse gang. More recently, all four of the military vets were working together on a construction crew on a project in downtown San Diego. D.J. was their foreman. It all links up."

"Nice work, Detective!"

"It wasn't me," Richard asserted. "Kelly's part of the investigative team now. She's kept me in the loop. Where are you now, Micheline?"

"I'm out on the town. I thought I'd catch a show tonight."

"You shouldn't be out in public. You're all over the news. People are sure to recognize you and to call it in eventually."

"I'll just have to take my chances. I've got line-of-sight on Wade Branigan."

"Do you want some backup?"

Micheline considered the offer as a white flag of truce.

"I just followed Wade to the old Imperial Theater at Fifth & Island. He had keys to the front door."

"Wait for me there. I can be there in ten."

"Sounds like a plan. Do you have anything on the prison gang they all belonged to?"

"All I know is they called themselves the Wild Wolves. Each member had a black and red tattoo of a wolf's head as their signature brand. Kelly's tracking down their known associates, determining who was also incarcerated at Lompoc during the time these men served their prison sentences, and any background or former arrests that might lend some light."

"Right."

"Micheline?"

"Yeah?"

"The four dead military vets were working on the demolition project at the Imperial. That might be where the bank robbers who escaped are holding Jenny hostage."

"That was my thought as well," Micheline said.

"We have to be careful. It's not just the bank robbers who are a threat. The cops are gunning for you, too. To them, you're an escaped convict responsible for the deaths of fellow officers. Lieutenant Salvatore and Sergeant McCaffrey weren't the only officers killed at the bank during the robbery. Four other uniformed off-duty officers were on the scene that morning. They died during the bomb explosion at the front of the bank. One of the female officers was pregnant."

"Oh, that's horrible."

"The police force doesn't consider you to be a trusted friend and colleague like I know you to be. They only see the black and white, not the gray in between."

"Quite the pickle I'm in, huh?"

"I realize you want to solve this and to prove your innocence. But if you do come across the thieves who escaped from the bank before the police do, they're not going to be any friendlier to you."

"I kind of figured that. Our last encounter wasn't a picnic, you know. I have three bullet wounds that ache like hell every time I move."

"My guess is they're also former vets. They're probably from the same battalions or naval squadrons as our deceased bank robbers. They'll be ruthless, and they'll shoot first without any regrets. It's all about survival now. You know that, right?"

"Well, guess what, Richard?"

"What's that?"

Micheline pursed her lips and tightened her jaw. "Maybe I'm the one they should all be afraid of. Because right now, I'm back on duty and I'm ready to kick some ass."

"Amen, girl. I'll be there as quick as I can. Wait for me."

"Thanks, Richard. Call me back when you get here."

Micheline ended the call. She took a deep breath and slipped the cell phone into an enclosure on the right side of her pants leg.

It was time to get the party started. Micheline moved forward quickly, alone. The band was already playing inside the empty theater, and she wasn't about to wait for her prom date to ask her to dance.

Forty

Micheline crept stealthily through the front entrance doorway of the decrepit Imperial Theater. Everything inside was shrouded in austere darkness. Only the dim light cast by the nearby cityscape invaded the foyer through wide gaps in the plywood sheeting that covered glassless exterior window frames.

The theater had a storied history. Built in 1927 in the American Renaissance Beaux-Arts style, the Imperial Theater and Performing Arts Center seated more than three thousand people. Over the years, its performances included operas, symphonies, Broadway-style stage plays and musicals, rock & roll concerts, and stand-up comedy venues. Its attendees had included business tycoons, Hollywood celebrities, former presidents and high-ranking government officials, and the members of foreign royal families.

The room was silent. There were splintered wood planks, sawdust, and broken glass shards strewn haphazardly across the torn-up and dilapidated carpet. A distinct aroma of fish tacos and French fries filled the air.

Micheline treaded forward steadily alone. She listened intently for any hint of a human presence within the abandoned palace.

The smell of fish tacos was making her hungry.

She moved forward quietly to the right along a side corridor. Directly ahead, a set of carved wooden double doors led toward a vast open room. Within that grand hall, an opulent theater auditorium had once received thousands of guests and occupants adorned in tuxedoes and fancy ball gowns.

Micheline crouched low to the floor and pushed the door open a tiny crack. Voices echoed lightly from farther away.

She switched off the flashlight attached to the handguard of her rifle and silently pushed the door open several inches.

Thank goodness the door hinge didn't squeak.

She quickly entered the room from a low stance. She held the door as she did so and closed it again without creating a disturbance.

Micheline was cloaked in darkness at the back of the theater. She got down on her belly and allowed her eyes to adjust to the black void around her. She moved slowly, quietly, and nestled her shoulder against the back of the frame of a metal arena seat.

A soft glow of lantern light was emitted from the raised stage at the front of the empty theater. Micheline looked up. The auditorium was immense. The cathedral ceiling was several stories high. Three separate rows of ornate balconies lined the perimeter of the outer walls.

Ahead, the seating section sloped downward toward the orchestra pit. A divider railing, which separated the seating section from the orchestra pit, ran across the entire floor span from side to side. Voices were coming from the raised illuminated stage beyond the orchestra pit. Access to the stage was from side entrances only.

Micheline maintained her prone position on the floor. She silently crawled along a downward-sloping side aisle to improve her vantage point closer to the stage. The voices became clearer.

"Thanks for bringing the food," a woman's voice said. She had a distinct accent. "I could eat a half dozen of these things."

"I'll go back to get more if I need to," Wade Branigan said. Micheline recognized his voice immediately. "I only have two hands, you know."

The sound amplification and acoustics within the theater were well propagated. Micheline realized that any sounds she might make would be equally generated to the group on stage she was surveilling.

"Fish tacos and fries are my favorites," said an unknown male voice.

"Are there any more jalapeño poppers?"

"Yes. Here you go."

"Would you pass me a bottle of beer, please?"

"What's this dip called again?"

"It's queso fundido dip. Try it on the fish tacos. Just dip one of the ends into it."

"It's amazing! You made a great choice for our last meal in San Diego."

"I picked it up at a Mexican joint down the street."

"Do you have any vinegar, salt, or ketchup packets for the chips?" the woman asked. Her British accent betrayed her identity.

Jackie Henshilwood?

"They should be in the bag," Wade answered. "So, guys. What's the plan? Do you have any updates yet?"

"Good news," another male voice replied. The man's voice sounded vaguely familiar to Micheline, but she couldn't place it right away.

"What's that?"

"The cruise ship is due into port tomorrow morning. It was delayed since last Wednesday because of the Siberian storm that swept in past Alaska and western Canada."

"I would have preferred to stay at a hotel in the meantime," Jackie stated.

"Of course. We've all hated being holed up in this crummy demolition zone of a theater for the whole damn week. But it was necessary to ensure a clean getaway."

"Better safe than sorry," another unknown woman's voice replied. "Right?"

"Thank goodness D.J. was a foreman on the construction crew. They were working on the demolition project for the theater. We needed a haven to lay low since the cruise ship was delayed into port, and he had the keys to this lovely castle, so to speak."

"Not much of a castle if you ask me. Feels more like a mausoleum or an old, haunted house from a Frankenstein or vampire movie. It gives me the creeps."

"You're right, I guess."

"We wouldn't have wanted to return to any of our homes after the bank robbery went down the way it did. With four of our members killed in action, it's just a matter of time before the cops identify us. Once they review the military history and prison records for Donny, Jeff, D.J., and Al, they'll check for known associates. It's better that we're not taking any chances. We're so close to gaining our freedom right now."

Micheline crawled forward a few more seat rows. She wanted to get a better visual of the people talking from the stage.

"I wish I was going with you," Wade said. "I know that was the original plan. But I'm going to stay with Laura and make the best of it. I've made up my mind. I can't leave the kids behind."

"You were basically ready to leave them all before. What's changed your mind?"

That was Greg Slater's voice. Holy fuck!

"Samantha's gone," Wade answered somberly. "I can't keep holding on to a memory that was never real to begin with. Even if I'm not in love with Laura, and I haven't been for years, I've got to face facts and learn to be responsible for the kids' sakes."

"Well, how are you going to hide the fact you've got a couple of million dollars in cash stored in a locked filing cabinet at your business?"

"I've got it all worked out," Wade replied confidently. "I'm going to hire a manager to oversee day-to-day operations at the shop. I'll tell Laura the business has shown a nice profit and she can quit her part-time job. Maybe I'll pay off the mortgage on the house and start taking life a little easier."

"I wouldn't do that, Wade," Greg suggested. "That would be a huge mistake. Just keep making the normal monthly payments and keep things simple. Don't change your routine or habits too drastically too soon. No one will ever be the wiser, then."

Micheline crawled forward several more seat rows. She still couldn't make out the faces of the people on the stage.

Was Jenny up there with them? Did they have her bound or gagged? Had they hurt her?

"Thanks. I'll keep that in mind. So, where's this cruise ship taking you off to?"

"We set sail from San Diego to Puerto Vallarta, Mexico on the Oceana Vista," Greg said. "It's a luxury cruise liner. I saw a drawing that compared the size of the Oceana Vista to the Titanic. It made the Titanic look like a little tugboat."

"Geez, that's got to be a big ship."

"It's one of the largest in the world. We'll spend a few days chilling out at a beachfront resort in Mexico. Then we have reservations to board the Atlantic Quest, which will take us through the Panama Canal and on into the Caribbean Sea to the Cayman Islands."

"It sounds like paradise."

"It will be," the other male voice said. "We're making our new home on Grand Cayman Island, where the rum is cheap, the sex is orgasmic, soft breezes run warm and mild, and the banking institutions don't recognize the FBI's authority."

"Brilliant!" Jackie called out.

"Yes, it is," Greg proclaimed.

On the stage, a half dozen battery-operated camping lanterns had been stationed in a wide circle. Within the circle, a clump of suitcases, air mattresses, and folding chairs had been set up. There was a pile off to the side of rifles and other protective gear from the bank heist.

Micheline could see Greg and Jenny, Wade, and another male and female couple seated next to one another. Jenny didn't appear to be tied up, but she was sandwiched in between them. The woman next to her was Jackie Henshilwood. The male seated on the other side of Jackie looked hauntingly familiar. Short, stout, wavy hair. He wore a long-sleeve shirt with the cuffs rolled up, a pair of cargo shorts, and canvas sneakers.

"What about all the gear from the bank heist?" Wade asked. "You can't take that with you on the cruise ship."

"Just leave it here."

"But won't the construction crew find it and report it to the police?"

"Not to worry."

"That's all I seem to do these days," Wade admitted.

"We've already got a contingency plan in place for that."

"Really?"

"Yes. Before the heist, DJ and Al had gotten their hands on demolition explosives for the project. It wasn't clear yet whether they would need it or not."

"So?"

"So, learning to set explosives was part of my military training a few years back. I've got the structural supports throughout the theater lined with C4. One push of the button and all this will become the largest rubbish pile on the west coast."

"But..."

"It'll be years before the city council puts a budget together to clean up the mess we leave behind. I'll use a battery-operated water sprinkler timer to have it go off a few days after we've left, just to make sure we're in the clear."

"You've thought of everything."

"I can't wait to get to the hotel on Grand Cayman and to order my first cup of coffee," he said. "I want to see the look on the barista's face when I pass them a one-hundred-dollar tip."

No way! Harrison Murray from the Books & Coffee Café. How can he be involved in this?

Micheline was shocked that she knew all five of these individuals on the stage.

Four of them are murderers and thieves. What does that say about me as a detective?

"Jackie says I shouldn't. That I should keep a low profile. What do you say?" he asked the group.

"Same advice I gave to Wade," Greg answered. "Don't go around flashing your newfound wealth. Play it cool. Live a quiet life, but one in which you never have to think about how much stuff costs ever again."

"We can have nice houses, though, right?" Jackie asked.

"Yes, of course," Harrison replied. "Once all the bank transactions have cleared and our individual accounts are set up, you'll be able to do what you want. Nice beach houses. Nice cars. Nice toys. I just suggest we play it safe in the beginning. That's all."

"Okay, I think I can handle that."

"We'll start with a resort vacation on Grand Cayman and take our time to get acquainted with the island. We'll stay at the hotel and eat in fancy restaurants. We'll act like a group of tourists, which is exactly what we will be."

"I agree. That should be an easy part for us to play."

"Later, when things calm down, we'll seek out a credible realtor. We'll purchase our new homes, and we'll act like we're a bunch of ex-pats looking to retire in style."

But what were they planning to do with Jenny? Were they going to shoot her or leave her behind to die when the building exploded?

"I can't wait for us to set sail on this new adventure in our lives," Jackie exclaimed. "Thank you, Harrison, for including me in your far-out scheme. I feel like we're a modern-day Bonnie and Clyde."

Harrison pulled her close and kissed her. "We're going to have a blast eating fancy food, driving exotic cars, getting ourselves wasted, and fucking our brains out on those sandy beaches, babe."

"Oh my," Jackie said. "And watching beautiful sunsets and sunrises, too."

Micheline continued to crawl forward toward the stage. She scowled angrily with each new comment she overheard.

Enough of this Fantasy Island bullshit!

She intended to quietly position herself between the bank robbers and their weapons stash. If she could do that before they became aware of her presence, she could hold them at gunpoint, rescue Jenny in the process, and call in the cavalry.

That will be the plan. Now, how to get there without being noticed?

Micheline pressed her body closer to the floor and crawled in between a row of seats. Each chair was scarred with torn fabric.

High-density molded foam protruded from beneath the frayed and well-worn surfaces.

Micheline estimated she was only ten rows away from the perimeter railing at the orchestra pit. Her plan was to make her way silently and swiftly to the center aisle. When the time was right, with the shadowy darkness of the theater as her backdrop, she would quietly make her way across the seating section to the stairwell exit at the side of the building.

Before they know what hits them, they'll think they're surrounded by a team of SWAT officers with high-caliber machine guns and sniper rifles trained on them.

She would take down the murderous team of bank robbers. She would save Jenny. She would call the police to swarm in to take charge.

And then she would prove her innocence beyond a reasonable doubt.

Forty-One

The front row was less than ten feet distant to the railing that separated the seating gallery from the orchestra pit. But it might as well have been a mile away.

Micheline stayed low to the floor behind the tenth row of center stage seats. She only occasionally poked her head above the top of the seats to check the positions of the bank robbery crew and their hostage on the raised stage in front of her.

"Does anyone want more food?" Wade asked. "I'll make another beer and taco run if you'd like."

"Nah, I think we're good," Greg said. "I know I'm stuffed. Harrison, how about you?"

"I'm okay," Harrison replied. "Those tacos were mighty tasty, too. I'll finish the last beer if no one wants it."

"Ladies?" Greg asked. "Last call for midnight snacks."

"No, thank you," Jenny mumbled softly.

"No more for me, either," Jackie agreed. "My tummy's full, and I've got everything I could ever hope for sitting right here next to me."

"All right, guys," Wade said. "I guess this is where we say goodbye. It's been a real pleasure while the fun lasted. I hope you all make it safely to your island paradise and live a rich and happy life."

"You mean that, Wade?" Greg asked callously. His words were coated with a thick veil of anger and suspicion.

"Of course, I mean it, Greg. Why wouldn't I?"

"I don't know," Greg replied. "You seem to forget our fallen heroes. They died for your sake. For all of our sakes."

"I don't forget, man. I spent time with them in the joint. We were brothers."

"So, why did you change your mind at the last second and decide not to come along with us? Tell me honestly, why you did that."

"I just had a change of heart, I guess," Wade replied with a deadpan expression.

"That decision could put us all in jeopardy," Greg argued. "What happens if you're caught with the getaway vehicle at your shop and you squeal to the cops before we make it out of the country?"

"Greg, seriously. I would never do that. And besides, they couldn't recognize the SUV the way it looks now. It's completely restored and painted a different color."

"Are you sure?"

"Of course, man. You and your brother came up with the perfect plan for a heist, and you included me in your crew. I would never betray that trust."

Brother? What does he mean by that?

Wade extended his arms out to his sides. "Look, the truth is, I loved Samantha more than anyone in my entire life. If she hadn't been killed by some psycho ex-boyfriend, I was planning to ask her to come with me to the Caribbean."

"Seriously?" Harrison asked. "You loved her? You thought she'd be a willing participant in all of this?"

"Yes, I loved her. No doubt about it. I don't think she felt quite the same way about me. But the promise of a lifetime in the Caribbean and loads of cash. I think I could've persuaded her to appreciate me more."

"She was already rich," Jackie said. "You were just a toy to her. Nothing more."

"Yeah, but she and I got along so great together. It was weird how she was killed like that, right after I had left her at the park, too. Man, I can still see the way she looked at me with those gorgeous green eyes of hers. It would have been awesome to take her to the Caribbean and to spend forever together."

"You can be so dimwitted, Wade," Greg said.

"Huh?"

"You think that numskull ex-fiancé doctor followed you to the park and killed her?"

"Well, yeah," Wade said, dumbfounded. "Who else would've wanted her dead? Who else would've had reason to carve her up like that? The TV newscast said she'd been stabbed something like forty times. That's psycho rage if you ask me. That doctor was so jealous she was with me instead of him. You saw the way he reacted at the restaurant that night. It had to be him."

"Well maybe your wife was upset and jealous about your fornicating with other women," Greg suggested. "Did you ever for once consider that perhaps Laura knew about you and Samantha? That maybe she wished you both dead?"

"Yeah," Wade replied, shrugging his shoulders. "She called me out on that. But she's no killer. She made me promise I'd be faithful to her from now on."

"And do you think you can do that?" Harrison asked.

"I don't know," Wade said. "But I've got to try."

"Do you realize Samantha had a trust fund since she turned twenty-one worth over ten million dollars?" Greg asked. "And all we needed was her thumbprint to gain access to it."

"What?"

"That's right," Greg said. "You left a business card with Samantha's phone number in your pants pocket, you dumb fuck. Laura found it when she was doing the laundry. We've known all about it for a long time now."

"Oh, no! Greg, please tell me you didn't have anything to do with Samantha's death."

Wade's face turned a shade of green. He looked as though he were about to be sick. In the back of his mind, he knew the answer.

"Of course, I had a hand in it," Greg admitted. "But I can't take full credit. It was all part of our team's master plan, and it serves you right."

Greg stood and walked casually over to the pile of suitcases. He surveyed some of the items spread on the floor of the stage.

"Why?" Wade cried. "I was finally happy. You had to go and ruin that. I never did anything wrong to you."

Greg bent over and reached for something hidden behind a large Pullman suitcase.

"Because you did more than just to hurt Laura's feelings, Wade!" Jackie accused. "You ruined her life. And all for meaningless sex with a woman who would never love you back. You said so yourself. Samantha served her purpose well, I'd say."

"No, I don't believe it," Wade stammered nervously.

"Face it, Wade," Harrison said, "we used her, just like she used you. And you think Jackie just showed up at the murder scene as a coincidence because they play on the same softball team?"

"What do you mean?" Wade asked alarmingly. "That was totally by a freak accident, wasn't it?"

"She's been watching Samantha for almost two years now. She was the lookout that day. She knew where Samantha parked her car. She knew when Samantha was going to meet you at the park. She led us straight to the perfect spot to take her cell phone and her thumbprint. That gave us direct access to Samantha's bank accounts."

"No!" Wade cried. Tears began to stream down upon his reddened cheeks.

Greg laughed mockingly at Wade. "The only reason Jackie was screaming and pretended to the police to be a witness was that that blind guy and Micheline showed up unexpectedly. She had to make it look good to cover our tracks. Otherwise, she would've disappeared from the murder scene without a trace."

"I can't believe this!" Wade shrieked in horror. His eyes bulged with rage. "I don't care what happens to you now, Greg. This changes everything."

Before Wade could take a step forward to protest further, Greg picked up the M4 automatic rifle on the other side of the suitcase. He calmly selected the three-round-burst firing mode.

"Wait, no!" Wade cried. "I didn't mean it."

Greg established a firm base position with his legs, just as he had been taught in the Army. He aimed the barrel of the gun at his new-found nemesis and proceeded to punch three gaping holes into Wade's unprotected chest cavity.

Blood spurted to the uneven floorboards at the edge of the stage. The force of the three blasts knocked Wade's body backward off the stage. His lifeless corpse slammed into the orchestra pit below.

"Damn," Greg said as he peered curiously over the edge of the stage. "What a mess! I should've remembered, we still have to sleep here to-night. It'll be kind of creepy to have a dead body so close by. It reminds me of Afghanistan."

"It's only for one night," Harrison said. "And he had it coming to him. We could never trust him to keep our secret. You know he'd end up in the joint again someday. We'd always be wondering if he'd offer us up to receive a reduced sentence. It's cleaner this way."

"Seems a waste of all that money he stashed at his auto body shop," Jackie said.

"Not a waste," Greg added. "We'll make sure Laura finds it after we're safely on our way."

"But her husband is dead. Now she's a single mom again. Haven't you made things worse for her?"

"Not really," Greg replied. "Wade was nothing but poison in her life. She was too blind to see that. Now she's rich and she's free to meet somebody who may really care for her. Somebody who'll be a good father to her kids, too. Somebody better than that piece of garbage."

"I see your point."

"Think of it this way," Greg added. "Now there's no one left who could snitch to the police about us. It's the perfect ending to an epic story. What do you say, bro?"

"I'm all for that," Harrison said. "I've got my girl, and we've got more money than we'll ever be able to spend in this lifetime."

Harrison raised his bottle of beer into the air.

"Cheers!" he called out.

Forty-Two

Micheline lifted herself away from the floor and got to a one-kneed stance. She pushed the safety selector switch above the pistol grip of her Smith & Wesson semi-automatic assault rifle to the fire position.

It's now or never.

She carefully surveilled the area around her. She was enshrouded among the shadows of the seating section of the theater. It was doubtful anyone from the stage would be able to detect her movements. Still, she had to be careful.

The problem was the orchestra pit railing stood between the first row of seats and the raised platform of the stage. The distance across the orchestra pit was at least twenty-five feet. To make an approach to the stage even more difficult, there were no stairs or direct access to the stage from the recessed floor of the orchestra pit.

There's got to be another way.

Micheline nudged the selector switch of her rifle to the safe position. She bent down low and crept back along the row of empty seats to the side aisle. She listened attentively to the conversation from the stage while she silently plodded forward toward the exit doors at the back of the theater.

"Is everything all set for the fireworks display?" Greg asked.

"All set," Harrison replied. "It's on a sprinkler system timer, so I could set it for a few days from now when we'll be long gone."

"What about the power source? There's no live electric feed from this site, is there?"

"It's connected to a car battery I lifted from Wade's shop."

"That's poetic justice for you. He'll be buried under a million tons of rubble sparked by one of his own batteries."

"Knowing the political history of this site, it'll be weeks before they consider a clean-up operation. Probably more like months or even years. By that time, we'll be comfortable living the good life with our new identities in an extradition-free country. No more looking back over our shoulders."

"I think you deserve some special treatment for devising such a perfect plan," Jackie said, her tone sounding overtly sexual and flirtatious.

Micheline turned and gazed back toward the lighted stage area. Jackie had straddled Harrison's lap. The couple was embraced in a passionate kiss.

"Let's find a quiet place and I'll show you," Jackie suggested.

Yuck!

Micheline flexed her jaw and forced herself to turn around. She continued to head back toward the exit door. Within seconds she had quietly escaped into the lobby.

An obscure shadow flickered near to the main entrance doors. Micheline crouched low and immediately pressed her body against the wall. Her index finger pushed the selector switch of her rifle to the fire position.

"Micheline?" the voice whispered.

Micheline's heartbeat settled. "Richard, thank goodness it's you."

"What's the situation?" Detective Richard Tuller asked. He approached closer to Micheline's position next to the heavy wooden doors. He wore a gray hooded sweatshirt, blue jeans, and black canvas sneakers. A Glock 22 nine-millimeter pistol was secured in a waist holster on his right hip. His badge was snapped in place next to the holster. A handcuff clip and a tactical LED flashlight were attached to the belt on his left side.

"We have three bank robbers. They're holding a hostage on the main stage."

"They're armed?"

"If we're not careful, they could start a war. They have all their equipment from the bank heist nearby. That includes fully automatic military rifles. But they're not expecting us. The guns are off to the side. They just finished having dinner and drinking beer. If we can advance on them from the side stage entrance, we can surprise them and take them down."

"Who are they?"

"All of my best friends."

"You're joking."

"Not entirely," Micheline said. "One is Greg Slater, my former supposed boyfriend. The other two are Harrison Murray, the barista at the coffee shop I go to every morning near the courthouse, and Jackie Henshilwood, the witness from the Samantha Miller case."

"And they've taken Jenny Casella as their hostage?"

"Yes. Jenny doesn't appear to be injured. But she may be restrained to a chair in the middle of the group."

"What about Wade Branigan? Isn't he the one you followed here in the first place?"

"His body is on the floor in the orchestra pit. They thought he might give them up at some point, so they executed him with three rounds to the chest from close range. He took his final bow right off the edge of the stage."

"You saw that?"

"Yeah. It really shook me, too. The theater's dark as a crypt. The group is hanging out on the stage with camping lanterns set nearby."

"I smell fried food."

"Wade brought them their dinner tonight. Fish tacos, French fries, and beer."

"Right, and that's the thanks he gets. So, what are we going to do now?"

"I say we exit stage left and take them down. Are you with me?"

"Right by your side, Detective."

"Are you wearing a vest?"

"Yes."

"Okay, then. Let's go, and let's be quick about it."

Richard nodded toward Micheline. They simultaneously turned and scampered across the main lobby toward a corridor on the left side of the building.

Debris and garbage were scattered everywhere across the tattered floor.

"Housekeeper's day off, huh?"

"Yeah, definitely overdue. Wait."

"What?"

Richard shone his flashlight high up on a weight-bearing column. There was a tiny flash of red light blinking every thirty seconds or so.

"Fuck! They've got this place wired with explosives. That's C4 strapped to the top of the column. Lots of it."

"I heard them say something about a fireworks display. The devices are running on a battery-operated timer. They're set to go off in a few days. They wanted to have time to make their getaway."

"All right. Let's apprehend our suspects, call it in, and then let's get our asses the hell out of here."

The two detectives moved quietly along the corridor. Ahead, soft whispers emanated from the shadows away from the stage. There was grunting and the reverberations of subdued resistance.

Micheline switched off her flashlight. Richard did the same. They moved forward silently, one step at a time. They didn't want to inadvertently kick an unseen object on the floor and create a sound that would give their positions away.

They had the element of surprise on their side. They intended to use that to their fullest advantage.

Forty-Three

There was a scuffling movement coming from the black void of the corner ahead. Micheline held up her forearm with a closed fist, signaling Richard to pause and remain silent.

"Don't fight me on this," Greg Slater growled tersely. "I have my mind made up in this matter, Jenny. It's going to happen whether you agree with me or not."

Greg had forced Jenny Casella into the corner. Her back was to the wall. Greg was attempting to assault her. His arms encircled her torso. Jenny's body was locked in a defenseless position.

Greg's hands groped Jenny's body all over. He was attempting to kiss her neck. Jenny's head was tilted back against the wall. Her hands were raised in the air and shook wildly back and forth. Her fingers clawed at the air in desperation but found nothing to grasp onto.

Richard gently touched Micheline on the top of her shoulder with his left hand and flashlight. He motioned to alert her of his intentions. He would move in first to apprehend Greg Slater. Micheline would cover him. She nodded her consent.

Richard moved forward agilely and immediately placed the barrel of his Glock 22 against Greg Slater's back.

"Freeze, Slater," he snarled. "Police. Get your hands off her. Place them on the back of your head. Now."

Micheline switched on the flashlight attached to her rifle. Jenny's face was a silhouette portrait of shock, panic, and worry.

"It's all right, Jenny," Micheline called out. "We're here now. Richard, cuff the bastard, please."

Detective Tuller attached his flashlight to the belt around his waist. Then he holstered his gun. He placed a handcuff on Greg Slater's right wrist and firmly locked it in place. He pulled Slater's right arm down behind the back, palm facing outward, and then locked the stainless-steel cuff onto the left wrist.

"Now we've got you," Richard said firmly. "Where are your partners?"

"I'm not telling you shit," Greg fumed.

Jenny squirmed away from the wall and moved toward Micheline.

"Oh, Micheline. Thank you for arriving when you did!" she blurted. "He was going to rape me."

Micheline lowered her rifle and wrapped her right arm tightly around Jenny's shoulder. Jenny was quaking with anxiety and the disquieting horror of having been attacked by someone known to her.

"It's all right now. We're going to get Harrison and Jackie, too. Stay right here until it's safe, okay?"

Jenny nodded slowly. "Yes, okay. I'm so sorry about what I said to you before. I'm sure you hate me."

"Don't worry about that, Jenny. You're safe now. That's all that matters."

"Thank you," Jenny said. "Both of you. You're heroes."

"We're not out of the woods yet," Micheline said.

"C'mon, Greg," Richard ordered. "Let's go find your pals."

Richard escorted Greg toward the stage. He had unholstered his Glock 22 and kept it pointed forward. Micheline followed from behind and to the left. She was more determined than ever now. Her fingers held tightly onto her rifle. She could taste her freedom and vindication of the charges filed against her coming soon.

"Keep it quiet, Slater," Richard ordered tersely.

They moved into the outer perimeter of the lighted area of the stage. There was movement at the far end off-stage.

As they approached, Richard identified Harrison Murray and Jackie Henshilwood on the floor. Harrison lay on his back with his pants pulled down to his knees. His arms and legs were spread wide. Jackie had removed her lace panties, which had been tossed aside on the floor nearby. She was fully engaged on top of Harrison with his other appendage.

"Well, don't you two look cozy," Richard called out. "Police. Remain still and stay where you are."

"Bloody hell!" Jackie cried sharply. "You scared me."

"This is just the beginning," Richard promised. "You'll need to get used to it. Get up, slowly."

"How did you find us?" Jackie asked angrily with the tension of a scowl etched upon her face.

"Your buddy, Wade, led us straight to you," Micheline called out. "I saw what you did to him."

"Detective Avila?" Harrison asked in a surprised tone. "How is it that you're here? Aren't the police looking for you, too?"

Jackie lifted herself from atop Harrison's body and stepped aside. She didn't appear so innocent or humbled by her current circumstances.

Harrison quickly pulled up his underwear and blue jeans to cover himself. His facial expression registered dejection and contempt.

"You can get up slowly," Richard commanded. "No funny business, Murray."

Richard turned back toward his partner. "Micheline, do you have an extra set of cuffs? I carry two sets on my duty belt. I'll take care of both of our male suspects. Will you do the honors with our female culprit, please?"

"Yes," Micheline said. "Jackie, turn around and place your hands to the back of your head."

"Can I please put my panties on first?" Jackie asked.

Micheline nodded. "Yes. Hurry up."

Jackie bent over and retrieved her pink cotton undergarment from the floor. She slipped into the panties one leg at a time, exposing her thighs and bikini tan line as her dress shifted upward during the process.

Richard snickered. "Consider this the first and last conjugal visit you two will ever share."

"Oh, you think this was the first time, huh?" Jackie grumbled. "We've been together a lot longer than you may think."

"We'll be checking into that for sure," Richard replied. "But none of it matters now. We've got you."

Micheline reached for the handcuffs that were clipped in a plastic holder on the belt around her waist.

"Micheline, you've captured them all!" Jenny cried out excitedly. She was standing immediately behind Micheline.

"Jenny, please stand back," Micheline instructed. "We've got to take them into custody first."

"Shouldn't you call in to report them?" Jenny asked impatiently. "Don't you have backup coming to assist the two of you?"

"We will," Micheline confirmed. "One step at a time. We have to subdue them in handcuffs first."

"Yeah, that's right," Greg challenged maliciously. "You call it in, Micheline. Some girlfriend you turned out to be. Warm hands and an ice-cold heart."

"Let's just get through with this please," Micheline suggested.

"I doubt your police colleagues will even believe you when this all comes to light," Greg sneered. "You're just a bitch who used to have a badge. Now you're nothing but a disgrace within your own department."

"Sticks and stones, Greg," Micheline said. "I'm going to enjoy having the last laugh on this one."

"Are you sure about that?" Greg taunted abrasively. He abruptly squirmed on bended knee and jerked away from Richard's grasp on his elbow. Richard had been concentrating on placing his second pair of handcuffs on Harrison's right wrist. He reacted a moment too slow toward Greg and pivoted awkwardly to regain control of his suspect. He was off-balance.

Micheline fumbled with the snap on her belt. She used her right hand to release the handcuffs from the plastic clip that held them in place.

From out of nowhere, a three-inch knife blade suddenly cut sharply across Micheline's right forearm. The wound drew blood. Micheline dropped the handcuffs to the floor.

"What the hell?" she screamed in pain.

From behind Micheline's left flank, Jenny grasped the carry handle of the rifle with her right hand. She brandished the three-inch folding knife threateningly with her left hand in front of Micheline's unbelieving face.

Jenny scrutinized Micheline with a fiery expression of poisoned indifference. "We're not going anywhere, Detective. It's time for all of us to lay our cards on the table."

Jenny immediately jabbed the knife blade's edge wildly toward Micheline's exposed throat.

Micheline countered by pivoting inward toward Jenny. She stepped close and raised her wounded forearm in a defensive block of the savage assault.

"That's the same knife you used to carve up Samantha Miller, isn't it?" Micheline accused.

Both women were at a standstill. Each had one hand that gripped the rifle while their forearms pushed against each other as if in a contest of arm wrestling.

"You're a good detective, Micheline," Jenny mocked her. "A little too slow on the uptake, though."

"How do you mean?"

"I used it on J.P. Ballard, too. You were just too naïve and trusting to consider me a suspect back then."

Micheline instinctively released her grip on her rifle and brazenly pushed Jenny backward to the wall. She had mere seconds before Jenny would recover, and Jenny now had control of the gun.

Micheline pulled a two-ounce pepper spray throw grenade from her waistband. She immediately flipped the plastic cap off and snapped the release mechanism down. A fine mist of pepper spray began to emit from the nozzle.

Micheline forcefully advanced the nozzle toward Jenny's face and pushed her adversary backward. She stuck her foot strategically behind Jenny's leg as she did so and used the momentum to knock Jenny to the floor.

Jenny helplessly dropped both the rifle and the knife from her grasp. The weapons clattered to the floor on either side of her writhing body. The pepper spray had elicited an incapacitating haze of inflammatory effect.

Jenny's eyes felt as though they were on fire. She cried out and squeezed her eyes shut in a useless attempt to ward off the searing pain. The more she wiped her eyes, the more it stung.

Harrison attacked Richard from behind. He grasped the detective's Glock 22 handgun and bent Richard's arm backward. Within seconds, Harrison had control of the gun in his grasp.

Micheline spun quickly on her heels and flicked the pepper spray throw grenade at Harrison's chest. The canister struck him squarely and bounced to the floor. But not before the agitating mist had spewed its contents into his open orifices.

Harrison released his hold on Richard and dropped to his knees. He maintained a solid hold on the gun in his hand. But the grenade had taken its effect.

Micheline grabbed Richard by the arm and pulled him toward her. She swiftly uncapped a second pepper spray grenade and tossed it toward Greg Slater. She wasted no time and withdrew the third canister, deployed it, and tossed it toward Jackie Henshilwood.

"Richard, we've got to get out of here," she ordered harshly. "Now!"

The two detectives scattered haphazardly across the stage. They attempted to shield their faces from the compromising effects of the airborne mist. Harrison used Richard's Glock 22 and blindly fired a half dozen shots at the officers as they made their withdrawal.

A single shot clipped Richard in the back of the right leg. He grunted loudly and hobbled forward.

"I'm hit!" he shouted to Micheline.

"Come on," she beckoned. "Keep moving. We've got to get away from them."

They made their way to the corridor. They turned left and tramped awkwardly along the hallway. Their forward progress was slow. They needed to make their way to the front entrance of the theater. Richard limped heavily.

Ahead, gunshots fired toward them from the direction of the lobby. Their captives had somehow turned the tables on them and had out-flanked them from the main entrance. Shots were being fired at them from two separate directions, both front and back.

"They've got us trapped," Richard gasped alarmingly. "There's no-where to go."

"We passed a stairwell door back the other way," Micheline said. "We have to get back there. It's our only chance."

Gunshots strafed wildly through the corridor. Micheline wrapped an arm around her partner and helped him toward the stairwell exit door. She pried the door open as it squealed stubbornly on its ancient iron hinges.

"Quick, let's head up to the roof," she stammered. "We'll call it in from there."

Richard managed to click his flashlight on. The powerful LED beam penetrated the eerie blackness above them on the marble stairwell.

Loud bursts of gunshots reverberated beneath them. They were being chased up the stairs toward the roof.

"How are you doing?" Micheline asked.

"I'll manage," Richard mumbled through gritted teeth. He struggled to force himself up the wide staircase.

They had to be careful. Even with the flashlight's LED beam, the stairwell was dark and obscure. There were frequent obstructions, cinder blocks, bricks, piles of broken concrete, and pipe littering the steps at each level.

Below them, the perpetrators of the bank heist chased after them and were gaining ground quickly. Micheline focused her attention on getting them safely to the rooftop. She still had a few aces up her sleeve. But she would need time and a defensive position from which to activate them.

"Let's go, partner!" she prodded. "We're almost there. How high can it be? Six or seven stories, tops. Right?"

"I guess," Richard agreed. He was in no mood to argue.

After ascending two more flights of stairs, Micheline and Richard reached the rooftop door. Like its counterpart below, its rusted iron hinges squealed like fingernails against a blackboard as Micheline forced it open. She slammed it shut behind them and then quickly viewed the limited hiding places on top of the roof.

On any other night, the view of the surrounding downtown Gaslamp Quarter district would be considered both romantic and amazing. But Micheline had much more pressing matters to attend to. She needed to find cover or shelter immediately. A single mistake could cost both detectives their lives.

"Over there," she instructed Richard. "Behind the AC unit. Let's take cover."

"Got it," he replied.

The air conditioning unit was a square steel-plated cube. It was four feet wide and barely three feet in height from the rooftop. Still, it was the only protective blockade available to them.

Richard settled himself to a sitting position behind the metal unit. Micheline reached into a side pocket and withdrew her backup handgun. It was a Glock 19 nine-millimeter pistol, the same model as she carried in her side holster on her left waistline.

"Take my backup gun," she said. "I've got my primary."

Micheline quickly removed her jacket and tied it around the wound of Richard's right leg. Then she unclasped the pepper spray canister belt from around her waist. She placed three remaining pepper spray grenades into a pocket on her left side and tied the belt as a tourniquet around Richard's upper thigh. Richard grunted loudly as Micheline tightened the strap and set it in place.

"That should hold for a short while at least."

Micheline reached into another of the zippered pockets on her pants leg and withdrew the cell phone. She was ready to call in the cavalry. All she had to do now was to hold a defensive position until that could happen.

She pushed the phone app, selected contacts, and pressed Kelly Van Horn's number. A call failed error message displayed on the screen. Micheline glanced more closely at the phone.

No bars. There was no service inside the demolition zone.

What am I going to do now?

"There's no cell service," she muttered.

Darkness was closing in fast.

Forty-Four

M icheline held the cell phone in front of her and shook her head. "There's no bars."

"It might just be your position," Richard suggested. "Try moving around to the other side of the AC unit."

Micheline stepped around Richard's legs and checked her phone.

Two bars appeared.

She redialed Kelly Van Horn's number.

"Micheline, we hit the jackpot!" Kelly sputtered excitedly.

"That's great! Kelly, I've found them," Micheline informed her.

"You found who?"

The steel rooftop access door shrieked loudly as it was forced open from below in the stairwell. Shots fired randomly across the darkened rooftop.

Micheline fired four quick shots in succession toward the open doorway.

"The bank robbers," she yelled immediately following the gunshot concussions. "They've been waiting it out at the old Imperial Theater in the Gaslamp Quarter. We're at the corner of Fifth Avenue and Island Avenue on the rooftop."

"Were those gunshots?"

Micheline fired two more shots toward the doorway.

"Yes. Richard and I are pinned down on the roof behind an AC unit. We're holding them off for now."

"Who are they?" Kelly asked.

"Everyone in my recent life, it seems."

"What does that mean?"

More shots were fired from the open doorway directly at the AC unit. Micheline ducked behind the boxlike steel structure next to Richard.

"Greg Slater, for starters," Micheline grunted.

"What? Your boyfriend?"

"I sure know how to pick 'em, huh?"

"Unbelievable."

"It's true. And Jenny Casella was not taken from the bank as a hostage as we thought. As it turns out, she's the mastermind behind the whole thing."

"Whoa!"

"She had access to all the bank's accounts. She confessed to killing J.P. Ballard and Samantha Miller, too. Remember Jackie Henshilwood, the witness from the Samantha Miller murder?"

"Yes, of course."

"She was in on it, too. She only acted as a witness, when in fact, she was Jenny's lookout during the Samantha Miller murder. She knowingly followed Samantha to the rendezvous point in the park and waited for the right time. They're all in it together. And with them is Harrison Murray, the barista from the coffee shop near the courthouse."

"What about Wade Branigan?"

"He was a part of it, too. He was Samantha's lover. But he's got nothing more to say on the matter. They shot him. He's dead."

A hail of three-round bursts of gunfire erupted from the rooftop stairway door. Richard leaned over on his side and fired back in return.

"Was that more gunfire?" Kelly asked alarmingly.

"They've got us cornered on the roof right now. Richard's been shot."

"Holy shit! Hold tight, Micheline. I'll be there as quick as I can."

Micheline could hear Kelly's heavy breathing. Kelly sprinted toward her parked car.

"You'd better make it fast," Micheline implored. "I don't know how much longer hold them off. They're just as likely to make a run for it, too."

"I'm still a good twenty minutes out. I'll punch it with lights and siren."

"Thanks, Kelly."

Micheline peered around the corner of the AC unit. The rooftop was shrouded in darkness. But there was enough light to make out shapes and to detect movement. She didn't see anyone lurking among the shadows near the doorway.

On her phone, she could hear a car door slamming shut and air disturbance.

"Kelly?"

"Yeah? Hold on. Let me put you on speaker."

Micheline waited a moment and fired three more rounds toward the stairwell doorway.

"They're making their getaway on a cruise ship tomorrow afternoon," she said. "They're headed for Puerto Vallarta in Mexico, and then on to the Grand Cayman Islands sometime after that."

"You're sure of that itinerary?"

"Yes. I heard them talking about it. The ship's coming into San Diego port tomorrow morning. They mentioned it was delayed into port due to the storm up north. They think they're on their way to Fantasy Island. Only, I want to turn that dream into the worst nightmare of their lives."

Several more gunshots struck the AC unit. Micheline peered around the corner. Their antagonists were stationed in the open doorway at the top of the stairwell. The structure offered their adversaries complete protection. It also created a blockade that prevented Micheline and Richard from any chance at an escape.

Micheline set the phone on the rooftop deck and fired several quick shots at the open rooftop doorway.

"That'll back 'em up a bit," she cursed out loud.

She picked up her phone.

"We're at a standstill right now," she said. "They're pinned inside the rooftop stairwell. They can't come out, but Richard and I can't leave, either."

"Just hold tight, Micheline. I'm on my way as fast as I can make it there."

"Thanks for having my back, partner."

"I found out a few more things tonight, Micheline."

"What's that?"

"Based on what you've told me, it's all beginning to make sense now. I did the background check on Jenny like you asked."

"I can only imagine what that turned up."

"First off, she didn't come from a large family in Chicago as she told you. And she never took a trip on the weekend of the Miller murder. There's no record of her on file with the airlines."

"Obviously she was attempting to create a false alibi for herself."

"She was an orphan from the age of seven. She grew up in foster care. After high school, she moved to Vegas and then later to San Diego. She worked as an exotic dancer at various clubs. She was employed at the Paradise Club downtown in the Gaslamp Quarter while Samantha Miller also worked there. They knew each other. Do you want to take a guess as to what their stripper names were?"

"If you say Clarissa and Hillary..."

"Bingo! Jenny later earned an associate degree from UCSD."

"Not a bachelor's degree or a master's in finance?"

"Nothing like that. I think she fudged her resume or outright lied during her interview at the bank."

"It makes you wonder how she ever got away with that."

"It turns out, our murder victim J.P. Ballard is the one who hired her. I think he knew she was a stripper."

"So, it was all a lie and a fabrication."

"There's more."

Micheline traded gunshots with the assailant who was still taking refuge in the covered stairwell.

"What's that?"

"Greg never worked for a luxury car dealership. He's a former Army Ranger who got himself dishonorably discharged from the service. He worked as a bartender at the strip club after having served four years at Lompoc on bank robbery charges. Harrison Murray, your favorite coffee barista, is his half-brother. Same mother but different fathers. He was also incarcerated at Lompoc for the same crime."

"How is it that all these people from my personal life turned out to be so goddamn bad?"

"I think they sought you out, Micheline. You met Jenny during the J.P. Ballard murder investigation. She must have pegged you back then and continued her ruse as a trusted friend to gain your confidence. She probably got you to spill police intel on the murder investigations without you even realizing it."

"She had me completely fooled," Micheline admitted. "I never would have guessed that she'd be capable of such sinister and abhorrent behavior. Two counts of cold-blooded murder, computer and financial crimes, armed robbery, and now assault and attempted murder of a police officer."

"The CSIs came upon some other interesting details when they searched through the debris at the bank."

"Such as?"

"In Jenny's office, they found used ketchup packets in the wastebasket. Now, she may have used them on a breakfast egg sandwich or some other food item. But a dozen of them? I'd bet next week's paycheck that an examination of Jenny's blood-streaked blouse from the robbery turns out to be nothing but ketchup stains."

Micheline could hear the squeal of tires from her phone and then the connection with Kelly went dead.

An extended burst of automatic gunfire suddenly strafed against the AC unit. The robbery crew was getting restless and wanted to end it all here and now. Several of the bullets exited through the rear panel of the metal box.

"Christ, that was close!" Richard grunted uncomfortably. He needed medical attention soon.

With too few options left to her, Micheline grasped the microphone from her police radio and switched it on. She heard static. She depressed the call button.

"Nine-Nine-Nine! Officer in distress. One of us is shot, and I'm taking automatic gunfire from the bank robbers of the Fidelity Savings and Loan Bank heist last week. The location is the rooftop of the Imperial Theater at the corner of Fifth Avenue and Island Avenue. Please hurry!"

"Identify yourself," squawked the voice on the radio. It was Ana Kapileo's voice.

Micheline depressed the call button.

"Detective Micheline Avila, badge number five-one-zero-nine. In need of immediate assistance. Over."

"Micheline, what the hell?" Ana responded.

"I'm under heavy gunfire on the rooftop of the theater, Ana. Detective Richard Tuller is with me. He was shot by the bank robbers from the Fidelity National bank heist last week. I've identified who the bank robbers are. Their names are Jenny Casella, originally thought to be their hostage. Turns out, she's the mastermind behind the whole thing. With her are Greg Slater, Harrison Murray, and Jackie Henshilwood."

"You're insane!"

"They've got all the same weapons and artillery they had at the bank heist. Please advise caution to initial responders and tell them to light a fire under their asses. I need their help now."

"You realize they'll be coming to arrest you, too."

"Yes, I do," Micheline responded boldly. "Send them all and send them now. Detective Tuller requires medical assistance."

"As you wish, Micheline."

"And one more thing."

"What's that?"

"Wade Branigan is another of the bank robbers who were on scene tonight. Jenny Casella executed him from point-blank range to keep him from snitching on them."

"Got it. And Micheline?"

"Yeah?"

"Good luck, Detective! There's still a few of us who refuse to believe you're bent."

"Thanks, Ana. We'll talk about that in person when this is all over."

The line went silent for a moment and then squawked again with Ana's clear, concise instructions to all units in the field.

"All units, nine-nine-nine! Officers in distress. Please respond immediately to the intersection of Fifth Avenue and Island Avenue in the Gaslamp Quarter. The location is the abandoned Imperial Theater. Bank robbers from the Fidelity Savings & Loan heist are confirmed to be inside. They are heavily armed and extremely dangerous. Officers are on the scene on the rooftop. They are under heavy fire and at least one officer has been shot. Please respond urgently with lights and sirens."

There was a momentary pause.

"Bank robbers have been identified as Jennifer Casella, Greg Slater, Harrison Murray, and Jacqueline Henshilwood. Also, on scene and responsible for the call-in are Detectives Micheline Avila and Richard Tuller."

Ana paused for another moment. She realized this could cause her to lose her job. She took a deep breath and let it out slowly.

"Repeating. All units, nine-nine-nine! Officers in distress at the Imperial Theater in the Gaslamp Quarter at the intersection of Fifth Avenue and Island Avenue. Please respond immediately and be careful out there!"

Micheline replaced the hand microphone back to the strap on her right shoulder pad.

"You still with me, partner?" she asked Richard.

"I'm holding on as best I can," he replied.

"Let's both give them some return fire," she said. "On three. Ready?"

Richard nodded and stiffened his muscles in preparation for the next assault. His consciousness was fading fast.

Forty-Five

On any other night, the skyline view from atop the Imperial Theater would have provided a magnificent vista of colorful Gaslamp
Quarter festivity and a clear darkened sky full of constellations. A glass
of wine along with a rhapsodic accompaniment of music would have
added the perfect touch to create a sense of romantic ambiance.

But not tonight. On this night it was a death trap.

"The shooting's stopped," Micheline whispered in Richard's ear.

"Uh-huh," came his faint reply.

"We've got to get you out of here. You've lost too much blood."

"I can hold on a bit longer."

"There's no telling how long we could be here, Richard. That's not
our only problem, either."

"You mean the C4?"

"Exactly," Micheline said. "We screwed up their plans. They can't
afford to sit around and wait for the police to show up. My bet would
be they'll set off the detonation switch early to make a diversion. It
would assure their safe getaway."

"What choice do we have?"

"None, unfortunately. We wait it out, they could raze the building
right from under us. We move forward, they might be baiting us into
an ambush. Either way, I have a plan."

"I trust you, Micheline. You call it."

"Can you stand on the leg?"

"I think so. Give me a hand and let's give it a go."

"Not just yet," she said. "I'm going to storm the door. I could sure use your cover fire to keep them at bay. They still might be hiding in the doorway."

"Let's reload our clips. We'll give them everything we've got."

"Good thinking."

Micheline pulled two nine-millimeter standard ammunition magazines with fifteen rounds each from a pocket on her right leg. The detectives reloaded their Glock 19s.

"You have one in the chamber?" Micheline asked.

"You know it."

"Good. That gives us thirty-two rounds. You unload your magazine straight into the doorway. I'll go wide to the right. When I get there, I'll toss two pepper spray grenades down the steps."

Richard nodded. "Let's do it."

Micheline rose to a squatting position on both feet. "On three, start shooting. I'll take off on your second shot."

"Affirmative."

"Ready for the countdown. Three. Two. One."

Richard immediately rolled onto his belly away from the AC unit. He extended his arms into a perfect firing position. He aimed toward the rooftop doorway and pulled the semi-automatic trigger in a steady, consistent cadence. This would allow Micheline to count the rounds fired. He continued his firing sequence until all sixteen bullets had been expended. There was no immediate return fire.

Richard rolled back behind the AC unit and pressed the magazine release button. He removed the empty magazine and replaced it with one that still held a dozen rounds.

Micheline scurried in a defensive crouch position across the rooftop. She made a wide right curve toward the stairwell and fired only one shot for every four shots that Richard fired into the open doorway.

She wasn't prepared for the act of running across an open space with live fire going off around her. It was a terrifying ordeal. But Micheline kept her focus sharp and covered the distance in under seven seconds.

When she arrived at the doorway, Micheline pressed her body tightly against the outer brick wall. She holstered her weapon and quickly retrieved two pepper spray grenades from the pocket on her left leg. She popped the plastic caps off the canisters and depressed the activation tabs.

Fire in the hole!

She reached around the corner of the doorway and gently tossed the first grenade so that it would bounce off the far inside wall and fall farther down the staircase. Then she tossed the second grenade so that it would stay in the doorway on the topmost landing. She fell back around the corner and waited.

Seconds passed as slowly as molasses in January. Of course, Micheline realized, that phrase only worked in colder northern regions outside of California. In San Diego, it would drizzle like honey in hot tea all year round.

Stay focused!

Micheline wanted to be certain the entire contents of the pepper spray grenades had dissipated before she made her next move. She waited another thirty seconds and then quickly peered around the corner of the doorway. There was no one in sight, nor was there any sound coming from the stairwell below.

She returned to the AC unit.

"Richard, it's all clear," she said. "Richard?"

As she stepped around the corner of the AC unit, Richard lay prone and unconscious on the rooftop. She touched his shoulder and shook him.

"Richard? Wake up. Come on now."

She took his face in her hands and continued to rouse him more forcefully this time.

Richard's eyes fluttered slightly.

"You still with me, partner?"

His body fell limp.

"No! Richard, I need for you to wake up, honey. Come on now. We've got to get our asses out of here."

Micheline shook his body hard. She hoisted him to a sitting position with his back against the bullet-riddled AC unit.

"Come on now. We've got to go."

"Uh, Micheline?"

"Yes, Richard. It's me. Wake up, please. We have to get out of here."

"Oh, it hurts."

"I know it does. Be strong. Be brave. We can do this together. You and me."

"Okay, I'm with you."

Richard opened his eyes.

Micheline helped Richard to his feet. He grimaced painfully as he applied pressure with his right foot. But he knew it was life or death, and he preferred to keep on breathing.

"I'll manage," he said. "Let's go."

They made their way to the rooftop door. Micheline kicked the door open wide and fired two quick shots with her Glock 19 into the dark recess below. She waited a few seconds and fired two more rounds. There was no response.

"C'mon, let's start heading down."

When they reached the balcony designated Row C at the highest level of the theater, they veered away from the stairwell and made their way along the outer perimeter of the building toward the front. Then they began to work their way down the stairs which descended directly to the front lobby.

As Micheline poked the lobby door open a crack, she caught a glimpse of Harrison Murray. He fervently twisted a control dial on top of a workbench near the door by the main front entrance. He swiftly flung the exit door open and disappeared to the outside. The main entrance doors remained slightly askew, allowing streetlights to filter into the darkened enclosure.

"Quick! We've got to move now," Micheline beckoned to Richard. "Harrison toggled some sort of control device on the table."

Gunfire erupted from outside on the street. Bullets strafed inside the front foyer of the theater entrance.

328 | ROBERT VALLETTA

Micheline and Richard traipsed their way across the dilapidated theater foyer amid a hail of gunfire from the outside. Slowly, they maneuvered their way closer to the massive double front entrance doors.

Another fifteen feet and they would be at the doorway.

Without warning, the rumbling and cacophony of thunder blasted its way across the room. Both floor and ceiling shook with a mighty vibration. It was as if heaven and hell were suddenly enflamed by a tumultuous burst of incredible energy.

The Big Bang!

There was no flame or conflagration. Everything shook and then the entire building imploded upon itself. Multiple explosions in two-second intervals ripped throughout the circumference of the immense structure.

The cathedral of the arts immediately collapsed inward upon itself. Its fortified walls were sucked into a chaotic storm of imminent destruction.

Within a matter of seconds, the Imperial Theater was reduced to a monumental trash heap of mangled rock, brick, and twisted steel beams. Thick plumes of smoke and dust filled the air.

Everything beneath the Grim Reaper's toxic darkened cloud was dead, obscure, and forever silent.

Forty-Six

Micheline's eyes fluttered open convulsively. She choked and gasped for breath. The toxic air that enveloped her in a polluted haze smelled like burnt metal and wind-blown concrete dust. For a moment, Micheline imagined she was back home in New Jersey.

She lay on the ground, motionless. A searing pain erupted from her left elbow. Detective Richard Tuller lay unconscious on his back nearby.

The flashing lights of an oncoming battalion of police cruisers with the dissonant clamor of sirens invaded the surrounding scene.

Micheline twisted her head from side to side. Around her, blackened smoke permeated the air. Her eyes squinted in vain to comprehend what was happening.

"Richard, are you all right?" Detective Kelly Van Horn's voice beckoned alarmingly.

"Micheline, are you still with us?" she shouted.

"I'm here, Kelly," Micheline muttered somewhat incoherently.

"Get the EMTs over here now!" Kelly's voice commanded. "We have wounded officers."

Micheline attempted to sit up. Her left arm was useless. She could barely twitch her fingers. The left elbow remained locked in a cradled position. She stretched her neck to release the tension in her shoulders and back.

"Did you get them? How's Richard doing?"

"I need an ambulance now," Kelly shouted. "This officer's been shot. Micheline, hold tight. We'll get you medical attention soon."

"But did you get them?" Micheline inquired. "All four of them exited the building right before the building came down on top of us."

"Paramedics! Get over here now," Kelly screamed again. Her face showed anguish and concern.

"I'm sorry, Micheline. There's no one here," Kelly affirmed. "I just arrived on scene, myself. The rest of the department is coming in waves. Don't worry. We have an APB out on them. We'll catch them."

"That's not good enough!" Micheline cried. "Let's go get those motherfuckers."

Micheline attempted to rise to her feet. Her head swooned and she fell backward.

"Medics, over here now," Kelly called.

Three uniformed paramedics and emergency medical technicians surrounded them. One tended to Micheline while the other two assessed Richard's wounds and condition.

"What's wrong with me?" Micheline asked.

"Hi, Micheline," an EMT said. "My name is Brian. Can you bend your elbow for me, please?"

"I can't," she replied. "It hurts too much."

"How about your fingers? Can you move them for me?"

"Just a little," she said. Micheline attempted to move her fingers. There was only a slight flutter of movement.

"It looks like a dislocated elbow, or possibly a broken arm. I'll immobilize it until we get you to the hospital. They can do an x-ray there."

"How's Richard? Is he going to be all right?"

The EMT turned to see how his team members were making out. One gave him a nod and a thumbs-up signal.

"They're working on him now," Brian said. "He'll be okay. They have to get him stabilized before they can take him to the ambulance."

"Brian, how's your patient doing?" a man's voice barked.

"We're good, Lieutenant," Brian said. "A dislocated left elbow, a laceration to the right forearm, and some minor cuts and abrasions to the face. I'll immobilize the elbow and get her other wounds cleaned up."

The lieutenant immediately turned toward the other men nearby. "Denny, what's this officer's status?"

One of the EMTs kneeling by Richard's side looked up. "Critical, sir. We have a GSW to the rear right quad. His partner tied a belt as a tourniquet, which probably saved his life. We're getting him stabilized for transport now."

"Keep at it, guys. Thanks."

The lieutenant turned back toward Micheline. "Detective Avila, was there anyone else inside the building?"

Micheline looked up with discomfort. "No, sir. Detective Tuller and I were the last ones out before the building came down on top of us. We were lucky to make it out the doorway."

Brian looked Micheline in the eyes. "Detective, I need to slip this uninflated orthopedic sleeve over your arm. This may hurt a bit."

"Go for it," Micheline said, gritting her teeth.

"Tell me something," Brian said. "You've been on the news all week. It sounds like they got the story wrong."

"Not even close," Micheline replied.

"Did you catch the bad guys? The people who robbed the bank?"

"No, we didn't. Not yet. They're the ones who blew up the theater. Detective Tuller and I were on to them, but they escaped."

"I'm going to slip this over your arm now. Take a deep breath."

Micheline did as she was instructed.

Brian slid the transparent plastic sleeve over the top of the full length of Micheline's left arm. He used a push-pull valve attached to the sleeve to inflate it with air.

Micheline could feel the pressure of the sleeve tighten around her arm.

"That'll keep it in place while we transport you to the hospital. It's transparent, so they can do the x-ray without having to remove it first."

"Thank you, Brian," Micheline said. "For taking good care of me."

"It's my job, Detective." He smiled at her. "We'll get you patched up good as new. You need to be out catching those bad guys responsible for the mess behind us, right?"

Micheline attempted to smile. It was a weak attempt at that.

A stretcher arrived with two other paramedics. The EMTs lifted Richard's body and carefully strapped him in place. Within seconds, they hoisted the stretcher up so that the wheels locked in place. The EMTs held an IV bag above Richard's head. A moment later, they hurried away with their patient toward the back end of a waiting ambulance.

"Let's clean up some of these cuts and abrasions, Detective. That forearm looks like a nasty cut."

"Please, call me Micheline."

"You got it. Let's push your sleeve up toward your elbow so I can treat the laceration, please."

Detective Kelly Van Horn suddenly knelt in front of Micheline. "I'm going to ride in the ambulance with Richard," she said. "You're in good hands here, Micheline. Thank you. They said you saved his life."

Micheline nodded. "I'm the one who brought him here, remember? We almost had them, too. We were so close."

Kelly patted Micheline on the shoulder. "You did good, Micheline. We're not through yet. We're going to put the collar on those four. I'll keep you posted. Take care."

Kelly turned and walked briskly toward the waiting ambulance. "Captain Kovacs, over there," she called out, pointing toward Micheline on the ground.

Captain Phillip Kovacs, head of the San Diego County Robbery Unit, approached Micheline and the EMT attending to her wounds.

"Micheline," he opened softly. "I'm sorry. I had it wrong. Tell me what you know."

Micheline wanted to cry. She stiffly held the tears at bay. "Four suspects," she stated firmly. "Jennifer Casella is the leader. She confessed to the murders of J.P. Ballard and Samantha Miller. She had the knife used to commit those murders on her person. She cut me with it on the right forearm."

"And who else?"

"Greg Slater, Harrison Murray, and Jacqueline Henshilwood. Slater and Murray were part of the bank heist. They both have a military and a prison connection to the bank robbers killed during the heist."

Micheline inhaled a deep breath. Her entire body ached with pain. A jolt of electricity raced up her right forearm as Brian applied an antiseptic to the knife wound.

"Henshilwood was an accomplice to Jenny Casella at the Miller murder scene. All told, they're a tight-knit group of killers."

"I've gathered that," Kovacs said.

"And Wade Branigan was in on it, too. He was at the bank heist. You'll find his body in the orchestra pit of the rubble behind me."

"I understand you uncovered their getaway plan. Where are they headed?"

"That's correct, sir. They had planned to board a cruise ship tomorrow bound for Puerto Vallarta, Mexico."

"Why did they wait so long after the heist? Why not leave sooner?"

"The ship was apparently due into port last week, immediately following the bank heist. That was their original plan. The ship was delayed due to the storm up north. They needed a place to hide until the ship came in. Some of their crew worked on the theater construction project. They had the keys to the front door of the theater, and they had access to explosives for the demolition project."

"We'll be waiting for them at the port if they attempt that escape route. Any other thoughts as to how their plans may have changed since you and Detective Tuller tossed a monkey wrench at them?"

Micheline took a moment to think. The foursome would need an immediate place to hide. Then perhaps a new plan to get them across the border into Mexico.

"Definitely keep watch at the port tomorrow. That was their planned escape to Mexico. For right now, I'd make sure the filing cabinets from Wade Branigan's office are locked up in the evidence room. I heard them say the cash stolen from the bank was stashed there. They will likely need money to get them out of the country."

"Good to know. Other thoughts?"

"Check out the Paradise Gentlemen's Club down the street. Slater used to be a bouncer there, and Jenny Casella was a stripper. They might use their contacts there to help them hide until things blow over."

Kovacs nodded. He lifted a portable two-way radio in his hand. He pressed the call button.

"Yo, Valentino," he called.

"Yes, sir," came the prompt reply from a female officer. "Standing by."

"Take a team over to the Paradise Gentlemen's Club on Island Avenue. Search every room, nook, and cranny for our escaped convicts. They have a known association there."

"Copy that. Right away, sir. We're on it. Out."

Kovacs looked back at Micheline with raised eyebrows.

Micheline winced again as she shifted her sitting position. Her elbow brushed against the ground.

"Branigan's Mercedes was parked at the curb on Fifth, near the Mexican restaurant. I think he still had the keys with him when they killed him. But I'd check to confirm that. Lockdown the Gaslamp Quarter, and check the trolley stations, too. They're most likely on foot. I don't know how long I was out. But they couldn't have gotten too far."

Kovacs nodded.

"Other than that, put surveillance on their known home addresses, and the Books & Coffee Café where Harrison Murray was employed."

"I appreciate your thoroughness on this, Detective. I'm clearing you of all previous charges. Now, get yourself to the hospital. We're going to need you back on the job as soon as possible."

"Thank you, Captain."

Kovacs turned abruptly and left Micheline and the EMT behind. He was barely two steps away when he began barking orders rapidly into his two-way radio again.

"Detective," Brian said. "Let me take care of the abrasions on your forehead. Turn to the right, please."

"Thank you, Brian," she said. "It's been a while since anyone has taken such good care of me."

"Well, I could get used to this," he said and smiled at her. "I've never seen such beautiful blue eyes before."

Micheline looked up at the emptiness of the nighttime sky ablaze with the flashing of red and blue police strobe lights. Then she turned around to observe the demolition zone that had once been a mighty and opulent cathedral for the performing arts.

She closed her eyes tightly. There was still much work to do. The killers were still on the loose, and she only had a few vague ideas as to where to search for them before they disappeared forever.

Forty-Seven

Micheline stood in the corner of the district attorney's vast office and leaned against the tinted glass window overlooking the urban downtown landscape of the Gaslamp Quarter. Her arm was supported by a sling around her neck.

"Are we ready to begin?" DA Rosalyn Whittaker, playing the part of judge and executioner, asked the group assembled before her.

Everyone present in the room seated themselves quickly around an elongated conference table. Everyone except for Micheline. She remained expressionless against the window awaiting her fate.

"To be clear," Assistant Prosecuting Attorney Mark Longfellow opened, "all criminal charges previously filed against Detective Avila are now dropped. Her reinstatement status to Homicide Division is effective immediately. For me personally, I can't say loud enough how sorry I am for everything she's been through."

"I concur with that sentiment," Phillip Kovacs announced. He turned toward Micheline. "I'm sorry I ever doubted your testimony, Detective."

The DA looked around the room to view the unanimous consent from all those seated around her.

"Detective Avila," she began with a bold proclamation. Her voice softened. "Micheline, I offer my sincere apology and my thanks for everything you've contributed toward identifying and nearly apprehending those responsible for the recent spate of murders and bank robberies in our city."

Micheline remained silent and nodded to the DA.

"Do we have any updates to report this morning?" the DA asked her team.

"Yes, ma'am," Kelly Van Horn announced.

"Let's hear it," the DA prompted.

Kelly cleared her throat. "A statewide APB has been issued for the four individuals involved. They remain at large. U.S. Customs officials at the Mexico border across California, Arizona, New Mexico, and Texas are on high alert status. The U.S. Coast Guard is preemptively blockading and searching all vessels attempting to sail away from coastal ports in southern California, including up north from Long Beach and San Francisco."

"We know where they may be heading," Phillip Kovacs interjected. "Media attention is across all networks right now. We'll catch the bastards."

"Was any evidence recovered from the debris at the Imperial Theater?" the DA asked.

"Yes," Kelly replied. "A three-inch Tac-Force spring assisted folding knife was recovered at the scene. We believe it's the same knife used in the J.P. Ballard and Samantha Miller murders by Jennifer Casella. It was also used by Casella to wound Detective Avila on the forearm during their altercation at the Imperial Theater."

"That's good," the DA said. "Having the murder weapon and an established M.O. will help us lock this one down."

"The lab is running tests now," Mark Longfellow stated. "The CSI team has their hands full with the debris field. They've uncovered some of the gang's weapons. They're still searching for Wade Branigan's body. The K-9 unit is involved in the search. It will likely take weeks or even months until they've gone through all of it."

"I'll approve any necessary overtime to keep operations moving along at the demolition site," the DA offered.

"Thank you, Rosa," Mark said.

"Anything else?" the DA asked.

"Yes, ma'am," Kelly replied. "I was able to uncover a few more details pertaining to the case."

"Such as?"

"Much of the background story the gang provided to Detective Avila was a complete fabrication. We now know both Jennifer Casella and Jacqueline Henshilwood attended the same high school in Cleveland, Ohio. They both headed west and worked as exotic dancers in Las Vegas and later here in downtown San Diego. The only true statement they told appears to be Jackie Henshilwood was originally from London."

"Both women had good jobs that would have required experience or a college degree. How were they able to do that if they were only skilled at taking their clothes off?" the DA inquired.

"We're working on a theory these two ladies slept with or blackmailed men in key positions within their respective companies to gain employment opportunities."

"I see. What do we know about the two men?"

"First of all, they're brothers."

"Really?"

"Half-brothers, actually. Same mother, different fathers. They entered foster care when the boys were nine and twelve years old. They both served as Army Rangers with distinction and were honorably discharged. But then later they were apprehended following a bank heist in Carlsbad. They served four years at Lompoc, during which time Wade Branigan and the other four men killed during the Fidelity Bank heist were interred."

"What's their connection to the women?"

"Prior to their incarceration at Lompoc, Greg Slater worked as a bouncer at the same strip club in the Gaslamp Quarter as both women. We've collected documentation of conjugal visits by both women to visit these two men during their time at Lompoc."

"So, they have a history of sexual activity pre-dating the current crimes they're accused of," the DA said.

"It's more than that," Kelly said.

"How so?"

"While the women never changed their maiden names, they're both married."

"The women are married to each other?" the DA asked for clarity and confirmation.

"No, ma'am," Kelly replied. "Harrison Murray is the husband to Jackie Henshilwood, and Greg Slater is married to Jenny Casella."

"You're fucking kidding me!" Micheline wailed loudly from across the room. "What kind of sick weird game were they playing?"

Kelly nodded and shrugged her shoulders. "Apparently, the two couples had a double wedding at a Las Vegas chapel the year before the men went down for the Carlsbad robbery. Both couples are legally married."

"Did they stay in contact the entire time?"

"Yes, they did. Prison records indicate the wives made bi-monthly visits to Lompoc on the same dates and times throughout the four-year period."

"And did they remain employed at the strip club during that time?"

"We've established both women left the stripping profession and began their new professional careers shortly after the men went to prison. Jenny Casella completed an associate degree at UCSD and became a part-time teller at Fidelity National. Jackie Henshilwood worked in facility operations at the Systole Biosciences campus. A year later, she was promoted to become an assistant sales representative with the company."

"They wouldn't have done it for the money," the DA stated. "I'd assume they had a much broader plan associated with their changes in occupation. It might have given them a foot in the door, so to speak. Separate doors that led to where the big-time dollars are kept. A bank vault and a billion-dollar pharmaceutical company."

"That's certainly a theory we'll be tracking down," Mark Longfellow confirmed.

The DA smiled. "Thank you, everyone, for staying on top of this case. Not only are your efforts pertaining to the families of the victims and the dismissal of charges against Detective Avila, but the outcome of the next election may depend on this as well."

The DA slowly gazed around the room at her colleagues and team members.

"Micheline, it's good to have you back. I assume you'll be out on medical leave for the next two weeks, and you'll be fully reinstated for duty following the recommendation of the clinical psychologist."

"Yes, Rosa," Micheline confirmed. "I'm eager to get back to work soon. I've already scheduled an initial appointment with the department shrink."

"Take some time for now," the DA cautioned. "Get your mind and your body back in shape. Take some time at the beach. There's no hurry. We've got your back while you're recovering."

Micheline smiled. "Thank you, Rosa. I may do just that. You're right, of course. My wounds need to heal properly. It's best I take some personal time to take care of myself."

"We'll keep searching for the robbery crew," Mark added. "They can't get too far. We've got every agency in law enforcement across half a dozen states on the lookout for them. Mexican authorities have been alerted as well."

Micheline nodded courteously to everyone seated around the table. She'd play the game and say what they wanted to hear for now. She was already plotting to schedule some time off at a resort villa on Grand Cayman Island.

Maybe she'd catch some big fish while she was there.

Forty-Eight

The view from the wide glass windows overlooking the tarmac at Terminal 2, West concourse, Gate 40 of the San Diego International Airport, formerly known as Lindbergh Field, provided a vivid display of tall palm trees and downtown office buildings in the distance. From another angle across the way, the view of Point Loma and the San Diego Bay was clearly visible.

Micheline stood next to Ana Kapileo, Elena Dobrovic, and Shayna Vasquez. Elena held loosely onto the extended handle of her Pullman-style carry-on bag.

Detectives Richard Tuller and Kelly Van Horn stood nearby, holding hands. Richard held a wooden walking cane with his right hand to help steady his balance.

A display board along the wall listed United Airlines flight UA2474 as on time for a 12:08 p.m. flight to Houston, Texas. Elena was booked on a connecting flight from Houston to her hometown city in Detroit.

"All of you didn't have to come to see me off," Elena said with wonder. "I'm a big girl now."

"Yes, we did," Shayna replied. "We're all part of an exclusive club. Empowering one another and sticking together are some of the perks that come with the membership."

"Oh, really," Elena said with a suspicious smile. "And what are the requirements for membership in this special club?"

Shayna pointed toward Micheline. "First, you have to be a known associate of the notorious fugitive Detective Micheline Avila. Second, you must acknowledge she's both a great friend and one badass cop."

This elicited smirks and gentle laughter from the members of this supportive, close-knit group.

"And third," Shayna continued with a devilish glint in her eye, "you had to be a willing participant to help her to escape not only from police custody but also from the murderous bank robbery gang who all pretended to be her former best friends."

"Ouch!" Micheline gasped. "That really hurts, Shayna. But seriously, everyone. I know who my true best friends are now, and it's all of you gathered here today. We still have a lot of work ahead of us. But without each of you, I wouldn't have been able to clear my name and to identify the killers in the first place."

"You earned our trust, Micheline," Richard said. "I put my life in your hands, and you came through for me. I'll back you up any day, on the job or off."

"I'll second that," Kelly declared.

"It's the same for me," Shayna added. "I wouldn't be where I am today if Micheline hadn't shown up at my door and kicked my ex-husband's ass. She showed me there's a better life ahead. A life full of possibilities. I won't ever forget that."

"Everyone here has such a remarkable story," Elena commented. "All I did was to offer her refuge in my hotel room."

"Same here," Ana confirmed. "I just answered a call into dispatch. That's my job."

"Elena, you answered my call when I needed you most," Micheline said. "I'll never forget that. This all could have ended badly if you hadn't helped me when you did. I could be sweating it out with a life sentence behind bars right now."

Elena blushed.

"And Ana," Micheline continued with a gentle smile. "You could have presented my call in a more unfavorable way. You directed the entire force to come to our aid instead of to arrest us. What you did helped Richard and me to escape the building before it blew up. Your immediate nine-nine-nine announcement allowed Richard to receive medical attention in a much timelier manner than would have been possible otherwise. We both owe our gratitude to you."

Ana shrugged. "Okay, so I believed and trusted you. It was a split-second decision. I'm glad I made the right one."

Micheline's smile widened. "Thank you, my friend."

"So, Elena, will you ever come back to San Diego for a visit?" Kelly asked.

"I'm sure I will," Elena replied. "I feel like I've gained a whole new family here."

Elena turned toward Micheline. "This is one work trip I'll never forget. I may consider writing a human-interest feature about it. What do you think?"

"I suggest you hold off on that until after we have the culprits locked up," Micheline remarked. "I'll give you the exclusive rights to the story after that for sure."

"I'll look forward to it," Elena said. "Perhaps you'll come to visit me in Detroit for our debriefing."

"That's an excellent idea," Micheline said. "I'll need a vacation after all of this is said and done. There's no telling when that might be, though. It could be a while."

"But we'll stay in touch," Shayna added. "The sisters have to stick together."

"Hey, what about me?" Richard asked.

"Well, since you took a bullet for her, I guess we can count you in, too," Shayna quipped. She winked at Richard.

Richard smiled back. He leaned to his left to take the weight off his injured right leg.

A uniformed flight attendant at the gate announced that boarding for the flight to Houston would begin in a few minutes.

Micheline, with her left arm in a half-cast suspended by an adjustable canvas sling, wrapped her right arm around Elena. She squeezed tight.

"Thank you for being such a good friend, Elena. I'm looking forward to getting to know you even better in the future."

"Me, too," Elena said. "This has been quite an adventure. Murders, bank robberies, and police chases. I need to return home just for the quiet time. Good-bye, everyone." Elena gave a quick wave before she turned and took a position in the boarding line for her flight.

"C'mon, everyone," Micheline said. "Lunch is on me. What's everyone hungry for? Barbecue or Mexican Grill?"

"Barbecue for me," Richard replied.

"Me, too," Kelly agreed.

"That's fine with me," Ana said.

"Shayna?"

"Barbecue sounds fine," she said. "And you need the extra protein."

"Good," Micheline stated. "My nurse tells me I need to get my strength back if I'm going to take down the bank robbers?"

"You really think they're still around?" Kelly asked. "I mean, still here in San Diego. I'd hightail it out of here if it were me."

"I tend to agree," Richard said. "I'd be across the border to Mexico by now."

The quintet turned and walked through the busy airport terminal toward the food court.

"I have a sneaking suspicion we haven't seen the last of that group," Micheline said. "I don't care whether they're holed-up in a backroom somewhere in the Gaslamp Quarter or basking on a beach in Puerto Vallarta or the Cayman Islands. I won't stop my investigation until I find them. That's a promise."

"We're here to help you accomplish that, Micheline," Kelly said.

Micheline gazed across the terminal to the wide windows overlooking the tarmac. She distractedly watched a plane take off in the distance.

Somewhere out there, a menacing danger lurked like a storm cloud approaching the shore. That threat was comprised of a group of liars, cheaters, murderers, and thieves who were on the run.

Micheline would need to be stronger and smarter than they were. She took a deep breath and vowed to continue her search for them with her heart beating fast and her blood running hot.

Dear Reader,

Thank you for purchasing ***Blood Running Hot***. If you enjoyed reading this book, I would appreciate it if you could leave a brief review on social media (Instagram, Goodreads, Twitter, Facebook, TikTok, etc.), or at the bookstore or online retail site that you purchased your copy from.

Your review needs only to be a Starred Review and one or two sentences on how you felt about the book. It does not need to be a long or detailed account.

Online reviews allow other readers the opportunity to discover great books they otherwise would never have found or selected.

I certainly love to see my readers take pictures of their copies of my books in creative settings and post them on social media blogs. Thank you again for reading. I sincerely hope you enjoyed the book, and I appreciate it if you would be so kind as to provide an honest and positive review.

ABOUT THE AUTHOR

Robert Valletta grew up in the greater Lehigh Valley of eastern Pennsylvania. After graduating from high school, he spent two years backpacking his way throughout Europe and lived along the coastline of the Mediterranean Sea.

He has earned a B.A. in Business Management and an MBA in Supply Chain Management from Moravian University in Bethlehem, Pennsylvania.

Over the years, he has worked in management positions for global companies in the consumer electronics, life sciences, and pharmaceutical industries. He has lived outside the metropolitan areas of Philadelphia, New York, Boston, and San Diego. He now lives with his wife in the majestic desert canyons of southern California.

To learn more about the author or to order personalized, signed hardcover editions of his books, including the 2021 American Fiction Awards Techno-Thriller Finalist *Crossfire*, the poignant, descriptive, and a heartwarming coming-of-age novel based on his real-life European adventures *A Foreigner's Heart*, and a collection of his short stories and poems entitled *When School Let Out*, please visit:

https://linktr.ee/robertvallettabooks

Printed in the USA
CPSIA information can be obtained
at www.ICGtesting.com
LVHW090214171123
764223LV00006B/13/J